GIANT STEPS

*the new
generation of
african american
writers*

*edited
and with
an introduction
by*

KEVIN YOUNG

Perennial
An Imprint of HarperCollinsPublishers

FIRST EDITION

Designed by Bernard Klein

Library of Congress Cataloging-in-Publication Data has been applied for.

ISBN 0-688-16876-0

00 01 02 03 04 WB/BP 10 9 8 7 6 5 4 3 2

GIANT STEPS

Also by Kevin Young

Most Way Home

for my parents

and for all our ancestors,
literary and otherwise

i say
who will name this Renaissance
i stand knee deep in
who go tug the elbow of Langston Hughes
tell him we are yesterday again
to McKay and Cullen and Hurston
Walker and Baldwin
we doin it again

—Ruth Forman,
Renaissance

CONTENTS

CONTENTS

GIANT STEPS

THE BLACK PSYCHIC HOTLINE, OR THE FUTURE OF AFRICAN AMERICAN WRITING

DIAL NOW

The future can be hard to predict—yet I am here, like a weatherman or a late night television psychic, to tell you what you already know. No, not that the man you think is no good is indeed no good, nor that you should follow your passion, nor that money will follow you (though it might if you bought this book in your hands). Rather, as you already suspect and know, the future is now—and is made up, in part, of the writers contained here.

For *Giant Steps* features a cross section of cutting-edge black writers. Much like the famous New Negro anthology of the 1920s, *Giant Steps* highlights the present-day directions in and diversity of what many call the current renaissance in African American letters. By including in one volume some of the best poetry, fiction, and nonfiction of our time, *Giant Steps* seeks to take a great leap forward while recognizing the formidable footsteps we are following in—both adding to and honoring our rich literary tradition.

The title also of course pays homage to John Coltrane's groundbreaking *Giant Steps*—which, with its "sheets of sound," its tender ballads, and bursts of saxophone, changed the way we hear and see. It is in the spirit of this landmark artistic endeavor, an event that marked a bold new direction for Coltrane's powerful voice and style, that this anthology was conceived. The title seems all the more fitting given that it was 1960 when Trane released *Giant Steps*—the same year, it turns out, that the oldest of the writers represented here were born.

FIRST MINUTES FREE

That said, *Giant Steps* began like most projects—with pleasure and a certain necessity. A pleasure in that in the past few years, I have been fortunate enough to read many of the writers now published here—from Elizabeth Alexander to Natasha Trethewey to Colson Whitehead—in manuscript, as books-to-be (though not necessarily their first books). My immediate thought upon reading these and other eventual contributors to *Giant Steps* was that something brilliant was afoot—had somehow fallen into my hands—and that I wanted the world to know.

Which is not to say I in any way "discovered" these writers—they needed no introduction then and need even less of one now. In fact, one of my major contentions with *Giant Steps* is that it is *not* an anthology of "emerging writers"—a term that has come into vogue recently and initially helped many of us gain a wider audience—but rather, that these writers have already arrived. The contributors have achieved honors as diverse as National Book Award finalist and Oprah's Book Club; they have earned the Pushcart Prize, NEA grants, and the Zacharis First Book Prize from *Ploughshares*; they have been featured in *Best American Poetry and Short Stories*; they publish in and are reviewed by major magazines, such as the *The New Yorker, Time, Essence,* and *Vibe*. The writers included here are the future of African American writing, and a crucial part of contemporary American letters. My pleasure, then, or wish, was not to see them in print for the first time—this has already taken place.

Without exception the writers here already have at least one book published; some, as of this writing, have authored as many as four. Rather, my wish was to see these writers, as we say, *conversate* with one another—to talk back and forth as in some existential barbershop or beauty parlor or kitchen table or surreal radio show or whatever paradigm of the black experience these writers have taken as their own. To work it, and work it out.

Giant Steps, in the tradition of the jazz combo, goes to this new yet familiar territory—a place where its many, fresh, and even avant-garde voices compete and complement and contribute to the larger African American tradition.

PLEASE HOLD

Which brings me to necessity: It has grown apparent that in our evolving sense of the tradition, both American and African American, the younger generation has too often been left off the chart. This results as much from timing as from the times, for African American literature has begun to set its official canon. While certainly anthologies of black writing date back at least to James Weldon Johnson's *Book of Negro Poetry* (1922) and flourished during the ensuing Harlem Renaissance (which ended a decade later)—as well as the Black Arts movement of the late sixties and early seventies—the current, even millennial need to look back and evaluate is greater than ever. Thanks in part to such recent high-quality anthologies of African American literature as the Riverside and the Norton, we have solidified our sense of the past several hundred years of African American literary history—its bounds and movements, its arguments and associations. The Select Bibliography at the end of this book gives a brief sense of some of the classic and contemporary anthologies that have helped define black letters.

But where the future? Even the best anthologies skimp on younger writers, perhaps a function of their mission to establish a strong and unassailable tradition. (A notable exception is novelist and poet Clarence Major's *The Garden Thrives,* which has a varied selection of young writers.) Meanwhile, those national magazines, whether popular or literary, that have had issues dedicated to the current "black renaissance" often leave us out completely, relying as may be expected on the tried-and-true at best, at worst on the trendy. Quite rare is a journal such as *Callaloo* and its remarkable editor, Charles Powell, who has consistently and early on supported young writers—often with groundbreaking issues devoted to them alone. Across the aisle (or isle, as it were), a recent cover story in *Harper's* on the new fiction mentioned no writers of color at all—this despite the fact that many young writers fit its profile of smart, even experimental writing in pursuit of the unsaid, difficult, and even dangerous.

Certainly one should be wary of counting who is included and who is not; this can lead to counting our losses instead of our blessings. Yet it is just as easy to grow weary of having no forum for writers to interact with one another, to build on the tradition, or to complain. Far better then, as James Brown said, to "Get Up, Get Into It, Get Involved"—or, if you prefer, this motto's recent incarnation: "Get up, get out, and do something"—I listened to the Godfather of Soul, and *Giant Steps* got born.

For by neglecting the generation of this anthology, we neglect the transformative possibilities of youth. This proves strange, because in previous "renaissances," from the Harlem Renaissance to the lesser-discussed Chicago (and arguably Midwest) Renaissance of the mid-twentieth century, to the Black Arts movement, it was black youth who pushed these movements forward. After all, we cannot imagine the rise of folk forms without their championing by Langston Hughes, Zora Neale Hurston, and Sterling Brown; or the vision of the city life as subject matter offered by Gwendolyn Brooks and Richard Wright; or this vision contested by everyone from Amiri Baraka to James Baldwin; or the important takes on tradition offered by Sonia Sanchez and Lucille Clifton, by Michael Harper, Jay Wright, and Audre Lorde. It was the Black Arts explosion—and its discontents—that addressed street songs and prison life (following Sterling Brown's *Southern Road* north), explored sexuality and feminism, and argued forcefully against war, oppression, and a literary presumption of whiteness. While in previous generations, the young have determined how the tradition was seen, currently we young guns are too often those under the radar gun.

Part of this of course is natural—there is a long line of folks for us to acknowledge, to praise, to owe our current literary lives to. I see it as the writer's job, especially the African American writer's job, not to "kill the literary father" but rather to celebrate our ancestry. The influential Dark Room Collective, of which I (and a few other contributors) was once a part, used to be quite conscious of ancestry, celebrating the achievements of literary antecedents while also recognizing what we called the "living legacy"—celebrating writers from Alice Walker to Yusef Komunyakaa (who, before winning the Pulitzer, won the first Dark Room Prize for Poetry). We prided ourselves on being ahead of the curve—not out of some self-conscious sense of the avant-garde, but as a means of survival. We prized the living legacy, its sense of community and its convictions. "Total Life Is What We Want" went one slogan, taken from a Clarence Major essay; "So Hard to Canonize!" went another.

Between this shadow of canonization and the act of "total life" falls the literature of our generation, some of which is included here: uncompromising with regard to subject or voice, questioning in terms of what it means to be alive, to be African American, to be what Du Bois called "behind the veil." (But sometimes secretly loving the view from the so-called cheap seats.) What is often called the post–Civil Rights generation should not be thought of as at the tail end of "The Movement" but rather at the start of another "new thing," as experimental jazz was known in the 1960s. We are the front lines of a new century.

EIGHTEEN OR OVER TO CALL

It may seem odd to think of 1960—the debut of Coltrane's album—as a cutoff point for *Giant Steps* contributors, since decades and eras and generations are not as neat as a New Year's Eve (or even a millennium, I suspect). Yet generally speaking, 1960 is the cutoff for the birth of Generation X, that hazy rubric that these writers also may be considered under, or alongside. Regardless of the labels, there is a wide gap between the baby boomers who popularized both protest and popular culture— and too often fail to see the co-option of each by the other—and the generation represented here, who take both pop and protest for granted. And unlike so many boomers, our generation has not renounced either pop or protest, ironically becoming yuppies or buppies or advocates against the popular—in a word, their parents.

Our generation seeks to understand the ironies of both pop and protest—figuring out, as Terrance Hayes's poems do, how Marvin Gaye can write about violence but be taken by it; how, as Ruth Forman writes, "blaxploitation" icons like Cleopatra Jones can be personally liberating; how, in the end, we take and make our heroes where we can. How, even if, as Elizabeth Alexander's inaugural poem relates, we love Betty Shabazz at first for superficial reasons—her superheroic name (SHA-BAZZ!)—we come to love her entire being, her sense of what Alexander calls "expectation." Indeed, such expectation characterizes the *Giant Steps* generation and its writing.

Of course, it is perhaps a symptom of the times that what was originally written as a celebration of Shabazz now resonates as an elegy. Our elegies, such as Terrance Hayes's powerful "Some Luminous Distress," come from public mourning for a lost leader, as did Robert Hayden's "In the Mourning Time," written for Shabazz's husband, El-Hajj Malik Shabazz, for Malcolm X; they may also come from a personal relationship, as Alexander's does, as were the elegies for Malcolm X by Sanchez and Baraka. Regardless, we are far from the notion, largely false, of X as merely an image on a hat—just look at how *Giant Steps* contributor Joe Wood's anthology *Malcolm X: In Our Own Image,* makes claims on history, both personal and public. In fact, the writers in *Giant Steps* seem profoundly engaged in and with history in a way the Harlem Renaissance was engaged with origins (both folk and African) and Black Arts with politics and identity (and "identity politics"). Of course, these are generalizations, and all generations have engaged with history in some way—yet there is a clear sense in which history and attendant myth apply to these writers (such as Edwidge Danticat, Darieck Scott, and Colson Whitehead) that a glance through past anthologies does not reveal.

I hope by now it is clear that despite the age bonds, the writers here are bound not merely by age—either their years on this earth or the era around them. Rather, the writers of *Giant Steps* hang together as a generation because they address several shifting yet recurring themes in their writing: next to history, music; a willingness to use popular culture and/or experimental narratives; a focus on ancestry, especially slavery; a fluid yet frank manner in discussing sexuality, race, or biracialness; a freedom of form and technique, even ranging across genres; the travelogue; and a combination of popular culture, folkways, and wisdom beyond their years. There is also concern with violence, not as the transformative metaphor of the 1960s (think *Dutchman,* think revolution) but as a reality (as in Carolyn Ferrell), as a state of mind (Scott), or both (Hayes).

While there is not enough space here to address all these common themes, those of music and pop culture seem to demand further inquiry. We are, among other things, the hip-hop generation, having grown up alongside that art form; what this means is not simply that the writers here are rappers or even urban. Rather, they use, quite comfortably, hip-hop's aesthetic and sense of history—that is, that history is ever-present, the past easily taken from ("sampled"), repeated ("looped"), collaged together, unified often only by voice and by the rhythm of day-to-day life ("flow" and "beat"). These last elements' focus on language as a means of holding together the work of art cannot be overstated—certainly it informs the writing found in *Giant Steps*. These writers flow and then are willing to interrupt that flow, to challenge the aesthetic of quiet storm "smoothness" or sitcom solutions that are hallmarks of a public need for "positive images" or easy uplift. In other words, what previously was seen as fragmentation, these writers see as unity; what once was heard as siren, we hear as song.

Ultimately, what folk culture was to the Harlem Renaissance, popular culture is to the post-soul writer: a common language, a structure that can be referred to, a destination that some want to vilify but which we grew up with. Do not forget that it took our New Negro writers to make the blues visible as literature (and not as sinful backwardness); it has taken the writers here to make *Jet* magazine and blaxploitation and disco vinyl acceptable themes for literature (and not just "negative images"). We see no problem breakfasting with the Black Panther Political Party while reading a *Black Panther* comic book. And as is often the case in soul music, questions of suffering are implicit and subtle (take Danticat or Scott); our voices, like that of any street singer, from doo-wopper to rapper, presume their public stance and private pain. No need to state over and over "This is a protest" when declaring "We're a Winner," even though the protest is clear. Here, as with the best of hip-hop or in Ellison's *Invisible Man,* there are lower frequencies that it is the listener's job—as dancer, DJ, conductor—to discern.

To this end, *Giant Steps* hopes to counter our expectations of what black writing should be with what it be. Likewise, with the Discography at the back of the book, we hope to honor those who go before (with the best albums since 1960), just as we explore the notion of what hip-hop is. Hip-hop is more than just rap: It is an aesthetic approach, a flexible form, which, at its best, is unafraid to take from any source, then turn the beat around and let us hear it new. It is hip-hop's premise—"hear it new"—that matches modernism's urging the writer to "make it new," recognizing that much of this work is up to you, who hear the music and these words, to hear these writers' unique combination of originality and influence.

FREE SAMPLE READING

As we have seen, in this long conversation—full of calls, responses, shouts (ring and otherwise), scats, jukes, hot combos, and solos—that is African American literature, the writers here talk back to their ancestors and to each other. What further distinguishes the writers of the *Giant Steps* generation is a willingness to find ancestors anywhere the ghost takes them, whether in history (from runaway slaves to Medgar Evers), literature (Phillis Wheatley to Paul Laurence Dunbar), music (Robert Johnson and Josephine Baker), or popular realms (from Cleopatra Jones to Shaft). Indeed, the writers here seem to argue for a lack of distinction between such categories.

Just as previous generations made a way of no way, forging not just themselves but a brilliant array of opportunities for us to occupy, we are taking culture, both black and popular, and attempting to make it sing. This may be another aspect of being what may best be called post-soul writers, those writing after the 1960s and "soul power" gains. Coined by Nelson George, *post-soul* describes the world after Motown and Mayfield, the birth of funk and hip-hop and, yes, disco (originally a gay African American and Nuyorican form, lest we forget) and its current amalgams taking over our airwaves. Soul, another parallel to Black Arts, for me also parallels, if not creates, the rise of a black popular culture. (Which raises the question: Are there any non-black forms of American popular culture, from blues to rock and roll to the twist? Television, perhaps.)

In a post-soul society, however, the essentialist and often easy answers to questions of race—which have never been easy; just ask Bert Williams or Paul Robeson or Josephine Baker or Muhammad (Ali, that is)—are as complicated as ever. In recognizing the diversity of "the black experience," the poets here ask: Where do Shaft and Langston Hughes meet? The answer may often be in the Parliament-Funkadelic mothership, or in a memory from childhood or in coming to reading—but it is never simple, nor simply "never." Likewise, our nonfiction writers confront family and the past—whether in Anthony Walton's trip to his "father's land," Mississippi; or Daniel Jerome Wideman's trip to "the motherland" of Africa. Or the form of memoir itself, as in Natasha Tarpley's selection from *Girl in the Mirror*—perhaps best called a nonfiction novel—written in her grandmother's voice. These writers define nonfiction not as the opposite of fiction but as prose that takes many of the effects of fiction—from point of view to dialogue to character—and applies them to a form that inherently questions the meaning of truth.

In Hilton Als's attempts to recognize "the Negress" (often in himself), in Rebecca Walker's reclaiming of black skin, and in Phillipe Wamba's reconciliation of the "madman," our nonfiction writers also recognize the impact that gender roles play in our formulation of "blackness." This questioning of blackness—along lines of politics, gender, place, sexuality, and sexual orientation (or is it preference?)—makes up a large part of the concerns for the nonfiction writers. Our fiction writers often take up the concerns and voices of what once was called "the oppressed": from the so-called inner city (or as Lucille Clifton said, "like we call it/home") to rural poverty, from Haiti to Hollywood.

In this, we are the daughters and sons of James Baldwin and Ralph Ellison, of Zora Neale Hurston and Langston Hughes, of Jean Toomer's *Cane*, and Gayl Jones's *Corregidora*—writers who attempted the whole of human experience in their writing, often in the many forms imaginable, from memoir to criticism to novel to theater to short story to song. These writers felt no limits on what could be said, and said it loud and proud. We hope to do the same, which is why you will find a writer like Elizabeth Alexander—who leads the volume in a happy accident of alphabetizing, but who is also often seen in the forefront of this generation—writing in and across several genres. Not just poetry, but criticism; photo-essays and other essays; a verse play; inclusion in anthology after anthology: Alexander's output alone, listed in the Bibliography (useful to scholars and students and seekers of these writers' other works), also proves emblematic of this generation's output and interests.

Alexander's work clearly confronts questions of ancestry, whether in the tale of a relative who "passed" for white ("Race") or the legend of the black cowboy Nat Love ("Deadwood Dick") or the unsung story of "Frank Willis," the security guard who discovered Watergate and set in motion events that would change our country forever. (And in some small way, Alexander counters the recent troubling trend, in films from *Forrest Gump* to the more recent *Dick*, that treat Watergate, and by extension history, as a whites-only water fountain.) In celebrating her own heroes, and realizing that heroism in America does not necessarily ensure immortality, Alexander examines the consequences of being a "cog" in history, while also lifting Mr. Willis up out of the everyday, our American amnesia, and even an easy martyrdom—and into her life and ours.

We could take, for another example of the anthology's themes, of its writers' use of multilayered meaning, fiction writer Colson Whitehead, whose first book took the world of elevator inspectors and made it a powerful allegory for race and moving on up; often compared to Ellison, he may be more like Ellington, attempting with his new book on John Henry, previewed here, to take on a range of myth and meaning that Duke would be proud of (and that Ellison's second, unfinished novel could only imagine). Or take Randall Kenan or Edwidge Danticat or Carolyn Ferrell, whose writings, like Faulkner's, imagine and flesh out a whole community: whether Tims Creek, North Carolina; Port-au-Prince, Haiti; or Queens, New York City, USA.

OPERATORS STANDING BY

Above all, however, these writers are funny and filled with a sense of life's complexities, what Ralph Ellison called "the jagged edge of existence." From positions as varied as biracial or Caribbean, rural or urban, funk or folk, the contributors here have managed to expand the term *African American*—or more accurately, to recognize that now, as always, we contain multitudes. What's more, the writers have managed to make music—some that you can dance with, some that you can mourn either a lover or a life, some that makes you just want to sit back, sway, and say amen.

The writers here hail from poetry slams and the reading circuit; from intensive workshops such as Cave Canem, started by Toi Derricotte and Cornelius Eady, to the Dark Room Collective; from the Furious Flower conference and subsequent publications and recordings that helped to cement the new renaissance; from universities and cities and country roads; from upstart papers to national magazines; from established writing programs and homegrown, unnamed writing groups (not to mention the one you, fearless reader, may start tomorrow); and ultimately from the lone, long-standing practice of putting words to paper.

From the start I set out to capture some of the range of the writing experience, to remain not merely expansive but selective—to provide a peek at what's next, and who. Certainly others may have their own preference in writers, and other talented ones I am sure have managed to slip under even my radar gun, but this has been a necessary and exciting part of the process of selecting from a thriving, ever-growing literature. Indeed, on several occasions, writers I admired and would have included—especially in the longer forms of fiction and nonfiction— were simply between projects and unable, either because of contracts or timing, to produce shorter works in time. In the end, I was interested here in good writers who would stand the test of time, not just good pieces of individual writing. By way of example, the following selections do not represent merely a few "hit" poems but provide a sense of the poet's progression over time and thought. If this is my sense, then so be it—but in the space available I have sought to provide, both in selections and author notes, a healthy sense of tradition, "the changing same," while emphasizing those writers who best challenge that tradition and, by extension, our lives.

As a result, *Giant Steps* strikes a healthy balance between pieces that are uncollected in book form, those that have quickly become, for lack of a better phrase, "instant classics," and those exciting pieces that appear here for the first time. Such preservation and presentation I see as a powerful purpose of this anthology—a principle that guided me in my final, often difficult, selections.

No event brought the necessity of this process into clearer relief than the sudden loss of Joe Wood in July of 1999. After speaking with Joe about his work, the state of contemporary letters, the power of the all-too-often-underread James Baldwin, and about his excitement over the anthology, I found that his disappearance a few weeks later weighed heavily on this book's completion. In the time since, I have been struck over and over not just by Wood's brilliance, but by his relation to Baldwin himself: Wood's challenging insights on race and identity, as in his piece I am happy to see reprinted here, will be surely missed. It is in the spirit not just of our great loss with Joe Wood's disappearance, but in the spirit of his even greater achievement at such an early age, that this anthology seeks to preserve what will surely be our literary heritage.

In this way, I hope this anthology will introduce readers to writing they might otherwise not know, and broaden their knowledge of writers they may already know. May you discover, as I have, that the voices of *Giant Steps* are as varied as a jazz symphony and provide an art and future worthy of Coltrane's prophetic title.

—KEVIN YOUNG
Athens, Georgia

ELIZABETH ALEXANDER

b.1962

In *The Venus Hottentot* (1990), Elizabeth Alexander addresses history with a wary and wise eye, whether in the voice of Mexican artist Frida Kahlo, the versatile cool of Duke Ellington, or the spirit of collagist Romare Bearden. *Poetry* magazine praised the title poem, saying "it will be a landmark in American poetry, and that *The Venus Hottentot* is a superb first book."

Alexander's second book, *The Body of Life* (1996), contains fierce narratives about redemption and her childhood, including "Blues" and "Frank Willis." Her latest poems continue to merge the personal and the public, contemplating the black body—and the body politic—with a tough humor. Noted by *The Oxford Companion to African American Literature* as "emblematic of the promise and wide range of variegated voices that have sprung forth during the first half of the 1990s," Alexander is a founding member of the Cave Canem workshop retreat for African American writers.

WHAT I'M TELLING YOU

If I say, my father was Betty Shabazz's lawyer, the poem can
go no further. I've given you the punchline. If you know
who she is, all you can think about is how and what you
want to know about me, about my father, about Malcolm,
especially in 1990 when he's all over t-shirts and medallions,
but what I'm telling you is that Mrs. Shabazz was a nice
lady to me, and I loved her name for the wrong reasons,
SHABAZZ! and what I remember is going to visit her
daughters in 1970 in a dark house with little furniture and
leaving with a candy necklace the daughters gave me, to
keep. Now that children see his name and call him, Malcolm
Ten, and someone called her Mrs. Ex-es, and they don't
really remember who he was or what he said or how he
smiled the way it happened when it did, and neither do I,
I think about how history is made more than what happened
and about a nice woman in a dark house filled with
daughters and candy, something dim and unspoken,
expectation.

NINETEEN

That summer in Culpeper, all there was to eat was white:
cauliflower, flounder, white sauce, white ice-cream.
I snuck around with an older man who didn't tell me
he was married. I was the baby, drinking rum and Coke
while the men smoked reefer they'd stolen from the campers.
I tiptoed with my lover to poison-ivied fields, camp vans.
I never slept. Each fortnight I returned to the city,
black and dusty, with a garbage bag of dirty clothes.

At nineteen it was my first summer away from home.
His beard smelled musty. His eyes were black. "The ladies love my hair,"
he'd say, and like a fool I'd smile. He knew everything
about marijuana, how dry it had to be to burn,
how to crush it, sniff it, how to pick the seeds out. He said

he learned it all in Vietnam. He brought his son to visit
after one of his days off. I never imagined a mother.
"Can I steal a kiss?" he said, the first thick night in the field.

I asked and asked about Vietnam, how each scar felt,
what combat was like, how the jungle smelled. He
listened to a lot of Marvin Gaye, was all he said, and
grabbed between my legs. I'd creep to my cot before
morning. I'd eat that white food. This was before I
understoodthat nothing could be ruined in one stroke. A
sudden storm came hard one night; he bolted up inside
the van."The rain sounded just like that," he said, "on the roofs
there."

FRANK WILLIS

I am in the four percent
of adults 18–29 who told
George Gallup they know
"a lot" about Watergate.
"Watergate" was the building
near the Howard Johnson's where
we'd go when school let out for summer
and eat clam strips. Water-
gate was where we stopped
in carpool one year to fetch
the sickly boy for day camp,
where I danced in toe shoes
to the Beach Boys, in shame.
Growing up in Washington
I rode D.C. Transit, knew Senators,
believed the Washington Monument
was God's pencil because my friend
Jennifer said so, never went
to the Jefferson Memorial,
climbed the stone rhino
at the Smithsonian, cursed tourists,

took exquisite phone messages
for my father, a race man,
who worked for the government—
I held his scrawled hate mail to the light.

I don't care now that Chuck Colson
has a prison ministry, or that G.
Gordon Liddy ate a rat.
The summer I was eleven Watergate was something I watched
with my grandmother on TV like the best
soap opera but also like something
she would have called "civic," the things
you had to know. Today in some way
I somehow care that Frank Willis lives
with his mother, without employ,
was arrested for stealing
a $12 pair of sneakers, told Jet
it was "a total mix up," somehow know
there is meaning in Jet's tending the fate
of this man who saw the tape
on the office door latch. Cog, cog,
cog in the wheel of history, Frank
Willis in Jet these years later,
like the shouted spray paint on an empty
garage in my parent's back alley:
"Aaron Canaday," his name alone
enough, and then a sentence,
a song: "Slick was Here-O."

STELLA BY STARLIGHT

(after the tune, played by Monty Alexander on
piano and Othello Molyneaux on steel drum)

Red hair in summertime,
ashy toes, dust-knuckled,

the slim curve of autumn
in sight. In summertime
rhiney, shedding burnt skin,
petticoats, pantaloons.
I'm a rusty-butt sun-
baby, summer is gone.

No more corn and no blue-
berries. Sweet tomatoes
overripe. No more ice
blocks with *tamarindo,*
sweaty love in damp white
sheets, sunflowers, poppies,
salt in summertime,
sun-stoked bones. Summer jones.

Starlight cool as the edge
of fall. "Stella by Star-
light" steals stars for letters.
Each *l* and each *t* pricks
the sky like a star or
a steel drum quiver on
a note 'til it shimmer.
Who is Stella? Summer's

DEADWOOD DICK

"Come on and slant your eyes again, O Buffalo Bill."
—Carl Sandburg

Colored cowboy named Nat Love,
They called him Deadwood Dick.
A black thatch of snakes for hair,
Close-mouthed. Bullet-hipped.

One knee bent like his rifle butt,
Just so. Rope. Saddle. Fringe.

Knock this white boy off my shoulder.
Stone-jawed, cheekboned man.

Mama, there are black cowboys.
A fistful of black crotch.
Deadwood Dick: Don't fuck with me.
Black cowboy. Leather hat.

OVERTURE: WATERMELON CITY

Philadelphia is burning and watermelon is all that can cool it,
so there they are, spiked
atop a row of metal poles,
rolling on and off pickup trucks,
the fruit that grows longest,
the fruit with a curly tail, the cool fruit,
larger than a large baby, wide
as the widest green behind, wide
vermillion smile at the sizzling metropole.
Did I see this yesterday? Did I dream
this last night? The city is burning.
is burning for real.

When I first moved here I lived two streets over
from Osage, where it happened, twelve streets down.
I asked my neighbors, who described
the smell of smoke and flesh,
the city on fire for real.
How far could you see the flames?
How long could you smell the smoke?
Osage is narrow, narrow
like a movie set: urban eastern seaboard,
the tidy of people who work hard for very little.

Life lived on the porch,
the amphitheater street.

I live here, 4937 Hazel Avenue, West Philly.
Hello Adam and Ukee,
the boys on that block
who guarded my car, and me.
They called him Ukee because
as a baby he looked
like a eucalyptus leaf.
Hello holy rollers
who plug in their amps,
blow out the power in the building,
preach to the street from the stoop.
Hello, crack-head next-door neighbor
who raps on my door after midnight
needing money for baby formula,
she says, and the woman
who runs in the street
with her titties out, wailing.
Hello street. Hello ladies
who sweep their front porches each morning.
In downtown Philadelphia
there are many lovely restaurants,
reasonably-priced.
Chocolate, lemon ice,
and hand-filled cannoli
in South Philly.
Around the corner
at the New Africa Lounge
in West Philadelphia
we sweat buckets
to hi-life and zouk,
we burn.

RACE

Sometimes I think about Great-Uncle Paul who left Tuskegee,
Alabama, to become a forester in Oregon and in so doing
became fundamentally white for the rest of his life, except

when he travelled without his white wife to visit his siblings—
now in New York, now in Harlem, USA—just as pale-skinned,
as straight-haired, as blue-eyed as Paul, and black. Paul never
told anyone he was white, he just didn't say that he was black,
and who could imagine an Oregon forester in 1930 as anything other
than white? The siblings in Harlem each morning ensured
no one confused them for anything other than what they were,
black. They were black! Brown-skinned spouses reduced confusion.
Many others have told, and not told, this tale.
When Paul came East alone he was as they were, their brother.

The poet invents heroic moments where the pale black ancestor
stands up on behalf of the race. The poet imagines Great-Uncle
Paul in cool, sagey groves counting rings in redwood trunks,
imagines pencil markings in a ledger book, classifications,
imagines a sidelong look from an ivory spouse who is learning
her husband's caesuras. She can see silent spaces
but not what they signify, graphite markings in a forester's code.

Many others have told, and not told, this tale.
The one time Great-Uncle Paul brought his wife to New York
he asked his siblings not to bring their spouses,
and that is where the story ends: ivory siblings who would not
see their brother without their tell-tale spouses.
What a strange thing is "race," and family, stranger still.
Here a poem tells a story, a story about race.

BLUES

I am lazy, the laziest
girl in the world. I sleep during
the day when I want to, 'til
my face is creased and swollen,
'til my lips are dry and hot. I
eat as I please: cookies and milk
after lunch, butter and sour cream

on my baked potato, foods that
slothful people eat, that turn
yellow and opaque beneath the skin.
Sometimes come dinnertime Sunday
I am still in my nightgown, the one
with the lace trim listing because
I have not mended it. Many days
I do not exercise, only
consider it, then rub my curdy
belly and lie down. Even
my poems are lazy. I use
syllabics instead of iambs,
prefer slant to the gong of full rhyme,
write briefly while others go
for pages. And yesterday,
for example, I did not work at all!
I got in my car and I drove
to factory outlet stores, purchased
stockings and panties and socks
with my father's money.

To think, in childhood I missed only
one day of school per year. I went
to ballet class four days a week
at four-forty-five and on
Saturdays, beginning always
with plie, ending with curtsy.
To think, I knew only industry,
the industry of my race
and of immigrants, the radio
tuned always to the station
that said, Line up your summer
job months in advance. Work hard
and do not shame your family,
who worked hard to give you what you have.
There is no sin but sloth. Burn
to a wick and keep moving.

GIANT STEPS

I avoided sleep for years,
up at night replaying
evening news stories about
nearby jailbreaks, fat people
who ate fried chicken and woke up
dead. In sleep I am looking
for poems in the shape of open
V's of birds flying in formation,
or open arms saying, I forgive you, all.

FEMINIST POEM NUMBER ONE

Yes I have dreams where I am rescued by men:
my father, brother, husband, no one else.
Last night I dreamed my brother and husband
morphed into each other and rescued me
from a rat-infested apartment. "Run!"
he said, feral scampering at our heels.
And then we went to lunch at the Four Seasons.

What does it mean to be a princess?
"I am what is known as an American Negro,"
my grandmother would say, when "international friends"
would ask her what she was. She'd roller-skate
to Embassy Row and sit on the steps of the embassies
to be certain the rest of the world was there.

What does it mean to be a princess?
My husband drives me at six A.M.
to the airport an hour away, drives home,
drives back when I have forgotten my passport.
What does it mean to be a prince? I cook
savory, fragrant meals for my husband
and serve him, if he likes, in front of the TV.
He cooks for me, too. I have a husband.
In the dream we run into Aunt Lucy,
who is waiting for a plane from "Abyssinia"

to bring her lover home. I am the one
married to an Abyssinian, who is already here. I am the one
with the grandmother who wanted to know the world.
I am what is known as an American Negro princess,
married to an African prince,
living in a rat-free apartment in New Haven,
all of it, all of it, under one roof.

HILTON ALS
b. 1960

Whether in his articles as contributing editor of *The New Yorker* or in his nonfiction book, *The Women* (1996), Hilton Als courts controversy. In prose precise as James Baldwin's, Als confronts race, soul music, sexuality, and the 1970s without regard to sacred ground—including Baldwin himself. *The Women* provides an autobiography by proxy, discussing Als's mother, Warhol scenemaker Dorothy Dean, and Harlem Renaissance figure (and Als's sometime lover) Owen Dodson with equal insight into their characters. By suggesting that all three were "Negresses," Als ultimately describes himself, forcing a discussion of race, sexuality, and identity. As seen in these two excerpts, Als brilliantly combines cultural studies with the memoir form, challenging both racial and sexual stereotypes.

FROM *THE WOMEN*

Until the end, my mother never discussed her way of being. She avoided explaining the impetus behind her emigration from Barbados to Manhattan. She avoided explaining that she had not been motivated by the same desire for personal gain and opportunity that drove most female immigrants. She avoided recounting the fact that she had emigrated to America to follow the man who eventually became my father, and whom she had known in his previous incarnation as her first and only husband's closest friend. She avoided explaining how she had left her husband—by whom she had two daughters—after he returned to Barbados from England and the Second World War addicted to morphine. She was silent about the fact that, having been married once, she refused to marry again. She avoided explaining that my father, who had grown up relatively rich in Barbados and whom she had known as a child, remained a child and emigrated to America with his mother and his two sisters—women whose home he never left. She never mentioned that she had been attracted to my father's beauty and wealth partially because those were two things she would never know. She never discussed how she had visited my father in his room at night, and afterward crept down the stairs stealthily to return to her own home and her six children, four of them produced by her union with my father, who remained a child. She never explained that my father never went to her; she went to him. She avoided explaining that my father, like most children, and like most men, resented his children—four girls, two boys—for not growing up quickly enough so that they would leave home and take his responsibility away with them. She avoided recounting how my father—because he was a child—tried to distance himself from his children and his resentment of them through his derisive humor, teasing them to the point of cruelty; she also avoided recounting how her children, in order to shield themselves against the spittle of his derisive humor, absented themselves in his presence and, eventually, in the presence of any form of entertainment deliberately aimed at provoking laughter. She avoided explaining that in response to this resentment, my father also vaunted his beauty and wealth over his children, as qualities they would never share. She was silent about the mysterious bond she and my father shared, a bond so deep and volatile that their children felt forever diminished by their love, and forever compelled to disrupt, disapprove, avoid, or try to become a part of the love shared between any couple (specifically men and women) since part of our birthright has been to remain children, not unlike our father. She avoided mentioning the fact that my father had other women, other families, in cities such as Miami and Boston, cities my father roamed like a bewildered child. She was silent about the fact that my father's mother and sisters told her about the other women and children my father had, probably as a test to see how much my mother could stand to hear about my father, whom his mother and sisters felt only they could understand and love, which is one reason my father remained a child. My mother avoided mentioning the fact that her mother, in Barbados, had had a child with a man other than my mother's father, and that man had been beautiful and relatively rich. She avoided explaining how her mother had thought her association with that relatively rich and beautiful man would make her beautiful and rich also. She avoided explaining how, after that had not happened for her mother, her mother became bitter about this and other things for the rest of her very long life. She avoided contradicting her mother when she said things like "Don't play in the sun. You are black enough," which is what my grandmother said to me once. She avoided explaining that she had wanted to be different from her mother. She avoided explaining that she created a position of power for herself in this common world by being a mother to children, and childlike men, as she attempted to separate from her parents and siblings by being "nice," an attitude they could never understand, since they weren't. She avoided recounting memories of her family's cruelty, one instance of their cruelty being: my mother's family sitting in a chartered bus as it rained outside on a family picnic; my mother, alone, in the rain, cleaning up the family picnic as my mother's aunt said, in her thick Bajan accent: "Marie is one of God's own," and the bus rocking with derisive laughter as my heart broke, in silence. She avoided mentioning that she saw and understood where my fascination with certain aspects of her narrative—her emigration, her love, her kindness—would take me, a boy of seven, or eight, or ten: to the dark crawl space behind her closet, where I put on her hosiery one leg at a time, my heart racing, and, over those hose, my jeans and sneakers, so that I could have her—what I so admired and coveted—near me, always.

By now, the Negress has come to mean many things. She is perceived less as a mind than as an emotional being. In the popular imagination, she lives one or several cliché-ridden narratives. One narrative: she is generally colored, female, and a single mother, reduced by circumstances to tireless depression and public "aid," working off the books in one low-paying job after another in an attempt to support her children—children she should not have had, according to tax-paying, law-abiding public consensus. Like my mother. Another narrative: she can be defined as a romantic wedded to despair, since she has little time or inclination to dissemble where she stands in America's social welfare system, which regards her as a statistic, part of the world's rapacious silent majority. Like my mother. Another narrative: she gives birth to children who grow up to be lawless; she loves men who leave her for other women; she is subject to depression and illness. Her depression is so numbing that she rarely lets news of the outside world (television news, radio news, newspapers) enter her sphere of consciousness, since much of her time is spent fording herself and her children against the news of emotional disaster she sees day after day in the adult faces surrounding the faces of her children, who, in turn, look to her to make sense of it all. Like my mother.

What the Negress has always been: a symbol of America's by now forgotten strain of puritanical selflessness. The Negress is a perennial source of "news" and interesting "copy" in the newspapers and magazines she does not read because she is a formidable character in the internal drama most Americans have with the issue of self-abnegation. The Negress serves as a reminder to our sentimental nation that what its countrymen are shaped by is a nonverbal confusion about and, ultimately, abhorrence for the good neighbor policy. Most Americans absorb the principles of the good neighbor policy through the language-based tenets of Judaism and Christianity. These laws lead to a deep emotional confusion about the "good" since most Americans are suspicious of language and spend a great deal of time and energy on Entertainment and Relaxation in an attempt to avoid its net result: Reflection. If the Negress is represented as anything in the media, it is generally as a good neighbor, staunch in her defense of the idea that being a good neighbor makes a difference in this common world. She is also this: a good neighbor uncritical of faith, even as her intellect dissects the byzantine language of the Bible, searching for a truth other than her own. Which is one reason the Negress is both abhorred and adored: for her ability to meld language with belief without becoming sarcastic. Take, for instance, this story, reported in the *New York Post*: "The Trinidad woman who lost her legs in a subway purse snatching is not looking for revenge—but she hopes her mugger becomes 'a better person' in prison . . . Samela Thompson, 56, fell onto the tracks in the Van Wyck Boulevard station in Jamaica, Queens . . . She was trying to jump onto the platform from an E train as she chased a homeless man who had grabbed her sister's purse . . . The feisty mother of five's attitude is 'you have to take life as it comes.' Thompson wished [her attacker] would know God."

To women who are not Negresses—some are white—the Negress, whether she calls herself that or not, is a specter of dignity—selfless to a fault. But eventually the Negress troubles her noncolored female admirer, since the latter feels compelled to compare her privilege to what the Negress does not have—recognizable privilege—and finds herself lacking. This inversion or competitiveness among women vis-à-vis their "oppressed" stance says something about why friendships among women are rare, let alone why friendships between noncolored women and Negresses are especially so.

For years before and after her death, I referred to myself as a Negress; it was what I was conditioned to be. And yet I have come no closer to defining it. In fact, I shy away from defining it, given my mother's complex reaction to Negressity for herself and me. I have expressed my Negressity by living, fully, the prescribed life of an auntie man—what Barbadians call a faggot. Which is a form of kinship, given that my being an auntie man is based on greed for romantic love with men temperamentally not unlike the men my mother knew—that and an unremitting public "niceness." I socialized myself as an auntie man long before I committed my first act as one. I also wore my mother's and sisters' clothes when they were not home; those clothes deflected from the pressure I felt in being different from them. As a child, this difference was too much for me to take; I buried myself in their clothes, their secrets, their desires, to find myself through them. Those women "killed" me, as comedians say when they describe their power over an audience. I wanted them to kill me further by fully exploiting the attention I afforded them. But they couldn't, being women.

Being an auntie man enamored of Negressity is all I have ever known how to be. I do not know what my life would be, or if I *would* be at all, if I were any different.

To say that the public's reaction to my mother's being a Negress and my being one were similar would be egregious. My mother was a woman. Over the years in Brooklyn, she worked as a housekeeper for a relatively well-off Scotsman, as a housekeeper for a Jewish matron, in a beauty salon as a hairdresser, as an assistant in a nursery school. My mother responded to my being a Negress with pride and anger: pride in my identification with women like herself; anger that I identified with her at all. I could not help her react to any of this any differently than she did. This failure haunts me still. I have not catapulted myself past my mother's emotional existence.

Did my mother call herself a Negress as a way of ironically reconciling herself to her history as that most hated of English colonial words, which fixed her as a servant in the eyes of Britain and God? I don't think so, given that she was not especially interested in Britain or history. But "Negress" was one of the few words she took with her when she emigrated from Barbados to Manhattan. As a Negress, her passport to the world was restricted; the world has its limits. Shortly after arriving in New York in the late forties, my mother saw what her everyday life would be; being bright, a high school graduate, and practical, she looked at the world she had emigrated to, picked up her servant's cap, and began starching it with servitude. In her new country, my mother noticed that some New Yorkers retained the fantasy that in writing or speaking about the "underclass," or the "oppressed, silent" woman, or the "indomitable" stoic, they were writing about the kind of Negress she was, but they weren't. My mother was capricious in her views about most things, including race. As a West Indian who lived among other West Indians, my mother did not feel "difference"; she would not allow her feelings to be ghettoized; in her community, she was in the majority. She was capable of giving a nod toward the history of "injustice," but only if it suited her mood.

I think my mother took some pleasure in how harsh the word "Negress" seemed to the citizens in her adopted home. I have perhaps made more of the word "Negress" than my mother meant by it, but I saw and continue to see how it is used to limit and stupidly define the world certain women inhabit. I think my mother took pleasure in manipulating the guilt and embarrassment white and black Americans alike felt when she called herself a Negress, since their view of the Negress was largely sentimental, maudlin, replete with suffering. When my mother laughed in the face of their deeply presumptive view of her, one of her front teeth flashed gold.

My mother disliked the American penchant for euphemism; she was resolute in making the world confront its definition of her. This freed her mind for other things, like her endless illness, which was a protracted form of suicide. From my mother I learned the only way the Negress can own herself is through her protracted suicide; suffering from imminent death keeps people at a distance. I was so lonely knowing her; she was so busy getting to know herself through dying. When my mother became ill with one thing or another, I was eight; by the time my mother died, I was twenty-eight. When she died, I barely knew anything about her at all.

❑

Because my mother spent most of her time dying, many women she knew—my father's sisters, my sisters, one or two of her neighborhood friends—created a circle around the event of her long-anticipated death. These women knew there was power in it. Some of them even co-opted it as the greatest event, the greatest story of their lives. These women marveled at the defeat and loss, the bitterness and recrimination, the silence and cunning, the love and generosity, that my mother, living and dying, had borne with the alacrity of a stoic. In their lives, these women had experienced similar emotions, but had tried to obfuscate them with the vows of motherhood and marriages which no illusionary veil could obscure the pain and boredom of. To these women, my mother was a kind of Cassandra, who saw their future as well as her own. What they saw in my mother was a woman who, having disavowed the conventions of marriage, chose to control her own demise instead. I have yet to stop considering either as life's only options.

The central link in this circle of women was my father's sister, who remains the first Negress I ever knew who did not avoid recounting the facts of her life. My mother was attracted to her because of this, but she also shied away from my aunt's speech; it made my mother's silence more pointed and my aunt's Negressity more entertaining. My aunt had already established her presence in the world by becoming a dramatic alcoholic. When I went to stay with her—generally when my mother was in the hospital for one thing or another—I would watch her turn large and green with alcohol. Her alcoholism was the event of her life, and it dwarfed the emotional life of those around her: her widowed mother, her husband, her daughter, my father, and (sometimes) me.

My aunt made up her internal physiognomy far too garishly; and her rouge pot consisted of violent language. Like the poets my sister would eventually introduce me to in Harlem, she was too rhetorical in her stance. There was no way into her language, but her performance resonated for her audience. She poured glass after glass of scotch and the brown liquid gurgled as her large eyes became larger, then her neck, and then her entire body. She observed the events of her life as if from a great distance—that distance being the land spit of her mind and body. And as I observed her—the way my mother sometimes did—she became literature: that is, she took on the contours of a figure who could engage my imagination. She was a Negress. She drank to forget the fact that she felt dwarfed by my father's exceptional beauty. She drank to mourn her older sister's renunciation of a promising career as a jazz musician because their father had told her that playing jazz is for whores. She drank because her second child, a boy, was born dead—twenty years before I knew her—and I, who was alive, was named after him. She drank when she suggested that she "killed" him. She drank because her mother had not wanted her to be born. She drank because she was a woman. She drank because she was a nurse. She drank because of the fecklessness of men, the despair of all women, and the fact that she could not write her language and somehow claim her life—it was too oratorical, too rhetorical.

So she replaced her life with its mundane exigencies. Every day of her married life, she argued with her husband about what he had not turned out to be, what her daughter would turn out to be ("a bitch"), how the world had turned against her. She had the gift of language, but she couldn't use it. Her drinking brought forth the sense that language had turned to waste in her twilight mind, which lived in the past while she went on uttering the old, old female story: her inability to forgive life for what it had not allowed her to claim: herself.

Until I knew my father's sister, I did not know that class issues had an effect on the daily life of the Negress. I realized this when I observed that my father's sister and her daughter had more of most things—money, clothes—than my sisters and mother had. When I noticed this, I was five, or twelve; at any rate, I was a child, and impressed by the glamour of their prosperity. My admiration was made more delicious by the fact that I experienced economic envy of another Negress. Until then, it had not occurred to me that the Negress world I had been born into was not the entire world. My daily life with my mother and sisters was so different from my aunt's. My mother, my sisters, and I spent a great deal of our time going to the storage bins that families on public assistance were required to go to then, to pick up large tins of ketchup, corned-beef hash, empty calories. We filled up on the empty calories we consumed. A social worker came to our home to find out if my mother worked, or whether she had a boyfriend who helped her financially. I learned how to be a conversationalist as I amused the beleaguered, suspicious social worker while my sisters and brother hid the possessions my mother had acquired through her employers: frying pans, a small black-and-white television set, a typewriter.

My aunt knew very little about all this. She was fat with drink and privilege. As my aunt drank, her eyes took in her possessions and numbered them: the beautiful house with dark wood paneling, heavy drapes, and wooden blinds, all of which my grandmother had acquired through thrift and fortitude, ostensibly for her children, who could not see any surroundings without projecting their despair onto them.

In certain photographs taken at her marriage, my aunt wears a wedding dress of green satin and carries a small corsage. Copies of the same photograph were on prominent display throughout my grandmother's house. My grandmother cleaved to achievement of any kind. My grandmother's children—my aunts, my father—had achieved nothing in this common world except marriage and children and maintaining a sense of their own privilege. And alcohol on my aunt's lips could never dispel the words that tumbled over each other, picking over each bitterness. When she looked at her wedding photograph, she saw not how the dress fit her, but its creases.

In the privacy of my home, I consider certain facts: that my mother died in Barbados, our ancestral home. Before she left New York for Barbados, I did not visit her to say goodbye; this was only one of many leave-takings. When my mother left New York for Barbados, she did not say goodbye to many people who had known her. My mother could not bear to say goodbye to anyone, although she did it continually. I have acquired this tendency of my mother's without quite knowing how. I have also acquired her drive to suicide. But I have only shown it once. I had learned from many years of watching my mother that one way to join the body and mind together was through suicide. After she died, I tried to kill myself. But I laughed so hard watching myself do this in the bathroom mirror that the pills in my mouth spilled out. How could a handful of pills compare with the years my mother spent dying?

In Barbados, my mother did not say goodbye to her sister who lives there still. "I knew she wouldn't come back. I knew she would die there," my mother's sister told me when I went to Barbados after my mother's death to see where she had died and perhaps retroactively to spend time with her (I was so lonely knowing her alive; now that she is not alive, she is everywhere, like words). My visit meant nothing to my mother's sister. She is not interested in the facts of anyone's life—a family trait. She said several things when I went to visit her in her ugly house surrounded by coconut trees on a pitiful plot of land. She said: "Your mother was so angry at the end." She asked: "When did you know you were going to be an auntie man?" She asked: "When will you write a story about me?"

I did not ask: Am I not a Negress too? Incapable of making a gift of myself to myself? In that ugly house in Barbados as the trade winds blew, my aunt was telling me I could.

ANTHONY BUTTS
b. 1969

The poems of Anthony Butts serve as a self-portrait of the city of Detroit, though for Butts his hometown proves less the Motor City than a city of stagnant lives, as in "Machines" and "Self-Portrait with Clark Street Cadillac." Butts's first volume of poetry, *Fifth Season* (1997), describes a unique state of mind and time, often through quiet lyrics that hint at his growing up in a school for the blind. As in "A Poe Story," Butts treats Gothic material such as violence as an everyday occurrence—or the ordinary becomes Gothic and ominous, as does the orchestra in "The Loudest Sound." In any form, Butts's poems challenge our sense of reality and responsibility.

GIANT STEPS

A POE STORY

Three a.m. smoke rises from underground
gas lines, the hissing louder than the murmurs
of pigeons, louder than the white winter
clouds passing, heavy with the burden of snow,
nothing released here in Kalamazoo,
neither snow, nor rain, nor any item dropped
from the clenched purse of a woman walking
to her car, footsteps growing louder, quickening
as she spots me walking towards her, towards
the computer center, open twenty-four hours
for people like me, her car between us, gun metal
gray and slush beneath the fenders, the sky
forbidding as my brown face must seem,
her legs making ostrich strides, high heels
scraping the pavement, maybe thinking
my University book bag isn't a knapsack
but a rucksack concealing a gun or knife
bigger than any she's seen in any beefcake
action film where the hero can save a woman like her
from a guy like me, as beautiful as any Poe story,
the spires growing steeper, the icy
smoke of winter puffing faster through her lips, my strides
lengthening like any man who's tried to avoid looking
like a criminal, easing and slowing down as if the indictment
has already been filed, as if suspicion alone
could sentence a man before the crime,
before the thought has entered his mind, before the need
to steal ever took him from the arms of the starving children
he hasn't fathered, or from the woman waving good-bye
to her mother in the window of that first foster care home.

BECOMING THE GHOST

They sit on the window ledge
and her liver spots disappear
as he takes her hand in his
while they watch leaves fall
at the conspicuous feet of ghosts
like the cat Chucky Mastaw hung
from his neighbor's lamppost
last Halloween. Today they pretend
that they're invisible, invincible
to the rotten broomstick
leaning in the laundry room.
In this embrace—at the showing
of the moon through fat-cheeked clouds—
her arms dangle down his back.
Theirs is an economy of imitations.
Her cinnamon lipstick smile mimics
the one in his mind, the one
his mother couldn't give him.
Body guards need to guard bodies
only, the best mother raising the best
little boy in a neighborhood of paroled
drug dealers dealing on the time
left to them. No, this woman is not
his mother or anybody else's: the slightly
puffy veins in her arms are a kind of comfort,
a protection. Her forgiving limbs
could shield him and soften the impact
of stones hidden in his mind,
from the memories of snowballs hurled
across a school yard, from the memories
of that kiss, that smack of the wet rock
against his arm.

SELF-PORTRAIT WITH CLARK STREET CADILLAC

Old age seems like a palette of watercolors
to the child who visits his aunt at City Hospital,
watching her sip orange juice through the green straw
in her arm. On the window's canvas, his face looks back
from the street below—concealing those hollow plains,
those dusty low places of stone gristle and rusty
crisscrossed nails, bleeding beneath his face
like the face of Clark Street Cadillac half-demolished.

DETROIT, ONE A.M.

Slabs of steel for luxury
cars are piled neatly behind
this 1950s diner, like the ones
their fathers took them to, years ago,
after picking them up from school.
The young men remember the time
as a gloaming in the distance of history.
Blacks work here now
under the cold brilliance
of fluorescent lights hanging
above the counter,
while the customers—big like their fathers—
stuff their faces with sandwiches.

Pairs of Japanese girls
pass through the doors, land
smoothly on the bar stools—
sit up straight as rooks,
shaking the slight chill
of a Detroit autumn from their hair.
They smile like the blonde girls
from the play they've just seen,
the pained look
of their faces in compact

mirrors reminding them
of their alien sex.

The men already have that beaten down
look of divorce, smiling
because they must appear
normal and unattached
if it's going to work this time.
They can make it different
if only they learn
how they can shine brighter
than the punishing lights.

MACHINES

Outside of town, thousands of frogs chortle
And whistle like the frantic sirens and screams
Of an apocalypse, but only the theaters
Are full. Aliens have invaded the earth

Once again. We are never alone, not even
The man who pulls his wife closer in bed
To keep her silent. Her thoughts are like pigeons that crowd
The sidewalks of city parks. The sun rises

Over a misty lake in a starving artist's
Painting. It's the last thing they agreed upon.
Throughout the town, public art stands
At the ready like unnamable metallic

Creatures awaiting a secret message to strike.
A dumpster bears the spray-painted warning:
HEAVEN OR HELL AWAITS YOU as children twirl
Yo-yos with Copernican precision.

A man whispers how machines control
Us all as he watches the toys churn gears.
Pizza delivery vehicles careen
Around corners like the National Guard

GIANT STEPS

On maneuvers. There's a price for being first.
Morning has returned, the sun between
The slats lacing their arms like rubber straps.
Late night static on television gives way

To a commercial involving local store owners,
Toddlers and canines at their sides. Families are
Truth. In Hartsburg, children smelly as goats
Or dogs run through lawns covered with pumpkins.

All is calm, but the festival crowds are days
Away when cars will jam the road through town.
Proclamations will shine like copper doorknobs,
Their closing sentences held together by hinges.

THE LOUDEST SOUND

The creatures seemed to disappear as snow
fell in flakes the size of buttons, the gray
noon fastened down like a sofa cushion,
the muffled air laboring to breathe.

The limbs of trees flashed their charcoal
lightning overhead, their green leaves
withheld like winter's thunder, each branch
bobbing like wrists in a violin section.

A man sat on a park bench, allowing
the snow to hem his shoulders beneath the silent
white garment of winter. He watched as flakes
filled the footprints, erasing the evidence.

Others remained in the still cocoons
of their living rooms like caterpillars snoozing.
The concert hall held an orchestra practicing,
the white cuffs of their shirts poking out of

the black cylinders of their suits like prairie
dogs. They carved their strings as a slender Ukrainian
pianist deftly killed each previous chord,
damning the keys with her long white fingers.

EDWIDGE DANTICAT

b. 1969

Born under Haiti's dictatorial regime, Edwidge Danticat writes of oppression and possibility in her works of fiction, which include two novels: *Breath, Eyes, Memory* (1994) and *The Gathering of Bones* (1998). *Krik? Krak!* (1995), her collection of short stories, was a National Book Award finalist and a Pushcart Prize winner. Although her parents emigrated to the United States when she was four, Danticat did not follow until she was twelve; perhaps as a result her work confidently holds many voices, even worlds, at once, fusing a postcolonial, Caribbean perspective with a style all her own. Much like Toni Morrison, Danticat tackles difficult subjects while gaining a popular appeal for her work, selected for Oprah's Book Club and appearing in a recent *New Yorker* issue on "the future of American fiction." "The Book of the Dead," reprinted here, further explores the often rough terrain of family, memory, and exile.

THE BOOK OF THE DEAD

My father is gone. I am slouched in a cast-aluminum chair across from two men, one the manager of the hotel where we're staying and the other a policeman. They are waiting for me to explain what has become of him, my father.

The manager—"Mr. Flavio Salinas," the plaque on his office door reads—has the most striking pair of chartreuse eyes I have ever seen on a man with an island-Spanish lilt to his voice.

The officer is a baby-faced, short white Floridian with a pot belly.

"Where are you and your daddy from, Ms. Bienaime?" he asks.

I answer "Haiti," even though I was born and raised in East Flatbush, Brooklyn, and have never visited my parents' birthplace. I do this because it is one more thing I have longed to have in common with my parents.

The officer plows forward. "You down here in Lakeland from Haiti?"

"We live in New York. We were on our way to Tampa."

I find Manager Salinas's office gaudy. The walls are covered with orange-and-green wallpaper, briefly interrupted by a giant gold-leaf-bordered print of a Victorian cottage that somehow resembles the building we're in. Patting his light-green tie, he whispers reassuringly, "Officer Bo and I will do the best we can to help you find your father."

We start out with a brief description: "Sixty-four, five feet eight inches, two hundred and twenty pounds, moon-faced, with thinning salt-and-pepper hair. Velvet-brown eyes—"

"Velvet-brown?" says Officer Bo.

"Deep brown—same color as his complexion."

My father has had partial frontal dentures for ten years, since he fell off his and my mother's bed when his prison nightmares began. I mention that, too. Just the dentures, not the nightmares. I also bring up the claw-shaped marks that run from his left ear down along his cheek to the corner of his mouth—the only visible reminder of the year he spent at Fort Dimanche, the Port-au-Prince prison ironically named after the Lord's Day.

"Does your daddy have any kind of mental illness, senility?" asks Officer Bo.

"No."

"Do you have any pictures of your daddy?"

I feel like less of a daughter because I'm not carrying a photograph in my wallet. I had hoped to take some pictures of him on our trip. At one of the rest stops I bought a disposable camera and pointed it at my father. No, no, he had protested, covering his face with both hands like a little boy protecting his cheeks from a slap. He did not want any more pictures taken of him for the rest of his life. He was feeling too ugly.

"That's too bad," says Officer Bo. "Does he speak English, your daddy? He can ask for directions, et cetera."

"Yes."

"Is there anything that might make your father run away from you— particularly here in Lakeland?" Manager Salinas interjects. "Did you two have a fight?"

I had never tried to tell my father's story in words before now, but my first sculpture of him was the reason for our trip: a two-foot-high mahogany figure of my father, naked, crouching on the floor, his back arched like the curve of a crescent moon, his downcast eyes fixed on his short stubby fingers and the wide palms of his hands. It was hardly revolutionary, minimalist at best, but it was my favorite of all my attempted representations of him. It was the way I had imagined him in prison.

The last time I had seen my father? The previous night, before falling asleep. When we pulled into the pebbled driveway, densely lined with palm and banana trees, it was almost midnight. All the restaurants in the area were closed. There was nothing to do but shower and go to bed.

"It is like a paradise here," my father said when he saw the room. It had the same orange-and-green wallpaper as Salinas's office, and the plush green carpet matched the walls. "Look, Annie," he said, "it is like grass under our feet." He was always searching for a glimpse of paradise, my father.

He picked the bed closest to the bathroom, removed the top of his gray jogging suit, and unpacked his toiletries. Soon after, I heard him humming, as he always did, in the shower.

After he got into bed, I took a bath, pulled my hair back in a ponytail, and checked on the sculpture—just felt it a little bit through the bubble padding and carton wrapping to make sure it wasn't broken. Then I slipped under the covers, closed my eyes, and tried to sleep.

I pictured the client to whom I was delivering the sculpture: Gabrielle Fonteneau, a young woman about my age, an actress on a nationally syndicated television series. My friend Jonas, the principal at the East Flatbush elementary school where I teach drawing to fifth graders, had shown her a picture of my "Father" sculpture, and, the way Jonas told it, Gabrielle Fonteneau had fallen in love with it and wished to offer it as a gift to her father on his birthday.

Since this was my first big sale, I wanted to make sure that the piece got there safely. Besides, I needed a weekend away, and both my mother and I figured that my father, who watched a lot of television, both in his barbershop and at home, would enjoy meeting Gabrielle, too. But when I woke up the next morning my father was gone.

I showered, put on my driving jeans and a T-shirt, and waited. I watched a half hour of midmorning local news, smoked three mentholated cigarettes even though we were in a nonsmoking room, and waited some more. By noon, four hours had gone by. And it was only then that I noticed that the car was still there but the sculpture was gone.

I decided to start looking for my father: in the east garden, the west garden, the dining room, the exercise room, and in the few guest rooms cracked open while the maid changed the sheets; in the little convenience store at the Amoco gas station nearby; even in the Salvation Army thrift shop that from a distance seemed to blend into the interstate. All that waiting and looking actually took six hours, and I felt guilty for having held back so long before going to the front desk to ask, "Have you seen my father?"

I feel Officer Bo's fingers gently stroking my wrist. Up close he smells like fried eggs and gasoline, like breakfast at the Amoco. "I'll put the word out with the other boys," he says. "Salinas here will be in his office. Why don't you go back to your room in case he shows up there?"

I return to the room and lie in the unmade bed, jumping up when I hear the click from the electronic key in the door. It's only the housekeeper. I turn down the late-afternoon cleaning and call my mother at the beauty salon where she perms, presses, and braids hair, next door to my father's barbershop. But she isn't there. So I call my parents' house and leave the hotel number on their machine. "Please call me as soon as you can, Manman. It's about Papi."

Once, when I was twelve, I overheard my mother telling a young woman who was about to get married how she and my father had first met on the sidewalk in front of Fort Dimanche the evening that my father was released from jail. (At a dance, my father had fought with a soldier out of uniform who had him arrested and thrown in prison for a year.) That night, my mother was returning home from a sewing class when he stumbled out of the prison gates and collapsed into her arms, his face still bleeding from his last beating. They married and left for New York a year later. "We were like two seeds planted in a rock," my mother had told the young woman, "but somehow when our daughter, Annie, came we took root."

My mother soon calls me back, her voice staccato with worry:

"Where is Papi?"

"I lost him."

"How you lost him?"

"He got up before I did and disappeared."

"How long he been gone?"

"Eight hours," I say, almost not believing myself that it's been that long.

My mother is clicking her tongue and humming. I can see her sitting at the kitchen table, her eyes closed, her fingers sliding up and down her flesh-colored stockinged legs.

"You call police?"

"Yes."

"What they say?"

"To wait, that he'll come back."

My mother is thumping her fingers against the phone's mouthpiece, which is giving me a slight ache in my right ear.

"Tell me where you are," she says. "Two more hours and he's not there, call me, I come."

I dial Gabrielle Fonteneau's cellular-phone number. When she answers, her voice sounds just as it does on television, but more silken and seductive without the sitcom laugh track.

"To think," my father once said while watching her show, "Haitian-born actresses on American television."

"And one of them wants to buy my stuff," I'd added.

When she speaks, Gabrielle Fonteneau sounds as if she's in a place with cicadas, waterfalls, palm trees, and citronella candles to keep the mosquitoes away. I realize that I, too, am in such a place, but I can't appreciate it.

"So nice of you to come all this way to deliver the sculpture," she says. "Jonas tell you why I like it so much? My papa was a journalist in Port-au-Prince. In 1975, he wrote a story criticizing the dictatorship, and he was arrested and put in jail."

"Fort Dimanche?"

"No, another one," she says. "Caserne. Papa kept track of days there by scraping lines with his fingernails on the walls of his cell. One of the guards didn't like this, so he pulled out all his fingernails with pliers."

I think of the photo spread I saw in the *Haitian Times* of Gabrielle Fonteneau and her parents in their living room in Tampa. Her father was described as a lawyer, his daughter's manager; her mother a court stenographer. There was no hint in that photograph of what had once happened to the father. Perhaps people don't see anything in my father's face, either, in spite of his scars.

"We celebrate his birthday on the day he was released from prison," she says. "It's the hands I love so much in your sculpture. They're so strong."

I am drifting away from Gabrielle Fonteneau when I hear her say, "So when will you get here? You have instructions from Jonas, right? Maybe we can make you lunch. My mother makes great *lanbi*."

"I'll be there at twelve tomorrow," I say. "My father is with me. We are making a little weekend vacation of this."

My father loves museums. When he isn't working in his barbershop, he's often at the Brooklyn Museum. The ancient Egyptian rooms are his favorites.

"The Egyptians, they was like us," he likes to say. The Egyptians worshipped their gods in many forms and were often ruled by foreigners. The pharaohs were like the dictators he had fled. But what he admires most about the Egyptians is the way they mourned.

"Yes, they grieve," he'll say. He marvels at the mummification that went on for weeks, resulting in bodies that survived thousands of years.

My whole adult life, I have struggled to find the proper manner of sculpting my father, a man who learned about art by standing with me most of the Saturday mornings of my childhood, mesmerized by the golden masks, the shawabtis, and Osiris, ruler of the underworld.

When my father finally appears in the hotel-room doorway, I am awed by him. Smiling, he looks like a much younger man, further bronzed after a long day at the beach.

"Annie, let your father talk to you." He walks over to my bed, bends down to unlace his sneakers. "*On ti koze*, a little chat."

"Where were you? Where is the sculpture, Papi?" I feel my eyes twitching, a nervous reaction I inherited from my mother.

"That's why we need to chat," he says. "I have objections with your statue."

He pulls off his sneakers and rubs his feet with both hands.

"I don't want you to sell that statue," he says. Then he picks up the phone and calls my mother.

"I know she called you," he says to her in Creole. "Her head is so hot. She panics so easily: I was just out walking, thinking."

I hear my mother lovingly scolding him and telling him not to leave me again. When he hangs up the phone, he picks up his sneakers and puts them back on.

"Where is the sculpture?" My eyes are twitching so hard now that I can barely see.

"Let us go," he says. "I will take you to it."

As my father maneuvers the car out of the parking lot. I tell myself he might be ill, mentally ill, even though I have never detected anything wrong beyond his prison nightmares. I am trying to piece it together, this sudden yet familiar picture of a parent's vulnerability. When I was ten years old and my father had the chicken pox, I overheard him say to a friend on the phone, "The doctor tells me that at my age chicken pox can kill a man." This was the first time I realized that my father could die. I looked up the word "kill" in every dictionary and encyclo-pedia at school, trying to comprehend what it meant, that my father could be eradicated from my life.

My father stops the car on the side of the highway near a manmade lake, one of those artificial creations of the modern tropical city, with curved stone benches surrounding stagnant water. There is little light to see by except a half-moon. He heads toward one of the benches, and I sit down next to him, letting my hands dangle between my legs.

"Is this where the sculpture is?" I ask.

"In the water," he says.

"O.K.," I say. "But please know this about yourself. You are an es-pecially harsh critic."

My father tries to smother a smile.

"Why?" I ask.

He scratches his chin. Anger is a wasted emotion, I've always thought. My parents got angry at unfair politics in New York or Port-au-Prince, but they never got angry at my grades—at all the B's I got in everything but art classes—or at my not eating vegetables or occasionally vomiting my daily spoonful of cod-liver oil. Ordinary anger, I thought, was a weak-ness. But now I am angry. I want to hit my father, beat the craziness out of his head.

"Annie," he says. "When I first saw your statue, I wanted to be buried with it, to take it with me into the other world."

"Like the ancient Egyptians," I say.

He smiles, grateful, I think, that I still recall his passions.

"Annie," he asks, "do you remember when I read to you from *The Book of the Dead*?"

"Are you dying?" I say to my father. "Because I can only forgive you for this if you are. You can't take this back."

He is silent for a moment too long.

I think I hear crickets, though I cannot imagine where they might be. There is the highway, the cars racing by, the half-moon, the lake dug up from the depths of the ground, the allée of royal palms beyond. And there is me and my father.

"You remember the judgment of the dead," my father says, "when the heart of a person is put on a scale. If it is heavy, then this person cannot enter the other world."

It is a testament to my upbringing that I am not yelling at him.

"I don't deserve a statue," he says, even while looking like one: the Madonna of Humility, for example, contemplating her losses in the dust.

"Annie, your father was the hunter," he says. "He was not the prey."

"What are you saying?" I ask.

"We have a proverb," he says. " 'One day for the hunter, one day for the prey.' Your father was the hunter. He was not the prey." Each word is hard won as it leaves my father's mouth, balanced like those hearts on the Egyptian scale.

"Annie, when I saw your mother the first time, I was not just out of prison. I was a guard in the prison. One of the prisoners I was questioning had scratched me with a piece of tin. I went out to the street in a rage, blood all over my face. I was about to go back and do something bad, very bad. But instead comes your mother. I smash into her, and she asks me what I am doing there. I told her I was just let go from prison and she held my face and cried in my hair."

"And the nightmares, what are they?"

"Of what I, your father, did to others."

"Does Manman know?"

"I told her, Annie, before we married."

I am the one who drives back to the hotel. In the car, he says, "Annie, I am still your father, still your mother's husband. I would not do these things now."

When we get back to the hotel room, I leave a message for Officer Bo, and another for Manager Salinas, telling them that I have found my father. He has slipped into the bathroom, and now he runs the shower at full force. When it seems that he is never coming out, I call my mother at home in Brooklyn.

"How do you love him?" I whisper into the phone.

My mother is tapping her fingers against the mouthpiece.

"I don't know, Annie," she whispers back, as though there is a chance that she might also be overheard by him. "I feel only that you and me, we saved him. When I met him, it made him stop hurting the people. This is how I see it. He was a seed thrown into a rock, and you and me, Annie, we helped push a flower out of a rock."

When I get up the next morning, my father is already dressed. He is sitting on the edge of his bed with his back to me, his head bowed, his face buried in his hands. If I were sculpting him, I would make him a praying mantis, crouching motionless, seeming to pray while waiting to strike.

With his back still turned, my father says, "Will you call those people and tell them you have it no more, the statue?"

"We were invited to lunch there. I believe we should go."

He raises his shoulders and shrugs. It is up to me.

The drive to Gabrielle Fonteneau's house seems longer than the twenty-four hours it took to drive from New York: the ocean, the palms along the road, the highway so imposingly neat. My father fills in the silence in the car by saying, "So now you know, Annie, why your mother and me, we have never returned home."

The Fonteneaus' house is made of bricks of white coral, on a cul-de-sac with a row of banyans separating the two sides of the street.

Silently, we get out of the car and follow a concrete path to the front door. Before we can knock, an older woman walks out. Like Gabrielle, she has stunning midnight-black eyes and skin the color of sorrel, with spiralling curls brushing the sides of her face. When Gabrielle's father joins her, I realize where Gabrielle Fonteneau gets her height. He is more than six feet tall.

Mr. Fonteneau extends his hands, first to my father and then to me. They're large, twice the size of my father's. The fingernails have grown back, thick, densely dark, as though the past had nestled itself there in black ink.

We move slowly through the living room, which has a cathedral ceiling and walls covered with Haitian paintings—Obin, Hyppolite, Tiga, Duval-Carrié. Out on the back terrace, which towers over a nursery of orchids and red dracaenas, a table is set for lunch.

Mr. Fonteneau asks my father where his family is from in Haiti, and my father lies. In the past, I thought he always said a different province because he had lived in all those places, but I realize now that he says this to keep anyone from tracing him, even though twenty-six years and eighty more pounds shield him from the threat of immediate recognition.

When Gabrielle Fonteneau makes her entrance, in an off-the-shoulder ruby dress, my father and I stand up.

"Gabrielle," she says, when she shakes hands with my father, who blurts out spontaneously, "You are one of the flowers of Haiti."

Gabrielle Fonteneau tilts her head coyly.

"We eat now," Mrs. Fonteneau announces, leading me and my father to a bathroom to wash up before the meal. Standing before a pink seashell-shaped sink, my father and I dip our hands under the faucet flow.

"Annie," my father says, "we always thought, your mother and me, that children could raise their parents higher. Look at what this girl has done for her parents."

During the meal of conch, plantains, and mushroom rice, Mr. Fonteneau tries to draw my father into conversation. He asks when my father was last in Haiti.

"Twenty-six years," my father replies.

"No going back for you?" asks Mrs. Fonteneau.

"I have not had the opportunity," my father says.

"We go back every year to a beautiful place overlooking the ocean in the mountains in Jacmel," says Mrs. Fonteneau.

"Have you ever been to Jacmel?" Gabrielle Fonteneau asks me.

I shake my head no.

"We are fortunate," Mrs. Fonteneau says, "that we have another place to go where we can say our rain is sweeter, our dust is lighter, our beach is prettier."

"So now we are tasting rain and weighing dust," Mr. Fonteneau says, and laughs.

"There is nothing like drinking the sweet juice from a green coconut you fetched yourself from your own tree, or sinking your hand in sand from the beach in your own country," Mrs. Fonteneau says.

"When did you ever climb a coconut tree?" Mr. Fonteneau says, teasing his wife.

I am imagining what my father's nightmares might be. Maybe he dreams of dipping his hands in the sand on a beach in his own country and finds that what he comes up with is a fist full of blood.

After lunch, my father asks if he can have a closer look at the Fonteneaus' back-yard garden. While he's taking the tour, I confess to Gabrielle Fonteneau that I don't have the sculpture.

"My father threw it away," I say.

Gabrielle Fonteneau frowns.

"I don't know," she says. "Was there even a sculpture at all? I trust Jonas, but maybe you fooled him, too. Is this some scam, to get into our home?"

"There was a sculpture," I say. "Jonas will tell you that. My father just didn't like it, so he threw it away."

She raises her perfectly arched eyebrows, perhaps out of concern for my father's sanity or my own.

"I'm really disappointed," she says. "I wanted it for a reason. My father goes home when he looks at a piece of art. He goes home deep inside himself. For a long time he used to hide his fingers from people. It's like he was making a fist all the time. I wanted to give him this thing so that he knows we understand what happened to him."

"I am truly sorry," I say.

Over her shoulders, I see her parents guiding my father through rows of lemongrass. I want to promise her that I will make her another sculpture, one especially modelled on her father. But I don't know when I will be able to work on anything again. I have lost my subject, the father I loved as well as pitied.

In the garden, I watch my father snap a white orchid from its stem and hold it out toward Mrs. Fonteneau, who accepts it with a nod of thanks.

"I don't understand," Gabrielle Fonteneau says. "You did all this for nothing."

I wave to my father to signal that we should perhaps leave now, and he comes toward me, the Fonteneaus trailing slowly behind him.

With each step he rubs the scars on the side of his face.

Perhaps the last person my father harmed had dreamed this moment into my father's future—his daughter seeing those marks, like chunks of warm plaster still clinging to a cast, and questioning him about them, giving him a chance to either lie or tell the truth. After all, we have the proverb, as my father would say: "Those who give the blows may try to forget, but those who carry the scars must remember."

THOMAS SAYERS ELLIS
b. 1963

Thomas Sayers Ellis well earns the description of a "literary activist," whether as contributing editor for the journal *Callaloo*, or
cofounder of the influential Dark Room Collective. In his collection *The Good Junk* (1996), Ellis does for his native Washington, D.C., what Seamus Heaney does for the Irish landscape,
serving as a self-described "urban naturalist"—showing us life in
a "Chocolate City" complete with block parties and playgrounds,
film crews and go-go music. This desire to catalog the world
around him does not mean Ellis's work is without metaphor; instead, his poetry insists on transformation and redemption, as
much out of this world as in it. Witness the cosmic and comic
surrealism of "Hush Yo Mouf," a series of epigrams for black
best poet Bob Kaufman, or Ellis's recent poems on funk fore-
fathers Parliament-Funkadelic. The latter poetic series manages
to tell the history of the band while making language—its edges,
puns, and play—the real star. The result is poems that—like
"Atomic Bride," selected for *The Best American Poetry*—live
somewhere between music and the mothership.

VIEW OF THE LIBRARY OF CONGRESS FROM PAUL LAURENCE DUNBAR HIGH SCHOOL

For Doris Craig and Michael Olshausen

A white substitute teacher
At an all-Black public high school,
He sought me out saying my poems
Showed promise, range, a gift,
And had I ever heard of T. S. Eliot?
No. Then Robert Hayden perhaps?

Hayden, a former colleague,
Had recently died, and the obituary
He handed me had already begun
Its journey home—from the printed page
Back to tree, gray becoming
Yellow, flower, dirt.

No river, we skipped rocks
On the horizon, above Ground Zero,
From the roof of the Gibson Plaza Apartments.
We'd aim, then shout the names
Of the museums, famous monuments,
And government buildings

Where our grandparents, parents,
Aunts, and uncles worked. Dangerous duds.
The bombs we dropped always fell short,
Missing their mark. No one, not even
Carlton Green who had lived in
As many neighborhoods as me,

Knew in which direction
To launch when I lifted Hayden's
Place of employment—
The Library of Congress—
From the obituary, now folded
In my back pocket, a creased map.

We went home, asked our mothers
But they didn't know. Richard's came
Close: Somewhere near Congress,
On Capitol Hill, take the 30 bus,
Get off before it reaches Anacostia,
Don't cross the bridge into Southeast.

The next day in school
I looked it up—the National Library
Of the United States in Washington, D.C.
Founded in 1800, open to all taxpayers
And citizens. *Snap!* My Aunt Doris
Works there, has for years.

Once, on her day off, she
Took me shopping and bought
The dress shoes of my choice.
Loafers. They were dark red.
Almost purple, bruised—the color
Of blood before oxygen reaches it.

I was beginning to think
Like a poet, so in my mind
Hayden's dying and my loafers
Were connected, but years apart,
As was Dunbar to other institutions—
Ones I could see, ones I could not.

FATAL APRIL

Thomas Leon Ellis, Sr. (1945–1991)

The phone rang. It was Doris,
Your sister, calling to say
April had taken you, where,
In your bedroom, when, days ago,
How, murder, no, a stroke.

You left a car (but I
Don't drive) and enough cash
In your pockets to buy
A one-way train ticket
From Boston to Washington.

Let's get one thing straight.
I didn't take the money, but
I did take your driver's license
And the Chuck Brown album,
Needle to groove,

Round and round,
Where they found you.
Both were metaphors.
The license I promised, but knew
I'd never get—now I have yours

And the album because
Of what you may have been
Trying to say about writing,
About home. James keeps
Asking me to visit your grave,

When will I learn to drive
And why I changed my name.
He's your son, stubborn with
An inherited temper. I keep telling him
No, never, there's more than

One way to bury a man.

BEING THERE

Kennedy Playground
Washington, D.C.

We forced our faces
into the circular frame
a stringless hoop made,
hoping more than silence & light

would fall through.
We fought for position.
We fouled & shoved.
We high-fived God.

Our Converse All-Stars
burned enough rubber
to rival the devil and his mama.
Hoop, horseshoe, noose.

We aimed at a halo
hung at an angle we couldn't fit,
waiting for the camera
to record our unfocused

need to score.
We left earth.
We lost weight.
We disobeyed bone.

Our finger rolls
& reverse layups
were rejected by angels
guarding the rim,

same as prayers
returned to sinners.

HUSH YO MOUF

for Bob Kaufman

1

Pretty soon, the age of the talk show
Will slip on a peel left in the avant-gutter.

2

I refuse to write for more people
Than I can listen to.

3

I tripped over a tongue last night
And failed to wipe up the metaphors.

4

The world is held together by the word
Of one person who ignores everybody.

5

The Space Race is foolish;
NASA will never catch up with Sun Ra.

6

Since Virginia Beach, I've added Heckle and Jeckle
To my list of endangered mythical beasts.

7

My father and I have my mother in common.
She does all the talking.

8

A slap in the face is the most corrective form of punctuation,
Sentencing.

9

Bomb coffee houses, not abortion clinics.

10

The preachers of plasma say Give the gift of life,
Rhetoric.

11

Talk, talk, talk.
Lies, lies, lies.

12

A thousand pubic persons, all publicly pissant, politicians.

14

Talk, rumor, he say she say, word of mouth,
History.

15

Wanted Dead or Aloud
Someone to rinse the tongue stuff from my eyes

16

I, too, write writing:

17

We bony V's
Trying to make a W.

18

And drink ink.

19

Child, please.

20

I came to this planet to escape walkie-talkies.
I failed.

PHOTOGRAPH OF DR. FUNKENSTEIN

after Christian Witkin

A crazy evil grin, eyelids flipped
Inside out, red hot and pink as pork.
The tongue slipping out the mouth
Suggests fellatio, and a pussy taunting dogs.

He is arrested, in custody,
MOST WANTED, an atomic shaman
With a scratch-and-sniff beard. I'll bet you he
Was dreaming of Venus, about to say something nasty
When the photographer bopped him
With a nickel bag of light into a permanent

Type nod, sizzaleenmean, somewhere
Between a mugshot and maximumisness.

Judging from the shirt and tie,
He's well hung and may have been
About to make a house call (reach
Way up and give Sir Nose a splanking
Or photosynthesize, a dandy lion)
When the booty snatchers slapped him
With a warrant, shoving him, handcuffed,
Onto a death row of commodes,

A zone of zero funkativity,
Violating his right to hold
His own thang, his right to pee.

ATOMIC BRIDE

for Andre Foxxe

A good show
Starts in the
Dressing room

And works its way
To the stage.
Close the door,

Andre's cross-
dressing, what
A drag. All

The world loves
A bride, something
About those gowns.

A good wedding
Starts in the
Department store

And works its way
Into the photo album.
Close the door,

Andre's tying
The knot, what
A drag. Isn't he

Lovely? All
The world loves
A bachelor, some-

thing about glamour
& glitz, white
Shirts, lawsuits.

A good dog
Starts in the yard
And works its way

Into da house.
Close your eyes,
Andre's wide open.

One freak of the week
Per night, what
A drag. Isn't

He lovely? All
The world loves
A nuclear family,

Something about
A suburban home,
Chaos in order.

A good bride starts
In the laboratory
And works his way

To the church.
Close the door,
Andre's thinking

Things over, what
A drag. Isn't
He lovely? All

The world loves
A divorce, something
About broken vows.

A good war starts
In the courtroom
And works its way

To the album cover.
Close the door,
Andre's swearing in,

What a drag.
Isn't he lovely? All
The world loves

A star witness,
Something about
Cross-examination.

A good drug starts
In Washington
And works its way

To the dancefloor.
Close the door,
Andre's strungout,

What a drag,
Isn't he lovely? All
The world loves

Rhythm guitar,
Something about
Those warm chords.

A good skeleton
Starts in the closet
And works its way

To the top of the charts.
Start the organ.
Andre's on his way

Down the aisle,
Alone, what an encore. All
The world loves

An explosive ending.
Go ahead Andre,
Toss the bouquet.

CAROLYN FERRELL
b. 1962

Carolyn Ferrell's *Don't Erase Me* (1997) won the *Los Angeles Times* Book Prize for First Fiction and the Zacharis First Book Prize from *Ploughshares*; one story from the collection appeared in *The Best American Short Stories*. *Ploughshares* describes the book as "eight first-person stories, eight singular voices that incandescently mix lyricism and street patois to portray the lives of mostly poor black girls." As Ferrell herself says, the book finds "the black/interracial/overweight girl everywhere: in California, in New York, in the South Bronx, in Germany." The result, as seen in the following selection, is something like Flannery O'Connor sending her characters up north, out west, or overseas—Ferrell's narrators prove naive yet ironically without innocence, witnesses to a modern world of violence and compromise.

CAN YOU SAY MY NAME?

We have two facts in front of us. One: babies, once they're here, stay, and can do our work for us; and two: men love love. Bri threw up in homeroom almost every day and it seemed like a awful commotion. But whenever she turned around and saw Roc two rows back and felt his blue eyes reciprocating love and understanding, it was like it was *his* hands that were wiping up her mouth, all the baby throw-up, and not the teacher's, Mr. Hancock's, who was scared shitless, and so Bri didn't have anything to fear. Me, I'm still waiting. I'm trying to reciprocate, but I'm doing it alone. Boy Commerce bops past me in the hall on his way to practice and sometimes has a stone frown, or sometimes he laughs all in my face when he catches me rubbing my belly. He don't talk to me anymore. He pretends to dis me any chance he gets. Like when he knows I'm following him down the hall, he'll put his hand up some other girl's ass and say, "Did I do that? Sorry," like it's supposed to really make the girl laugh, like I'm supposed to get jealous and shit.

He pretends to dis me. But it ain't no real disrespect, cause it's strange, but you know deep in your heart that one day your waiting will come to an end. My plan is gold. I can even go so far as to say this: that whenever I look at Boy Commerce, I see him as the black ship sailing out to the wide free sea, and me as one of the slaves in the hold. Like we learn about in school and are supposed to feel proud of. The waves are crashing against the side of the boat and the dolphins are trying to catch the sun rays in their open mouths with their tiny rows of teeth and I am licking the toes of the other slaves lying around me. Maybe there is something else out there, but I am the one who dies in the hold, on the trip to the New World, the new life. I will never leave. I will stay on the ship. There is not a damn thing to fear.

Do you like tongue kissing a dog? No, I ain't tried that shit. *Would you try it for me?* Hell, are you crazy? *No, I ain't, it's real simple, all you do is pretend you got someone in your arms that is ready for you to do just about anything, and you're hot tonight.* Shit, that's some sick shit, I will never put my mouth on a dog's. *Then you won't ever put your mouth on mine.* Don't say that. *I just did.* Why you treat me like this, don't you know my loving is all for you, you my number one, ain't nothing gonna come between us? *Look, I'm not asking for too much, just something little and crazy, you want to prove you will do anything I say, that's what I call love!* But that dog been licking his ass. *The dog's mouth is clean, and I just want to see you do it, please baby.* I only want your kisses. *I just want to see.* Will you promise to never leave me, I'm doing this crazy shit only for you and you better not fucking go nowhere. *I just want to see.* Look, I'm the boss now, and I want you to promise you will never leave, because you can't imagine how much I love you. Please. *Please.* Please.

Bri and me decided in ninth grade that we were going to be wives in school. The homegirl cheerleaders turned up their noses and shook their asses at us. One of them, Sam, said to me, "You got to lose that shit, girl! There *are* other ways to get out, and the one you doing is crack open for a dick and get a public assistance check shoved up there instead. Don't get it too wet or they won't cash it." Vulgar. Another one, Mandy with the imported African box braids, said, "Become a cheerleader! This way you can save yourself all by yourself, and *then* the shit that the adoring homeboys serve up to you is choice!" Teeny, cornrow cheerleader, said, "Geez Christ, mens do pain us!" The last time any one of them said anything, it was Marge, real name Margarita Floretta Inez Santamaria, who really could've had any boy in the whole damn school: "You will go through all that work but you ain't gonna have the reward. You gonna be two women sitting alone in the laundromat, dreaming about humping a tube of toothpaste when you get home."

Me and Bri laughed them off. Yo yo: we are homegirls and you know we know the deal better than anyone else and their mama and their mama's mama.

The teachers didn't think we were so crazy. One of them, the old science lady, puckered up: You folks are all the same. Laying up under men like that. It's a God-honest shame. Don't you ever wonder where you'll be?

Mrs. Mary, the Irish teacher who used to be in Catholic school, chimed in: No, they sure as hell don't. We show them the history of the world, and they are doomed to repeat all the mistakes. They just want to spend the rest of their born days right here!

Mrs. Faulkner, Elizabeth Taylor lookalike, sewing homeroom: Here? But they'll just wind up statistics! Heavens! Don't you think we should perhaps guide them . . . at least a little into the light?

Blond sissy-ass Mr. Hancock, math teacher and homeroom: You mean *our* way! Are you kidding, Althea? We don't want them our way! Let them stay the fuck where they are. They ain't got a clue. And I ain't gonna be the one to give it to them.

(*Wrong*, of course, because that dumb fake-English-accent ass was the one who didn't have the clue! We had the clues, we were on the money. Somehow. Still, all this talk tended to make Bri get all nervy, and she would start asking, "Toya, do we know what we're actually gone do? I mean, should we have babies or become junior-year cheerleaders?" Bri was always the unsteady one. I started to get sick of that shit, but then again: I didn't want to do it all alone. So I calmed her down, because she couldn't figure a damn thing out. The only thing she seemed to get together was this Africa thing. Wearing the African-looking clothes, gold bamboo earrings, a map of Africa on her jacket. She was really into that before-slavery shit. She called me her sister under the skin. She even wanted us to give each other African names, like Tashima and Chaka, Myesha, Zenzile, Aminata, and things. Like that is going to solve some shit! Sometimes she made me sicker than the baby throw-up.)

Bri was always freaking about the baby, but I managed to talk her out of her commotion and even got her to make a compromise: she relaxed her hair like the cheerleaders but wore T-shirts that said BABY = 1 + 1 and SOMEBODY DOWN THERE LOVES ME.

There was no question for me. I was going to be a wife in school. Boy Commerce was planning on a basketball scholarship so I'd have me an educated man. I *do* have a clue. It's just that people have clouded-up, fucked-up minds, and they refuse to see the truth and they live like snails underground in a garden, slimy. Blind. Dark. Like that hold.

Why you being so good to me all of a sudden, I thought you was mad at me, baby. Me, hell no, I just think I'm finally ready to give you all my loving. What's that supposed to mean, what I ain't already got? Me, the whole me, my heart. Well then, hurry up and give it. It's yours for the taking. *I like that shit, lemme feel your lovin.*

*   *   *

My Uncle Marion busted his best pair of glasses upside my head. "You what?" He rammed me into the refrigerator, so hard the door popped open and the milk crashed on the floor. *Big-time dis!* "Ho, ho, you been ho'ing in my house!" He had the wooden spoon, the one that used to belong to my mother and me on Delancey Street, and he was drumming out a funeral march on my ears. (I admit, it was hard not to bust out crying, but I kept my plan in mind, and that was like my light at the end of the tunnel.) "Ho! You get what you deserve! Grinding up neath that boy! You worse than a African! Is that how I raised you? Is that how I done?" Uncle Marion grabbed one of my cheeks and tugged till his nails left his permanent mark of love on me. "Ho! What was you thinking?"

Don't say nothing till it's too late to have an abortion.

It took a lot out of me to try and learn this scared-ass Bri the basics. I told her to keep on going to gym class, keep on doing the fifty warm-up pushups, hundred situps. Volunteer to be the kickball team captain, not just a regular player! Keep on wearing Wah Wah lipstick and doing your hair up like if someone better came along, you'd go for him and leave that other sorry ass—the one who was going to be your husband—behind. Don't put your head down on the desk because you say you're tired, or other kinds of baby-related shit. Be like you were in the old days and get the right answers and say them in front of the rest of the class: *you are still a genius like before.* Just don't zip up your pants, just wear a big sweater over so nobody sees you can't bend over no more. The gold plan. That's how you become a wife in time for Homecoming and Thanksgiving break.

I have been in love since the seventh grade. One day I sat in Reading with my large-print version of *Tale of Two Cities* propped up on my lap and dreamed of what I am doing now: being big with somebody's love. My destiny was as clear to me then as it is now. You might say that since I was a child then, I was illing because I was thinking I would be Boy Commerce's wife in tenth grade. But not so. You're only illing when you dream of things that can't possibly come true.

Bri took it upon herself to fall in love with Roc, and at first the cheerleaders said they wouldn't even consider looking at me or Bri because of this move of hers. Sam said that Bri was taking some white girl's boy away, and they didn't go for that, man-snatching, the cheerleaders. The only way the girls could be sure you wasn't playing dirty was if you had some homeboy or some Puerto Rican dude as yours. But I ask you: what do a white boy want with one of us for? What do Roc want with Bri, who's dark and not the prettiest girl you ever seen? That's some fucked-up shit. In my opinion, men like that only see the girl as a dark-skinned beauty, like some Pam Grier in the action movies, and they want to experience some bad pussy. Bri ought to have known that shit. And if it ain't that, then some white girl is crying her eyes out because her boy has left her for some dark ass. And that ain't right, because it's the same thing as man-stealing, and that goes against all cheerleader rules of order. We *are* all sisters when you get down to it.

Bri said love never happened like it was planned. She said love was a flower with no name in the garden of mankind. A flower like the kind that grew in the Motherland, *Africa*. She said, "You all are *illing*. This man wants me for me!" So she said she was going to prove it. Roc followed her around like a puppy. Once I caught them in the science lab, and it was like Roc's hands was straightening Bri's whole body like a relaxing comb. Smooth, broken, knotting-out movements. I laughed out loud. Bri flushed and was ashamed, and Roc said, "You can't stop me!" He looked scared like a true skinny white boy, but he did put his arms around big Bri to try and cover her up. I think that was the real reason Bri said she was going to be with Roc as his wife in school. Maybe if I hadn't a caught them planting the seed, maybe she would have left him afterwards. I had wanted to apologize, but they ran off dragging their clothes down the hall.

Bri was ashamed, and so I made it my job to convince her to stay with him because first: I knew she would never get a man like him (who loved love) again in this world, and two: I didn't want to be alone.

You know, I feel like I want to open up to you, ain't that weird? *Why? I feel the same way.* Nah, really, I'm not used to that kind of shit, and now I'm feeling like: hey, I want this girl to know a part of the real me. *I'm all ears, forever.* You know my father, he ain't raised me to be a sissy, he raised me to be a real man, and so it's hard, it's hard. *You want to lay your head on my shoulder?* I got things to do, I got places to see—

but don't talk to me about any of that when I'm lying next to you making some good love. *What do you mean, places to go?* Baby, I got feelings, sometimes I just look at all the people in the street lying around, or sometimes I see my father dealing out a deck of cards and kissing my mother's cheek, and I start feeling so low. *Don't worry, you always got me.* Do you know I feel like killing my fucking self, getting on the track and touching the third rail? *Baby, don't say that shit, don't!* Word. *Don't.* That's how it gets to me sometimes, and I wonder: am I going to get a chance to kill myself, or will I just be buried alive? *BUT WHERE YOU TALKING ABOUT GOING, AM I GONNA BE WITH YOU, HOW DO I FIT IN BABY?* There you go talking all that shit, you don't listen to a word I say, do you? *Sure I do, baby, it's just I don't know where you thinking about going, that's all, and I always want to be there with you, understand?* I ain't talking about you, I'm talking about staying the fuck alive! *Don't worry, baby, with me, you will always be alive to the one who matters, now go on.*

I used to be five-foot-six with pretty box braids, skin the same color as the singer in that movie *Mahogany* and a nice voice. I could sing me some beautiful songs, like "Reveal Him to My Soul" and "Precious Is the Son." I used to be skinny and used to could dance to music. I used to go to parties with my mother's, then with Uncle Marion's permission. My nose came out in a perfect point, and I used to have dimples. Cute, you could've called me, or even a fox.

Then there is this time where everything disappears, everything. I make up my mind, I look in the mirror and make up my mind. Tired of all this being alone and shit. They all think they can book whenever they like.

Therefore, now I am five-foot-three with relaxed hair in a runt pony-tail. I travel with a belly now. My face is spread out like a ocean, with rocks and seaweed in every wave. I always have throw-up in my mouth, sometimes I carry a little cup with me in the train. I don't dance at parties to the record player no more. I dance underneath a boy who says, "Put your butt this way, I am almost *there.*"

I look into the mirror and still see a fox. Hell, I will go so far as to say: I am badder than bad.

*   *   *

I took Bri to the new Stop-One Supermarket and to Tinytown's. She had to learn the good sides that were to come. This was part of the gold plan. It's like we learned about in school: this was a science.

Look, I'ma show you what you don't learn in Home Economics. This here is the most important aisle: Borax, Mr. Clean, 2000 Flushes, Fantastic. You got to know how to keep your man happy, and this is gold. This is the surefire way. This is the way so that when his boys come over to check out the crib and hang and smoke some herb, you earn a A+.

This aisle is the lifesaving ring to the new wife and mother: Alpo, KittyKat Delight, Friskies, Yum Pup. Now, you can bet your bottom dollar that once you're in, the husband is going to want to get you a pet so you have some hobby to take your mind off the kid sometimes, because you don't want to go having a nervous breakdown on me, right? If it's a cat, then you also got to think about kitty litter, and somehow boys don't like cats too much, all that rubbing up on you and shit. Boys get jealous when they see the cat laying up with you in the bed and then they act like: it's them or me, and you about ready to fall out laughing because they sure as hell don't seem like grown husbands but like spoiled kids. But you don't laugh, you take the cat to a shelter. Let em get you a dog. Boys like to be around dogs because it makes them into men faster. It's the kind of thing where they can go out on a Sunday morning to the park and jog and run and play catch and think in the back of their minds: Hey, this shit is *down*, I'm feeling good. Husbands need to feel good. And that's when they thank their lucky stars they got us back at home. Dogs' breath sure do smell like shit, but just think of him in the park. You take the dog out for a walk in the weekday morning and let it protect the baby.

Here's my favorite aisle, because it always changes: diet foods and ethnic. They got all these Slim Control foods, like Slim Control Salad Dressing, Slim Control Apple Snack'ems, Slim Control Malted Milkshake. Slim Control is what's going to keep us going, girl! And they keep on getting more: Slim Control Ketchup, Slim Control Jelly. You can eat all this shit, then take one or two of their Slim Control Diet Pills and you aren't hungry for three days. Get it? You lose weight that's really not weight at all. And you can laugh at the men getting their beer bellies in front of the TV, because you ain't going to be in the same boat. Then the homies that come by the crib start checking you out. Wouldn't you love to stay skinny forever? Not blow up the way all those mothers do? We got to hold on to our world, honey, and this is the way we going to do it. I want Boy to fucking love me forever. I love Slim Control Cheddar Cheese Popcorn.

Bri, like I had figured, loved Tinytown's. She kept saying, "Oooh, I'ma get me this for the baby, oooh, I like this toy machine gun if it's a boy." Bri held the black baby dolls like they were her own and kissed their cheeks. She said they looked like African goddesses! I was thinking, This store is too goddamn expensive. My child will do like me in the old days: play in the bathtub with the spatula, the wooden spoon, the rice pot, the strainer. Man, I had me some good times once.

Bri asked the Tinytown saleslady how much the black baby doll was that said, "Can you say my name?" The saleslady said eighty-nine fifty. And do you believe Bri was thinking about asking her mother for the money for that thing? *Typical.* Ugly-ass doll. *Can you say my name!* But at least I got Bri to look for a moment at the positive side of motherhood and being a wife in school. I told Margarita Santamaria in the school cafeteria, Yeah we know what the hell we are doing.

Listen up I'm only gonna say this once I know I done some fucked-up things in life but it's never too late to make things change for the better, *you ain't done anything that fucked up and listen we got more important things to talk about like what's gonna be the name and when you coming over to spend the night with me again,* shit Toya you ain't gonna let me get a word in is you, *sorry,* sorry my ass, sorry.

Listen up we can still be together but don't you want to go to college like me or you was talking about that business school where you could learn something useful, *man all that stuff's in the future we got other things to think about,* no THIS IS WHAT WE NEED TO THINK ABOUT, *no this is what we need to think about: are you always gonna be there for me in other words are you always gonna be faithful?*

I want you to be happy even if I been doing some fucked-up shit, *you mean with them other girls,* yeah I mean like that, *shoot I know you don't really care about them,* yeah you right I don't, *so why you bring them up?*

Because I want the chance to care about them, baby.

Listen up you: I ain't going to college or business school or nothing, when it comes you are gonna give it a name or else!

Else what?

Don't do like that because I know that what you really want deep inside is love love love and that's what I got to give let me show you again.

Listen to me, LISTEN TO ME, listen to me, listen to me.

In seventh grade, my mother was still alive. The house on Delancey Street was cold indoors because the bricks were falling off outdoors. When I came home from school, I used to have to feed her applesauce and overcooked vegetables from a spoon. Uncle Marion called from his house on the other side of the city, Washington Heights. He used to check on us and ask how my mother's breasts were doing. I used to have to hold Mother's head in my arms like a warm ball and smooth out her hair with my hands, she couldn't take no brush. She would ask me to sing "Unforgettable You" and "Breakaway" to her so she could sleep better. My voice was high in those days. I was in the after-school gospel singers. I used to love to sing, but only songs like "In Times Like These" and "Send a Message"—songs that gave you a good feeling, like you *are* in seventh grade and your whole life *is* spread out in front of you like a red carpet, but I hated it when her head dozed off in my arms. It made me too ancient.

Her favorite animals were fishes. She dug them all, angelfish, blue whales, sharks, dolphins. She liked the free way they swam the ocean. They moved without seams, without giving a thought to where their next breath was going to come from. They traveled light and always in a direction. They never dreamed about getting caught, about being on a dinner plate, about swimming in a tank before hundreds of hungry eyes. They let the currents brush them along, and they tasted ocean water the way we tasted the air in the room with the air conditioner on. Mother had the kind of wishing talking that cut deep when she spoke and when I held her head in my arms.

It was going okay, I thought. I did take good care of her. But then one day, sure as shit, Mother announced like she was a loudspeaker in a subway station, I am going to kill myself. She said, I won't be here for you when I do that, but you will have Uncle Marion. You can hold on to him.

I said, under the water of tears, "Don't you think you could change your mind? Don't you think you could think again and decide to stay with me till I am a grown-up? I want to hold on to you."

She said, You just don't understand the pain, Toya. It has to give way. I have to make it give way.

So she sent me off to Uncle Marion's house and she drowned herself in poison air with her head laying in the gas oven. Uncle Marion said that was because her breasts were on fire on the inside, that's how he explained that shit to me then.

She couldn't stay for me. Damn, she couldn't even do it in the water, take her life where I knew she'd like to do it the most.

Mandy with the imported box braids said, "You *gots* to be crazy, baby! I ain't giving up being a cheerleader for nothing! And I don't want to have stretched-out legs!" Mandy had seven brothers and sisters and you could understand that she needed to spend all that time at cheerleader practice to get the hell away from them.

Margarita Santamaria said, "Bri, you aren't stupid. Do like I did."

Sam, head cheerleader, told us, "Naw, I see things different now. You girls is *on!* Lemme be the godmother, okay? I can give it a godname, right?"

Boy Commerce got cheerleader Sam's boyfriend, Big Daddy Dave, to let us into the biology lab. He had some big secret for me, Boy, he even held my hand on the way there from the boys' locker room. Big Daddy unlocked the door, and Boy held it open as I walked on through. He was like a real gentleman when he said to Big Daddy, "Catch you in a sec, bro."

I made sure to keep my hands off my belly. I didn't complain one time about my big swelled-up feet. I wore my old raincoat so Boy wouldn't have to notice my shape if he didn't want to. One time I even linked my arm in his and pressed a little and said, "Are we really here?" Boy lit up a cigar in the lab and just let the smoke out his mouth like a chimney. In the dark I could see the outline of his pick sticking out the front of his afro.

So I asked him, "Do you want my loving now, baby?"

So he waited a moment and pulled me by the hand over to a table with glass jars and beakers on it. There was a row of fat glass cylinders.

When he went to turn on the light, I saw little baby mice bodies in the cylinders. They were just little baby mice floating in gray water. They were holding their hands in prayer.

Boy Commerce said, "If you have this kid, it might come out all twisted and small like this, Toya. Why you want to do some nasty shit like that?"

He said, "Toya, you think you gonna trap me like this baby here? You gonna tie my hands up? Well, *think again*. That's some stupid-ass shit. And you're a stupid-ass girl." It looked for a second like he was going to put his hand on one of the cylinders.

His eyes were red-lined. By accident, the basketball under his arm slipped out and fell on another table and knocked a beaker to the floor. "You see what you made me do, asshole?" He swept the broken pieces under the table with his foot. The smell of something fierce hit my nose, but it wouldn't make me do something stupid like cry. That was the way to lose them. Wives in school didn't cry. They just carried their load and thought their thoughts just like old women. I didn't say a word. Silence was the golden plan.

Boy switched off the light and opened the door. "Toya, get this fact through your head: I won't let you end my fucking life. I always thought you were smart."

Silence.

"So forget it, bitch. You ain't nothing but a animal." He left.

But he never said he wouldn't change once the baby got here. He had turned off the lights and I was alone in the dark lab. I slipped off my shoes and put my hands just like the praying babies and thought: God, I do love him. Let him recognize my love for what it is. Let him follow Roc's example of loving love.

Then I let my own damn self out.

Boy is the ship, I am in the hold. Mrs. Mary taught us in history that that was how the slaves traveled. They couldn't see the outside, they were in chains. (They could maybe hear it, though. Maybe it was a dolphin flying through the air, telling them that their iron buckles would be off in about four hundred years, and maybe they were grateful for that dream from the fish. They might've even got so happy, they woulda wanted to kiss each other, this shit wasn't going to be forever, but the chains wouldn't reach, so the one who was able to slip the chains went around kissing the others for joy. She kissed their feet. That made them more together. But then the smell was bad.)

Mrs. Mary told us that the slaves had been a primitive people. That's why they didn't rebel—they had been too primitive. And sure, they had the hardships of slavery to endure before them, but that would be only a short chapter in their history, and then they would be free! Mrs. Mary said that Negro people in our country had always had it so much better than the Africans that were still in Africa. Some of them still didn't even live in houses. The Negro has definitely come a long way in America. The Negro has become—*sophisticated*.

All I knew was that Bri was wrong. I couldn't have no African name. I had me my slave name, and I wasn't going away from it never.

Bri called me up all hysterical and shit, and I wanted to say: Like I don't have enough of my own problems, but I didn't say that. She cried so hard I thought the phone would melt.

"Toya," she whimpered, "what if I wake up one day and realize I don't love Roc?" Her crying was impossible. We had agreed not to do it.

I said, "Bri, calm the hell down. You haven't come to that point. Wait till you get married before you start in with all the soap opera shit. By that time you will need to have an affair, maybe we can fix you up with Big Daddy Dave." I was still grateful to him for that night in the lab.

She screamed, "But I don't love Roc *now!* The day in the future was this morning, and the baby throw-up almost choked me! Fuck!"

I told her to calm the hell down, but secretly I was afraid. Bri had heard about a place that would get rid of it almost at the same time it could be born, and she was going around school trying to get the information. She didn't have to become a school wife, I had told her before, because she could just *be* with him and *be* his woman. But she had to go through with the kid. How the hell could she have her anchor if she backed out now? And Roc was a white boy, an ugly one by white girl standards, flat nose and a caved-in chest, only he had this thing for Bri's hair when it wasn't relaxed, just natty afro and shit, and he had this thing for her African ass, and logically we all knew that that meant he would be easier to keep. Even the cheerleaders knew it, even if they were too stuck up to admit it. That white boy was not going back.

"Bri, just think about it for a moment. He won't ever make you work a day in your life. All he will want is children. Baby, most people would say you got it made."

She must a fallen out her seat because the phone hit the floor and I could hear her sniffling close by. "Toya, he told me that he got me pregnant on purpose, that I didn't have a damn thing to do with it! He wanted to have me forever! That's some sick shit! I don't want his fucking hands to touch me again. I'ma throw me down the bleachers at school."

I said, "It doesn't matter who got who. Point of the matter is, you got the prize at the end of the rainbow. You got your whole life ahead of you."

Bri whispered, "I don't want his fucking hands to touch me."

I ain't your goddamn vacation home! You think you can come and go if you like? YOU THINK I'MA ALWAYS BE HERE? Look me in the eye! I got feelings, too. You think you can come and go and it ain't gonna make me break inside? No, don't be looking at me like that! I got pride, damn you, and I got me, yeah that's right, ME! And it's about time I took care of me! Yeah, I know you been fucking with Margarita Santamaria, and I know she told you she came after the first time! Well, that's bullshit! It's hard for girls to come, they only say that to make you feel like a man! Yeah, I'd like to see you try and make me come! Try it! Just remember: when you're done, you ain't gonna have me to push around no more. That's not how my mama raised me! She raised me with good loving! What you talking about: good loving? Is that what you been wanting all this time? Good loving from a good woman?

Well, baby, that's what I been offering you all this time, you just been too blind to see. Let me love you. Let me show you what loving is all about. It's all in here, just for you. Just relax on me. Let's you and me reciprocate. Let me be sure. Let's reciprocate. You don't have to make me come, neither.

Boy Commerce wrote a poem for the school newspaper. Well, that was about the craziest shit I ever heard! He don't even know how to spell, and he hates English class! He hates books and he hates using your brains to do what you can do with your mouth in two seconds flat.

He wrote a poem, and he had all the cheerleaders sighing in the hallway. Bet they wished they was in my shoes.

FOR YOU

I want to say
but then I stop and think
Did you think I
could keep this song
in the bottom of my heart
with my everlasting love?
Don't keep me
let me run my wild manly course free.
I'm just an ordinary man,
doing all I can.
Wandering around
till it's true love I found.
Where's my future?
Is it you?
I'm a bird
but you want to be the sea.
So let me spread my wings, you done yours.
Let's stay that way
And I'll never forget you down there
If you ever learn to forget me.

Mother, Mother, Mother, Mother.

(I want you.
  I am in the ship.
  I need you.)

(This was the beginning of my own poem. I would never show it to anybody cause there ain't anybody.)

I don't want a African name. I know we should be proud. Bri calls herself "Assata" and when she isn't thinking about the future, she is feeling proud like there is something else to live for. I know we should be proud.

But face it, why don't you? Here Mr. Hancock is telling me that I could get a vocational diploma and go on to do work in food service like he used to say I could do when I was back in his class reading *Tale of Two Cities* and not paying attention really. Here he is. He said, "Toya, you still have a chance for an okay future, you don't have to throw it all away." Right? Only a primitive person would turn their nose, like I did. *Right?* Fuck Mr. Hancock. Shit, I knew damn straight I wanted a better future than in food service.

Slave of a slave. I don't want a African name. I'll keep my slave name.

Boy was voted Most Valuable Player. Margarita Santamaria was voted Homecoming Queen. Bri went and had the secret abortion but promised me she would always be my friend. Big Daddy Dave asked her to check out a private party at his crib and she said yes she would sneak out her mother's house at four A.M. in the morning. Mr. Hancock asked me if I would want Boy's newspaper poem dedicated to me in the yearbook, as someone had anonymously requested, and I said, What the hell, it's his loss. Roc called me up late one night at Uncle Marion's and asked me if he could start coming over and shit, and I said, Why the hell not? Sam the cheerleader came up with Katherine as the godname. She is down with the program. She and I are going over to Tinytown's next week to check out what's new and happening.

RUTH FORMAN

b. 1968

Winner of the Barnard New Women Poets Prize, Ruth Forman's first book, *We Are the Young Magicians* (1993), announces the presence of "young magicians," or young African American poets, while recognizing the powerful tradition of black women writers. Forman futher invokes the notion of literary rebirth in the very title of *Renaissance* (1998), her second book of poems; the title poem asks "who will name this Renaissance/i stand knee deep in/who go tug the elbow of Langston Hughes/tell him we are yesterday again." Forman continues the tough tradition of poets like Sonia Sanchez and June Jordan, who helped form and refine the Black Arts movement, mixing vernacular voices and folk forms such as the blues with the precise images of haiku.

GIANT STEPS

HAIKU I

> Sometimes I Wonder
> why did I have to be Black
> I get over it

THE WILLIAMS SIDE OF THE FAMILY

We all women here
big boned and sassy
been so since we dropped from our mamas

we all sisters here
long talk and evenin
early and work hard

we all mothers here
babies and patience full
quick tongue and love

we all children here
looking for God at the end of our prayers

How long for y'all to see
who we be
your relative
long long at the end of the dirt road
pot fulla collard greens
n waitin on company

BLUES POEM III

> las nite you said you'd bring me the moon
> o las nite you said you'd bring me the moon

but tomorrow imma get me the sun
if you don't fetch it soon

cuz all you bring today is bruises and scars
yeah all you give today is bruises and scars
and ma cryin eyes too swoll
to wish on stars

SHOW ME THE ANKLES OF JUSTICE

the ones on which we claim our strength
they itch like ghosts who still exist

show me the ankles solid and unafraid
of children sucking sugar from the peel
of withered oranges
and I will say this is a country
worthy of the name

let's not deny the skeletons
this page is filled with corners you already know
democracy pardons its absence
but who will bring it home
who will plant it worthy of the name
we are hungry
and our bellies don't know how to explode gracefully

the scent of change makes the mouth water
for oranges long gone and we gnaw our own bones
show me ankles solid and unafraid
of ready teeth and rumbling bellies
show me ankles not stumbling from voluntary blindness

show me your ankles we are many
show me your ankles and how we stand
and I will say this is a country

CANCER

The end is coming
can see it on every plateau of breath inhaled
Johanna your eldest daughter/a deer
bends for water
at your palm

you Margaret
looking for your peace song
angels writing it
the chorus the first part finished
your son your sister brother mother father they all singing
you the solo
the chorus the first part
the harmony done
the melody they write
pens in hand
Margaret the peace song is in your tongue
dry from open mouth calling in breath
drinking air like kisses
holding time like a big hand

our eyes red
skin pale from being inside
I watch you search for your song
woman on water
looking for the next stone
i witness the growing marks on your cheeks from the rub of oxygen
    tubes
the brows come together like praying hands
the mouth not knowing the right words to say
the direction home or what time
there are hands of a child holding yours

somehow the air tells me not to break this spell not to leave this
    room at 10:15
silver hair mother from apple vinegar rinse
wrinkle wrists from blood stolen by I.V.s those thirsty worms
the feeding tube hangs from the I.V. stand a suitor

your coughs
scraps of sandpaper
we have to wait for you to find your voice

i've had to get used to so many things in its absence
the whir of fans
the grumbling of the oxygen machine
your slow morphine nod growing slower
to tapes of Romans and Corinthians

how fortunate i am to write this while your breath blesses this room
I catch it in my hands
like shallow water

MOMMA DIED WHEN MY WISDOM TEETH COME IN

push their way through the holes
not there yet
n stand like a new home

have to
hold my jaw different now

careful when i chew or i cut my cheek
careful how i hold my mouth when i talk
stay away from meat
keep food at the front of my mouth
where i can handle it

dont know how to wield them wisdom teeth yet
just set my jaw in the place it hurt least
and chew

EVEN IF I WAS CLEOPATRA JONES

Even if i was Cleopatra Jones
wild cane and sugar in the raw
honeydip dark n lovely gift of the gods
best bootie in the house
and your inspiration

i would not be the one.

i would not be the Nile at the end of your long long day
i would not be your ebony queen in this misplaced land
i would not be the Nubian princess who wanna get wich ya
i would not be the be strong sista
i would not even be poetry brushing past your thigh.
i would not be the stroker of good thoughts above and below
i would not be the guide the wise one the concubine mistress
    partner or best friend
well maybe best friend
but i would not be the one to crawl into or keep safe from myself
hot with the waiting for your mouth chill with the waiting for your
    mouth
naw
i would not be those rose hips on the fly girl round the way straight up
i would not be your world your baby or your mother
i would not be your milk or your honey although i do come close

i would not be any or all or any of these things
if i was yours the one you choose to choose
the one you say you choose

today remember
i would not be any of these things not just at the start of rain
i would not be any of these things, ever.

just the source of some damn good imagination.

TERRANCE HAYES
b. 1971

Shaft and Fat Albert, Billie Holiday and Betty Shabazz all appear in the poetry of Terrance Hayes. As in the early work of LeRoi Jones (Amiri Baraka), Hayes is comfortable playing with both popular and high culture; as with the blues, even when he is being humorous Hayes is saying something quite serious. The title of Hayes's first book of poems, *Muscular Music* (1999), aptly describes the style and subjects of the poems in which, whether writing about Esau or his own grandmother, Hayes is acutely aware of tradition. Often this leads Hayes to treat popular culture icons, from Marvin Gaye to *Sanford & Son*, as family. As a result Hayes provides recipes, not just for soul food, but for a unique, post-soul poetry.

SHAFRO

Now that my afro's as big as Shaft's
I feel a little better about myself.
How it warms my bullet-head in Winter,

black halo, frizzy hat of hair.
Shaft knew what a crown his was,
an orb compared to the bush

on the woman sleeping next to him.
(There was always a woman
sleeping next to him. I keep thinking,

If I'd only talk to strangers . . .
grow a more perfect head of hair.)
His afro was a crown.

Bullet after barreling bullet,
fist-fights & car chases,
three movies & a brief TV series,

never one muffled strand,
never dampened by sweat—
I sweat in even the least heroic of situations.

I'm sure you won't believe this,
but if a policeman walks behind me, I tremble:
What would Shaft do? What would Shaft do?

Bits of my courage flake away like dandruff.
I'm sweating even as I tell you this,
I'm not cool,

I keep the real me tucked beneath a wig,
I'm a small American frog.
I grow beautiful as the theatre dims.

I WANT TO BE FAT

I want to be fat,
I want a belly big enough to hold
A refrigerator stuffed with trout,
Big enough to house a husband with a beer gut,
A wife with a baby in her belly.

I want to be fat like a Volkswagen bug,
Candy-apple red, or cabbage green
With a burping engine and curving hood
Which opens to reveal my penis tucked
Safely between the crowbar and spare.

When I am fat,
Ladies sipping diet colas will whisper:
Look at him. My God how'd he get so big?
And beneath those questions they'll think,
I wonder if he still makes love?
I wonder what he looks like naked?

Love me skinny girls,
As you love jenny craig and vegetables,
Love me fat girls,
As you love insecurity and everything filling.
I'll let you kiss my triple chins,
I'll let you swim in the warmth of my embrace.

When I am fat
I'll scramble a dozen eggs each morning,
Brush my teeth after every meal
—this, of course, in the years
Before I am eight-hundred pounds,
Before I marry my mattress,
And lay all day swallowing
The light of tabloid TV.

I'll cry elephant tears
When *Cooking with Betty Crocker* is cancelled,
I'll curse flexing biker-shorts and ESPN,
And I'll never forget you, Fat Albert,
Your ass like heaving pistons of flesh,
Your stomach like a massive tit
Beneath your tight red shirt.

"You motherfuckers will have to give me
My own seat on the bus!"

I want to be the champion of excess,
The great American mouth with perfect snapping teeth,
I want fat children to send me letters
Of self-love and gratitude,
I want to swell thick with love and gratitude.

I want to be buried in an ocean of dirt,
This ocean of flesh, this heart
Like a fish flopping at the center of it;
This heart like a skinny man gasping
at center of it;
This heart. This heart. This heart

NECKBONES

4 pounds neckbones
¼ teaspoon sage
1 tablespoon salt
3 tablespoons bacon fat
1 teaspoon blackpepper
1 medium onion

Wash meat in warm water—
used to frown at my folks'
nigga-tongue
In public

I'd sweat cause I understood
every broken sound
    Heat bacon fat & brown on all sides
This was America
And we were spose to speak English
At night they sat round tellin stories
I listened and felt dumb.
    Simmer until meat pulls away from bone
They improvised; made magic
    Add flour to liquid if gravy is desired.
On their lips poetry was born,
I saw Sweet wearing a cheap burlap dress,
proudly.
She placed steaming neckbones
before me. Said,
This is America,
    Eat.

CANDIED YAMS

3 boiled whole yams unpeeled and sliced,
into a saucepan
1 stick melted butter
2 big tablespoons nutmeg
¼ teaspoon cinnamon
2 tablespoons lemon juice
1 cup brown sugar

1 brown-sugar woman
quietly slices yams
at a wicker table.
She does not melt
into the ruckus of
a rumbling house.
2 boys who never stop
to listen.
Listen. Listen.

She gives each
1 brown yam topped
with marshmallows;
gives each a love
for the impossible;
for the majesty
of soul food;
a love
for remembering.

I want to write
something about that;
the saucepan's infinite scent,
the dip & tenor of tablespoons,
the brown hands   blacker
than these scratches I make.
I want to write something
about my mother's yams:
I want to make magic
magic.

WHAT I AM

Fred Sanford's on at 12
& I'm standing in the express lane (cash only)
about to buy *Head & Shoulders*
the white people shampoo, no one knows
what I am. My name could be Lamont.
George Clinton wears colors like Toucan Sam,
the *Froot Loop* pelican. *Follow your nose,*
he says. But I have no nose, no mouth,
so you tell me what's good, what's god,
what's funky. When I stop
by McDonald's for a cheeseburger, no one
suspects what I am. I smile at Ronald's poster,
perpetual grin behind the pissed-off, fly-girl

cashier I love. Where are my goddamn fries?
Ain't I American? I never say *Niggaz*
in my poems. My ancestors didn't
emigrate. Why would anyone leave
their native land? I'm thinking about shooting
some hoop later on. I'll dunk on everyone
of those niggaz. They have no idea
what I am. I might be the next Jordan-
god. They don't know if Toni Morrison
is a woman or a man. Michael Jackson
is the biggest name in showbiz. *Mamma se*
Mamma sa mamma ku sa, sang the Bushmen
in Africa. I'll buy a dimebag after the game,
me & Jody. He says, Fuck them white people
at work, Man. He was an All-American
in high school. He's cool, but he don't know
what I am, & so what. Fred Sanford's on
in a few & I got the dandruff-free head
& shoulders of white people & a cheeseburger
belly & a Thriller CD & Nike high tops
& slavery's dead & the TV's my daddy—
    You big Dummy!
Fred tells Lamont.

GOLIATH POEM

I am always sorry for the big ape falling
from the Empire for love. Or Esau, a big man,
begging his father for even a breadcrumb
of thy Grace—sly brother-Jacob scampering
off to seed a nation. Dudes like that.
All muscle and hands weeping on the shoulder

of regret, which is a kind of blindness,
a recognition come too late. Sometimes I am sorry
for Rick, whom I love, where ever he may be,

six-foot-eight hurling stones through the window
of another woman who's turned him away,
and I too far this time to drive to him in the night.

Who will save the big men of this world?
Earlier I watched *King Kong* and was sorry again
for those building-size fuckers we see falling
from miles away. Those we thought invincible,
almost permanent like the sun which burns,
truthfully, only a few hours each day.

Once when his girlfriend called me, I drove in the rain
from college to his house. Nintendo cords roped
his shoes, a bottle of pills between his thighs, he sat
on the couch. In the darkness we could have been the same.
Perhaps I thought of holding him, my twin,
or thought of another door and my father weeping

beyond it a month before. I could have talked
about the horse on its carousel; how each man lowers
his head to circle, blindly, his life. But we said nothing.
We listened to rain like the sound of a big man's tears,
the sound God made before the Word or Light,
And the moon curved above us like an ear.

WHEN THE NEIGHBORS FIGHT

The trumpet's mouth is apology.
    We sit listening

To *Kind of Blue*. Miles Davis
    Beat his wife. It hurts

To know the music is better
    Than him. The wall

Is damaged skin. Tears can purify
    The heart. Even the soft

Kiss can bite. Miles Davis beat
    His wife. It's muffled

In the jazz, the struggle
    With good & bad. The wall

Is damaged skin. The horn knows
    A serious fear.

Your tongue burns pushing
    Into my ear. Miles Davis

Beat his wife. No one called
    The cops until the music

Stopped. The heart is a muted
    Horn. The horn is a bleeding

Wife. Our neighbors are a score
    Of danger. You open

My shirt like doors you want
    To enter. I am tender

As regret. Mouth on the nipple
    Above my heart.

There is the good pain
    Of your bite.

SOME LUMINOUS DISTRESS

for Betty Shabazz

Not even tomorrow morning can save us—
    Not even this great American space,
Palatial and white with stars can save me

    Or the burning house engines holler
Off to douse: curtains flaring at the windows
    Like hair, the black woman locked

In bright sleep—None of it.
    Yea, though I walk this stone
Unraveling valley, I shall fear no evil. Do I follow

    The siren, the men with red hats
And hoses—angels on their chariot,
    The yawn of smoke there—

Just over the hill; some luminous distress?
    Why not burn, star bright? I fear no evil,
Nor good will guide me. Only this night

    Which takes my eyes, these limbs
Shedding their secrets,
    Young scabs falling from wounds.

How else do I say it? The leaves
    Are falling. Three blocks from here:
The flame, and somewhere else, the white-

    Palmed child who set it. Do you see
How smoke & absence can blow
    The heart from its branch? Sunday's over,

It's Fall. Only softskin sinners
    And the butterbean moon; the siren's
Dirge just over the hill, the lit sky,

    The limbs black against it.
Where is my shepherd and his rod?
      Yea, though I walk . . . Where ever

This night is headed, I'll follow,
    Where ever I'm going, I've been.

SUMMER

In Oakland a white girl sings
what sounds like the blues,
song Summertime splashing
in her throat & I start thinking
I'd like to sing it too: a classic.
But nowadays brothers don't sing
the Gershwin tune,
a white man's vision
of plantation paradiso:
pretty black Bess, pickaninnies.
Porgy and thick cotton coons.
Enough is enough.

It's Summer so I hum.
Let bass slip around
my runagate tongue.
I have lived watermelonless,
I have scorned my languorous youth.

These days, I listen too closely
to your music, deaf
to the pit & patter of Politic.
O Summer, let me sing a song for you,
Let me be the king of something,
O Summer, let me spread my wings

ALLISON JOSEPH
b. 1967

In *What Keeps Us Here*, winner of the 1992 Women Poets Award competition, Allison Joseph re-creates her childhood experiences with an age-old wisdom. Her poems combine nostalgia and clarity with forceful detail and narrative, qualities continued in *Soul Train* and *In Every Seam* (both 1997). Like her fellow Jamaican and Harlem Renaissance predecessor Claude McKay, Joseph tells her story in an uncompromising manner, challenging presumptions of what black is—whether in "On Being Told I Don't Speak Like a Black Person" or through her "Home Girl" character. She is founder and poetry editor of *Crab Orchard Review*, a journal based at Southern Illinois University.

SALT

There's a kind of glory in it,
I think, though doctors warn
of havoc it can do set loose
in the body, able to rocket
blood pressure way past danger.

But I crave it nonetheless,
reaching for the fullest shaker,
whitest crystals, pouring it on
everything, anything, adding it
to the pale trickle of flavor

that passes for soup in the
cafeteria, sprinkling it on
the tame grains of rice
and tepid wilting leaves
from the market's salad bar,

not denying its sting
over chicken noodle casserole
or macaroni and cheese,
homey foods too plain to eat
without salt, too boring

to consider without that
familiar burn, that fall of white
raining down on warmed-over leftovers.
How else could anyone eat
dingy washes of boiled broccoli

or formerly frozen carrots faded
beyond recognition, vegetables
far too blanched to think of
without salt's savvy tossed
on top? And when I say I'll cut

down. I'll take the shaker off
the table, there's always butter,
molten and balmy in saltiness,
always cheese, its sharp tang
of sodium intact whether you

grate it, slice it, melt it.
Yes, my thirst is incredible,
lush, wanton, so thick I drink
far too many glasses
of water per day, that fluid

swelling membranes, cavities.
If I could, I'd return
to that childhood Jamaica trip:
salty water, bluer than I knew
water could be, buoying me up,

slipping past my lips into my mouth,
beloved taste of home in seas
I'd never seen before. Relatives
still say I couldn't get enough,
child who didn't want to leave

the sea, who drank that water
deeply, flooding my mouth with it,
loving its prickle on my tongue,
knowing it belonged far within,
where nothing else could reach.

LEARNING THE BLUES

for Jon

You taught me testimony,
slow-dragging the night until
our mouths kept time together,

GIANT STEPS

arms around each other,
silhouette huge, rocking
silent on the wall.

Nothing to that dancing,
one foot forward, other
back, pulling me closer

as the music grew, growled—
thunk of Lightnin's guitar,
Willie Dixon's sinuous pleas,

I just wanna make love to you
sung over and over, sear
of love undone in his voice.

Lights down, just one bulb
glistens mid-ceiling,
furnace rumbling the house.

I've got you close, under
fingertips, near enough
to lick salt off your neck,

for you to whisper all about
Slim Harpo, Koko Taylor,
Sonny Boy's porkpie grin,

and Bessie's sweet shimmer,
all that woman loose upon us,
her holy, holy voice.

FAMILY LIFE

The couple upstairs can't decide
whether to break it off. Her sobs
come down to us, spectral,

continue longer than anyone
should cry. He sounds surly,
but we can't make out his words,
can tell they hurt her, petty
for all they've lost.
They make me think nothing's safe,
that one day I'll walk into
my apartment, find it all broken
or gone. They make me think
no one's ever safe, not my mother
at the sink, hands in suds,
turning to deflect my father's
quicksilver anger, his temper changes
so sudden he'd soon try to hold her,
though she'd want none of the embrace.
His anger, fleeting like the money
that didn't pay our bills,
returned, eventual testimony
to our house, his loss.
Her funeral was near his birthday,
and he leaned over, said,
So this is what your mother leaves me.
Better this, I thought, than to be
fighting still, squabbling over
money, religion, utility bills.
I keep hoping the woman upstairs
will leave, hoping she'll rise,
spine straight, eyes unaverted,
walk right out his door, down
the stairs, out of his life.

HOME GIRL TALKS GIRLHOOD

Remember that longing for hips
and breasts, the rising curves
of womanhood? Honey, I was

so skilled at wishing
for a body I didn't know
what the hell to do with:

round, proud, everything
high and firm, long legs
curved just so, a dancer's

bearing. Just who I was
going to lure with all this,
I didn't know—all I did know

was that I quaked, afraid
each time I had to pass
those boys on the corner,

their eyes inspecting me,
finding what wasn't there,
calling after me—*you ugly,*

too skinny, for real.
How much time did I waste
longing to be a woman,

fooling around in Mother's
make-up—slashes of red vivid
against my lips, loose powder

freed on her dresser top.
I'd forage among bottles
of perfume, spray myself

with musk's dark odor,
fingers stained by mascara,
rouge. And when she'd find

me, she'd demand *just what
you think you doing, you
no damn woman yet,* and I'd

wait again, hoping my body
would begin, hoping to be
like her—all business,

all woman as she wiped
the paint from my face,
smoothing on cream to clean

my skin, bringing me back
to my ashy girlhood self,
muted child of color.

ON BEING TOLD I DON'T SPEAK LIKE A BLACK PERSON

Emphasize the "h," you ignorant ass,
was what my mother was told
when colonial-minded teachers
slapped her open palm with a ruler
in that Jamaican schoolroom.
Trained in England, they tried
to force their pupils to speak
like Eliza Doolittle after
her transformation, fancying themselves
British as Henry Higgins,
despite dark, sun-ripened skin.
Mother never lost her accent,
though, the music of her voice
charming everyone, an infectious lilt
I can imitate, not duplicate.
No one in the States told her
to eliminate the accent,
my high school friends adoring
the way her voice would lift
when she called me to the phone,
A-lli-son, it's friend Cathy.
Why don't you sound like her?,

they'd ask. I didn't sound
like anyone or anything,
no grating New Yorker nasality,
no fastidious British mannerisms
like the ones my father affected
when he wanted to sell someone
something. And I didn't sound
like a Black American,
college acquaintances observed,
sure they knew what a black person
was supposed to sound like.
Was I supposed to sound lazy,
dropping syllables here, there,
not finishing words but
slurring final letters so that
each sentence joined the next,
sliding past the listener?
Were certain words off limits,
too erudite, too scholarly
for someone with a natural tan?
I asked what they meant,
and they stuttered, blushed.
said *you know, Black English,*
applying what they'd learned
from that semester's text.
*Does everyone in your family
speak alike?* I'd question,
and they'd say *don't take this
the wrong way, nothing personal.*
Now I realize there's nothing
more personal than speech,
that I don't have to defend
how I speak, how any person,
black, white, chooses to speak.
Let us speak. Let us talk
with the sounds of our mothers
and fathers still reverberating
in our minds, wherever our mothers

or fathers come from:
Arkansas, Belize, Alabama,
Brazil, Aruba, Arizona.
Let us simply speak
to one another,
listen and prize the inflections,
differences, never assuming
how any person will sound
until her mouth opens,
until his mouth opens,
greetings familiar
in any language.

JOHN KEENE
b. 1965

Annotations (1995), John Keene's first book, goes back to the roots of the word *novel*—creating a new form that is part prose poem, part jazz solo, and completely his own. Through short lyrical chapters—a series of "annotations" on a boy's life—Keene explores coming of age in St. Louis, once "Gateway to the West," home of Charlie Parker and T. S. Eliot. Indeed, Keene combines jazz impulses with modernist methods, suggesting in the end that they may be the same thing. Though perhaps better known as a fiction writer, Keene is also a formidable poet, bringing the same sensitivity to history and language to his verse. As the title *Annotations* suggests, often Keene is concerned with writing as writing, willing to express a self-consciousness and lyricism both rare and thrilling.

GIANT STEPS

JACKIE ROBINSON IN SPORTSMEN'S PARK, 1949
for my father

Throw me a colored river city, beer, blues and patent leather shoes:
Stan the Man, Slaughter, Schoendienst rule this bandbox.

I brought three suits and one borough to town: nine
pins before me, wind 'em up fair or dirty, I knock 'em all down.

Today I'm facing Red Munger, whose fastball's as fat as a melon.
Still, you gotta be wary of Marion, who could catch a gnat

in his fingertips, back turned. Just two years ago some of them
    threatened
to walk off if my black ass graced the diamond. I did, we played.

Now Newk's got their number, his curve like a carving knife
across their stares, this big blue Jersey rookie their boogey man,

while Roy C., half-Negro, half-dago, guards the plate,
peppers the corners like stickball in a Philly alleyway. The colored folks

still sing my name out up in the rafters like a battle cry,
their hopes so near it's as if they're standing on first base.

I'm as ready for war as I was in '42, what man who wins
doesn't thrive on fear? Furillo's on second, I'm bringing him home.

Full count, when someone—a fan—shouts *sit down, boy!* again, the
    outfield shrinks,
even Pee Wee Reese blinks as if he's just looked into the sun—not me.

Instead I step behind the chalk, look at Burt, draw a line in the thick
    Missouri
dust: I take the sign, the ball swells as huge as the hate in these walls:

Here comes

                        a bullet:

          I dare you

                        to catch it.

CECIL'S CONSOLATION (1942)

A spry tomcat, Cecil crafts the shortest route
through the trolleycars and Duesenbergs
crisscrossing Aloe Plaza at noon
aware and not fully there
vasts grids of numbers shifting between his ears
like constellations

every season a new tally of disappointments
no places for a Negro engineer
Depression's depredations
add a nephew fallen to a bookie's straight razor
and his wife to the charms of Irish whiskey
the ever burgeoning nightmare of the European war

remember the beauty of variables he reminds himself
fingering the brass buttons of his livery
figuring the percentage rise in share price of his boss's firm
as he waits behind the wheel he knows where differentials disappear to
even in the organ's wheezing or printing press's hack
he can always diagnose and cure the sickness

twilights he steals away
to the basement of Sumner High School
donning a tattered mechanic's apron
often he has to stroke and caress
his old and indomitable mistress
until he hears the lathe softly humming

ONE REVOLUTION

Outside the street is ablaze with Portuguese.
I stand in the door of the tailor's with twenty cents
in my pocket, twenty dollars in my billfold, my only
money and already committed. Boombox
beats blast backwards from the square
where the hard light is. Laughter. I offer
my lighter to a woman with French nails like straight razors
since I don't smoke. Alright, take it. It's a day
to linger and drink lattes and steal art supplies
I'll never use and think about the Revolution. I am dying
to speak Spanish with a man I know can understand
me if his eyes were not so coal, his tongue a terra cotta
shard but English silts beneath my own. Give me a Pepsi.
Thanks. If I start walking I'll reach the Institute
in twenty minutes, the river in half an hour. Noon
sweats on the pavement. Yesterday I got a haircut and I finger
the ridge where the spears surrender to skin
which is called a fade, as something ignites
where my change sits, then the crown of my head
piercing the air two and a half inches, because I got
a flat-top which makes me feel beautiful. In there
everyone there was going on about the revolution
as if the showdown was happening tomorrow
and they might miss it and I might miss it too if I didn't listen
and not in Africa. Where the true light is. That same man
passes me with a glance I remember from daydreams then turns
away. I know this too. One of the patrons
of the dime store stops to chat with a streetwalker
I've seen too many evenings only at this moment
she's an activist distributing flyers. Union. He moves
behind them. I kneel to retie my new sneakers and suck
on a peppermint. Pardon me, which if I say
it fast enough would convey my intent

even to a native Kreyòl speaker. Buses rush
up and slither off to the Boston-side. Call that
the pathetic fallacy. I ought to get on. Maybe I'll recall
the contours of his cheekbones when I'm drawing him
from memory a week from now, or later
tonight when my fingers pause
on his brown collarbone as he leans
into my kisses. Next light you take
a left. It's nothing, you're welcome. I make a flute
of my can as best I can, and step forward till I am
nearly facing him. What the light gives. It is a day
to live and drink in these voices and think
about revolutions and Africa and men, I'll take it.
Maybe it's myself I now hear speaking or it's his voice
whose eyes commit me and maybe it's not Spanish
but English and he understands me if I really want it.

WINTER ELEGY

Suddenly those mysterious faces filling the telescreens
in the waning light of the edge-city mall
I take you glowing inside me like a candle

the darkest man exits through the backdoor
where questions pool like shadows
what exactly then was anyone asking for?

to hear the president's frail voice fading on the radio
to see desire parsed, down to its constituent elements
to stark cries and unbearable crackling

ultimately the point is to endure
because after all is whispered and agreed to in the boardroom and the
    union meeting hall
memory's aftermath shrouds us like fallout

winter upon the water as in a white mirror and the utter infamy of it
    all
they are gay now and can barely see beyond their industry
needing once more the arms held in those own arms the night before

snow fell, setting fire to the comforter
still one fears writing on the blackboard and the bill of sale
alone I wander through gray and desolate districts

the meaning of evening evaporates like esters
or the star where your tongue pierces my hipbones
pinpoint the moment of our deliverance

at the appointed hour someone surrenders you as if out of vengeance
with an answer but you are blind and cannot understand him
exactly what does it mean to feel

when the final verdict is rendered
what does it mean when the avenues
where your absence ascends in me like nightfall

ultimately everything is forgotten at the proper frequency
or forgiven like the year they abandoned us the children at the river fair
black embers of your fingers rewriting my back

new fog hovers above the city like a gallows

WHY I LOVE MY FATHER

Is not a matter for literary study.
That kind of feeling festers like sepsis
in darker chambers. Each of those
Negro men had a story to tell, a song

and dance for sons as though a bar and hop
could do no wrong, redeem it. Did not.

Theme of a child he could not abide
in silence, rooms, vodka-soaked dramas.

Counter-theme: a mother, his savior.
But why was the one forgiven? Not act,
but process. Agony as redress. When
at last we arrived at the grave of loving I

abandoned words as a point of ceremony.
That much evolved into a first write-crisis.
We crossed, he and the one who favors him
in crow-eyes, sugar-tongue, blacker brow

as a seal of birthrite, deceit as the price
of living. (Rage was a bridge across glacial
embraces.) Later, after proving yourself worthy
of yourself came the task of forging on as in

forgetting, not another routine order. Provident-
ially I remembered. If, not like. Now you ask
the next question, son. How does it end, do you
forgive? Nothing clears the air like a leaving. I live

with what I was given, waive claims, decline
the chain. Truth is a valid way of beginning.

RANDALL KENAN

b. 1963

Randall Kenan's first novel, *A Visitation of Spirits* (1989), broke
new ground in southern and black literature, staking the crossroads of sexuality, superstition, and black religious life. His second book, *Let the Dead Bury Their Dead* (1993), is a collection
of stories that tell one larger tale of mortality and morality; the
title story is itself the "annotated oral history" of a Carolina Ma-
roon society in the self-conscious tradition of Borges and Nabo-
kov. His recent nonfiction book *Walking on Water* (1999)
journeys into the heart of African American identity, discovering
the many meanings of blackness at the millennium.

Kenan's fictional community of Tims Creek, North Carolina,
the setting of his first two books, is also the setting for the following story. In addressing the moral fiber of a recurring character from *Let the Dead Bury Their Dead,* Kenan, like Faulkner,
confronts the reader with presumptions and questions of race,
myth, and power.

NOW WHY COME THAT IS?

That squall. That squall: metallic and beastly, squalling, coming from the bottom of hell itself, a squall full of suffering and pleas for mercy, a squall so familiar since Percy's earliest days, from when he was a little boy feeding his daddy Malcolm's Poland China brood sows . . .

But he didn't want to hear it now, damn it, not now, no, for now Percy Terrell was deep inside a dream. He and Elvis were on the town—was it Memphis? New Orleans? Nashville?—he didn't really know, and it didn't really matter. Cause he was in this diner with the King after a wild night of drinking and pool—the velvet night as tangible as the sheets in which he entangled himself at this moment of the dream—at this moment when he and Elvis sat in the diner with the checkered red and white tablecloth with two blondes, one each, one for him, and one for the King; and Percy had his hand on the milky-red thigh of that big-legged gal who smiled through her smacking gum and that leg was so soft and so inviting and she smiled even bigger as Percy moved his hands up that thigh toward—

But that squalling got louder as if someone were murdering that damn hog over and over, calling Percy back to wakefulness, and Percy didn't want to wake up, not with this fine big-legged thing sitting next to him, practically begging for it, and Elvis looking on across the table through his sunglasses, his arm around his sweetie for the night.

What's your name again, hon?

Evangeline, she said.

Evangeline. What a pretty name. Yeah. Percy slid his hand a little higher. Yeah. What's that smell?

At that moment, the moment when the dreamer begins to lose the threads and fabric of his dream, Percy began to dwell more and more on that vile, that powerful and obnoxious odor. Was it the woman? No, hadn't smelled her before. She looked clean enough. And the squalling kept on and on and the smell of hog. Hog. *Hog.*

Percy sat up in the bed, wide awake. As he blinked and focussed, the squalling continued, but not in the bedroom now, and presently stopped altogether. Percy swung his feet over the side of the bed, and one foot landed in something warm and slick, the sensation at once comforting and sickening, ooey and gooey and warm. His bare foot slid on the Carolina blue carpet.

"Shit."

Shit. There it was, and Percy's heart almost leapt for joy. Almost. For his foot was in a turd. But he had proof. At long last the evidence he needed.

"Rose," he called to his snoring wife, turning on the bedside lamp. "Rose," he began to shake her. "Rose, wake up. Look, Honey, look. That damn bastard has been here and he's left his calling card. Wake *up!*"

Rose Terrell smacked her mouth absently, and frowned, the sleep so deep around her eyes. "Hmmm?"

"Look, Honey, look." Percy held his soiled foot perilously close to his wife's face. "See, Rose, see it there! I wont lying. He was here. That bastard was here."

Rose opened one eye, moved it from her husband's brown-stained foot to his gleeful face; she closed it and turned over. "Percy? Take a bath. You stink." Rose brought the sheet over her head, and almost as quickly began to snore.

Percy, a little dejected, removed his foot, and with a little hesitation began to wipe it clean with a tissue. Yet he was not completely deflated, no. He was not crazy, as his be-soiled foot and annoyed nostrils bore witness. This proof was what he had needed; he had finally gotten a physical sign, a residue; and with all the stubbornness his Scotch-Irish blood could muster, he was going to prove, at least to himself, that he was not mad: he was indeed being visited by a hog.

A reddish-brown rusty razorback, to be exact, an old boar hog with unpulled incisors long enough to be called tusks, kite-big, floppy ears, and massive testicles the size of a catcher's mitt. For now on six weeks this hog would appear out of nowhere, without warning or preamble, anywhere—in the living room, in the cab of his pickup, at the store, entreating Percy, staring at Percy, following Percy, and the damned fool thing of it was that nobody but Percy had—could—see it; and Percy had no idea how it came and went.

Rose Terrell had listened to Percy—who for not one minute believed

the hog to be a figment of his imagination—and was absolutely uncon-
vinced. In fact, seeing that Percy otherwise had all his faculties, she
clearly just assumed Percy was fooling again—like the time he swore
up and down that there was a snake in the plumbing (a very bad joke)—
and just ignored him. Percy could tell that was what she had figured,
and had given up on her, had simply stopped commenting on the hog,
even when it showed up and sat at his side all through breakfast. And
now he was assured the whole thing might be a practical joke being
played on him. But by who? He wasn't certain. But he'd find out in
time. Got your hog right here, Mr. So Percy would play along, cause
there was no way in hell she and everybody else didn't see that damned
hog.

But now, now he had evidence and substance. Now he knew the
whole damn thing could be explained away. Something someone else
could see, smell, hell, even taste. And though, upon reflection, he had
no idea what to do next, other than clean up the mess, sitting there on
the side of the bed, his foot encrusted with drying excrescence, Percy
Terrell felt a glimmer of something like hope, a sense that perhaps he
were not going mad.

That first night he had seen it madness was far from his mind; the
whole occurrence had simply been a matter of negligence, of chance,
of curious curiosity. He had been at his desk around eight o'clock in his
office at the back of the general store, deep in thought, pouring over tax
document after tax document, trying desperately to find a mistake his
fool accountant had made, cussing at this damn new machine that Rose
bought him, damn thing was supposed to be fast, digital and all, but it
kept losing the figures, coming up with zero or e, and . . .

Percy had heard something outside his office, in the belly of the store,
something clicking on the old hardwood floor. He stopped, tilted his
head to give a listen. A few more clicks. "Rose? That you?" He didn't
hear the clicks. "Malcolm? Percival? Philip?" Nothing, just the refrigerator going off, a car passing by outside, the buzz of the overhead light.
Percy went back to work. Presently he heard it again, but closer, decidedly a "click" or a "clock" or a "cluck" sound, of something hard, yet a
bit muffled against the wood. Something walking. Percy got up to inspect. Everything looked shadow-drenched and shadow-full, the ghostly
beams of the emergency lights enhancing the shadowscape, making the
rows of fishing rods and gun racks and boxes of mufflers and barrels of

three penny nails and the yarn section, the bubblegum machine, the pipes and monkey wrenches and shovels and babydolls, seem about to move. Yet all was bathed in after-closing quiet, and still. Percy saw this dim world every night and he had never given it a second thought: same as it was during the day. But for some reason, this night, at this moment, he felt a little spooky.

"Who that out there?" Nothing. "Store's closed, now." By and by, Percy began to feel silly, just a tree branch knocking against the roof, and turned around and set his mind to line 27e on page 12 of whatever the hell that form was. After a bit his mind was once again stinging with the unshakeable accuracy of what his accountant had ciphered true, and how much he would not be putting in T-bills this year, when he felt a presence. Someone was standing at the door. He didn't want to give in to the surprise, and his mind instantly went to the three rifles on the wall behind him, just below the flattened rattlesnake skin he had tanned himself. If they had a gun trained on him, he wouldn't be able to reach it in time. Reluctantly he looked up.

Percy actually hollered. And flung his chair back so hard that the wall shook and the bronze gubernatorial citation he had received in 1975 fell to the ground with a clank. Had it been a human being person, Percy would have been ready, but before him stood this great big ole hog, its head jerking here and there, inspecting the place, coming back every now and again to Percy, its eyes piercing and unhumanly human.

"Git!" Percy said from the chair, collecting himself, wondering how the hell a hog got in his store. "Git on, now, git." Percy sprang to his feet, now simply annoyed, annoyed that someone had obviously left the door open or it came open and this hog got in. He grabbed a broom from behind the door and waved it at the hog, no stranger to the dumb, docile nature of the creatures. "Git on, now. Git on." Wondering who it could belong to, hoping it hadn't shit in the store. Damn. Damn. Damn. The hog grunted and began to back up. In his frustration Percy hit the creature on the nose with the broom. "Git on out of here and back to where you belong!"

With that crack of the broom the hog backed up two steps and raised its head, opening its swine mouth wide, and let out a piercing, brassy bellow, a bellow of outrage and anger, loud enough to make Percy step back and almost drop the broom. And with a quickness that belied its enormous size, the hog leapt and ran, the clackety-clackety of its hoofy gallop reporting against the store's walls. Percy chased after it, but soon realized he didn't hear the hog anymore. He switched on the store lights, which momentarily rendered him blind with their glare. He didn't see the hog. He searched up and down each aisle, calling it, stopping to listen, but heard nothing. After about twenty minutes, his frustration at the boil, he got on the horn and called his sons and wife and the two men who worked in the store. "No, Dad. I don't know nothing about no hog." "Percy, I locked and checked all the doors fore I left. How could a hog get in there?" "Swhat I want to know, Ed!" When his youngest and dimmest son, Philip Malcolm, suggested, "Well, maybe he climbed in through the window," Percy just slammed the phone down, annoyed, angered, pissed-off beyond anything he could remember in recent memory. He sat at his desk, stomped his foot once, sighed, crammed all the tax forms and files into his satchel, turned out the lights and left.

Days passed and the memory of the mystery hog began to bore Percy with the equality of its nagging and its curiosity. He went about his days with the grim, quotidian joylessness and banal glory with which he filled each day. Rising at five to feed the dogs, watching the farm reports from Greenville, eating breakfast that Rose prepared herself since Agnes didn't arrive until eight; going to open the store, checking everything; driving around the farm, checking this, checking maybe having a meeting in Crosstown with his lawyer or his banker or the manager of the mill, lunch most days at Nellie's Cafe, a plate of barbecue that his doctor said he should at least cut back on, with a glass of ice tea—these were his days, as empty as they were full. And even Percy, Lord of York County, had dreams of going off away somewhere, maybe to go on safari, hunting big game. He had done that once, back in '52, and had a fairly good time in Kenya, got a good shot off at an antelope, but didn't bag a thing. These days it was too much trouble, especially since those uppity coloreds made it illegal. He'd met a man a few years back who said that they'd guarantee a big kill in one of those African countries, Percy forgot which one, but it would cost him somewhere in the neighborhood of fifty thousand American dollars, the man had said, and Percy had said, Thank you kindly, and good-bye, cause Malcolm Terrell didn't raise no fool. No sir. Thank you sir. So he figured he'd content himself with deer and coon and ducks and the occasional big fish, though, truth to tell, at 58, Percy Terrell was losing his taste for killing things, something he'd never admit to another soul. Some days just being in the woods of an autumn or in a boat under the big sky was reward in and of itself. Perhaps Percy was at a point that he could even admit it to himself.

A week and six days passed, and Percy had damn near forgotten about the hog—he remembered really, mostly, that feeling of horror that had involuntarily gripped him upon the sight of the thing. That afternoon he stopped by one of the twenty-tree turkey houses he owned, a set of five over in Mill Swamp, where Ab Batts was fixing the feeding system that had been breaking with annoying frequency. This turkey house was about thirty yards long and Percy could see Ab bent over at work at the far end. Percy despised these dumb creatures, gobbling and gibbering about his feet and ankles, their heads just above knee level, the sight of their red and gelatinous wattles making him sometimes shiver with disgust. Turkeys were too dumb to walk out of the rain, but sometimes one would get its feathers riled and would peck at you. One tom turkey made him so mad once that he stomped it to death before Percy realized what he was doing, and which he later regretted cause the price went up that very day.

As Percy waded through the dirty white mess of jabbering poultry, kicking and shooing, he called out to Ab and Ab waved at him and went on working. As Percy got about halfway into the house, the turkeys started making more and more of a commotion, and started parting even before Percy got in their midst, bunching along the wire-mesh walls, hollering, crying even, it seemed to Percy's ears. Percy looked about, baffled, and even Ab Batts jerked up, amazed at the unruly fuss. Then Ab's eyes fixed on Percy with a mild degree of consternation and puzzlement, but Percy came to see it was not he Ab had transfixed in his glare.

"Boss," yelled Ab, "what you bring a hog in here for?"

Astonished and confounded, Percy stared at Ab, trying to make sure he understood what he was saying, and, as he said, "Wha . . . ," trying to understand, he looked round about him, and directly behind him stood that same damned hog, sniffing at the turkeys, whose racket was at this point of an ear-splitting quality. And ever so briefly, in the middle of this feather frenzy, this poultry pandemonium, ever so momentarily, eye to eye with this porcine beast, this stalking ham, Percy felt that he were not in Tim's Creek, North Carolina; that he was not Percival Malcolm Terrell, first and only son of Malcolm Terrell; not chairman and chief executive officer of Terrellco, Inc., county commissioner and deacon—he was a mere blip on some otherness, some twisted reality. He didn't know where he was.

Ab rushed after the hog and, after some effort, chased it from the turkey house. "Tweren't your hog, I reckon," Ab laughed off the situation, walking up to Percy, who had not really moved.

"Ah . . . no." Percy rubbed his eyes, not wanting to betray himself to Ab. "No, don't know where it came from. Must a just followed me in here. Didn't even see it. Ain't that something?"

"Must a been one of Joe Richards's. He been catching the devil with his hogs. Got one of them newfangled, fancy-dancy hog operations, over there he has, and can't keep em from getting out." A predicament that Ab clearly found amusing as he laughed some more.

Somehow, hearing Ab speak of the hog as a piece of a machine, a cog, an it, something that belonged to someone, and eventually on a plate, reassured Percy and filled in that momentary sense of a void; made him, oddly enough, whole again in his mind.

But that would be the last time he would feel that way for many a day, for, two days later, the hog again appeared in the back of his pick-up truck while he was driving back to Tims Creek from Crosstown. He stopped the truck and got out, worrying that the hog might vanish and convince him that he was more than a little touched. But the hog remained standing there in the bed of the truck, and Percy touched it, patted it, saying, "Whose hog are you, fella?" Feeling its warm, rough, hairy flanks flinch beneath his hand, the coarseness and the solid meat, Percy laughed out loud and shook his head and drove on to Tims Creek. He stopped at McTarr's Convenience Store in the middle of town and got out, seeing within the store Joe Batts and Tom McShane and Teddy Miller and Woodrow Johnson, standing around the microwave counter.

"Hey, ya'll," Percy said upon entering. "Anybody lost a hog?"

The men looked one to another, and all around out the window, searching with their eyes.

Woodrow took a swig of his Pepsi. "Where you see a hog, captain?"

"Out in my truck is where. Anybody heard anything about somebody losing one?"

Everyone went out to inspect the now empty truck.

"All right, now. Who took the hog out that truck?"

The men, smiling, a bit confused, watched one another, a little uneasy now.

Percy looked to see if anyone else were about. He noted a young woman filling up her compact Japanese-made piece a mess. "Hey, there. You seen anybody take a hog out this here flat bed?"

The teenager shrugged and said, "I ain't seen nothing and nobody. There wont nothing in that truck to begin with."

"There was!" Percy turned to the men, who were no longer looking him in the eye. He walked to the side of the store. Nothing. Just a lone tractor.

"All right, now." He came back before the men, who dared not look him in the face. "Where is it? There was a goddamned boar hog in this goddamned truck and I want to know which sonofabitch put it—took it—"

"Percy? You all . . ."

"Yes, I'm all right, god damn it, and when I find out who—" Percy heard himself, heard himself yelling, heard how ridiculous he was sounding, him, Percy Terrell, before these men who respected and admired him, men who he knew secretly all hated and dreaded him as well. And he caught himself, the way a snake handler catches the head of an angry snake; caught himself mid-roar, and started laughing, just like that, laughing, started exerting control of the situation and of himself. He winked, "Had you going, didn't I?" and he strolled past the men who were not laughing, yet, who followed him into the store where Percy went over to the drink cooler and hauled out a Pepsi and drank deeply, saying, "So, Tom, did you ever find that foaling mare the other night?"

Still a bit uneasy, Tom McShane sat down, clearly a mite rattled, and said: "Ah, yeah, Percy, yeah I did, but it was too late, they both died. Hated to lose that mare and that colt. Twas a colt, you know."

The men fell into commiserating and talking about this and that, and the queer spell Percy had cast over the meeting diminished by and by, though the specter of his curious behavior clung to the air like a visible question mark. And Percy, who was O so loathe to admit it to himself, knew that he had no idea what the hell was going on; knew that in some inescapable way he was, at bottom, more than a little afraid.

The visitations stepped up after that in frequency and in their curious and unexpected nature. The hog would appear of its own accord now in the house—once, when he was shaving, he saw it in the mirror; once, when he and Rose were in the living room watching a World War II documentary on cable ("Rose?" "Yes, Percy," she said, not looking up from her needlepoint. "Nothing." And the hog got up, during a commercial, walked out of the room and didn't return that night.)—now in town—once in a meeting at the mill with John Buzkowski, the general manager, the hog walked from behind the manager's desk, with him sitting at it, and the manager saw nothing, and Percy had to pretend he saw nothing; and once while attending a court proceeding over a bankrupt furniture store he owned a percentage in, Percy swore he saw the hog walk across the front of the room and expected someone to say something, anything, to acknowledge the animal. But no one said a word, not even Percy.

Every day now, the hog was sure to show, and everywhere that Percy went the hog was sure to go. He had given up asking if anyone else had seen it. He was even no longer certain that it was an elaborate practical joke that everyone was playing on him, a joke that would suddenly come to a crescendo, a punch line, and that everyone in the whole blessed county would have an enormous, gut-wrenching, wont-that-funny-as-hell laugh over and then Percy would come out looking the good sport and the business would be finished. But nothing of the sort occurred. So Percy waited, for days and days, and he became a little resigned to his swinish companion, and had even commenced to talking to it on occasion, when they were alone, sometimes in the cab of his truck, where it would sit, as tame as any dog. And, on these queer occasions, Percy would think how sanely insane it all was, and that he himself might be, without a doubt, crazy. But one stubborn and nagging fact remained: Ab had seen it. And as long as he didn't remark upon the creature, Percy's life was going along swimmingly.

However, one day his bafflement reached a new level of strangeness. He had gone over to his son Malcolm's house, where his daughter-in-law was bad-off with the flu. Rose, who was frantic with preparing and planning for a church trip to the Holy Land next month, asked Percy to take some food Agnes had prepared over to poor ailing Maria. Malcolm and Maria Terrell had five children, three boys, Percival, Malcolm III, and Richard (after Maria's father), and two girls Rose and Electra, and Percy felt awful proud of his progeny, especially the second boy, who not only bore his father's name but his father's likeness, but with a sweetness the old man had never possessed. That day, as he blew the truck horn, the children all ran out the front door to greet Granddaddy Percy, and he got out of the truck and reached into his coat pockets for the treats he never forgot to bring for them—much to their mother's disquiet, who had the unfortunate lapse of good judgment to tell him to his face that she disapproved of giving candy to her children, whereupon her husband Malcolm himself made it clear that you don't object to Percy Terrell's largess, and besides a little candy won't hurt em none, and so she now just grinned and bore it, the way Percy felt she should have from the beginning—but this day the children inexplicably ran to the other side of the truck. Percy walked around to discover them cooing and cuddling with the hog; little Malcolm had clambered onto its broad back, and, to Percy's amazement, rode the hog like a miniature pachyderm.

Percy stood there with a feeling like bliss and quiet resolve. "Ya'll see that ole hog, do you?"

Rose, age 8, looked up as if to say, What kind of question is that? "Where'd you get him, Granddaddy? He's BIG!"

Percy lit a cigarette and watched the innocent gallivanting for the duration of his smoke, a guilty pleasure he had promised the doctor he'd quit, while promising himself he'd just cut back; he watched with a feeling of warmth at the sight of his issue's issue having fun, a feeling that he rarely felt, a feeling that he actually felt uncomfortable feeling, yet felt good feeling when they were around. Over it all, in the middle of it all, under it all, was the strange stalking porker, whose presence, for a few moments, he actually accepted, accepted as a queer reality, and at the moment, even enjoyed.

Presently, Percy took the food in to Maria, who, from her bed, asked what the children were doing out there, and Percy almost said, "Oh, they're just playing with my hog," the reality behind the word "my" pricking his brain as he thought it, suddenly aware of the connotations, the meaning of the word "my." My hog. "They're just playing."

After sitting for a few minutes with the mother of the children who would carry on his family name, his name, Percy kissed her upon the brow and ordered her to get better—she was a good-looking woman, even when she was under the weather—and returned to the playing children, now three of whom were perched on the back of the patient, ever-suffering, ever-enormous hog. Percy gently lifted his grandchildren off its back, one by one, and slapped its rump, "Go on, now. Git on."

The hog didn't move. "Go on now, go on back to where you belong." Percy kicked it.

"Granddaddy! Don't!"

"Quiet now, honey. This ain't my hog. Sgot to go on back to where it came from."

"But Granddaddy . . ."

The hog turned around and looked at Percy with something that Percy felt to be an accusation. Without further adieu or prodding the hog trotted off in the direction of the house. Richard started to run after it, but Percy made him come back. "Leave him go, boy. Leave him go."

That very night the hog left his aromatic calling card.

But, as fate would have it, that next morning, Rose rose before Percy did, and she cleaned up the offending mound, leaving Percy with ring ears over letting those dogs come in the house, haven't I told you enough about that Percy, Land to Goshen! I'd swear you were brought up in a barn—Hog, hog, hog—just stop it, Percy, and also leaving him right back where he started from.

Having exhausted every avenue he could consciously consider short of going to a doctor—or a vet—Percy took what, for him, was a bold and unexpected step: He went to visit Tabitha McElwaine.

All the colored folks who worked for him swore up and down about Miss Tabitha, who was known throughout five counties as the best midwife and rootworker around. They mentioned her name with reverence and a touch of awe: "Went to see Miss Tabitha bout it." As if, Percy contemplated with scorn, she was the Lord Jesus Christ Him Damn Self. When they spoke to him of her, he called them damn fools to their faces, saying they'd be better off just burning their money. "But Mr. Percy, you just don't know." "I know damn well enough that that old fool can't do nothing but make piss and deliver babies, and God can take care of that without her around!" But the colored swore by her and gave her money left and right to cure ailments and make somebody fall in love with them; to make them prosperous and to take out revenge, happily handing over hard-earned currency to that lying heifer. And if he discovered a white person doing such a thing, Percy would refuse to speak to them for years on end.

The old witch, who was about Malcolm's age, lived alone in the old McElwaine mansion that proudly stood in what was left of her granddaddy's two-hundred-and-eight-acre spread, purchased after the civil war. Now only five acres remained, the balance now belonging to the Terrell family, as his own father had seen to. Legend had it that his daddy had killed her daddy over it, and they had in turn killed Malcolm. But nobody could prove anything, and Percy kept the land, and they kept their hatred.

Percy stood there now, at the front door of the old Federal style house, improbable in its competence and simple grandeur, well kept up, recently painted, red brick and white trim, fearfully large crepe myrtle bushes ringing the yard, and Percy wondered how an ex-slave could have possibly built it alone, thinking the story to be a lie in the first place. As he stood there Percy dared not admit to himself how desperate he had to be to come to this lowliness, how perplexed and damned, and, at base, simply bored with this intrusion, this haunting; how his other-wise simple and orderly life had been thrown into chaos, and how he, Percy Terrell, was at his wit's end. How he wanted an old black woman to tell him, an old white man, what he must do to release himself. But at that time, though he knew this all to be true, he would not allow the thoughts to form in his noggin; he just moved forward with an inexorable logic and a bitter will for exorcism. So he told himself nothing, as he stood there knocking, knocking, repeatedly, annoyed and calling out, finding the door to be open and just inviting himself on in.

Grudgingly impressed again, he marveled at how finely wrought and finely attended the house's interior had been, how cavernous its halls and rooms seemed—larger than the ones at his house—fixed up like a New Orleans cathouse with lace and doilies over the velvet upholstered chairs and with ferns and potted plants aplenty, gossamer curtains, da-guerreotypes of some solemn-looking Negroes staring down at him from the walls.

Without prologue he saw her straightway, on the other side of a big room, through yet another between them, standing by a big and dark stone fireplace. She stood there, still a tall and slim woman, her head now white with grey, a red shawl over her shoulders, wearing a long blue dress that looked modern and fine, as if she'd just ordered it out of a Spiegel catalogue. Percy walked down the carpet toward her.

"Nice hog," she said, not cracking a smile or moving a muscle.

"Um," Percy grunted, not wanting to acknowledge his co-visitor, walk-ing by his side, his head febrile with the fact of his being there, in her damn house, fighting with the inevitable fact of humility, of asking, of a need he for once could not solve with a credit card or the writing of a check.

He came within a yard of her and stopped, seemed his legs refused to take him any closer. The room sparkled with light from the windows, nothing hanty or frightening about it, as he had imagined it. He could have been standing in some resort hotel, somewhere far and away. "Look, Weird Sister, I got this little problem and I was wondering—"

"Well, Percy Terrell," she said, taking a pipe out of her pocket. "I ain't heard you call me that since 1952." She scooped and worked the pipe in a leather pouch full of tobacco.

Dismayed, Percy's eyes grew wide and even amused. "What?" He even grinned, involuntarily, so taken aback was he. " 'Weird Sister?' You remember the last time I called you that? Hell, I ain't talked to you in over thirty years."

Tabitha drew on the pipe, squinting in the cloud of sweet fog, and, blowing out the match, giving him a look as if to say, Boy you don't know your asshole from your mouth, do you? said, "I made up the year."

"Look," Percy said, after clearing his throat, feeling more than a little betrayed, more than a little stupid, more than a little. . . . "Look, I ain't got time for this. I need—"

"Know what you need. Why you came here. Answer's no."

"Huh?"

"Can't do nothing for you."

"Wait a minute. What you mean, you 'know'?"

"Want to get rid of that damn hog a yourn, don't you?"

"Can you?"

"Oh, I can." Tabitha stopped and blew out a long stream of smoke, like a ghost's train, and looked upon him vaguely with a look of pity that quickly transformed into scorn. "But you ain't gone be willing to do what you got to do to get rid of him. So why waste my time? Can't help you." She turned to the window, clearly having said all she would say.

Percy felt his face go red. When had someone last told him flat out no? No song, no dance? Refused him anything? After he had done such a thing as to actually come to this freakish old colored bitch for help, after . . . He stood there staring at this woman who had dismissed him so rudely, and it never once occurred to him that he might plead, beg, pour out his heart, that he might say *please*. He just got angrier, hotter, redder. Finding his voice he finally said, shaking, "Well, why don't you just go right on to hell then, you crazy witch. You just crazy. Ain't a bit a nothing to that old foolishness you preach. Just a old charlatan. You just go right on to hell."

He watched himself storm out of the old house, wanting to break something, wanting to burn the entire abomination to the ground, vowing to himself that he'd break that old witch one day. So twisted with hate and malice and anger was he that he couldn't even frame his own thoughts, at that moment, so inarticulate with rage, such a rejected little boy that he almost came to tears. And, indeed, at the wheel of his truck, with the hog sitting quietly, peacefully beside him, driving down and away from the old house, the unfamiliar sting and pain and torment began moistening his cheek, and he did.

By the time he reached home, twilight had darkened past dusk, and, it being a Saturday night, Rose had already left for bridge and wouldn't be back until after eleven, and he simply wanted to forget this whole business, to forget the hog, forget, indeed, the feeling the mystery of the hog precipitated within him, to forget how helpless and hopeless he was feeling. He locked himself in his study and snapped on the TV and popped *The Outlaw Josey Wales* into the VCR and opened a fresh bottle of his old friend, Jack Daniels, and took two enormous swigs before pouring four fingers neatly into a tumbler. He kicked off his shoes and loosened his belt and flopped back on the couch, before the flickering images of a West that never existed, concentrating intensely on the testosterone-deluded fantasy, and drank and drank. He had stopped drinking so much—well, during the week, now only on Fridays and Saturdays . . . except on special occasions; and he had stopped getting truly drunk . . . except on special occasions—but tonight that was exactly what he wanted, craved; he needed to erase, expunge; he lusted after what the bottle never failed to supply: power and ease and good feelings; he wanted to revisit the sweet veil of haze and be-bothered nothingness and the viscous warmth and head-fuzziness; he wanted to be released from tax codes and stupid children and orders and poultry and stocks and marriage, from maleness and the tug of gravity on his growing belly, to be released from the grey hair that he refused to dye out of a vanity stronger than fear and the red splotches and burst veins that would never vanish from his face and that signaled the end, years ago, of his virility and machismo energy; to be released from the memories of that once-youth, of his escapades and all the trouble his penis had seen and caused; away from memories of hunting and dancing and tomfoolery: released, yes, from the hog and all it seemed to signify. Percy drank. And drank. He swilled and slurped, he guzzled and gobbled, with a ferocious abandon, and with the swallowing, at his lips, and the fuzzy now-hum of his brain, somewhere in the amber liquid of the bottle, somewhere behind the black label, enlivened by the light of the TV screen, he saw his father, that old demon, with his big black hat with the huge brim, looking down upon his son with contempt. And Percy didn't want to see his father, never ever again, knew he was better than his father, could never be like his father, was a human being person unlike his father, an evil freak of nature, yes, he built it all up from nothing, yes, he started it, murdered for it, stole and beat for it, that sonofabitch, and left Percy with the blood, but Percy had, had—no, he didn't want to think of Malcolm, so he drank, and drank some more, the fire in his belly now out-stepped by the fire in his brain, he willed himself to stop seeing Malcolm, and, stumbling up and over, switched off the VCR and turned on the CD player and fell back on the sofa to the measured twangs and lonesome chords of Hank Williams, "Goodbye Joe, me gotta go . . ." and sang with Hank (Hell, Malcolm never could sing, never sang, never would sing) laughing and goofy in the clouds and fumes of mash and Benedict, Benedictine, and the deluged fretted in Antioch, O' Antioch, where the gladrags had orgies of ragout in Shiloh, O, by the door of Doomsday, yes, in Berlin where superior werewolves were sailors with head colds who lost the compasses in that distance, that joint—what was its name?—of pus-filled pushovers who submit, submit, wogs and Zeus, yes, zilch, in shampoo, Zimbabwe! Gomorrah! Dye. Die.

And somewhere, somehere, somethere, in the misfiring synapses and purple blaze of effluvium that had seized his brain and body, somewhere just before passing out, Percy saw his hog sitting there by him, by the couch, and felt a little love in his heart for this friend of his, and reached out to pet him, and, forgetting he held a glass, dropped it, and his mind went to black.

The next morning found the Head Deacon and Chairman of the Board of Trustees of St. Thomas Aquinas Presbyterian Church of Tims Creek, Percival Malcolm Terrell, sitting on the second pew along with the rest of the congregation, with a hangover that rivaled the worst hangovers of his youth—though knowing from half a century of heavy drinking that a bad hangover makes its own history. Percy felt he was indeed still drunk, for as he rose at seven after Rose banged and banged on the door to his sanctum sanctorum for him to get up and get ready for church, and as he washed and shaved and squirted drops of Visine into his eyes, and picked at his breakfast and drank four cups of coffee, the world was still tinged with a colorless aura, things were enveloped yet within a nimbus of gauze and otherness, and though he felt sick to his stomach, the alcohol had provided, at least for a spell and at a cost, a distraction from his mental confusion, had given his mind a respite from the hog which was nowhere to be seen.

Now he sat before Pastor Bergen, who could not preach to save his life, droning on and on about the faith of Zacchaeus up a tree, now he was playing the role he had part inherited and part worked for, a role so old it was capacious and well-worn and comfortable, and took so little effort he had barely to think upon it to be it: he was it: He was King of his little fiefdom of mills and poultry plants and fields and social rungs, richer than most men dared hope to be, and feared, respected, paid homage unto. Why on earth should he worry about anything other than cancer and taxes? And as Bergen drew thankfully near the end of his overlong sermon, Percy felt more than a little better and the nausea seem to abate and his mind to clear a bit and he thought of the football game he would cheer on after dinner with the kids and he realized he had not even thought of the hog all morning. As the colored light from the stained-glass windows played against the pristine whiteness of the church walls, Percy smiled to himself.

The commotion started as a low level rumble. Whispering turned to loud talk, and somebody said, "Git it, Frank!" By the time the minister stopped in mid-sentence and stared, Percy could hear people standing, some laughing, some angry, "How'd it get in here?" and before Percy could turn all the way around, he heard a grunt at his side: There was his old friend, his familiar, his companion and seeming advocate, his own and only hog. But the thing that Percy's mind latched onto was the fact that everyone saw the hog! Percy felt released. Yet, oddly enough, the hog had stopped by his side, as if to point a finger, or a snout, at him.

"What?" Percy hollered at the hog. *"What do you want from me?"*

With that the hog gave out his signature bellow and rushed toward the pulpit, around to the side and up toward the Reverend Paul Bergen.

The men in the front pews, unwieldy in their Sunday-Go-to-Meeting best, all jumped to their feet, and the pastor let out a girlish yelp, gathered up his robe like a woman's frock and ran, being chased by this boar hog, its oversized genitalia jangling betwixt its legs, its big ears flapping like the wings of a bat, its mouth wide and frothing. As the men of the church chased after the hog, and the women screamed, and the children laughed with unbridled wildness, Percy was just thankful and amazed that everyone, everyone, could see the hog, at last, at long last, and he felt that the whole six-week ordeal was coming to some end, was about to affix itself to a clear and final meaning.

The men tried in utter vain to grab the hog, but it proved too ornery, too sly, and kept slipping between their legs, knocking them over and down, for it was indeed a very large hog. At one point it actually bit Pernell Roberts on the hand, which made Pernell cuss ("Goddamnit!") in church, though no one bothered to scold him, for at that instant the renegade swine chomped down on the edge of the communion table-cloth and backed up, pulling the Eucharist, the silver pitchers full of grape juice, the little glasses, the silver platters containing wafers, all crashing, clattering, tumbling down with a metal thunk and splatter. Momentarily everyone stopped, the men, the pastor, the women, the children, Percy, the hog, stopped, witnessing the spectacle as if there was, in that brief wrinkle in time, some clarity, some hidden codeology in this bedlam. But the hog brought an end to that sober oasis of reflection when it moved first its head, with its bedazzling speed, toward Percy and grunted derisively, giving otherworldly language to its own unquestionably blasphemous actions, and with equal speed dashed down the aisle toward the door.

Without thinking, Percy moved in front of the great mass of pork, to stop it, calling out, "Whoa!" as one would to an intelligent, malevolent, comprehending entity. "Stop," he cried. But the hog didn't stop, poking its behemoth head between Percy's spread thighs and lifting him astride its wide neck, and continuing down the way, Percy being carted along and atop, backwards, yelling, through the throng of the agitated congregation. At the threshold of the church Percy fell off, unceremoniously and hurtfully, and the hog galloped away.

Percy scrambled to his feet, and, feeling somehow personally responsible, and even possessive, he gave chase, running down the side of North Carolina Highway #50, after that great boar hog, who had just

disrupted the services of St. Thomas Aquinas Presbyterian Church beyond conceivable imagination. Running, Percy didn't even give a second
thought to the fact that they were running, unmistakably, inevitably, to
his own home.

Though Percy's house was less than a mile from the church, he stood
in the doorway breathless, his heart pounding dangerously, sweat pouring copiously down his face, for he had not run this far, or this fast, in
years, not to mention the nausea he had been battling all morning. He
tugged off his tie and doffed his coat to the floor, and stalked to his
study. His mind was a red place, a hot place, a place of brimstone and
vengeance; he was not simply angry with a thing, but with an intangible
yet tangible circumstance, a situation, a tangle of happenstance and
botheration. He knew there was one way to get rid of it all, a way that
had never clearly presented itself before, since the creature had never
acted so hatefully.

Percy marched into his study, and, perhaps due to the anger and the
urgent need to strike out at something, broke the glass of his gun rack
with his elbow and a rebel yell, rather than waste time looking for the
key which was in his pocket. He reached for the old elephant gun he
had used once in Africa in 1952, and not since, though he had kept it
clean religiously. He loaded the shells, feeling the ungodly size of them
in his hands, himself feeling suddenly potent with each insertion, wondering to himself why he had not done this most obvious of things long
before.

Percy raised his head to the door, and, as he knew he would be, there
stood his hog, his hog, insolent, inquisitive, mocking. Percy sneered at
the beast, thinking and then saying out loud, for none would appreciate
this outsized drama more than he, like some celluloid cowboy show in
his brain: "End of the line, fella."

Percy had the hog in his sights, right between the eyes. They both
stood there, stock-still for a period of time Percy could not easily name.
Percy and the hog. The hog and Percy. The hog did not move, and by
and by, Percy thought: What a magnificent creature. Unaccountably he
began to tremble, and inadvertently he peered into the hog's eyes, into
the depth of them, perhaps toward the soul of it; and to Percy it seemed
the hog did the same to him. Percy's trembling increased and a feeling
began to wash over him and into him, and Percy began to feel puny.
Naked. Ashamed. Just as he had at that moment when he discovered

that his penis was not the largest in creation and that the juice of his testicles would neither save nor solve humanity; neither save nor solve himself; that all he had he and his father had stolen and robbed for, and that he had no right to any of it; that he was next to nothing, and that the mask of his flesh, once glorious, now wrinkling and withering, would in time be dust and ash, and that he was really not very, very much at all, not even as valuable as a hog.

Percy began to cry. He could not shoot. He would not shoot. He should not shoot. He understood in this moment of pregnant possibility, this showdown, this climax of it all, what the hog was. And in a moment of quiescence and acquiescence, Percival Malcolm Terrell let it all go, let the gun slip from his hands, and slumped to the floor of his study, a feeling like exhaustion settling into his bones. The great boar hog, on scuffling hooves, came rushing, and leapt, springing impossibly, up, into the air, and Percy, in chilled fright, watched as the mammoth creature sailed, like a gargantuan football, toward him; and he could only shield his face with his hands, and quake.

A few instants later he heard Rose run into the house, calling, "Percy, are you all right? My God, Percy!" He slowly uncovered his face to see only the open window, a breeze gently troubling the sheer curtains inward, barely a billow. Percy continued to sob, though the sob had altered in its tenor and meaning: now the sob was a sweet, deep wonderful and profound sob, his body shaking, snot running down his nose. Rose walked into the room, but Percy did not really see her or hear her, so intent was he upon this newfound and peaceful feeling. He felt just like that bird in the old Hank Williams song, the one too blue to fly, and tried to mouth: "Hear that lonesome whippoorwill": but only the mumblings of a child emerged. Lonesome, O so Lonesome.

HARRYETTE MULLEN
b. 1960

With *Muse & Drudge* (1995), Harryette Mullen has firmly established herself as inheritor of both avant-garde and vernacular
blues traditions. In her wild yet wise (and sometimes wisecrack-
ing) quatrains, Mullen takes on everything from Sappho to the
smart-talking Sapphire figure. Mullen continues her investigation
of language and the female body as in *S*Perm*K*T* (1992)—
the title a corruption of "supermarket," signifying on the sensuality of food—and *Trimmings* (1991), which takes Gertrude
Stein into the clothing store. Along the way, her work comments on labor in all its senses.

SHE LANDED ON THE MOON

She'd studied the science of motion,
applied physics to the wound
and her loneliness healed.

She landed on the moon,
alert in the snarl of machinery,
shining in complex uniform
with zippers and pockets
for emergency secrets,
a helmet to shelter her head.

Earphones played a musical wind
where not a tree was blowing.
Computers drove her there,
calculating her fall.

She landed on a soft spot on the moon,
evading the stony heart.
Emerging into greater solitude
she walked with new gravity,
her music parting the slow silence.

ROADMAP
for J. R.

She wants a man she can just
unfold when she needs him
then fold him up again
like those 50 cent raincoats
women carry in their purses
in case they get caught in stormy weather.

This one has her thumb out
for a man who's going her way.

She'll hitch with him awhile,
let him take her down the road
for a piece.

But I want to take you where you're going.
I'm unfolding for you
like a roadmap you can never again fold up
exactly the same as before.

FROM *MUSE & DRUDGE*

*Fatten your animal for sacrifice, poet,
but keep your muse slender.*

      —*Callimachus*

 1.

Sapphire's lyre styles
plucked eyebrows
bow lips and legs
whose lives are lonely too

my last nerve's lucid music
sure chewed up the juicy fruit
you must don't like my peaches
there's some left on the tree

you've had my thrills
a reefer a tub of gin
don't mess with me I'm evil
I'm in your sin

clipped bird eclipsed moon
soon no memory of you
no drive or desire survives
you flutter invisible still

4.

country clothes hung on her all and sundry
bolt of blue have mercy ink perfume
that snapping turtle pussy
won't let go until thunder comes

call me pessimistic
but I fall for sour pickles
sweets for the sweet
awrr reet peteet patootie

shadows crossed her face
distanced by the medium
riffing through it
too poor to pay attention

sepia bronze mahogany
say froggy jump salty
jelly in a vise
buttered up broke ice

10.

my skin but not my kin
my race but not my taste
my state and not my fate
my country not my kunk

how a border orders disorder
how the children looked
whose mothers worked
in the maquiladora

where to sleep in stormy weather
Patel hotel with swell hot plate

women's shelter under a sweater
friends don't even recognize my face

tombstone disposition
is to graveyard mind
as buzzard luck
to beer pocketbook

34.

if your complexion is a mess
our elixir spells skin success
you'll have appeal, bewitch, be adored
hechizando con crema dermoblanqueadora

what we sell is enlightenment
nothing less than beauty itself
since when can be seen in the dark
what shines hidden in dirt

double dutch darky
take kisses back to Africa
they dipped you in a vat
at the wacky chocolate factory

color we've got in spades
melanin gives perpetual shade
though rhythm's no answer to cancer
pancakes pale and butter can get rancid

38.

ain't your fancy
handsome gal
feets too big
my hair don't twirl

from hunger call
on the telephone
asking my oven for
some warm jellyroll

if I can't have love
I'll take sunshine
if I'm too plain for champagne
I'll go float on red wine

what you can do
is what women do
I know you know
what I mean, don't you

SUZUKI METHOD

El Niño brought a typhoon of tom-toms from Tokyo, where a thrilling
instrument makes an ok toy. Tiny violins are shrill. Their shrieks are
musical mice. The color of a mechanical clock is lost in translation.
Whatever you're telling me sounds like the straight teeth of rodents. My
dreams throw the book at the varmint. We both shudder as the
dictionary thuds. You've got to admit, our Esperanto's hopeless. Your
virgin is unfaithful. My savory hero boards the ship of Marco Polo,
loaded with soy from Ohio.

BLACK NIKES

We need quarters like King Tut needed a boat. A slave could row him
to heaven from his crypt in Egypt full of loot. We've lived quietly among
the stars, knowing money isn't what matters. We only bring enough to
tip the shuttle driver when we hitch a ride aboard a trailblazer of light.
This comet could scour the planet. Make it sparkle like a fresh toilet
swirling with blue. Or only come close enough to brush a few lost souls.
Time is rotting as our bodies wait for now I lay me down to earth.
Noiseless patient spiders paid with dirt when what we want is star dust.

If nature abhors an expensive appliance, why does the planet suck ozone? This is a big ticket item, a thickety ride. Please page our home and visit our sigh on the wide world's ebb. Just point and cluck at our new persuasion shoes. We're opening the gate that opens our containers for recycling. Time to throw down and take off on our launch. This flight will nail our proof of pudding. The thrill of victory is, we're exiting earth. We're leaving all this dirt.

KEVIN POWELL
b. 1968

Though he may still be best known as a star of the inaugural
season of MTV's series *The Real World,* where he was filmed
with six other strangers living in a loft in New York City, Kevin
Powell has emerged as a notable literary figure, co-editing *In the
Tradition* (1993), an early anthology of young writers, and publishing *Recognize* (1995), a book of poetry. Powell's music and
cultural criticism have kept him in the national eye, often as a
representative of "the hip-hop nation" he has helped define—
most notably, Powell interviewed rapper Tupac Shakur in a
groundbreaking cover story for *Vibe* magazine. Powell's nonfiction book *Keepin' It Real* (1997) is a series of letters to various
figures in his life in the epistolary tradition of James Baldwin
and others. "Letter to My Father," with its blend of direct-
ness and understatedness, attempts to reconcile a wayward father and an all-too-present past.

LETTER TO MY FATHER

January 1997

DEAR _____:

I haven't heard from you in over twenty years, not since that rainy spring day when my mother and I called you from a drugstore phone booth and asked you for money. You had been woefully negligent, and we desperately needed the extra dollars.

I was so happy that we were calling you; as my mother talked, I imagined your finally marrying her and rescuing us from poverty. Maybe, I thought, we will even have our own telephone and a big, red-brick house with a backyard, a swimming pool, and a swing set and a slide. When my mother put me on the telephone to say "Hey" to you, I remember that I beamed with joy after you said that you and I would get together again real soon. I gave the receiver back to my mother and returned to my fantasies.

But the sudden tremor in my mother's voice and the fury that washed the calm from her face snapped me out of my daydream. I couldn't hear what you said, but I learned later from my mother that you were accusing her of lying. You were insisting that I was not really your son, and you vowed that you would never give "a near-nickel" to her or me again.

My eight-year-old mind wasn't quite sure what "a near-nickel" was, but it sounded like something completely out of reach—like you. I didn't know what to feel, but I do remember thinking about the few moments we'd spent together up to that point. The one or two times I'd ridden with you in your tractor trailer—I will never forget those pinups of naked women inside your truck! Loungin' at your cozy, two-story house as you showed me how to play pool. Going to the barbershop with you: profilin' and smilin' for you—who cared if my two front teeth were missing?— as you took my picture with your new Polaroid camera. Standing impatiently by your side (I barely came up to your waist) as you pulled a fresh five- or ten-dollar bill from your bulging black wallet and handed it to me. The two trips to Journal Square, Jersey City's shopping district. The first one when you bought me my first Timex watch, and later when you bought me my first bicycle.

I kinda remember your family—most of all your older sister, who never stopped saying how much she loved me. She showed that love by taking me down South when I was just a few months old to meet your family. It didn't matter that I hardly ever saw you, or that I didn't really know you. You were my father, and all those instances, especially when you bought me the bike, had me amped about you. If you remember, my cousin Anthony's father had also gotten him a bike and Anthony, and I, and our mothers boldly bragged about which father was doing the most for his son. Because so many people knew you around Jersey City, it naturally seemed to me that you were *the* man, and that made this little boy very proud.

Word-life, though, my mother and you never being married messed me up something awful. I was embarrassed by the fact that I had been born "out of wedlock." While most of the other children in my neighborhood also lived in single-parent households, usually run by women, even at that young age I never felt that was right. Worse yet, it seemed that the other children around my way, or the ones I went to school with, at least got to see their fathers every week. In fact, some of their fathers regularly participated in their lives, visiting their teachers at school, taking them to ball games, teaching them about manhood— anything. I'd have to push my envy away when I heard boys call their fathers "Dad" or "Pop," or by their first names. I didn't know what to call you, so I never called you by any name. You weren't a constant in my life, so something as intimate as "dad" or "pop" just didn't work for me. Calling you by your first name (or your last as many people did) didn't cut it either. It would've made me feel like we were distant buddies at best, not related by blood.

And you can't deny that your blood runs through me deeply. I have your light-brown complexion, your reddish facial hair, your full lips, your medium-range height, and according to my mother, some of your ways. I am, I suppose, an extension of you, and you of me. But I've never felt your presence in any meaningful way, and that has tormented me my entire life. Your absence gave birth to an unbearable pain, so I did many things to avoid facing that grave dilemma. For example, at the beginning of each school year when teachers would ask the names of our fathers and mothers, I would conveniently give a different name for my father. That name would usually depend on what television show appealed to me at the time. One year it would be "Michael" as in Michael Brady from *The Brady Bunch*; another year it would be "James" as in James Evans from *Good Times*. Of course, most of my teachers knew what was going on, but they never put me on the spot. I often projected the pain I felt about lying onto my mother, whom I blamed for your not being in our lives.

At first I kept those feelings to myself. But as I got older I would confront my mother, falsely accusing her of driving you away. In the middle of one of our many arguments—it didn't matter what the argument was about—I'd yell back at my mother, saying if she'd been any kind of woman, you, my father, would have married her. I feel sick now just thinking of the things I used to say to my mother. She, in turn, took out her bitterness on me—with belts and switches, with extension cords, even her bare hands. If she couldn't confront you, then I was an easy enough target. What I realize now is that my mother was no child abuser. She was a young woman forced to raise a strong-willed male child alone after a man—you—had emotionally decimated her. I remember my mother trying to spank me into obedience, her voice pleading, demanding: "You gonna be good? Huh? You gonna be good?" I see now that she was preparing me in the only way she knew how for the cruel world that awaited me. And while my mother couldn't know everything I'd have to face, she did say, from the day you dissed her, that I'd better not grow up to be "no-good" like you. That was my mother's manhood prescription for me. Do not, under any circumstances, be like your father. But because I was a child, I didn't fully know or understand what had gone down between you and my mother—partly because my mother refused ever to discuss you, and would become visibly irritated whenever I asked about you. So I mentally distanced myself from her as best I could.

I was an only child, floating somewhere in limbo, "inwardly homeless," as bell hooks puts it. I felt not only that you had abandoned me, but that my mother, by virtue of her actions—which were really *reactions* to your callousness and your irresponsibility—had abandoned me as well. The worst thing a child can feel is that he doesn't have a true home, a place where he feels nurtured in a way that confirms his life. Without that, no matter how "smart" or "talented" that child may be, he is forever subject to bouts of hostility, paranoia, and serious doubts about his place and significance in the world. I mean, if he can't trust his own parents, really, whom can he trust? Whom can that child love if he feels he has never been loved by the very people who brought him into the world?

Even with you out of the frame for good, I thought about you all the time. When I played baseball and ran track, I wished you were there to cheer me on. All the times I was sexually curious and kind of fumbling around for answers, I wished I had you to talk to. My mother, being the socially conservative woman that she is, wasn't about to discuss the topic. All the times I got into trouble at school or with the police, my mother would have to get some other man—a cousin, a neighbor, any-one—to scold me for being bad. And of course I didn't pay any of those men any attention because, hell, they weren't my father. But neither were you, because you were not there. And my mother never let me forget that fact, either.

My life went on, through the loneliness of my high school years to my newfound political awareness at Rutgers University, to my ouster from college (I was quite a militant student). Next came a near nervous breakdown in my early twenties as I tried to make sense of my manhood and my place in the world. I've been homeless, a womanizer *and* a woman abuser, a careless lover, a complete jerk to my mother. I've been very irresponsible with my finances, and I don't even know how many people I've hurt and pushed away from me for fear of their getting too close. How could I allow that kind of intimacy when my experiences as a child said closeness among human beings did not exist? I was merely practicing what I'd learned from you.

That's when I needed you, I truly needed you, my father—a man—to tell me what I was doing wrong, how I could make things right. I needed you to tell me how I, a black boy, could survive in this hectic society which, when it paid any attention to me, seemed doggedly de-termined to annihilate me. I hate to sound like an echo machine, but those times I was harassed by the police or accused of stealing by em-ployers or dumbfounded because I had no clue how to make love to a woman, I wished you were there to show me the way, to chill me out (you would not believe how high-strung and bad-tempered I can be), to tell me things were going to be okay. You cannot imagine how many older men, and even men my age, I looked to for answers, only to be disappointed over and over by their shortcomings, perceived or real. You scarred me and, as a consequence, I am very hard on men who fall short of my super-high standards. All through my life, especially when I was a teenager, I fabricated an idealized father in my mind, someone I could male bond with, just as my homeboys actually did with their fathers.

This imaginary father would be so wise and so strong and so in touch with himself that, no matter how hard-core he appeared to be, he could also be gentle with my mother and with me, his son. My TV-addicted mind figured that kind of man would be a combination of Jimmy Stewart, Clint Eastwood, and Bill Bixby when he starred in that old show *The Courtship of Eddie's Father*. My imaginary father would, in a word, be *special*. You know, to be honest, to this day I have that imaginary father, that imaginary man, in my head. As a result, I have a very hard time relating to most men, especially men who do not open up, who are not sensitive. I can't deal with men who are not honest with *me*, who say they're mentors when they really are not, who say they're friends when they're actually jealous or insecure rivals, who cannot admit when they're wrong or afraid, who define their maleness only by their "machismo," who run away, as you did, rather than deal with the circumstances they helped to create. I don't think it's a coincidence that most of my closest friends are women. I feel with women, there isn't a lot of the defensiveness and B.S. going down, at least not in the way we men operate. I guess, maybe, I've internalized those things my mother told me you and other men were and that I should not become.

It's not that I haven't done a lot of predictable "man things" myself, because I have. Yet somehow, thanks to God or whatever higher spirit exists, I have survived. And somehow, without you, I've managed to do okay. My childhood dream of being a writer is being fulfilled, and I've learned to look out for myself. I'm also very thankful that I haven't brought any children into the world, because I would not have been prepared, emotionally or financially, to be a father. The reason for your disappearing act still escapes me since you were already in your thirties when you impregnated my twenty-two-year-old mother, and you had an above-average standard of living, as evidenced by the cars you drove and the homes you owned in Jersey City and down South. But I know that a father is so much more than loot, because you deprived me in ways that winning a million-dollar lottery could never have made up for. Nevertheless, my mother did a remarkable job. Other men sometimes paraded around, attempting to move in and live off my mother. But she'd always say, in obvious reference to you, "I can do bad by myself!"

Yet I can't lie either and say my curiosity about you has lessened over time. It hasn't, although I have never actively sought you out. But I was exhilarated a few years back when my mother told me that she'd run into you one morning while waiting for a bus. When my mother told me you asked about me, I bubbled with joy. I wanted to, uh, I wanted to meet you. My mother was perturbed by my reaction, but she said if she saw you again she'd get your number for me. A few weeks later, she did see you, but when she asked for your number, you told her you didn't have a pencil. She then gave you my number in New York City.

I waited for you to call. And I waited and waited. First days, then weeks passed. Nothing. In the interim, I imagined our meeting, how I was torn between saying, "It's good to see you," and kicking your ass for leaving my mother and me hanging all those years. But the phone call never materialized, and once again I had to deal with that old sense of rejection. Even though I was an adult it hurt me greatly. I cried like a baby. The pain was so great I couldn't even bring myself to leave my apartment for a few days. And that phrase, "a near-nickel," reverberated in my brain. I wondered if that was all I was worth to you. Later, when I visited my mother, she asked me if you had ever called. Before the response was out of my mouth she said, with disgust. "He ain't no good and he ain't never gonna be no good." Then my mother told me how, when she saw you, you had tried to hit on her, after all these years, more or less inviting yourself to her apartment. She said you went so far as to give her a picture of "Kevin's brother."

My brother? My mother always said you had mad kids all over the place and that you were "fast." But that was so wack to give my mother a photo of some sixteen-year-old boy whom I've never seen in my life, who has no relevance to me whatsoever, and pass him off as my brother. Yeah, he and I, like you and I, share blood, but that does not mean the circle is complete. The only common history between that "brother" and me is you. And you and I don't have much of a history. I took that photo from my mother, tore it up, and tossed it into a garbage can.

That meeting that did not happen was like pouring lighter fluid into a smoldering fire. And that photo of my "brother" was the match. You had burned me—again. And I realized that my entire life I've felt in-complete, empty, because you haven't been there for me. At times, I would somehow rationalize your absence, and call it fate or divine in-tervention. But even if those things are true, I cannot escape the fact that I have feelings for you. That you are my father, and that we are connected by blood and flesh and bone and history. In some dark spot in the recesses of my mind, I've got love for you. But to be completely honest, I hate you, too, and I hate that part of myself which is the part of you that abandoned me.

The question is: How do I resolve that hatred? Especially when it is that hatred of my life that makes me so angry to this day. Can you at least, somewhere in your world, wherever you are, understand that? If I hate you, then I hate myself. And I am tired of despising parts of who I am. I'm so tired of neglecting myself simply because neglect was the foundation on which my life began. My aim is to create a new foun-dation and to destroy that old foundation—that hatred—no matter what it takes. I pledge to myself that I will never abandon a child the way you abandoned me. No child, especially not a child born in the ghetto, deserves to be left to wander in this world by him- or herself. Nor should the mother, because of that father's absence, be forced to be both mother *and* father.

I can't really say what this letter may do for you, but it is very ther-apeutic for me. I've needed to say these things for a very long time. Whether you actually read these words or not doesn't really matter much. The point is that I've gotten it off my chest, and maybe some father somewhere will think twice about his relationship with his son. Or his daughter. Whether we realize it or not, we are all connected by time and space and circumstances, and my destiny is forever linked to yours. This manhood thing has been a hard journey, but it is one I will continue to explore and understand and define as best I can. Sometimes I wonder if I would've been on this kind of search had you been in my life. One can only speculate.

As I write this letter, after many years of agonizing soul-searching, I know that even if I never speak to you for the remainder of your life or my life, or if we never see each other again, I no longer harbor any bitterness toward you. I cannot make you accept me, but your accep-tance is no longer relevant to my existence. This has been a long battle for me, one that started in my heart and worked its way through my body and soul. Like the churchgoers who "get the spirit," I feel good, real good, about myself and the possibilities of one day becoming the man I wanted you to be.

Your son,
Kevin

CLAUDIA RANKINE
b. 1963

Born in Jamaica, Claudia Rankine writes of distance from the country of her birth and of displacement in the broader world. Some of the most successful poems in her prizewinning first book, *Nothing in Nature Is Private* (1995), are written in Jamaican vernacular, reminiscent of the early "dialect poems" of Harlem Renaissance writer Claude McKay.

As the title of her latest book, *The End of the Alphabet* (1998), suggests, Rankine's newer work concerns itself with the edges of language—extending the vernacular and "nature" into an even more "private" language of grief and loss. As with Gwendolyn Brooks, if her poems are occasionally challenging or formally dense it is simply because Rankine approaches form as hardship in order to best describe the difficulties—and delights— of American life.

AMERICAN LIGHT

Cardinals land
on a branch, female and male.
The sky shivers
in puddles created of night rain.
Speckled particles dance
in a path of light, so it seems
it doesn't matter what's in the road.
Then the shadow of a black oak
leans forward like a wounded man.

The lit landscape conceives
a shadow, its face dark, wide-open,
its eyes bloodshot
from what had come before.

.   .   .

In the lit landscape, in its peeled
back places, making the space
uncomfortable, representing no fault
in the self is a shadow
of a gesture of wanting, coveting
the American light.

A shadow on ships, in fields
for years, for centuries even, in heat
colored by strokes of red, against
the blue-white light—and in it
I realize I recognize myself.

And still the light
fills wind-tossed branches,
makes clouds iridescent
islands in the sky. And still
the same light (for nothing

in nature is private)
insists on a shadow in the road.

.   .   .

I step into my shadow
as if not to take it anymore,
and wonder where I am going.

Sweet sad shadow, sun charred
on the open road, I don't want
any trouble, don't wish
to be troubled, but when the sun
goes down on this aged,
dirt road, will I end
in dark woods, or make it home?

HIM

West Indian, him left like de rest,
to sail for New York, to plant and pot
whatever fi root in de new soil,
dasheen, callaloo, fevergrass.
From somewhere him find chickens
for de rented backyard as him wait—
Lord, how him wait—for him Alien
Registration card. And when it come,
him toast himself: *Immigrant! American
immigrant!* So him talk and laugh
with him lips quick parting, *Who
feel dem can bad mouth America
don't know a damn thing!* But
soon him voice quiet (*Yes, Sir.*) Him
newness slipping clean into de past.
Holding two, sometime three job,
(steward, carpenter, cook) him give up
a few things (sleep, Red Stripe,

dominoes) for him waan believe, pursue,
dream de dream though something
put shadow pon him. (*Boy*) Glasses pon
de table. Head in him hand. Please.
Please. Him break him back, and for
what? (*Boy*) A promise no nothing.
So then, American women, nuff new
woman, him go through dem like
butter: Ackee and saltfish. Cassava.
Stuffed breadfruit. Oxtail . . . till
one Sunday him wake, and as sun full
him yard, him kneel ina grass and begin
weed him garden. Him little one see him
and ask, *What's his name?* And de
bigger child answer, *He's our father*.

OVERVIEW IS A PLACE

*

Difficult to pinpoint

fear of self, uncoiled.

specter unstrung. staggering stampede. Which
sung? left the body open for the moon to break into,
unspooling disadvantage.

Give a thought, Jane: Did filth
begin in conversation? drag
the mood through before escaping the ugliness. Not to

dwell on but overhear footsteps again
approaching: immured,
not immune, then dumdum

bullet templed. rip the mind out. go ahead.

*

Dawn will clear though the night rains so hard. Rain

and Jane mix and mixing up, thinking shore but
    hugging floor.
What Jane must substitute for this year's substitute
for a mind intact? fire?

its greediness egged on, flame after flame
uninvolved
but still fueling the shifting onslaught.

Gray Jane
emphasize otherwise, not the eyes
but the cheek to the pillow. Bundle up and sweep

bare the mind. Land its ooze
at some other gate, soften
dead wood. Sea smoke, drizzle, distance. The moment

of elucidation snipped its tongue, its mouth water
dried out—
thought-damaged throat.

*

Remember a future
from another dream
and hold on. open your mouth

close to your ear: fear
in sanity lives. anatomy
as dissonance,

vertebral breaking. In spite
of yourself.
rising, the mercury

reaching out
to fever. fire. all your civilized
sense, Jane. disabled.

*

Assurance collapses naturally
as if each word were a dozen rare birds
flown away. And gone

elsewhere is their guaranteed landing
though the orphaned wish
to be happy was never withdrawn.

Do not face assault uncoiled as loss,
as something turned down: request or sheet. Pray
to the dear earth, Jane, always freshly turned,

pull the covers overhead and give
and take the easier piece.
to piece the mind.

to gather on tiptoe. Having lost
somewhere, without a name to call, help
yourself. all I want.

THE QUOTIDIAN

*

                  What we live
before the light is turned off
is what prevents the light from being turned off.
In the marrow, in the nerve, in nightgowned exhaustion,
to secure the heart,
hoping my intention whole, I leave nothing
behind, drag nakedness to the brisker air of the garden.

What the sweeper has not swept gathers
to delay all my striving. But here I arrive
with the first stars: the flame in each
hanging like a trophy in the lull just before
the hours, those antagonists
that haunt and confiscate
what the hardware of slumber draws below.

*

Night sky,

all day the light,

responding without proof, vigorously
embraced blue,
lavender-sucking bees,
a stone mouth spewing water to golden carp.

Light piled on indisputable light rekindled bits of garden
until bare-shouldered, coherent, each root, its stem,
each petal and leaf
regained its original name
just as your door opened and we had to go through.

Which is to know your returned darkness was born first
with all its knowledge—
routine in the settling down, little thumps
like someone knocking at the temple—arriving

within each soul growing old
begging, impatient
for these nights to end, wanting
never darkness—

its murmurous mirror:

GIANT STEPS

*

its drained tongue

as dead driftwood soaking the vein
as these words float up
out of body

in a joke sharpened in or sharpening
each myopic minute
met

and now dirtied up, or far too beautiful
for this

and now desperate for
the never would or could
or at least had not meant to mean).   Pity the stirred.

So stormed out, as in exhausted, my eardrums left watching.
Each nerve, in the mood exhumed,
hissing, *go away,*

go away,   night sky, did we come this far together?

I am cold. And in this next breath,
the same waking,

the same hauling of debris. I am
here in the skin of . . . otherwise) shoveling out, dryly

THIS LIFE

Each sensitive hour, every kicking day we sweep
the darkness mostly outside, wanting
the windows reflecting our lives to embrace a lit interior.

But then the blinds are closed, moths caught between
screen and window disappear, dust on the baseboard settling.

For what is hardest will persist in the world, an intrusion
that is forever; so it feels, of course,
we are open and vulnerable. Then the tears
start coming so fast nothing makes sense:
no blows, no blood, only hurt rearranging—

Who moves such pain?
its brokenness invisible, its breath at a loss.
And still the desire lives to shift its weight, to stand up
under it, to bring it forward out of its awkwardness,
out of our breast. Each of us, disappointment

covered over by flesh. All this life we are unable to rest.

DARIECK SCOTT
b. 1964

Darieck Scott writes fiction that addresses history both personal and political, much as James Baldwin did—always with an eye to confronting our sexual and racial roles and secrets. In *Traitor to the Race* (1995), this involved Scott writing about a black man's relationship with a white one, and the internal and community conflicts that relationship created. With his novel-in-progress, *Sex and Pancakes*, Scott seems to be taking on a larger setting, including a shifting cast of characters and time periods; the title indicates both the novel's humor and a willingness to confront stereotypes of blackness, from Sambo to Aunt Jemima. By showing us the unspoken, everyday life of adolescence in the following selection, "1979," Scott creates something more than simple nostalgia: the fun, funk, and expectation of the records his characters play over and over.

1979

It was the year 1979, twenty-one shy of the millennium, and gray skies brooded over Ansbach, West Germany. There, alongside primeval forest and medieval castles, lay one among scores of U.S. Army bases which pocked the Germany landscape and provided lodging and refuge for armored divisions, tanks and tank-drivers and tank-strategists, alert to what all believed to be the eternal Soviet threat. The morbid paranoia of this task was reflected not only in the sky that watched it getting done but in the daily routines of the soldiers and their families, who led lives that often seemed no more than tiny frozen ponds, anxiously awaiting the thaw of a belated summer. In Katterbach Kaserne, one of Ansbach's three major encampments, the junior officers and NCOs and their wives and children clustered in three- and four-storied works of indifferent stone and plaster. There they negotiated existences of skittish boredom: Up and down they traveled the stairwells to gossip with friends and choose teams for card games; round and round they fretted about the cold and planned road trips to Berchtesgaden and Amsterdam and Copenhagen for solace; over and over they pined for the day when they could say, "Two weeks short, man. Going back to the world."

"A rattrap," Langston's mother pronounced disgustedly of the place a day after they moved in, though perhaps, in view of the alternatives, she oughtn't to have complained. Langston's father was a lieutenant colonel with the Judge Advocate General, and so his family lived in their own duplex with their own little yard at Katterbach's border, just above a steep drop-off into rock and forest and winding road, and a discreet distance removed from the three-storied projects of the plebeians.

To his mother's disgust Langston added terror. His older sister and protector Nella had departed for the beginnings of grown-up life at Harvard, and now that he was unable to shelter in her shadow his parents had made it known that hers was an example to be followed and that they expected Big Things of him, too. He had in seventh grade discovered a respectable but by no means distinguished knack for contact sports (a carelessness, mostly, a fey willingness to cast aside concern for his bodily safety as long as someone else took the responsibility for his actions), and it had offered the hope of rescue from the terrible cliché with which his parents had saddled him—the doom of forever being a runt because he had skipped a grade as reward for his remarkably high reading level and proficiency in math. Dutifully, if diffidently, he plunged into a modest regimen of weight lifting that he hoped would free his real body from its runty chrysalis. This might have been sufficient to secure him had he remained in Fort Bragg for another year or so, but, uprooted once more as his father's commanders had decided they must be, he was again utterly at sea, again to be an outcast, doomed for a purgatorial term to roam the hallways of some alien school alone and unseen.

Rescue came far more quickly than he expected and convinced him that fate was arranged in his favor. In the first week of his American History class, Langston Fleetwood and Damian Garrow were seated side by side. They grimaced together at the teacher's poor introductory joke, the expression on Langston's face almost precisely mirroring Damian's expression. Somehow they knew this, though neither, of course, could see his own face at that moment. Soon enough, while the teacher fiddled with stripping the plastic from the new textbooks, Damian and Langston fell into an increasingly arousing conversation about the cover of the *Jaws 2* novel Langston had impudently brought with from him from home. The teeth, lookit the teeth on that thing!, they whispered, and I know someone who got bit by a shark, a friend of my dad's, and he went right into shock and doesn't even remember how he got out of the water, yeah, and I don't blame the shark, that girl looks like somebody *I'd* fuckin eat. (At which Langston, unable to keep it down, giggled.)

A day or so after Damian passed Langston a note across the aisle. In the hieroglyphic scrawl Langston made out, *Can you get drunk on wine?* Langston, who had never imbibed more alcohol than his mother gave him on New Year's Eve, wriggled his hand in the air and pursed his mouth in an expression which answered, *so-so.* "I prefer beer," he improvised—but since Damian knew a German place that, like many such places, happily sold wine but not beer to American minors, that was what they ended up getting drunk on.

This tack—lying—had borne such promising fruit that Langston soon made a practice of it. Langston did have a native talent for fantasy, for invention, for endless rumination on elusive dreams. At first he put this talent to use with a degree of reticence and modesty: only half-lies and untraceable lies, to the effect that yes, he had played first string JV football back in Bragg, well, he *started out* second string, but he was so good that . . . and he'd had this wonderful girlfriend, Vanessa, yes, beautiful name, huh?, Vanessa used to put out all the time for him, she loved him so much she never said no and he really, really missed her (all he had to do was think of his big sister and a little lump would rise in his throat for apocryphal Vanessa—the endowments and personality of whom, I might add, were vaguely based on photographs and interviews of Pam Grier he had seen in *Right On!* magazine). Whether these flights of fantasy were believed he couldn't be certain, but they didn't seem to hurt, as, little by little, he became acquainted with most of the athletes in the ninth and tenth grades, and even met one or two seniors.

On one particular occasion, some seven or eight weeks into autumn quarter, Langston got rolling with a good one.

"Yeah, man, you should have hung out with me like I told you to," he said to his new buddies Damian and Dillon, who feigned indifference but listened hungrily to every word. "Syl and Sam and James and me and the Maitland brothers were at the snack bar" (big athletes, this most-wanted list, football and basketball studs all; Langston flicked the names off his tongue with unctuous intimacy) "and the cheerleaders from Munich were there, and we started to rap with them, you know, and one of them was this *fine* girl with *big* titties. And she was *on* Sam, right, and I think she was wasted or else whatever Sam was saying was getting to her, because by the time we left there we were telling the other girls we'd see them at the all-area dance next week, but Sam had this fine one on his arm. He whispered to Syl and James, and then said, let's go over to James's because his parents weren't home. So we go over there, we drink a little bit, put on some music. I thought it was all mellow and relaxed, but then Sam stood up out of nowhere with the Munich girl falling off his lap—he was playing with her, she was giggling and slapping his hands—and he said to her like it was nothing, So let's get this train going. I do not lie, man. And I sweartaGod, man, chickieboom goes down in the middle of that living room floor, unzips homeboy's pants, *puts her lips on his dick*, and sucks him off, right there, man!" (During this pause for effect, Langston looked around wildly, to be certain no one who was really there had heard him.) "No, I'm serious! SweartaGod serious! And *then* he busted in her mouth! And she just went around like it was nothing to James, and blew him while he sat in the chair getting high! And then she did everybody, one by one, and man, I've had blowjobs, but this was good. She got everybody worked up, and I do not lie, we all went back to James's room and took turns fucking her. I even got a little wild, man, hadn't had any since I broke up with Vanessa, and *man*! She was tight, she had a grip, you know what I'm saying?"

Langston smiles (and gags) now, to remember this tale, because although not untrue in every detail, this virgin adventure was, of course, not as masterfully executed as he described. In truth Langston had not been party to the snack bar seductions he described but had heard about them subsequently, indeed some days subsequently, as he scrambled to get details of how the miraculous event of his participation in pulling a train had come about. He'd stopped by James's place that evening—not to see James, for he and James were far from equals and certainly not friends, but because his mother knew James's mother and wanted him to return a sewing pattern she'd borrowed to James's apartment. He rang the doorbell several times, and would have been ignored except that little Jerry Maitland, the younger of the two brothers and a hanger-on at these events, came drunkenly to the door and saw Langston through the peephole.

As it happened, Jerry and Langston had been designated lab partners in science class and had become friendly if not exactly friends, and so Jerry, feeling the expansive magnanimity that accompanied alcohol in his digestive system, unlatched the door quite against James's orders and invited Langston in. James gave the newcomer a sour look, and might well have issued him a pointed disinvitation—except that this was the fortuitous moment when the Munich cheerleader, who was even more drunk than little Jerry Maitland, decided to honor Sam's sixteenth repetition of "so let's get this train going" and fell from his lap to kneel between his knees. After that, nobody much noticed that Langston was there to take his place in the line right after Jerry.

The blowjob was in fact quick and perfunctory, more of a job, frankly, than a blow, and quite a bit different from Sam's and Syl's, which went on and on and on. And Langston was not sure that he was ever fully erect when he penetrated the girl, and it was true that it felt good, sawing into her, and the feeling of his balls slapping down there on a few of his awkward virgin thrusts. But it was all rather embarrassing, too: Sam—six-three, big-boned and nasty with sideburns, a mustache and chapped lips—was saying, "Yeah, fuck that shit, man, fuck that," and laughing to himself while he held his dick in his hands and lazily fondled it as it flopped beside the bed.

When Langston came, it felt funny—not like a full strong spurt the way it happened when he jacked off, but something more spasmodic and surreal. He wasn't sure he'd even ejaculated; and he felt so unsettled by this that for the next several minutes he kept wanting to get down there and take a look to find out. And there was no telling why Sam was laughing, or what it felt like for Sam (because of course Sam had to be doing it *right*) when Sam moved in between her legs after Langston finished and poked his partner-in-crime up there, and said, "Aaaaaah!" (That's how Sam referred to it: "my partner-in-crime," he'd say, and give it a pat.)

From time to time Langston looked to Syl for guidance: Cool, cool Syl, who shrugged off his shirt to show oily golden skin and a wire-taut, slender build, and fine, wispy hairs in the center of his chest. Syl's long fingers stroked the fleshy sides of the cheerleader's abdomen and ass as he did his duty with a slow, easy winding motion as if his butt were the handle of a spoon churning something thick but fluent, like syrup or ice cream. Cool, cool, catlike Syl, who kept a tiny smile on his face throughout, even when he came (his lips just parted a bit more, that was all), and who took swigs of James's daddy's bourbon straight from the bottle as dessert and reward for his labors. Once, when he caught Langston's eyes on him before Langston could pull his gaze away, the little smile seemed to turn up at one corner, and after another swig he handed the bottle to Langston. Langston accepted the offer, grabbed the neck of it gruffly to hide his trembling, and as he downed the stuff he tasted the smell and feel of Syl, sliding down his throat.

But if Langston had hoped for more camaraderie than that, he was disappointed. It wasn't as if the guys gathered around together after it was all over and after Sam had escorted the inebriated and worn-out cheerleader to her lodgings. (Langston would like to believe today that the girl's experience in some way represented empowered female sexual gratification, unfettered by bourgeois Victorian hypocrisy. But he feels guilty even today, and he suspects that for the cheerleader, the satisfactions of empowerment are not prominent among the night's memories.) Nor did anyone propose they go out and rehash events at the late-night snack bar (he hoped someone would compliment him, tell him he did a good job), and certainly no one said anything to welcome Langston into the fold, which would have made the whole rather gruesome incident worthwhile.

Yes, when the fun was at an end and the crew of train-pullers had been impressed into the duty of cleaning up the mess they'd loutishly created before Mr. and Mrs. James's Parents got home, good old Syl reached over and patted Langston on the shoulder, but with that awful enigmatic smile on his face, who knew what he meant? And then to sour even that feeble show of affection Langston was mobbed by soused little Jerry Maitland, who, under the cynical eye of his big brother Geoff, lurched around to each of the boys to dispense sloppy hugs and say, "Thanks, man, it was my first time, man," in a way that made Langston positively queasy.

Worse still was that Langston knew in telling his glamorous version of the story that Damian knew Langston was telling a story.

The three of them, Damian, Langston and Dillon, were walking home together after wrestling practice at the time, and Damian's half-gasps and affirmations ("Really?" "Damn!") seemed transparently patronizing.

Yet another grudge to hold against Damian.

Of course Langston's lie was small fry, as lying goes, and no taller a tale than many another spun daily amongst Langston's classmates. To hear a sizable proportion of the adolescent male population of Ansbach's combined junior and high school tell it, those three-tiered buildings were veritable temples of erotic celebration, sacred sites where young black and brown and white bodies discovered one another in the damp dark of basements and in the pink and ruffles of girly-girl rooms decorated with posters on the wall of Snoopy and Shaun Cassidy and Leif Garrett. "Two girls got fucked in this storage room," the tale-spinning stud of the moment might say, pointing to a mattress in a dark 10 × 12 cube that he felt to have been rendered seraglio-seductive by accoutrements like a cheap imitation oriental rug, a lamp that appeared to have taken from a Barbie doll townhouse and blown up to human size, and a stack of withered magazines. One was left to imagine the mouthwatering details.

Such stories were bread and butter to Langston. In them the promise of some form of human relation heavier and deeper, stronger and more intimate than mere kinship and consanguinity, lay hidden for the taking. Langston knew these accounts to be unreliable, but he cherished them anyway, for in their fancifulness they resembled and took on the luster of myths (or of *Penthouse* Forum letters, which amounted to much the same thing): not altogether believable, of course, but superior to reality and revelatory of some truth that no account of reality could articulate.

Therefore Damian's knowing smirks were threatening to Langston. It was not only his scoffing attitude about this latest and most treasured of Langston's lies, but the arrogant air with which he always seemed to regard Langston's excitement about sex stories: like some Enlightenment philosophe who had long since put away childish things to prove by sober experiment and rational deduction that lightning does not flow from the hand of a bearded fellow making sport at the top of a mountain and that earthquakes do not begin when the god of the sea strikes the earth with the tines of his trident. Langston could almost feel Damian gently patting the top of Langston's head.

Damian Garrow was the only child of a stern, burly master sergeant with stunning dark wavy hair and sallow, faintly African features. The master sergeant and his lovely young wife had adopted Damian shortly after they married, when Damian was eighteen months old. But not long thereafter the young wife soured on the demands of her sudden family and began to indulge in behavior less lovely than her looks. Hell broke loose when, at dinner one night when Damian was six years old or so, he innocently inquired after the "things" that the master sergeant's lovely young wife stuck in her arm when the master sergeant was away. The lovely wife, who had in recent months taken to wearing long-sleeved sweaters day and night and complaining about chills, and who put the boy down for his nap when she took her afternoon constitutionals, simply stared. As the story emerged, Damian, unsettled by his mother's silence, decided to mention the "Mex'can" fellow with the "big ears" who came by to play as well. The master sergeant tried to close his mind to fantasies about what this play entailed and how far it might have gone, but he could not come to peace with a weakness as horrible as heroin addiction, and after much shouting and endless days of sullen silence the lovely young wife became the lovely young divorcee, with only a token payment of alimony to show for her many, many pains.

The privation of his father's loss and the embitterment it engendered left a searing mark on Damian's subsequent years. Cold and relentlessly critical, fanatically perfectionist (he was probably a Virgo), the master sergeant revenged himself upon the world by demanding inhuman services from Damian: that the boy, no matter his tender age, learn to cook, that the boy clean the apartment within an inch of his life, that he never bring home a grade less than B, that he wrestle in the winter and pitch baseball in the spring, and that he never, never disturb his father's rest. They made an odd pair, this father and son, as they left wrestling matches together in the master sergeant's Volvo, Damian's small, dark head bowed against the backdrop of his father's massive shoulder.

Master Sergeant Garrow also did not approve of his son having friends—especially the spawn of arrogant college-boy officers as Langston and Dillon were—but he could not control Damian when the boy was out of his sight. Outside the master sergeant's house Damian could be vibrant and adventurous, and he had that attractive power of precociously robust young boy-men. In the hollows of Damian's cheeks beneath his cheekbones the shadow of a very young beard already grew at age fourteen; and Langston was envious of the dark dangling length between Damian's legs that he saw in locker-room glances.

Damian was intellectually able, friendly if perhaps too tenaciously competitive, and despite his occasional arrogance he gave his friends the sure sense of his absolute loyalty to them. Just don't ask Damian how he felt about anything you could have feelings about, and don't count on him to stick up for you or try to make you think he still respected you if you even looked like you might start to cry. Damian wouldn't ridicule you, but he was himself the sort who would recount without a waver in his voice a harrowing story of walking inside the door of his home one afternoon and being attacked by the master sergeant. In full fatigues, Damian would say with a blank smile, his father threw him to the floor and yelled, "Wrestle, boy! Wrestle!" This went on, he said, for five minutes before he finally relented, and then, standing tall while at his feet Damian's lungs heaved and muscles burned, he delivered a contemptuous critique of Damian's Greco-Roman technique. The irony, from Damian's perspective, was that he had shown the coach the same moves he'd used on his father, and the coach told him he had executed the hold the right way.

Langston (and Dillon, too) remained dumb when told of these horrors, reflecting back to Damian what Damian projected out and therefore seemed to desire: an attitude of resigned impenetrability that, even at the age of fourteen, when the charades of manhood usually are not so well practiced, would not deign to ask for comfort or sympathy or admit anything so sodden with femininity as hurt or fear.

Yet in the privacy of his thoughts Langston fastened upon Damian's misfortune with a secret gleefulness that was far from stoic. Damian's terror-filled home life made Langston's own struggles with his father look like a 1950s sitcom by comparison, and knowing that such demons as the master sergeant existed brought Langston a comfort in his relationship with Lieutenant Colonel Fleetwood which the relationship itself never provided. The more Langston could conjure in his mind the image of being wrestled to the floor by two hundred plus pounds of muscle and unremitting hatred, the more keenly he believed he could taste the salt of the dust layering the floorboards as his father's hand forced him down until either the bones of his face or the floor itself would have to yield, the more Langston and the lieutenant colonel seemed a father-son couple haloed by rays from heaven. It wasn't so bad, then, to have a father whose demeanor and function was like that of a sentry at a correctional facility. The colonel may have called his son "spoiled" or "sissified" from time to time, but he never laid hands on him.

Perhaps owing to having experienced the laying on of hands, or some other, unnamed experience, Damian seemed to possess a knowledge of something, painfully acquired, closely kept. The intensity of this—his knowing and not ever saying that he knew, or what he knew—drew Langston to Damian like a beacon. In this sense, Damian's deportment, his intensity always held in check like a wound spring you might struggle to hold fast in your hand, his patient impatience with so many of the things of the world he and Langston shared—girls and sex, wrestling matches and victory or defeat, the games of adolescent manners and insults and who-hangs-with-whom that decided one's status and chance for eternal happiness in the world—Damian's ironically earnest engagement with all these gave him the air of a priest of some hidden inner circle, privy to knowledge that would drive most mere mortals mad: it gave him the air, almost, of a wizard, if one could believe in such things. Damian's air of benevolent contempt for Langston's story hinted at the possibility of some experience that outstripped all the seemingly limitless pleasures and powers of the sexual congress Langston yearned for, some way of entwining one's body and soul with another that vaulted from the realm of the sexual to the super-sexual, the meta-sexual, the ultra-beyond-hyper-orgasmic-answer-to-life-sexual.

That the tension of eros ran between the two boys, like a hot pipe behind plaster molding, was undeniable. It found no outlet other than their inarticulate tenderness toward one another, but they celebrated it when they could. One afternoon, for example, there was a bright sun aloft in the sky, an event that one does not take for granted in the month of March in Germany. Damian and Langston skipped their last two classes (Dillon, doomed to after-school detention, could not join them), sprinted out from the doors at the end of the hall where the science classes were taught, and ducked into the faux marble stairwell in the building across the street. They panted and jumped at every sound in fear of truant officers who did not exist. After a cautious interval they peeked outdoors and then took boldly to the sidewalks to make an ex-hilarated trek to the post exchange annex, where they were accustomed to rifling the record bins in search of the few records whose names they could recognize from the Top Twenty Albums list of Colonel Fleet-wood's weeks-old *Jet* magazine.

They could not contain or restrain themselves when they saw an old album cover that each had heard but never owned, glistening in plastic: a tousled heap of orgiastic male limbs, heads and torsos, auburn and cinnamon-colored, sepia and ginger. They fought over it until they found another copy, and after each bought his own, they ran all the way to the Fleetwood duplex to keep in shape, and then repaired to Langston's upstairs sanctum, where they chattered at high speed about the album, about the group Foxy, about nothing much, about something for which they did not wish to select a name.

The static of the needle along the slick rim of the record heralded it, and with the optimism of youth they leaned forward to listen. To the brutal jackhammer, jackrabbit, jacking beat, and the call to which they longed to respond: *to get off/to get off/to get offf, to get—get off!* After one playing and a half, Damian was up. He snapped his fingers and pumped his lean brown hips maniacally, Langston felt, unsettlingly, but in perfect time to each insolent beat. Soon Langston followed, matched him, performed his own inner and outer gyrations. They sang the words. (*Sensuality excites my mind*) *it makes me GET OFF/(if I were you I'd get a good perspec-tive) on how to GET OFF/ (love me wild and love me crazy) so we can GET OFF!*

Damian probably got a whipping with the master sergeant's paddle for his tardy arrival home that night. Probably nothing special, no more painful or brutal than was the custom in Master Sergeant Garrow's dominion.

Although—maybe not.

At first things went along just as they had. At school Langston and Damian told a jealous Dillon all about it, and between the three the beat and lyrics became a little anthem, the punch line to every joke, so that if Mrs. Beattie said that she loved the musical *Camelot*, Dillon might whisper, "It makes her Get Off!"; or if some haughty girl who routinely snubbed them kept to her routine, they might flick their tongues and pelvises at her, and recite, "(If I were you I'd get a good perspec-tive) on how to Get Off!"

This bliss lasted for a week. Then Damian stopped coming to school.

There had been an explosion early the morning he was absent, with the mysterious result being that the power in Katterbach and Bleidorn both had gone out, snuffed out as if its source were as fragile as the flame of a candle. Rumors traveled up and down the stairwells of a terrorist attack, the return of the Red Brigade. In Dillon's building a Soviet preemptive strike was even mentioned. The end result was that school began three hours later than usual, after power had been restored, but, owing to missed buses or fear of the rumors or indifference, a third of the student body didn't show up. Damian was one of the no-shows. Langston and Dillon cursed their poor luck, and consoled themselves with the anticipation of the story Damian was sure to tell them the next day. "He probably went and got high with those German guys he knows, and then they went and bought a whore," Dillon said. Langston thought this an unlikely (though exciting) scenario, but Dillon was curiously insistent upon it. "His dad's at work, he doesn't have a mom, he can do anything he wants," Dillon said.

But Damian didn't come to school the next day, either.

Langston and Dillon called Damian's home during lunch period. There was no answer. Another day passed, and Dillon called, and then another day Langston called. No answer. On the third day the wrestling coach annouced that Damian had been withdrawn from school, a fact confirmed by one or two teachers. Langston and Dillon were bewildered.

Vainly they called Damian's number repeatedly, but the phone was never answered, almost as if Damian's father had gone, too. Dillon, more forward than Langston, pestered their teachers, but received only shrugs and sighs.

Langston's parents liked Damian, so he was able to convince his father to call Master Sergeant Garrow at his job. In the abbreviated and scrupulously civil conversation that followed, the master sergeant informed the lieutenant colonel that young Damian had gone back to live with relatives in Mississippi, and there he would remain.

For an interval Damian's seemed an unlocatable absence. Without a word or cause to name or to blame, it was so lacking in context that it threatened to be inconsequential, merely the obverse of Damian's equally unlocatable presence. Yes, Damian wasn't there, but then wrestling practice was still there every day, and the girls they tried to rap to were there, and the hallway radiators they warmed their butts on each morning and used as a perch from which to gossip about passersby were still there, too.

But soon the comfort of these familiarities grew cold. Syl seemed to maintain an interest in Langston, but after a time even the bourbon-smooth, bourbon-sly Syl's smile and daily greeting chatter lost its power to soothe him. Langston began to detect, swimming all around him and clamoring to pierce his defenses, loss, deadly and invisible like the molecules of an airborne virus. Damian's absence changed, it transmigrated; it became Damian's disappearance, and a nastiness, a disquiet, lingered around that back-to-Mississippi story.

Langston was not knowledgeable about the exigency and capriciousness of grief; he could only account for his feelings in more elliptic, embroidered fashion: Once, not long ago, Langston, Damian, and Dillon had set their faces against the rushing wind and rode the running boards of a locomotive force that carried them fast and forward into an unknown, glorious future. Destiny—this is the word Langston savored; adolescence is nothing if not drama and apocalypse—lay bright before them; once they met it, they and the world they inhabited would be transformed. In this revolution Damian provided spark and leadership. Without him, Langston's life and his sense of himself was rendered inert, like wet flint. There was no force, no movement. The future promised not bright destiny but decline.

Langston sat upon the threadbare cushions of a chair, and everything in his sight hung, dangling and dissipated. Repeatedly he set a record upon his turntable and sang the lyrics of a song that had escaped his attention only weeks before. *I really wasn't caring/but I felt my eyes staring/at a guy who stuck out in the crowd/He had the kind of body/that would shame Adonis/and a face that would make any man proud/I wonder why (he's the greatest dancer) I wonder why (that I've ever seen).* Langston held the album jacket in his hands and studied while he sang the faces of the honey-complexioned sisters, their cordial expressions spiced with a slight hauteur.

So Langston listened and he sang, and so he spent his evenings: Sister Sledge and fretting about the cold, dreaming of going back to the world. And, little by little, thinking now and again about Dillon Lawrence.

(Not that I mean to say that Dillon was the greatest dancer, now: No, Langston had a different body in mind when he tried to imitate the religious hush and throaty jadedness of Sister Sledge's paean to unattainable male beauty.)

It had seemed likely that, with Damian gone, Langston and Dillon would become estranged. When Dillon and Damian's friendship had blossomed into Damian's and Dillon's and Langston's friendship, it was Damian who glued them together, who centered their triad. Their shared devotion to Damian made the other two allies, certainly, but the fierceness of this devotion also preserved a dynamic of rivalry between them. While neither said an unkind word about the other, at the heart of matters they had long regarded one another with a slightly wary coolness. They would not have made any explicit decision that their trio could not be pared to a duo. More likely they would simply drift away, Langston to his world and Dillon to his.

But their love for Damian proved stronger, and stranger, than they knew. It kept them bound, manacled together in grief. Few days would pass without one of them conferring with the other about whether he had heard from Damian (the answer was inevitably no). Generally it was little more than that—waiting together—but this laid a foundation. When it began to appear that the wait might stretch on longer than they first believed, Langston and Dillon began to talk. This they did secretively; it would have been unseemly to share their thoughts with others. When they could sneak away they drank wine in the old place, and they speculated. Damian's father had tried to kill him, and Child Services took him away, the same thing that had happened to that Yarborough girl; Damian had tried to kill his father; Damian left to go live with his former mother; Damian ran away and was now a street kid, snatching purses in Frankfurt and living in a haze of hashish.

One thing was clear. The official story was not to be believed. "Back to Mississippi," Dillon said with scorn, and gave Mississippi all his venom.

He did not say so, but this mockery comforted Langston. Dillon's tight anger had depth. It was a well of strength from which Langston could draw at need. In Dillon's sharply angled nose, high cheeks, and brown eyes, each fired with the high color of indignation, Langston found an embrace that kept him from feeling alone.

And there was that evening.

After practice, in the locker room, Langston pulled his towel across his narrow waist and walked out from the shower, weary and damp and looking forward to his mother's cooking. Dillon was there, as he usually was. There was nothing new in this, nothing to note about Dillon's unhurried approach to dressing himself. But that evening Langston came to a certain view of him. (We may infer that Langston's secret craving for a peg to fit Damian's vacated hole brought him to this moment and raised to the level of apperception what had once been mere clinical observation. Or we may speculate that this was one of those moments that hover at the flash points of history, marking a crucial epoch-deciding choice between the road not to be traveled and the road soon to be trod; that's how Langston likes to think of it, but I've already said he has a very dramatic imagination.)

Langston discovered or remembered something that he had always appreciated: the smooth, smooth white cotton of Dillon's admirable briefs, and along with them, in a package with them, the cannily hairless and cream-colored legs—canny, you see, because their hairlessness and creamy complexion highlighted, allowed Langston to see, as if etched, each cord of muscle in Dillon's thighs, and to follow the sharp, supple rounded line of Dillon's calves.

Dillon's back was to Langston, and Langston's locker was near Dillon's. Dillon bent and began to struggle with pulling his jeans over his feet and then over his thick legs. Langston watched the legs and the low, narrow pouch of cotton hanging below the curve of Dillon's ass, and a bit faster than he had begun he walked straight from the shower toward Dillon.

Muscle rolled beneath the skin of Dillon's back as he straightened and tugged at the worn white waist of his blue jeans. Up close, Langston discovered to his shock—almost as a terror—that Dillon had a smell.

Langston knew smells, of course: the locker-room smell, coarse, stale, fetid, the rank odor of socks worn one day too many, droplets of urine dribbled over the course of six class hours and spread thin across the tile around the urinal trough and now soaking into the rubber sole of your shower shoe, the smell of pimples and pimple cream, of the pus of minor scrapes and boyish wounds, the pinched medicated fumes of ointments rubbed into sore muscles, body lotion for bony ashy legs, and the smell of combs and fold-out black-power picks stored in back pockets, and new underwear on baby-fat skin, and the stench of someone else's shit in the open toilet and your own sweet fart in the air, and the odor of hair, hair, everywhere, his hair and my hair and your hair, little floating hairs in the air, on the shower floor and in the sink, plastered to the blue-grey surface of the mirror.

Oh, yes, Langston knew his smells—but not this one, this new, distinct one. What I mean to say is that Langston loved smells, he could categorize them; he could taxonomize: the smell of a baby, a boy, a youth, a man, an athlete, an athlete before practice, an athlete at practice's end. But it had escaped him, he had not known before or he had not pursued the implications until that evening, of the particular smell of a particular person at a particular time: That someone, another guy, could have a smell all his own. And that that smell could register in a certain way. That it could have meaning.

Dillon, up close, had a smell, a scent: soapy, fresh, fragrant. Turbulent. With his arms at his sides, dark brown hair bulged out from Dillon's armpits, and this, too—the way he stood, the white briefs and the armpit hair—together these had a smell, too. Murderous. Dillon was the kind of guy, Langston thought, who could murder you.

Well—they did the deed. Langston did not campaign openly to bring this to pass. But he trusted, with some joy and a great amount of fear, that he was once again within the tow of a powerful locomotive force. Langston needed only to ruthlessly suppress all conscious knowledge of what he desired (he put the Sister Sledge album away) and to let his desire, unfettered, do its work for him. At times he would find, to his surprise, that he was staring at Dillon's crotch; and at practice and in class (but particularly in practice; in the future, Langston will discover that sweaty, drooping Adidas athletic shorts are an aphrodisiac) he would wait—quite unconsciously, of course—until the exact moment Dillon felt Langston's eyes on him before he looked away. Langston might smile then, as if to himself, and he knew Dillon was watching him smile. He could not have attempted such a thing with anyone but Dillon. Only Dillon could be trusted. Dillon, and Damian, who was not there.

Dillon responded greedily to these advances. First he complimented Langston on his legs, and Langston let that sink in for a lengthy, locked-gaze moment before he laughed and deflected the compliment with "Not as nice as yours." Next Dillon went out of his way to have his arms full of books he obviously would never read so that he could ask Langston, four feet away, to tie his loose shoelaces for him. Langston bent agreeably to the task, and by the way his head took its sweet time rising up after he was finished, Dillon knew that their friendship was taking on a rather different shape.

Dillon could scarcely be restrained once this knowledge came clearly to his mind; the opposite of Langston, he had only to recognize his desire before putting it to work. Since the two were frequently alone, it was not long before they stood toe to toe in the deserted boys' bathroom, hours after a Saturday meet. Dillon stood perhaps half an inch taller than Langston, and for the first time they noticed this. "I always thought you were shorter than me," Langston said, and lifted his eyes upward like the whore he was swiftly becoming. Dillon did not respond, even with a smile, but his head came down, and while one hand cupped in a palm suddenly grown bear-sized the curve of Langston's skull where it met the top of his neck, Dillon's salty tongue burrowed between Langston's wide-open lips (*such* the whore) and into Langston's mouth.

So they kissed, and Langston, one eye open, could see the rough poetry of their image in the bathroom mirror.

(Outside the door they heard, one million miles away and a thousand years in the past, the sound of the coach and his assistant, talking down the hall.)

Langston had the feeling that Dillon was trying to ingest him, from the insistence of Dillon's tongue and the way he held Langston as if trying to enmesh Langston's body into his own. Langston, more and more in his element, worked by smell: He inhaled the warmth of Dillon's skin and the light musk of his upper lip, and his hand dove straight past those pop-fly buttons for Dillon's dick. Its thickness filled Langston's grip. Langston felt himself awash with something; he felt he reached a culmination, he was on the brink of an apotheosis. Then Dillon broke their kiss and let his head fall back and closed his eyes tight.

"Oh, God," he hissed. "You're even hotter than Damian."

Then Dillon pushed Langston into a stall and latched the door and they, as I said, did the deed—after or during the time it took for Langston to extract a few mumbles from Dillon to the effect of Yes, he'd done this with Damian, too. Langston's shock and fury propelled, rather than checked, him. Dillon stripped down his pants so he could stick that fat thing somewhere, anywhere, but Langston shoved Dillon down by the shoulders and fed him his balls. He meant it meanly, but Dillon's mouth was as tropical and questing below as it had been above. Langston groaned and jerked all over Dillon's knee the moment Dillon's slathering tongue expertly slithered between Langston's cheeks, and, dazed, he let himself drop to the floor and be folded over the open toilet seat while Dillon jammed two fingers coated and re-coated in a small pool of saliva and then half the length and all the width of his dick into Langston's ass.

Later Langston reached back there with his finger and gave it a gingerly touch. He could not believe it had happened, he did not remember how it had happened that the entry, though excruciating, had at the same time not been unduly painful, and that despite the burning sensation in his rectum and the odd discomfort of it all he had ridden his ass back in time with Dillon's quick, every-which-way strokes. Langston even heard himself moan. The only sensation he remembered as pain was Dillon squeezing his shoulders as if he'd fall off him without the support.

After a moment or so of collapse Dillon stood, pulled up his pants, tucked in his shirt, and exited the stall. He was fixing his hair in the mirror when Langston finally emerged, fully dressed. Langston's stride was slightly askew, and he was afraid that he had suddenly been rendered incontinent and would be doomed to live out his years like his great-grandfather, who spent the better part of his days being wiped by a nurse. Despite this Langston managed a smile, which Dillon warmly if somewhat distractedly returned.

"Smells like butt in here," Dillon said and shook his head, then tucked his comb into his back pocket and exited.

Langston was left to peer at the reflection of his clone—its new face grafted onto the old, its bright new body at last free of the chrysalis, its disarrayed clothes and lopsided afro.

Dillon lived closest to the school and his mother worked at the commissary three days a week, so the Lawrence residence at lunchtime became the most frequent site of the boys' rendezvous. These were often not explicitly planned: It was simply understood, an unspoken pact, that they would get some whenever the getting was good.

The liaison was not without consequences for Langston. He had read the Book of Leviticus and knew that God had decreed homosexuals should be killed, and this gave him pause. "The penalty is death for both parties," God saith, which was certainly awful, but it was the line "They have brought it upon themselves" that troubled him most, especially since it came from the Living Bible, which was so full of black and white photographs of young people of all races hanging out on steps in city squares and playing sports and holding hands and generally looking like the fun-loving sort of people Langston hoped one day to become that it was hard to believe that everything the book said didn't apply to him, right here, today, in 1979. He promised God each time that he wouldn't ever do it again, but then Dillon would come looking for him, and if Dillon didn't make a move, he would go looking for Dillon. This seesaw of repentance and recalcitrance itself became limned with the shimmer of sexual excitement, its inexorable rhythm of hold, wait, circle, and surrender inevitably linked to and parcel of the lure and pleasures of orgasm. He was far yet from knowledge of terms like "closet queen," and thankfully five years or so away from having to consider the strictures of "safe sex," a concept which he would have found particularly baffling and mean-spirited. If, after all, you were going to commit a sin, if you were going to step off the edge of a moral cliff, what was the point in doing it safely? It was the lack of safety, the near certainty of condemnation and shame, that made Langston hunger for more and more and more. It was humiliating, to get fucked and like it and look forward to it, to throw himself with ardor at another male and find that he did not think about whether he had done it correctly and that when he did what he did he thought about nothing at all. Oh, sure, Dillon liked to put his legs up in the air, too, and certainly everything the two of them did was enjoyable, but Langston knew (but never said he knew) that, for himself, there was a more electric charge in bottoming as opposed to topping. Shame and humiliation were fun; being closeted was fun; being unsafe was fun. They were the elements of a new craft. They were the habits of a novitiate.

This sordid turn of events had been prepared for him, by forces beyond his ken, and if they were not quite the forces imagined in the laws and whimsies of a tent-dwelling desert tribe, then so let it be written, so let it be done, amen. Sometimes Dillon—never quite predictable as to how, when, where, or whether his desire would ignite—personified these forces. More often, the memory of Damian stepped into that role, as smoothly and confidently as if it had been written for him, a Broadway vehicle for a comeback super-diva. Langston drafted this memory to slave for him, he sank his teeth into the image of Damian and shook it like a dog, he tore at it with the savagery of a cuckold: Again and again he coaxed Dillon to tell him in detail what Damian had done with him and how often, and then, steeled by jealousy, Langston set about bitterly and joyfully to surpass him.

Revenge was the twine that lashed together shame, humiliation, and passion in one bundle; revenge Langston sought, a vengeance searing enough to match, and quench, the fire of his loss.

He could not then and cannot now quite name this loss. The betrayal was not only sexual or romantic, and indeed at base may have been neither. The vaguer and keener loss had something to do with belonging, the hope and promise of someday truly belonging. If Damian had not disappeared, if Damian had not crept behind Langston's back to seduce Dillon (well, that's how Dillon told the story, anyway), then . . . But the *then* was a blank space, forever to remain incomplete. Nothing belonged to it anymore.

Now, Langston vowed, now I will fuck Dillon in every way known to man, and do it thrice over, until by sheer volume nothing Damian touched in Dillon (and withheld from Langston) will not have been touched by Langston as fiercely if not more so. It was as if Langston were going to lift his leg and spray so that no inch of Dillon's body did not bear his mark, too. He would undo Damian's undoing of what might have been.

Naturally this didn't quite work out.

Gradually—perhaps no more than three weeks or more later—their affair puttered out, lost its heat and steam. One imagines two horny boys, the indefatigable lustfulness of adolescence, the allure of taboo and the satisfactions of secrecy, and it seems inconceivable, a waste, that the two of them shouldn't have been able to keep it up (as it were). Not at least without some bitter scene of guilt and blame and denial topped off with vengeful heterosexual reassertion, or some teacher or parent or parent's friend happening upon the wrong room at the wrong time and the onset of a scandal. Yet no such drama came to pass. Dillon's interest waned. They avoided one another. Perhaps, for both, the sex, no matter how nasty they tried to make it, no matter how dangerous, did not quite measure up, either to what they had known before or to what they had hoped to know. When they were together, somebody's cock up somebody's ass, there would be panting and heaving and all that good stuff, but nevertheless after the novelty of it had worn away, they were in limbo, or in some other universe parallel to the real one, the one they truly desired, and the doorway to this better universe was sealed shut by the silence of a friend's disappearance.

But not silence alone: a silence made more awful by the echoes of memories and fantasy.

In June the school year came to a close, and Dillon, his father having been reassigned to the Pentagon, departed for a suburban home in Maryland. Dillon promised to write but didn't, and Langston promised to write but didn't.

Langston waited, steely, cold, impassioned, to hear from Damian.

There's more, of course, but Langston is gnawing on his memory now, and can't be bothered to revise the past in view of the present. He should be thinking about his work, student essays to grade in the class he TAs, books to return and books to check out, the paper he needs to write for the conference he'll be speaking at next week, the many, many things that everyone else in his department knows that he still doesn't know, but instead he ponders that loss. Still inclined to a certain melodramatic imagination of his life, he thinks about how he may never have transcended it, about how it kept growing, like lichen on the mind. He thinks that there is a corner in his psyche from which emanates the heat that warms half his thoughts, and that in this corner there is a spotlight and a photograph and a record player playing over and over again tunes masking secret words and abstruse formulae, and that until the mystery is solved, his only offering is a libation of tears and new salt for old wounds.

DANZY SENNA
b. 1970

Centering on interracial and intraracial issues, Danzy Senna's first novel, *Caucasia* (1998), charts the territory of children and color; its title, Senna notes in an interview, turns "race into a place instead of a condition." Realizing both the construct and confusion of race while also recognizing its reality, the novel joins the tradition of James Weldon Johnson's fictional *Autobiography of an Ex-Coloured Man*. In the following story, "The Land of Beulah," Senna writes ironically about an urban paradise, again questioning whether "race is geography." By linking the promised land (Beulah land of the Bible) with pop culture (Beulah the maid from TV land), Senna investigates black and biracial female identity in a voice popular yet profound.

THE LAND OF BEULAH

The bitch was a mystery. She didn't look mixed, more like some breed that hadn't yet been discovered. Strangers on the street were forever trying to guess her background. They studied her appearance and behavior, searching for clues to her identity, but with each guess she seemed to shift into something else. In the face of such uncertainty, people saw what they wanted to see. Black folks thought she was mostly rottweiler. White people swore she was a Gordon setter. Puerto Ricans usually guessed an unlikely blend, such as German shepherd and miniature poodle, while the Arab guys at the bodega predicted she would grow into a wolf. The Korean grocer kept his distance, swearing she was the same kind of rare, vicious foxhound that had bitten him as a child.

Jackie—the girl who took the dog in off the streets—wasn't sure who to believe, and she wasn't sure she cared. Mixing, she understood, was a game of risk; a mutt could turn out pretty, or pretty damn ugly. And the bitch had won at least that round of Russian roulette. She was lovely: shiny black fur, long satiny ears, and little brown dots above her eyes that gave her a perpetual look of fierce concentration.

Jackie had stumbled upon the dog, quite by accident, one autumn afternoon while she was out jogging. Brooklyn was almost beautiful that day, a frenzy of disparate colors along brownstoned streets. But Flatbush Avenue was as ugly as ever. Seasonless, it stretched before her, a clutter of extinguished signs and dented vehicles. Jackie moved fast, the lone jogger, trying not to notice the men who beckoned to her, gesturing to their loins as if offering fruit for sale. She kept her eyes fixed instead on a giant billboard ahead. It was an advertisement for Newport cigarettes, but there were no cigarettes in the picture. Instead, it showed an ecstatic black woman holding a pin to the gigantic pink bubble emerging from her boyfriend's mouth. His eyes were wide open in mock fright. The words across the bottom of the billboard read: "Alive with

Pleasure!" Jackie couldn't decide whether the innuendo was racial or sexual, or both, and looked away. That's when she glimpsed the puppy.

It stood out, a lone spot of wildlife amidst the urban squalor. It was tied to a metal pole in front of a dry cleaner, and wore a sign around its neck. Curiosity, more than compassion, made Jackie slow down. She wanted to know what the sign said.

She approached with caution. The puppy was bound to the pole by an extension cord, so tightly that it couldn't properly sit or stand. Yet it grinned and squirmed excitedly at the sight of Jackie.

The sign around its neck was really just a large piece of torn card-board. Scrawled in orange marker were the crude words "Take me home. Ime Kold, Kute and Hongry." The author had tried to make it look as if the puppy had written the plea itself.

Jackie felt a surge of pity for the creature that took her by surprise. She reminded herself that the problem wasn't hers to solve. After all, there were stray mongrels all over Brooklyn—the scrawny and mangy creatures who wandered through traffic, wearing brindled coats, crazed, terrified grins, searching for some pack that had long since disbanded. She'd heard news reports saying the problem was worst in the autumn, when the weather began to change. People grew tired of the puppies they had enjoyed all summer and set them loose on the city. Jackie had noticed them everywhere—in parks, under bridges, in doorways of abandoned buildings. She'd also noticed the women who saved them. Dog women. Stray women. Jackie had glimpsed them around her neighborhood, wandering through traffic, wearing sensible shoes and foundationless faces, tugged along by a pack of dirty mongrels. Jackie wasn't one of them.

Yet as she stared down at the creature, she had to wonder if it had been placed in her path for a reason. She was recently single, unhappy, homeless for some land she couldn't quite remember. She was still a temp one year into her job search. She lived alone. She exercised alone. She ate her dinner alone at night in front of rented videos. She occasionally went to parties alone and left alone, with nobody to talk about the evening with. Sunday mornings were the worst. She woke awash with grief, imagining the entire city made up of couples, frolicking playfully under puffy duvets, surrounded by newspaper and pastel mugs containing pale, sweet coffee.

Jackie leaned down and began to struggle with the extension cord, attempting to free the puppy from its shackles. She heard somebody yell, "Suckah!" and whipped her head around to see who had spoken. A grown man on a child-sized bicycle cruised down the sidewalk in her direction. He leaned forward with his elbows raised to his side like chicken wings, his knees pumping up to meet his shoulders. He didn't meet her gaze, and she wondered if she was imagining things. But when she turned back to the puppy, she heard it again. "Suckah!" the male voice howled. She looked over her shoulder, but the man had already whizzed past her and was cruising away down the hill, out of sight.

A few minutes later, Jackie stumbled up Fulton Avenue toward her building, carrying the trembling animal in her arms. She felt flushed with good Samaritan pride and couldn't help grinning goofily at the strangers who caught her eye. They didn't smile back. A teenage boy loitering in front of Kansas Fried Chicken shouted out, "Don't your dog know how to walk?" Farther up the road, two old Caribbean women shuffled past her and one of them muttered, "Now that's what I call puppy love." Jackie sensed sarcasm in her voice but smiled anyway, as if the woman had meant it.

Jackie was new to solitude. It still felt strange to wake up alone. She'd been dumped two and a half months ago. Kyle was his name, but every-one called him Kip. He was tall, light-skinned, and dreadlocked, with a mole the shape of Italy on the small of his back. He had gone to prep school all his life, and had only discovered negritude somewhere late in college. Now he was a stockbroker. He claimed he wasn't really working for the Man: He was just making money so that later, when he joined the revolution, he'd have something to offer.

When he told her it was over, Jackie had been taken by surprise, but later, when she thought about it, there had been warning signs. He had refused to hold her hand when they walked through black neighbor-hoods, explaining that while he knew she was black, strangers might think otherwise.

Jackie was mixed—the product of a black saxophone-playing father and a white soul singer mother. She'd come out looking like the missing link between Sicily and Libya. Cabdrivers liked to claim her as part of their race just before they asked her if she was married. In the sum-mertime, she was the color of well-steeped tea. In the winter, she was paler, as if a dollop of milk had been added. Her hair was all that gave her away: a tangled mass of wiry curls. Kinky. It was her consolation prize. Kip liked her to wear it out around her face, so people would know.

Kip didn't believe in race mixing. He thought brothers who dated white girls should be called out on the street.

"But what if they really love each other?" Jackie had replied weakly, thinking of her own white mother and black father, who'd hated one another for as long as she could remember. "I mean, live and let live, right?"

He'd only laughed at her and patted the top of her head gingerly before saying, "There are casualties in every revolution."

It was always there, hovering over them. She recalled the night he broke up with her. They were at a soul food restaurant in Brooklyn, sharing ribs, greens, and macaroni and cheese.

"You can walk away from this any time," Kip had said out of the blue, sweeping his arm around the restaurant, although she knew it was blackness he was referring to. "For me, there's no way out."

She had rested her gaze on the baby-back ribs in front of her. They had looked gruesome to her all of a sudden, evidence of a crime.

After Kip told her it was over, he walked her to the subway, chivalrous till the bitter end. It was cold outside that night, and an old man dressed in a three-piece suit stood on the corner nearby, waving a Bible and raving about homosexuality. Kip had buttoned up Jackie's coat in an oddly paternal gesture, then punched her chin lightly and said, "Don't worry, Jack. I'm doing you a favor."

She sucked her teeth and looked away. "What's that supposed to mean?" She longed for the comfort of her own bed. She would cry later, under her duvet, out of his sight. For the moment, at least, she had to be hard.

Kip shrugged and stared at the ground, as if reading her future in the patchwork of chicken bones and candy wrappers. "Just wait and see," he said. "You'll end up with a white boy named Andrew, an architect or maybe a painter. You'll move to Nyack together and live in a big farmhouse. You'll remember me as a phase you were going through. Just wait and see. Girls like you never stick."

Jackie wanted to remind him that it was he who was leaving her. But instead she simply listened and wondered if what he said was true. Would she end up with a white boy named Andrew, in a farmhouse in

Nyack? It didn't sound so bad, especially the part about the farmhouse, but she had tried to look disgusted by the life he'd described.

Hidden underneath the sign, hanging from the dog's collar, was a silver tag engraved with the name BEULAH. Strangely, the tag listed no contact number, as if the dog's former owners had wanted her identity ensured, but not her safe return. Jackie vaguely remembered a television show that her grandmother used to watch that starred a black maid named Beulah. The name seemed demeaning somehow, like Aunt Jemima. But it was the only name the puppy had. Jackie felt obliged to keep it.

She called all her girlfriends that first night to tell them what she'd found. It was a mistake. She should have kept it a secret. They all laughed at her and said it would never last.

"I give it a week," said one.

"A dog in the city?" shrieked another. "Yuck. Picking up shit ain't for me."

Another one warned. "Watch out. You know what happens when a woman gets a dog."

"What?" Jackie had asked with a stab of fear.

"She stops being desperate."

Jackie shook her head and told them all they were wrong.

But later that same evening, when she looked around her apartment, she felt a shiver of horror. A soiled maxipad had been shredded across the kitchen floor. Black paw prints were smeared along the white wall of the hallway. A shoe—a silver open-toed pump jemson Jackie had worn at last year's birthday party—was now a mangled allusion to its former self. She tried to remain good-natured about it. She'd just saved a creature's life, after all. But she couldn't help feeling she'd turned a corner.

Jackie had never thought of herself as ill-tempered before. But that first evening, she walked into her bedroom only to find Beulah peeing on her bed. A yellow puddle spread across the snowy white duvet. The dog smiled up at Jackie with evident relief. Jackie felt something—a clicking in her brain. She'd never felt it before. In one swift motion, she picked Beulah up by the scruff of her neck and flung her to the floor. The puppy fell with a thud, then rose, whimpering, to her feet. Jackie kicked her sharply in the ribs, so that she fell again with a yelp. Jackie hungered to do more, but Beulah ran, tail between her legs, out of the room.

Later, when Jackie had cooled down, she found Beulah hiding under the kitchen table. She reached an arm out to pet her, but Beulah shrunk out of her reach. Jackie felt terrible and spent the rest of the evening showering the puppy with affection—kisses, tickles, a bouncing ball—feeling that she'd never loved anyone more, and possibly never would.

She promised herself it wouldn't happen again. She knew she wasn't supposed to hit animals. As a discipline technique, that had gone out of style in the late 1970s, maybe even earlier. She tried to be content with just hissing obscenities at the animal, but several times that weekend she lost control: She slapped the puppy on its butt when it tore her fancy sheets, and jerked its leash too hard when they went walking down the street so that the puppy's body lunged from side to side. Jackie found that small acts of violence—harmless ones, really—did help to quell her rage.

Monday morning, Jackie dawdled around the house before heading to work. She didn't want to go. She couldn't bear the thought of leaving Beulah alone. But she needed to get to the temp agency by eight or all the good assignments would be taken. As she put on her cheap pin-striped business suit, panty hose, heels, and lipstick, the dog watched from a corner with a disapproving glare. Jackie felt embarrassed under the dog's scrutiny. Her outfit suddenly seemed tartish, a whore's uniform, although it was perfectly presentable at the offices where she worked. She left the dog plenty of food and water and toys, but still whispered, "I'm sorry," as she went out the door.

At the temp office, black and Latino women of all hues sat lined up against the wall filling out applications and sipping Styrofoam cups of coffee. Four television sets blared from high corners around them, each displaying a different morning news personality. All the women were dressed to the hilt in four-inch heels and impeccable hairstyles. Jackie felt dowdy in her ill-fitting suit and scraggly hair. The temp agency had put out several boxes of Dunkin Donuts, but now only the jelly-filled doughnut holes remained. Jackie shoved one in her mouth and chewed unhappily as she waited for Vanessa, her agent, to find her work.

Fifteen minutes later, Vanessa—a whirling dervish of bottle-blond hair and orange polyester—did indeed come out of the office. She held a clipboard as she scanned the row of female bodies, tapping her foot and snapping her gum in time. Jackie wondered, not for the first time, if she was coked up. Her eyes fixed on Jackie.

"Jackie!" she shrieked, as if they were old college buddies.

Jackie slumped low into her chair, embarrassed. She was always one of the first to get hired, no matter how late she arrived. She'd noticed the pecking order immediately. They hired by complexion. Lightest, whitest, brightest went first. Dark-skinned girls were always last to go, no matter how fast their typing speed. The other women cut their eyes at her. She kept her eyes to the floor as she followed Vanessa into the back office.

Vanessa sent her to a Swiss bank on Park Avenue, where she was tucked in a corner with a stack of loan applications to enter into the computer. Her trainee was a small beige man named Chuck. He was a permanent employee at the bank. Mostly, permanents treated Jackie with open contempt. But Chuck was friendly—too friendly. He was giddy, like somebody who has been deprived of air and sunlight and sits for too long in the same position. That morning he spent over an hour showing Jackie how to enter the loan figures into the computer, a task so simple it needed no explanation. He sat too close, his knee pressed against hers, and kept resting his clammy hand on her exposed elbow when he wanted to underscore a point. He smelled of printer ink. When he could find nothing more to tell her about the data, he shuffled back to his own cubicle, giggling, about what, she couldn't imagine.

If Vanessa had taught Jackie anything over the past year, it was to work at a turtle's pace. The slower you took with your tasks, the longer the job would last. You couldn't be too slow, or they would notice. Jackie had worked out a perfect pace, but today she was slower than usual, distracted by thoughts of the puppy. She wondered what Beulah was doing. She imagined her dressed up in workout clothes, sitting human-style on the couch in front of a talk show, eating a bag of potato chips. She smiled to herself and couldn't help laughing at the thought. She began to doodle a picture of Beulah in exactly that posture, but felt someone watching her.

She looked up. Chuck was smirking at her from his cubicle. His feet were propped on his desk, and he leaned back in his chair. He held a sweating can of Fresca at his waist, just above his crotch, and she glimpsed a distinct bulge beneath his khaki pants. When he spoke, his voice came out croaky, like an adolescent boys, though he was way past thirty. "Did you get laid last night?" She wasn't sure she'd heard him right. "You have that postfuck glow," he added. The bulge in his pants seemed to move slightly. His own face glowed, like that of a wax figurine. She wondered what would happen if she held a match up to his skin, whether it would melt or burn.

She gripped her pen tightly in her hand and imagined herself jabbing it into his eye socket until the blue ink from the pen merged with his blood, becoming one stream of purple. He tilted his chair back at a more precarious angle. She watched him, willing him to fall and bite off his tongue. After a moment he seemed to see something on her face that made his smile disappear and the bulge in his pants withdraw from sight. He turned, quite abruptly, back to his computer, and Jackie could see that the tips of his ears were red. She too turned back to her screen, only to see her own reflection—pale, tense, her eyes dark hollows— staring out of its dark glassy surface. She whispered: "You've all been a terrible disappointment." She didn't know who the words were aimed at or what they meant.

On her way home from work that evening, she stopped at a pet shop in the Fulton Mall. The mall was really just a street in downtown Brooklyn made up mostly of sneaker shops, sportswear stores and fast-food restaurants. Jackie generally tried to avoid going to the mall when possible. She called it "Child Abuse Row." There was always a stream of teenaged mothers slapping their dazed children while Jackie looked on in horror. But there was a small, anemic pet shop at the far end of the mall, and Jackie wanted to buy Beulah a gift to make up for her leaving her alone all day.

The store was devoid of customers and smelled like a hamster cage, warm and dank and fertile. In the back sat a row of puppies—purebreds. They looked perfect, too cute, like the puppies of calendars and greeting cards. Jackie noticed how much calmer than Beulah they all were, almost languid as they stared at her from behind their plastic walls. She peered in at a beautiful golden retriever. It lay on its side, and its eyelids drooped. She tapped on the glass but it just blinked, unmoving.

Jackie wandered the chewies aisle, searching for gifts for Beulah. There were piggy snozzles, along with pig ears and hooves available—a use for every part of an animal's body. Nothing went to waste. She also found "bully sticks," which according to the sales lady were actually the dried penis of a bull. Jackie resisted the bully stick, but left the store with a Nylabone, a piggy snozzle, and a little squeaking bunny doll, promising to come back soon.

Out on the street, Jackie limped toward home, feeling the pinch of her toes crushed together in the tips of her work shoes and wishing she'd changed into sneakers at the office. All around her other women moved wearily toward their respective homes, and she felt herself to be part of a long and sad parade. It wasn't quite dark yet. In just a few moments the sky would turn to black. But for now it was a swirl of light and dark purples, the color of the moment before. The sky looked heavy to Jackie, like a swollen fruit—something inedible and on the verge of bursting. She watched that purple gourd as she walked, unbreathing, tingling with some inexplicable fear. As she turned onto her block, the sky slipped into black, the change nearly imperceptible. She breathed relief.

When she opened the door to her apartment, she found her living room covered in white feathers, like a cartoon vision of heaven. Beulah sat in the middle of the vision, grinning and slapping her tail happily against the floor. Jackie paused at the door, awestruck for a moment, before she realized that Beulah had destroyed the down comforter, the one she'd already stained with pee. Jackie dropped the bag of treats she had bought. An image flashed through her head: herself picking Beulah up by her scruff and slamming her small body against the wall.

Beulah wiggled her way across the room to greet her. Jackie knelt down and held out her arms, but the puppy shrunk back, sensing something. But Jackie had already caught her in her grip and held her by the scruff. The puppy didn't know whether it was being greeted or punished—her tail wagged slightly between her legs—and Jackie wasn't sure either. Some small voice told her to control herself. She pulled Beulah close and stared at her in the face, trying to decide on the best punishment. It was then that she noticed the hole.

It sat directly between the dog's two nostrils—small but perfectly round, as if a nail had been driven through it, or a large needle. It looked almost as if somebody had tried to create a third nostril. Jackie felt first repulsion, then horror, then pity. She began to cry. The hole was more than she could handle.

She stood up, sniffling, backing away from the mutilated animal, who wagged its tail playfully.

"Who did that to you?" she hissed. "Who did it?"

She had the urge to call Kip, but she knew that was impossible.

Instead, she paced her apartment as far as the walls would allow, trying to imagine where the hole in Beulah's nose had come from. It looked almost as if somebody had tried to pierce it. She had an image of a pack of Hell's Angels, laughing and swigging beer as they set upon her puppy with a needle or a drill. The hole reminded her somehow of slavery, of shackles and deformities too deep to ever heal. Jackie threw herself down on her empty bed and sobbed silently into her pillow. She felt a pain in her chest like a burn, and was aware that it wasn't just the hole she cried over. She whispered to herself, "It's going to be okay. It's going to be okay." After a moment she heard Beulah's clicking toe-nails coming down the hall. Beulah leapt onto the bed, where she wasn't supposed to be, and began to hungrily lick the salt off Jackie's cheek. Jackie held her close, gently this time.

The bitch was crazy. She never slept. She never even got tired. At night, Jackie tossed and turned, listening to the incessant click of the dog's toenails as she paced up and down the hallway. In Jackie's half-conscious state, she imagined the dog was supernatural, a laboratory escapee, and the hole in the nose was where the scientists had inserted crack cocaine.

Later in the week, she asked the veterinarian, a tall Waspish woman, whether the puppy was perhaps abnormal. The vet agreed with Jackie that the hole was mysterious—and disturbing—but swore the puppy was just behaving like a puppy. She simply needed more exercise.

She told Jackie about the dog gatherings in the center of the big park up the hill. The dogs and their owners convened before nine o'clock, when leash laws went into effect. They came in rain or shine, in winter and in summer, to tire their dogs out. It was the only way. It was Jackie's only hope.

Jackie went to see for herself one morning before work at the Swiss bank. She stood at the edge of the park, watching the dogs and their owners mingle on the grass. From a distance, they looked a bit like an AA group. The people stood in small clusters, chatting with one another under the cold white sunlight of late fall. Steam rose mystically up from their Styrofoam cups and disappeared into the crisp air. The dogs—there must have been at least twenty—swarmed on the grass around them, wrestling, fighting, humping, shitting, sniffing. Beulah pulled Jackie forward, trying to join the fray, wheezing from the friction of the collar against her esophagus.

Up close, the group appeared more like a cult than a support group—something better left in the seventies. Everyone looked as if they were waiting for something big to happen—a UFO to land or the Virgin Mary to descend from the clouds. They wore expectant believers' faces, and the manic dogs added an air of helter-skelter.

Jackie unhooked Beulah's leash and watched her romp over to a black Labrador who wore a red bandanna around its neck. They did their crotch-sniffing dance, then began to happily wrestle. Snippets of conversation, spoken in unfamiliar dialect, floated across the grass toward Jackie:

> . . . *you've gotta wait six months to spray* . . .
> . . . *lost his Booda Velvet* . . .
> *Can I have my Kong back, please?*
> *Purina One* . . .
> . . . *awful diarrhea* . . .

Jackie heard a voice behind her.

"You must be new here."

Jackie turned around.

A woman stood before her, swinging a leash in her hand like a lasso. She was heavyset, with rosy cheeks and big, horsy teeth. Her age was unclear: She was either a haggard thirtysomething or a young fortysomething. She reminded Jackie of a high school guidance counselor, somebody settled and sexless. She might have been pretty once; now she was practical and solid. She looked as if she'd dressed in a hurry: filthy Harvard sweat pants, shit-caked New Balance sneakers, and a beige cardigan that was buttoned wrong.

Jackie glanced at the dog by the woman's side and gasped. It was the ugliest mutt Jackie had ever laid eyes on—it appeared to be more wild boar than dog. Everything was off. It was barrel chested, and its legs were meant for a much smaller dog. Its fur was no color at all. One of its eyes was completely opaque, a cataract, and along its nose ran a raised scar. It wore a crazed joker's grin on its face.

The woman saw the look on Jackie's face and explained, matter-of-factly, "I found him that way. About six months ago. Abused, bleeding, stabbed in the eye. Somebody really did a number on him. He had a tag that said, 'Humpty Dumpty,' with a phone number, but I threw it out. Whoever did this to him didn't deserve him back."

"Oh," Jackie muttered, not sure what else to say. "How good of you."

The woman stuck out a hand and said, "I'm Nan, by the way. Welcome."

Jackie introduced herself; then, for lack of anything better, she nodded in Beulah's direction, where she was being mounted, unsuccessfully, by a toy poodle. "I found my puppy a few days ago. She was a stray."

Nan squinted at Beulah and said, "You *found* her? That's a good-looking stray. She couldn't have been on the streets long." Jackie felt a kind of one-upsmanship in the woman's tone. She wished she could show her the hole in Beulah's nose.

Nan began to give unsolicited advice about owning a dog. Jackie was hungry for advice. And happy to listen. Nan told her where and when to get Beulah spayed (eight months) and how to get the stray dog saver's discount on vet expenses. She told her what kind of food to feed her and how many times she needed to be walked. Jackie felt drawn to Nan's sensible enthusiasm. She seemed to know everything—about history, literature, dogs. She informed Jackie she'd been working on her Ph.D. for ten years. She was writing her dissertation on Victorian methods of birth control. Jackie listened to Nan chatter on and felt happy for the first time in months. The park around them was staggeringly beautiful in the morning light. The people continued to look expectant, as if they were waiting for something better to come, but the dogs seemed content, as if they'd already found perfection. The field itself was wide and lush, the forest of elms behind it like a clutter of secrets. The sky above was wide and unbroken by buildings. It was hard to imagine that beyond the green lay the filthy, groaning city. It reminded Jackie of Narnia, that land she'd been so obsessed with as a young girl. She'd spent hours in her mother's closet, eyes closed, trying to walk through the closet's back wall and into another world. She'd been surrounded by the smells of her mother—nicotine and whiskey and jasmine hippie oil—but for a second it had seemed that the wall really was melting away, giving rise to another country. The dog park resembled the land she had imagined she would find behind the closet, only without the dogs and their strange, lonely masters.

The sight of Beulah romping around made Jackie suddenly sad. She didn't want to take her home to her dingy fourth-floor walk-up and leave her there alone all day. Beulah had been liberated, but into what kind of bondage, she mused, while Nan chattered on about the trouble with rawhide bones.

Jackie learned a lot from Nan those first few weeks with Beulah, the basic and not-so-basic facts of dog psychology.

Dogs travel in packs, unlike humans, who tend to couple.

Fifty percent of all so-called purebreds are actually mixed.

The other fifty percent—the truly pure ones—are stupid and sickly, and susceptible to glandular problems.

Dogs have a denning instinct and therefore respond well to confined spaces. They feel safe, rather than trapped, in cages.

Among dogs, hierarchy rules. There must be an alpha dog, somebody to follow; otherwise, the pack is lost.

In public, at the dog park, Jackie acted like a slightly smug animal lover. She spoke with disdain about the imaginary person who had thrown Beulah onto the street. She nodded her head sadly when the other dog owners talked about euthanasia, puppy mills, dog abuse.

In private, Jackie continued to beat Beulah. Not every day, but nearly. It became a ritual, like a glass of wine with dinner. Beulah barely seemed to feel it. She wore an bemused, mocking expression while Jackie went at it. She didn't seem in the least bit scared. But Jackie was—scared of herself, the way she hungered to hit her. She would examine the house when she got home from work, searching for damage. She always found it, and then she would set upon Beulah with a newspaper or her hand, depending on the severity of the damage. It was like an itch, a tickle in her fist, the way she yearned for violence, and in the act of it she felt exhilarated. Sometimes Jackie restrained herself. Then she would settle for cursing. *I hate you, you fucking dirty mongrel. You're ruining my life. Get lost. Get lost. Get lost.* But usually those curses were not enough. They didn't satisfy her.

The beatings didn't work either. They only made things worse. Beulah continued on her path of destruction, undeterred by Jackie's raised hand. She ate Jackie's panty hose, broke the bathroom scale, peed on the wooden floors, and toilet-papered the living room. The house was transformed. Jackie spent her small salary on bull penises and pig ears, but

Beulah was unsatisfied by these gruesome offerings. She wanted more. She wanted to loot the bedroom closet, seize those objects most valuable to her master, and destroy them.

Outside, Beulah was just as bad. Jackie had never noticed before that the streets of Brooklyn were paved with discarded chicken wings. They were everywhere. And Beulah was like a metal detector, nose to the ground, scanning for silver. Beulah pulled so much on the leash that strangers on the street would often call out, "Who's walking who?"

And worst of all, she never came when Jackie called her. Sometimes, Jackie was forced to chase her for hours, trying to get her to come home. Beulah turned it into a game. She would stand still, grinning, until Jackie was within inches, and then at the last minute she would leap out of Jackie's reach, laughing, and run in circles around her. It was as if she was trying to humiliate Jackie in front of her new friends.

None of this behavior was lost on Nan, who tried to give Jackie advice on training Beulah. *Spray her with water when she barks. Shake a can when she jumps up on you. Spend fifteen minutes a day practicing commands. She must love and respect you as her alpha dog. All dogs long for a benign dictator.* Underlying all of her suggestions was the smug refrain: *There are no bad dogs, just bad owners.*

Jackie pretended to listen avidly to what Nan said. But she wasn't really listening. She was thinking about how she was going to kick Beulah's ass when they got home.

Even as Jackie kicked and beat and cursed Beulah, she loved her. Beulah was all that mattered to Jackie. Their relationship was one of extremes. Extreme hatred, extreme love. Violence seemed just another form of intimacy. Jackie wondered if you could truly love something without sometimes despising it. Jackie raged against Beulah, while simultaneously sacrificing everything for the beast.

She stopped going out to Manhattan so much for dinner or movies. Whenever she did, she would spend the entire time imagining Beulah at home with her bone and the television blaring out a language she'd never understand. She stopped jogging altogether—Beulah enjoyed group exercise more, so Jackie was forced to stand on the sidelines and watch the dogs play. Jackie learned to enjoy spending evenings curled up with Beulah in a filthy heap on the futon in the living room, which was permanently pulled out to serve as Beulah's bed.

Jackie began to lose touch with her old circle of friends—the pretty, manicured set of girls who lived in the city. She didn't miss them much. They had begun to annoy her, their constant chatter about men, their constant narrative of dates gone wrong. There was something so desperate about their endless parties and fancy dinners, as if they were in a perpetual state of meaningless celebration. The last time she'd been out with them, she'd still been smarting from the breakup. That night, she'd noticed how none of them looked at each other when they spoke. Instead, they looked over each other's shoulders, scanning the bar for eligible men. They were a sisterhood of fools, she'd thought, and had avoided them ever since. They all assumed it was because she was depressed, in mourning, because her man had turned out to be a dawg, just like all the rest. The truth was, she was too preoccupied with Beulah to really notice his absence.

Jackie grew close to Nan over the winter. They spent most mornings and evenings at the park, where they stood huddled together, watching their mongrels romp on the grass around them. It was an odd thing, the dog park. Everyone there was a stranger, but there was an intimacy to their encounters, particularly in the mornings, before they had put on their business suits and makeup. They saw each other in the natural state, sleep still stuck to the eyes, the way lovers see each other before the day begins.

Nan, she learned, hadn't had sex in ten years. Her last "encounter" as she put it, was with her ancient thesis adviser. He'd been in his early seventies at the time, and now he was dead. "It's weird," Nan said, wearing an oddly elated smile. "You stop missing it after a while. You learn to live without it." Nan liked to gossip meanly about the other dog owners. She seemed to have had a bad experience with almost all of them at some point or another. This one stole Humpty's Kong, that one didn't pick up her dog's poop, "making the rest of us look bad." It was hard to tell who Nan held a grudge against, the person or the dog. Whatever the case, she seemed to have no friends at the park except for Jackie.

There was a group of women whom Nan particularly hated. Like Nan, they were all single, all childless, and all white. But they, unlike Nan, hadn't quite given up hope yet. Nan had crossed an invisible line. She no longer wanted a man. These women still did.

Jackie called them the Weather Girls, after the early eighties disco duo famous for their hit single "It's Raining Men." She once, giggling, admitted the nickname to Nan, but Nan had just stared at her blankly until Jackie realized she was too old for that song.

The Weather Girls all owned purebreds, and for this Nan hated them most. Their dogs had the pretense of being status symbols—things they had purchased—whereas Humpty and Beulah had the air of the accidental. Nan liked to whisper mean things about their purebreds—how Carly, the obese chocolate Lab, resembled a piece of shit, or how Julie, the aged golden retriever, was nearly retarded, or Mindy, the cocker spaniel, was allergic to its own tear ducts. Nan hated one dog in particular. It was an expensive Japanese breed called a shar-pei, and its name was Kabuki. Jackie had to agree with Nan that Kabuki was funny-looking, a brown mass of wrinkles, like a crumpled fur coat. Jackie herself found the excessive wrinkles disconcerting; they reminded her of that disease small children get when they age prematurely. But for Kabuki it wasn't a disease. She had been bred to look that way, a cruel hoax by a mad scientist.

Nan liked to point out that Kabuki would never survive if left to evolution. "He'll get fungus infections between those folds in his fur that everyone thinks are so cute—and then he'll die of gangrene," she said flatly. Nan said Humpty and Beulah stood a much better chance of surviving in the wild. They resembled what she termed the "standard mongrel." Nan said that in the laws of Darwinian selection, the standard mongrel was the one that survived: thirty to forty pounds, short floppy ears, long nose. Beulah's ears and fur were a bit on the long side for natural selection, but she'd at least stand a chance, unlike Kabuki.

Sometimes when Nan wasn't around, Jackie would join the Weather Girls in conversation. They reminded Jackie of her friends in the city, the ones she'd stopped seeing. Those city friends were black, while the Weather Girls at the dog park were white, but they were basically the same. It struck Jackie that while she could be a black girl or a white girl, depending on how she decided to fix her hair, she was always a woman. There was no escaping that.

Winter came. The grass at the park turned gray and crunchy, and the sky above appeared streaked and dirty, like the film that coated Jackie's apartment windows. While once the park had been a pleasant ritual for Jackie, now it felt like a drag. Often, there was tension in the air, and fights broke out regularly between the dogs and between their owners. The people seemed to forget, at times, that the dogs were animals. They would argue, viciously, over whose dog had started the fight. Nan, meanwhile, had grown too close. She'd invited Jackie to join her for a movie and dinner several times, and Jackie had declined, not wanting to expand their friendship beyond the realm of the park. Nan was too possessive. If she caught Jackie talking to the Weather Girls, she would sulk angrily on the edges of their circle and leave without saying good-bye.

Jackie dreaded these petty dramas at the park, but she continued to go. It was still the only way to tire Beulah out. And besides, Jackie had no friends outside of the dog park, no real friends besides Nan. Her sisterhood of fools had stopped inviting her to dinner parties and bar hoppings, and she'd stopped wanting to go. She was too exhausted after a day of temping.

Jackie had begun to eat only when she was hungry, and she gave no thought to taste or calories or nutrients. She would scavenge the dark streets around her house for takeout, something near and cheap—kung pao chicken and fried shrimp, pizza, beef patties, jerk chicken, or roti— and carry it back to her apartment. There she wouldn't bother to put it on a plate. She'd just hunch over the container it had been served in, wolfing down what she could while Beulah stood waiting for leftovers.

Jackie no longer put much effort into her appearance, and she could see the women at the temp agency eyeing her with disapproval when she showed up for her assignments. She was no longer their favorite, no matter how light her skin. Whole days went by without her taking a shower or changing her clothes. Her fingernails were filthy, her hands callused from the pull of the leash. Her feet, ordinarily scrubbed and toenails brightly polished, were as tough as hooves. She had once been dutiful about waxing her legs every three weeks. Now the hair on them grew freely.

She'd hidden away her long mirror months ago, to keep it away from Beulah. The pea brain was always jumping against it, trying to play with her own reflection. Jackie had been afraid she would break it. One day, while rummaging in the closet for a tennis ball, Jackie pulled the mirror out and propped it against the wall. She glimpsed herself full length. She had taken to wearing her hair in twin braids, Pippi Longstocking style, so that its texture was unclear. She wore her usual dog walker's uniform: Adidas sweat pants and a sweater with a logo of a trucker's union across the front. She hadn't gained or lost any weight, but she looked different: raceless and ageless, almost virginal. There was a rough clarity to her features she hadn't noticed before—a wide blankness to her gaze. Her skin was clear, her features bold. She put the mirror away, vaguely troubled, but not certain exactly why.

One Sunday in late February, Jackie stumbled up Flatbush Avenue after Beulah. It was her weekend ritual. No matter what the weather, each Saturday and Sunday morning Jackie would spend two hours with Beulah at the park. She'd long since stopped imagining what the rest of the city was doing. Today the sky was a flat slate gray, and the frigid wind burned Jackie's cheeks. She hadn't dressed for the weather, and her gloveless fingers were numb around Beulah's leash.

A couple in the distance caught her eye. They were unremarkable except that the man was black and the woman was white. The man wore jeans and a red windbreaker, his head shaved neatly to his skull. The woman was tall and blond and wore jeans and motorcycle boots. They spoke to one another conspiratorially, one head tilted toward the other. Jackie stared at them, thinking for a moment of her parents. She wondered if they'd ever been in cahoots that way.

When the couple was a few feet away, the man looked up. Only then did Jackie recognize Kip.

He looked good, better than when they'd been together. She'd always disliked his dreadlocks; they'd made him seem vain and girlish. She'd fantasized about cutting them off. His new short cut made him look more vulnerable, naked, as if all the illusions had been cut away along with the hair. He was laughing at something the white girl had said. Jackie could see the girl better now. She was attractive in a flawed sort of way, with a slightly hawkish nose and a large mouth. She reminded Jackie of all the white girls she'd ever grown to hate. They had a casual, moneyed confidence to them that always made Jackie feel awkward and prudish in their midst.

Beulah was straining at the leash and half dragged Jackie to the little plot of dirt where a tree had been planted. There, Beulah squatted and began to take a immense shit in her hump backed position.

Kip was upon them now, and as he passed, he glanced up casually in Jackie's direction. She held her breath, waiting for him to smile, or frown, or blush with embarrassment beneath the light brown of his skin. But he only looked past her at the dog, and sneered slightly. Jackie held a plastic bag tightly in her hand, and the sweat made it slippery. His eyes moved over Jackie again, but showed no recognition.

They moved past her then. She watched their backs as they strolled away down the avenue. A block away, she saw them disappear into a greasy spoon diner. She recalled going there once or twice with Kip. They'd gone for a big bacon-and-egg breakfast after a leisurely morning in bed.

Jackie leaned against the slender tree beside her for support. She didn't know whether Kip had simply not seen her or had not recognized her. Or perhaps he had just pretended not to notice her. She wasn't certain. She left Beulah's mess where it was, thinking it would be okay to leave it just this once. Her cheeks felt warm with mounting clarity as she followed Beulah up the street.

When Jackie reached the park, she paused at the edge of the grass, confused by what she found. The dog park was more crowded than usual; the atmosphere was raucous. Balloons and a small folding table had been set up in the center of the grass. The dogs and their owners crowded around the table talking and laughing. Jackie saw the shar pei puppy, Kabuki, was wearing a pointy party hat on his head, and then recalled its owner, Doreen—the leader of the Weather Girls' pack— mentioning something last week about Kabuki's first birthday party. Nan had whispered afterwards that she wouldn't be caught dead at such a ridiculous event. They'd laughed about it together, but now Jackie could see that Doreen hadn't been joking. Some of the dogs were trying to get the party hats off by pawing at their heads, but most of the others were too busy surrounding the folding table, where Jackie could see the owners doling out treats. Barry Manilow's "Mandy" played from a tape deck.

Beulah romped joyfully off into the cluster of dogs and people. Jackie watched as one of the Weather Girls attempted to put a party hat on Beulah's head. Another one of them waved at Jackie and shouted "Join the fun!" Jackie waved back, tepidly, but kept her distance.

She didn't feel up to joining the group. She wished Nan was here, but she was nowhere to be seen. Jackie shoved her hands in her pockets and looked at the ground. She couldn't help thinking about Kip and the girl. She imagined them getting married, someday beginning to look alike, the way couples often did. She imagined they'd have children who looked like her—butterscotch babies. She could rouse no anger. The irony of their union was oddly comforting.

She must have stood thinking a long time, because when she did look up, the park was empty. The party had disappeared. The only evidence that anybody had been there was a lone party hat on the grass, and high in a distant tree, a bright orange balloon sat stuck between branches, its floating mission aborted. The cold had turned Jackie's face into something foreign and rubbery. She could no longer feel it. She looked at her watch. It was way past nine. Leash laws had gone into effect.

In the distance she spotted Beulah. The dog darted ecstatically through trees, hatless now, a lone speck of black and brown, oblivious to the cold and her master.

Jackie called softly, "Beulah, Beulah, Beulah."

Then a bit louder—Beulah!—the way they beckoned the maid on the show her grandmother liked to watch.

Beulah turned once, ears perked up. She grinned, wiggling her bottom in excitement, then pranced behind a cluster of trees. She wanted to play tag. She wanted to humiliate Jackie once again.

Jackie felt a dull clicking in her brain, a throbbing in her gums, and swore she'd kick the dog's ass when she caught her. She'd beat her right here, in the dog park. She didn't care who saw her. Nan could call the cops for all she cared. There *were* such things as bad dogs, not just bad owners. It went both ways.

She began to walk across the grass toward Beulah, but halfway there, something went out of her. She felt tired. Her throat hurt and her chest ached, as if she were coming down with something. She watched Beulah in the distance, as she ran insane circles around a tree, faster than seemed possible. She looked a bit like Little Black Sambo, running to escape the tiger. Jackie recalled the tiger had chased Sambo around that tree so fast that the tiger'd turned into butter, which later, Sambo, along with his mother and father, Black Mumbo and Black Jumbo, had slathered onto pancakes for their triumphant meal. Jackie imagined herself to be that tiger. She too would chase Beulah till she turned to butter. She too would melt and disappear.

She said the dog's name one more time in the weakest of whispers. Then she turned and trudged away, up the slope of mud and grass toward the big road. At the crosswalk, she felt something heavy shift inside of her, a sense of dread stronger than she'd ever felt before, and turned to look behind her—but the dog was not there and the feeling was gone as quickly as it had come over her.

*   *   *

She lay on a table in the back room of a midtown salon. She was on her lunch break from her new temp job at a law firm. A Russian woman stood hunched over her, concentrating on her eyebrows. She was giving Jackie an expression of perpetual surprise. Odd, Jackie thought, that women sought to look shocked. Not coy or delighted, but shocked. It was as if they wanted to look frozen in the moment before something happens.

The Russian woman was artificially pale, all bleached out. Her dye job seemed to mock her dark, Asiatic complexion. She didn't talk much, but when she pulled up Jackie's skirt to start waxing her legs, she whistled.

"When the last time you waxed?"

Jackie glanced down at her body. Her legs looked strong and useful, unintentionally toned and muscular. The hair on them had grown long and dark—Sicily and Libya revealed. It had been months and months since she'd touched them.

The woman shook her head, then took the spatula and stuck it into the pot of warm wax. She stirred it for a minute, then spread the wax along Jackie's leg, like butter on bread. It felt nice, warm and soft, but quickly hardening. Wax always felt so nice going on, Jackie thought, and so bad coming off. Her eyes began to water in anticipation.

REGINALD SHEPHERD
b. 1963

Reginald Shepherd could be called a classicist, as seen in the lush lyrics and narratives found in his first two books of poems: *Some Are Drowning* (1994), winner of an AWP Award, and *Angel, Interrupted* (1996). His work has also been selected twice for *The Best American Poetry*. With his latest book, *Wrong* (1999), Shepherd leaves narrative for lyric and fragment; the results are fascinating takes on death, Greek myths, and poetic predecessors such as Hart Crane. Like Crane, Shepherd expresses sexuality with a fierce combination of contemporary form ("S'il Meurt") and classical allusion ("Icarus on Fire Island"), while also investigating the black experience, from slavery to soul.

THE DIFFICULT MUSIC

I started to write a song about you, then I decided, *No.*
I've been trying to write about violence
for so long. (You were my mother; I love you more
dead. Not a day goes by when I'm not turning someone
into you.) A week of traffic jams and fog
filtered through glass, the country crumbling
in my sleep; old men in plaid jackets on the corner
drinking quart bottles of Old Milwaukee; the color black
again and again.
                    My first summer in Boston
a bum glanced up from tapping at the pavement with a hammer
to whisper *Nigger,* laughing, when I walked by.
I'd passed the age of consent, I suppose;
my body was never clean again. In Buffalo, a billboard
said, "In a dream you saw a way to survive and you woke up
happy," justice talking to the sidewalk on Main Street;
I thought it was talking to me, but it was just
art. (I've wronged too many mornings hallucinating
your voice, too drunk with sleep to understand
the words.)
                    Some afternoons
I can see through a history of heart attacks in two-room
tenement apartments, writing your silted name
on snow with which the lake effect shrouds
a half-abandoned rust belt city. (I've compared you
to snow's unlikely predicates, the moon's
faceless occupation. Some drift
always takes your place.) I was just
scribbling again. *Take it from me,* my stereo claims, *some day
we'll all be free.* If anyone should ever write that song.
The finely sifted light falls down.

DESIRE AND THE SLAVE TRADE

Contempt, my old inquisitor, across
the widening winter weeks our needs
converge, conquistador of manifest extinctions
and hemispheres, into a knot
my fingers have been bloodied
trying to untie, separating the raw fiber
from the seeds. I'm always calling you
my friend. *White people*, my mother
told me, *they stick together*. Some say
the Devil is a handsome man, some say
he isn't black as coal. *But a nigger'll
stab you in the back as soon as look
at you*. How could I accuse you of the miles
of milk-white cotton shrubs, the frost
that settled early on my countryside?

In 1721 in New York Colony the leader of
the first large-scale slave revolt in North America
was slow-roasted for eight hours as
a warning beacon. In Florida
they doused a black man from Detroit
with gasoline, kindling to put out the dark
where white skin wasn't bright enough
to light the way to Beulah Land. But that
was last year, and another state
of mind; he survived to testify. It was winter
then too.

In bed with books and faded photographs
I dreamed a walk with docent gusts, damp
dead leaves of sepia dioramas. We walked past
depots, chief among them shipbuilding Newport
of Rhode Island and Providence
Plantations, and mercantile Liverpool with its seven

miles of docks. (*By 1795 Liverpool*
had more than a hundred ships carrying slaves
and accounted for half of all the European
slave trade.) Wandered the hold of
the first American slave ship, the Desire, sailing
from Marblehead in 1637, *partitioned into racks*
two feet by six feet, with leg irons
and bars, conditions *among the best*
they had seen. Viewed auctions in major
market towns: Newport again, suffering much damage
in the Revolutionary War; Philadelphia
of the Quaker brotherhood, later a seat of abolitionist
agitation: deepwater Richmond at the head of the James,
not captured until 1865, much burned in the evacuation;
gracious Charleston of the Carolinas, chief entrepot
of the Southeast. Failed to bid. Centuries
of blood and urine clogged wooden gutters, blurred
black ink on yellowed bills of sale and frayed
advertising flyers. (*A Gang of 25 Sea Island*
Cotton and Rice Negroes, Ryan's Mart,
Chalmers Street.)
⠀⠀⠀⠀⠀⠀⠀⠀Then your quizzical face
behind rain-smeared glass, me taking the lash
or runagate brand, welts burning
ashy skin. As in a film (*The Birth*
of a Nation perhaps), there was no
sound. The dream that wasn't mine
but ours was smiling then, and brushing snow
from its white sleeves. Someone turning over
in his sleep, someone saying *please*.

Snowdrifts sleepwalk from window
to vacant window, waken a morning
when a touch is less than breath
against a cheek, a stranger's late December
history no boot has smudged. (Perhaps
I was never asleep.) It might be easy

to live among those muddled white
confessions. I could never be that man.

ANTIBODY

I've heard that blood will always tell:
tell me then, antigen, declining white cell count
answer, who wouldn't die for beauty
if he could? Microbe of mine, you don't have me
in mind. (The man fan-dancing from 1978
hit me with a feather's edge across the face, ghost
of a kiss. It burned.) Men who have paid
their brilliant bodies for soul's desire, a night
or hour, fifteen minutes of skin brushed against
bright skin, burn down to smoke and cinders
shaken over backyard gardens, charred
bone bits sieved out over water. The flat earth
loves them even contaminated, turned over
for no one's spring. Iris and gentian
spring up like blue flames, discard those parts
more perishable: lips, penises, testicles,
a lick of semen on the tongue, and other things
in the vicinity of sex. Up and down the sidewalk
stroll local gods (see also: saunter, promenade,
parade of possibilities, virtues at play: Sunday
afternoons before tea dance, off-white
evenings kneeling at public urinals, consumed
by what confuses, consuming it
too). Time in its burn is any
life, those hours, afternoons, buildings
smudged with soot and city residues. Later
they take your blood, that tells secrets
it doesn't know, bodies can refuse
their being such, rushing into someone's
wish not to be. My babbling blood.
What's left of burning

burns as well: me down to blackened
glass, an offering in anthracite,
the darkest glitter smoldering underground
until it consumes the earth
which loves me anyway, I'm sure.

S'IL MEURT

For Chris

If it die intestate, airless
If it lie all night half in state
If it live but as something with no wish to live
If it live but at the cost of whose
If it survive within the half-life of carbon
If it refuse to die
If it then you death too will die
If it born again but as what

If it remember prematurely
If it scale the course but fail the test
If it sacrifice incorrectly and is dejected
If it "abjection" instead of abjection
If it cancel the denominator and the numerator
If it cancel out the sum
If it find the forest minus every tree
If it count the yellow leaf, if it the rot

If it September to September
If it fifteen-wild-decembers in the manner of Emily Brontë
If it lost in the wold, lost on the moor
If it drown, if it breathe water, salt the lungs
If it ultramarine, if it indigo or perse
If it instead aquamarine, if it cold submarine rain
If it thunder forsaking rain
If it rage in several lights

If it like lions after slumber, if it refuse to rise
If it cry wolf, refuse to bear
If it render all pleas futile, if it interdiction
If it kiss the rod and kick the staff
If it the staff of life, if it wheat or if it chaff
If it sing somesuch out of tune
If it sing a somewhat overly familiar tune
If it the notes beneath the staff

If not the first person then the last

ICARUS ON FIRE ISLAND

Two loves I have, each one
too fair for me to be completed
in his eyes, summer open with Mediterranean blue
where care is left aside, the most
of available light. The Sunday beach with you,
spangled with tan men, their perfect skin
reproach and visible reward (until the sun abandons
them and they withdraw into the inked-in sky
to shine unseen for those who don't concern themselves
with light). I searched the air dazzled with kites
for them. I couldn't want them less. *Since shunning pain
I ease can never find*. I'll score the sky
with string, and there incise my name,
until the gusts decline.
                              I have dispersed
the clouds with one small wisp of breath,
his hand commands a paper dragon
through an insurgent breeze. The painted silk
is stolen by flight, the line snaps or he
lets go of the line, playing it out
against a sudden updraft. That was my future
life, lost track of all a summer
afternoon: a black point in a northeast corner of blue

descending, a mote across an open eye of sky
where light drains away.

AT THE GRAVE OF HART CRANE
For Michael Bonner

Mobile light paints me an undertow, trailing
a northeasterly hand through day, riptide
scattering coins of noon: silvers
surface currents to the key of water foaming

where it bickers with the rocks. Sings there
till sunset. This is my saltless sea, my
estuary, inlet, delta, eddy becalmed: no tides
in Lake Michigan, no shore this side, or

barely one. A drunkard preaching
to Lincoln Park asks late April, air, *What have
you given?* These five flat rocks bearded
with algae, quincunx, this cup-shaped crack

lakewater pours up into, overflowing,
pours away again, under itself. This
neap tide captured, something always
in-between, half solid water, half liquid

land, least difference washing itself away.
White-shining autumn, early, wave crest,
silver-tipped. I'm tired of the ocean
metaphors, old sea in me and thee:

a skeleton of sea, shape left behind
by what is left, just this idea of water. Someone
floating, someone sinking just out of sight,
drowning in earnest one more time. I believed

in his unsheltered sea, made my way
to cold fresh water, then lost heart.

SKIN TRADE

And then I said, that's what it means
to testify: to sit in the locked dark muttering
when you should be dead to the world. The muse
just shrugged and shaded his blue eyes. So naturally
I followed him down to his father's house
by the river, a converted factory in the old
industrial park: somewhere to sit
on threadbare cushions eating my words
and his promises, safe as milk
that dries the throat. If I had a home,
he'd be that unmade bed. He's my America
twisted in dirty sheets, my inspiration
for a sleepless night. No getting around that
pale skin.
   He throws things out the window
he should keep; he collects things
he should feed to the river. He takes me
down. While there, I pick them up.

The river always does this to me:
gulls squawking and the smell of paper mills
upstream, air crowded with effluents
like riding the bus underwater. I'm spending nights
in the polluted current, teaching sunken bodies how
to swim. My feet always stay wet. Sometimes
I leave footprints the shape of blood; sometimes glass
flows through broken veins, and I glitter.
Every other step refers to white men
and their names. The spaces in between
are mine. *Back of the bus with you,*
nigger. They're turning warehouses

into condos, I'm selling everything
at clearance prices: here's a bronze star
for suffering quietly like a good
boy.
     River of salt, will I see my love again?
Cold viscous water holds its course even after
it's gone. Throw a face into it and you'll never look
again, throw a voice and you'll hear sobbing
all the way down. Narcissus, that's my flower
forced in January, black-eyed bells echoing
sluggish eddies. Who hit him first?

The muse has covered his face
with his hands. It's just a reflex
of the historical storm that sired him:
something to say, "The sun is beating down
too hard on my pith helmet, the oil slick
on the river's not my fault, when are you going
home?" What he doesn't want to see, he doesn't
see. In the sludge that drowns the river, rats
pick fights with the debris. He calls them all
by their first names, he's looking through his fingers
like a fence. They make good neighbors. His friends
make do with what they can. They drink beer
from sewer-colored bottles in the dry stream
bed, powdered milk of human kindness and evaporated
silt. They stay by the river till past
sunrise, crooning a lullaby
to help it to sleep. The words
of their drinking songs are scrawled on the ceiling,
Mene, mene, tekel, upharsin: a madrigal
for the millennium's end.
                        I'm counting
down the days in someone else's
unmade bed, let these things break
their hold on me. The world
would like to see me dead, another gone
black man. I'm still awake.

NATASHA TARPLEY

b. 1971

Natasha Tarpley seeks connections and community in her writing, whether through poetry, nonfiction, or editing *Testimony:
Young African-Americans on Self-Discovery & Black Identity*
(1994), her anthology of college-age writers. The connections
are ancestral in *Girl in the Mirror: Three Generations of Black
Women in Motion* (1998); there, Tarpley honors her family
through both the recent practice of "creative nonfiction" and the
ancient art of storytelling. For *Girl in the Mirror* is not a typical
"memoir" from the author's own experience—rather, by writing
in the voice of her family and friends (as in the following passages from the book's "grandparents" section), Tarpley questions
our limited notions of self, identity, and ancestry. Tarpley takes
after writers such as Truman Capote who brought the freedom
and techniques of fiction to nonfiction in order to better understand our often lyrical inner lives.

FROM *GIRL IN THE MIRROR*

Some say our story begins in the middle of an ocean, in the belly of a monster, at the mercy of demons. Others say that we began with a hammer and a nail; that we laid our bodies down and raised cities along our spines. But I say it goes deeper than that, deeper than cotton fields and human cargoes, the thick and heavy links of a history we're constantly trying to break, to desire. The urge that stirs you in the middle of the night, grabs you by the spine and jerks your head upright. The story begins here, when we realize that we are no longer asleep, and the beat of our hearts sounds just like the beat of a faraway drum. And it is at this moment of unrest, when our hearts refuse to allow us to be still, that we realize what we must do, which is to gather ourselves up and move.

ANNA 1942

Dear Jack,

So there it was. The emptiness he left behind had beat me back to the house and was already in the kitchen, leaning back in Jack's chair and grinning with its feet propped up on the table. Don't look as you pass, just keep walking to the stove, eyes steeled on the coffeepot. Light the burner beneath the kettle. Reach for two cups hanging on the hook above the sink. Remember. Take down one. There's a clean saucer in the dish drain. Doesn't match your cup. Use it anyway. Stand on tiptoe to reach the coffee tin in the cabinet over the stove. Jack was supposed to finish that footstool before he left. Maybe you can ask one of the brothers. Maybe Buddy or Herb'll do it. Four tablespoons of coffee for the percolator. Too much. Three teaspoons of sugar in the cup. No, that's what Jack takes. Jack always did have a sweet tooth. Steady yourself against the stove. Get it together, girl. Get yourself together. Leave that cup and start over. One tablespoon coffee, one teaspoon sugar.

That's your cup. Already the kettle is singing and you haven't even got the cream out the box. Usually you end and the kettle begins on the same note. You slipping girl. Get it together. Get yourself together.

All of us here are doing fine.

Somehow when I turned around, I half-expected the emptiness to be gone. Chased away by the clatter of cups and saucers, the rattle of coffee grounds, the spoon clinking against the side of my cup as I stirred and kept stirring until I could get up the nerve to turn around. The emptiness was still there. And now that I was facing it, the only thing left to do was to go on over to the table and sit down.

"Mornin'," said the emptiness. I didn't say anything.

"Aw, come on, Anna. Don't be that way. I didn't do nothin' to you for you to be acting so mean. Can I at least have a smile this mornin'? Just one itty bitty smile?" I kept my eyes on my coffee.

"You know, sooner or later you gonna have to make peace with me."

I sat upright and opened my mouth but no sound came out.

"What you gonna say, gal? Wasn't nothin' you could say to keep that man here, and ain't nothin' you can say now that he gone. Face it. Me and you gonna be like two peas in this little house. That's all there is to it."

And sure enough, when I went to make the bed, the emptiness was there in the sheets still wrinkled in the shape of his body. It was there, pressed up against me as I cleaned the greens for supper, breathing down my neck and begging for a taste when I bent to check the ham browning in the oven. It was stretched back in the armchair as I dusted around the living room, rippling through the dirty water left over from the wash, swaying with the clothes blowing like ghosts on the line.

How was your ride? I hope I packed enough for you to eat.

I had to get out. Go somewhere away from the house where I could feel the heat prickling on my skin, and where there was air that wasn't already heavy with Jack's scent. Down the road, about a quarter mile, Jack's parents were working in the yard outside their house. The brothers would be out in the field rising over the horizon behind the house. Their wives and Jack's sisters would be home, cooking their part of the family dinner we would all get together and eat at Mom and Dad's later in the afternoon. All of the kids in Jack's family stayed on their parents' land. As soon as they were ready for a place of their own, or when they got married, Jack's parents would build them a house.

There was always someone within hollering distance, so there were places I could go. But I didn't feel like seeing anybody from the family just yet. And I couldn't go anywhere else because the food was almost done. I made myself content with a glass of iced tea and went out to the side porch which Jack had just finished screening in before he left. I had a chair out there in a dark corner where I liked to sit when I wanted to be alone with my thoughts. I could disappear in that corner, which is exactly what I needed to do.

It wasn't long after I got myself settled and comfortable that Iona Jackson, my friend from down the road, came strolling up the walkway. I never was so glad to see her. I figured with her here I could at least put off the emptiness for a while, get myself a little peace. Iona would ask what I was doing out in this heat, what smelled so good on the stove. And I would devote myself to answering. I would ask her about the quilting pattern she promised to bring, and did she remember how to do it by heart? And what was it she told me to try adding to my sweet potatoes? Orange rind? Lemon juice? Yes, I would stretch out the small details and string them together, a rope, a trap to harness the emptiness. I cracked an ice cube between my teeth anticipating the conversation, anxious for the company.

But Iona didn't even stop on the porch. She kept on into the house, waving for me to follow.

"Girl, it's too hot to be sitting out there." She sat down at the kitchen table and wiped her forehead with her palm. Iona, too, knew the emptiness and sniffed it out right away, turning up her nose and sucking her teeth at the familiar stench.

"He gone?" she asked.

"Yeah. Left this morning."

"Mmph," Iona snorted. "You be okay." For her the emptiness was a bitter taste on the tongue; the death smell that hovered over the sick and wounded, wafting up from a dark place in her heart. Her husband, Elijah, had gone up North, scattering promises to write and to send for Iona like rose petals in his wake. No one had heard from him since.

That man had wound Iona around his finger and just let her loose, like a pebble in some young boy's slingshot.

But for me, the emptiness was still just a space I was trying to figure out how to fill, like the scratchy silence at the end of a record, a kind of music unto itself that you listen to until you can decide what you're going to put on next. And maybe I should've been feeling different from how I was feeling. Maybe I should've been crying until I didn't have any tears left or cursing Jack for leaving. But I didn't feel anything but in between, suspended.

I watched Iona drain the glass of tea I had set before her. She stood up and smoothed down her skirt. I got up, too, and started wrapping the ham cooling on top the stove.

"Well, I s'pose one of the brothers will be by after a while to carry this food down to Mom and Dad's. You know how Jack's parents eat at four on the dot. You welcome to join us," I offered, not ready to relinquish her company.

"No thanks, sweetheart. I put a pot a beans on earlier and left them simmering. They should be ready by now. I'll be by tomorrow to check on you."

"At least take some greens," I said, rummaging for a bowl.

"Save 'em for lunch tomorrow," Iona said at the door. I nodded.

"You take care a yourself, honey, your Jack is fine. You'll hear from him soon."

I wanted to say that I wasn't worried about Jack, that I knew he'd call or write when he got settled, but the words wouldn't come. Instead, I waved my hand in front of my face, swatting away what Iona had said.

"I'll see you tomorrow," was all my tongue could grab, as I waved at her all the way down the walkway, and kept on waving after she had closed the front gate behind her and started down the road, even after she had stopped looking back.

Everything here is the same as you left it. Don't worry about me. I'll be alright until we can be together again in Chicago . . .

It wasn't until after dinner, as the night started closing in on the sun, like a finger pressed soft against lips, shutting out light like sound, that I began to really notice his absence. And when I was alone in the dark of our bedroom, this was when I started to feel again. The hurt came alive.

I talk to the air, Jack, because that's all of you I've got left. That's all that you left. All your shirts are gone. Ella came by here wanting to borrow a clean one for Buddy to wear to dinner, but the drawer was empty. Nothing but the newspaper lining and a few mothballs rolling around. Seeing that, more than anything, Jack, made me mad. Not because I think you're planning to desert me like Elijah did Iona. I know you're a better man than that. But I'm mad, Jack, because you took the comfort of our house, my grits and eggs warming your belly, our last night together, when we couldn't stop touching and kissing, and I was so soft for you; you took all these things for your strength, packed them away in that big trunk. You got up this morning, loaded the trunk onto Jackson's old rusty truck, and rode away.

Did you ever stop to listen to my heartbeat, Jack? I would've gotten up with you, traveled all those hours in that truck. I would've lived in one room and found some place to work in Chicago if I had to. Whatever we had, Jack, would've been enough. But you didn't hear me. You couldn't see all that in me. You took everything for yourself. And wasn't nothing left for me but the scraps, bones I got to find a way of piecing back together.

Everyone misses you and we wish you well. You are in our prayers.
Your loving wife,
Anna

JACK 1942

Night is a curtain drawing back its heavy, sleepy-eyed veil for us to enter its darkest part. You should see how Jackson has his truck rigged up for this trip. He's nailed some flat boards along either side wall like benches, and right before we left Alabama he picked up a nice, sturdy piece of canvas from the hardware store. We all helped him pitch it up over the hatch. We out here looking like a band of outlaws in a covered wagon, or Indians in a roving teepee, but at least there's something over our heads.

Jackson say this is his new business, carrying folks out of Alabama to Chicago. I guess with eight men paying fourteen dollars apiece for the ride and gas, and him making two, three trips a month, he'll make himself a nice piece of money. But then Jackson always could find some way to make a dollar, with his slippery self. Remember how he charged us for the hay ride at the church picnic? Or the time he drove down to New Orleans and came back with all those hoodoo potions, then set up that stand in the back of the truck to sell them? Jack could've been selling swamp water for all we knew, but folks sure lined up. Had their money out even before they got to the table. Yes, Lord. That's one man'll never starve.

Maybe if I had stayed, I could've gotten into something like that, carrying folks up North. Seem like so many want to go these days. Jackson can't handle all those folks by himself. Daddy has that old truck sitting out in the garage. It needs work, but me and Buddy could've probably fixed it up. You know how much my little brother likes to work with his hands. He can fix anything with a motor. But no use bringing it up now, I'm already on my way. Alabama is a cloud of dust rising from beneath the tires. Road already traveled. A fine-grain memory settling in our wake.

Ride's been smooth so far. No trouble. Except for when we pulled out of Warrior, this car full of white boys, kids really, trailed us for about ten, fifteen miles, hollering out the window, nigger this, nigger that. Damn, these folks just don't want to let us go. And it isn't even *us* really. It's the idea of us. The shadow of us. The way they feel like we're always empty and waiting for them to fill us up. Like that dented pail hanging in the pantry that's held everything: rainwater, piss, milk, bleach, dirt, soapy water. Whatever you want to load in that bucket, it'll carry. That's what we've been all this time. I'm not saying that's all we've been, but that's how they look at us.

Shit. I don't want to talk about them anymore. I don't want to talk about us anymore. I want to talk about the air out here. I don't know what makes it so different from the air anyplace else, but, Anna, I swear it runs through me like water, just as cool and clear. Yet there's something heavy to it, stale even. It's the musty smell spilling out from between the pages of those old books your grandmother keeps in her parlor, or the scent of mothballs escaping like a sigh from Mama and Daddy's closet. And still it's more than this. There's something in this air that I can't name.

You remember that time in New Orleans, right before we got married? I had come from Alabama to help your daddy with his harvest from the orchard, and one morning, before we went out, your mama fixed us some biscuits with this red meat gravy for breakfast. You know how much I always enjoy your mama's cooking, but this was something else. That gravy left this feeling in me, like I knew I had eaten it before, but couldn't remember when or where. Soon as I got back to Alabama, I asked Mama if she had ever fixed gravy that way. And Anna, you know what she told me? She said that she never made it herself, but M'Dear, my grandmother, used to make it and mash the biscuits in it and feed it to us when we were babies just starting to teethe.

That's how this air feels to me right now. Like something long forgotten, teetering on the brink of remembrance. But wherever it comes from, whenever I breathed it before, it is doing wonders for all of us right here, right now. Cleaning us out. Folks keep getting up to spit out of the back of the truck. It's the South coming up. All the stuff we kept inside, that dried and crusted on our ribs, hardened around our joints and muscles. The air is moving through my body. No blocked passages. Sinuses clear. Nothing weighing down my chest. No medicine you can buy can give you this feeling. Anna, I wish you could know this freedom.

Nothing to do out here but talk and sleep. I'm lucky I got my flashlight, or else I wouldn't have been able to see to write, though I'm sure my heart would've guided my hand across the page without it (smile). One of the men on the truck knows how to sing any song you can think of. The music is like candlelight, giving us a moment of brightness, a glimpse back into the lives now falling away with the miles.

People like us, who've been in one place all our lives, we get accustomed to things. Like the sky hovering over our heads and homes. We come to think of it as *the* sky. And how we can walk every inch of our land or from one end of town to the other with our eyes closed, or clock the distance between our house and the next town, even the next state over by heart. Then we pack our picnics for the roadside and call ourselves traveling.

But out here, you begin to understand that your sky is just a little thumbnail piece of sky. You begin to understand that no matter where you stop, the roads just keep going on and going on. Anna, the largeness of the world makes me feel so small; as though the wind could pluck me up and blow me away, just one more particle riding this ancient air. What anchors me here?

Above us, the moon shimmers white as a store-bought egg against this night. We toss up the loudness of our voices and dreams like a gigantic stone trying to crack it, to anoint ourselves in its yolk of possibility. The knowledge that the moon can't be broken ignites the talk, makes a man stand up and pace the three steps from the front of the truck to the back, pounding his fist in his palm, spewing out his plans. But it is the idea that it can that makes him settle down in a corner and sift through the ashes of his thoughts, asking himself how he can make it work.

It is the idea that saves us; keeps us hanging together, leaning on one another, here in the darkness. The idea that we all have destiny locked up in our suitcases or stuffed deep in our back pockets, hidden in our socks, strapped around our waists. The idea that our hands can build a new life, can carve for ourselves and our families a small space out of this vastness.

Some of the men on this truck, I grew up with and know as well as my name. Some of them have traveled from Birmingham and other towns and states just to make this ride. There're some out here dressed in plain clothes, and some out here bleeding, as they say, dressed sharp enough for their own funeral. Maybe it is a funeral of sorts, because some of us are dead now to the South, and the South is dead in us; the turn of a key in the ignition enough to cut ties to the land, to family. But I am one of those stroking around the navel, feeling the long cord that keeps us connected to home. My heart is the softness in me, the place where roots have grown deep. I am one of those who still remember.

But any way we've come, we're here now, standing at the edge of this night, black as a spit-cleaned slate. Our reflections, shimmering on its surface, beckon, *Come on, why don't you? Just jump in.*

NATASHA TRETHEWEY
b. 1966

Her family's history in and around Gulfport, Mississippi, informs Natasha Trethewey's forthcoming first book *Domestic Work*, recently selected by Rita Dove for the inaugural Cave Canem Prize. Recipient of an NEA Grant, Trethewey writes equally well about her grandmother's life in love ("At the Station") and at work ("Speculation" and "Drapery Factory"). Poems like "Flounder" and "Saturday Matinee" also address struggles over identity as a "mixed girl"—"someone like me,/a character I can shape my life to"—often through a struggle over poetic form. Both formal questions and racial themes inform Trethewey's latest work, which is based on the photographs of E. J. Bellocq, a white photographer in turn-of-the-twentieth-century Storyville, New Orleans. Trethewey writes about and from the perspective of the mixed-race black prostitutes who Bellocq photographed and history has left unnamed; by personifying them as "Ophelia, nameless inmate of Storyville," Trethewey invokes the tragic dramatic monologues of Browning and Eliot as well as the American classical music, jazz.

AT THE STATION

The blue light was my blues,
and the red light was my mind.

—Robert Johnson

The man, turning, moves away
from the platform. Growing smaller,
he does not say

Come back. She won't. Each
glowing light dims
the farther it moves from reach,

the train pulling clean
out of the station. The woman sits
facing where she's been

She's chosen her place with care—
each window another eye, another
way of seeing what's back there:

heavy blossoms in afternoon rain
spilling scent and glistening sex.
Everything dripping green.

Blue shade, leaves swollen like desire.
A man motioning *nothing*.
No words. His mind on fire.

SPECULATION, 1939

First, the moles on each hand—
that's money by the pan—

and always, the New Year's cabbage
and black-eyed peas. Now this,
another remembered adage,
her palms itching with promise,

she swears by the signs—*money coming soon.*
But from where? Her left-eye twitch
says she'll see the boon.
Good—she's tired of the elevator switch,

those closed-in spaces, white men's
sideways stares. Nothing but
time to think, make plans
each time the doors slide shut.

What's to be gained from this New Deal?
Something finer like beauty school
or a milliner's shop—she loves the feel
of marcelled hair, felt and tulle,

not this all-day standing around,
not that elevator lurching up, then down.

DRAPERY FACTORY,
GULFPORT, MISSISSIPPI, 1956

She made the trip daily, though
later she would not remember
how far to tell the grandchildren—
Better that way.
She could keep those miles
a secret, and her black face
and black hands, and the pink bottoms
of her black feet
a minor inconvenience.

She does remember the men
she worked for, and that often
she sat side-by-side
with white women, all of them
bent over, pushing into the hum
of the machines, their right calves
tensed against the pedals.

Her lips tighten speaking
of quitting time when
the colored women filed out slowly
to have their purses checked,
the insides laid open and exposed
by the boss's hand.

              But then she laughs
when she recalls the soiled Kotex
she saved, stuffed into a bag
in her purse, and Adam's look
on one white man's face, his hand
deep in knowledge.

FLOUNDER

Here, she said, *put this on your head.*
She handed me a hat.
You 'bout as white as your dad,
and you gone stay like that.

Aunt Sugar rolled her nylons down
around each bony ankle.
And I rolled down my white knee socks
letting my thin legs dangle,

swinging them just above water
and silver backs of minnows

flitting here and there between
the sun spots and the shadows.

This is how you grip the pole
to cast your line out straight.
Now put this worm on your hook,
throw it out and wait.

She sat and spit tobacco juice
into a coffee cup,
hunkered down when she felt the bite,
jerked the pole straight up,

reeling and tugging hard at the fish
that wriggled and tried to fight back.
It's a flounder, and you can tell
'cause one of its sides is black.

The other side is white, she said.
It landed with a thump.
I stood there watching that fish flip-flop,
switch sides with every jump.

SATURDAY MATINEE

When I first see *Imitation of Life*,
the 1959 version with Lana Turner
and Sandra Dee, I already know the story
has a mixed girl in it—someone like me,
a character I can shape my life to.
It begins with a still of blue satin
upon which diamonds fall, slowly at first,
and then faster, crowding my television
with rays of light, a sparkling world.

In my room I'm a Hollywood starlet
stretched across my bed, beneath

a gold and antique white canopy,
heavy swags cut from fringed brocade
and pieced together—all remnants
of my grandmother's last job.
Down the hall, my mother whispers
resistance, my step-father's voice louder
than the static of an old seventy-eight.

Lana Turner glides on screen,
the camera finding her in glowing white,
golden haired among the crowd.
She is not like my mother, or
the mixed girl's mother—that tired black maid
she hires—and I can see why the mixed girl
wants her, instead, a mother always smiling
from a fifties magazine. She doesn't want
the run-down mama, her blues—

dark circles around the eyes,
that weary step and *hush-baby* tone.
My gold room is another world.
I turn the volume up, over the dull smack,
the stumbling for balance, the clutter of voices
in the next room. I'll be Sandra Dee,
and Lana Turner, my mother—our lives
an empty screen, pale blue, diamonds falling
until it's all covered up.

BELLOCQ'S OPHELIA

from a photograph circa 1912

In Millais's painting, Ophelia dies face-up,
eyes and mouth open as if caught in the gasp
of her last word or breath, flowers
and reeds growing out of her watery grave,
floating on the surface around her.
The young woman who posed lay in the pond

for hours, shivering, catching cold—perhaps
with fish tangling in her hair or nibbling
at a dark mole raised upon her white skin.
Ophelia's final gaze aims skyward, her palms
curling open as if she's just said, *Take me.*

I think of her when I see Bellocq's photograph—
a woman posed on a wicker divan, her hair
spilling over. Around her, flowers—
on a pillow, on a thick carpet. Even
the ravages of this old photograph
bloom like water lilies across her thigh.
How long did she hold there, this other
Ophelia, nameless inmate of Storyville,
naked, her nipples offered up hard with cold?

The small mound of her belly, the pale hair
of her pubis—these things—her body
there for the taking. But in her face, a dare.
Staring into the camera, she seems to pull
all movement from her slender limbs
and hold it in her heavy-lidded eyes.
Her body limp as dead Ophelia's,
her lips poised to open, to speak.

REBECCA WALKER
b. 1969

Rebecca Walker has turned her concerns with feminism and race into a life of activism and writing, editing both *To Be Real* (1995), essays on the state of feminism today, and recently completing a memoir about growing up biracial. As daugher of prizewinning author Alice Walker, Rebecca Walker has continued family tradition while looking toward the future. In this activist vein—partly to continue the feminist struggle and partly to combat a media perception of the inactivity of Generation X— Walker helped form 3rd Wave, an organization designed "to encourage, inspire, and facilitate young women's leadership and activism." Walker writes about her own struggle to come to terms with skin and its meanings in the following essay, confronting society, the body, and our often warped mirrors.

HIGHER YELLOW

I am a woman obsessed with skin—others' and especially my own. I squint into the mirror, trying not to see the scars left from my bout with the chicken pox, the wrinkles appearing branchlike across my once satiny forehead, the dark spots reminding me of all the times I was too weak to practice restraint. I turn this way and that in carefully modulated lighting, keeping a fair distance from the looking glass, not wanting to know what it cannot help but say: My skin is not flawless. It ages, chafes, erupts angrily. It sags where I would like it to be taut, pebbles where I want it to be smooth. Ultimately I acquiesce, accept the unacceptable—I am human, a mere mortal like everybody else—and turn out the light.

But there is something else, a remnant of self-hatred that doesn't go away so easily, that doesn't fade when the light dims. This other thing is what makes me cringe when my lover pulls my jeans over my hips in the half-light of our bedroom. It's what makes me burn myself in the sun year after year, and idolize Naomi Campbell no matter how much I commit to honoring my own beauty instead of someone else's. Spots, scars, bumps and keloids just skim the surface of my neurosis. The depth of my obsession with skin revolves around color, and what I perceive to be my lack thereof.

I have always been light. Pale. Honey-colored. Yellow. Near white. Olive. Neon. Sallow. Jaundiced. Pasty. And I have, for most of my adult life, hated being so. While aunts and cousins told me I had "good" hair and was lucky to be light, I felt gypped, like my mother didn't do her part while I was *in utero*, like her melanin gene was no match for my father's hearty Slavic-Jewish stock. Sure there were moments when light wasn't light enough and I wanted to have straight hair and a mom named Jane, but for the most part I have wanted to be darker, with fuller lips and thicker, more chocolatey thighs. Darker is what my mother is, what my lovers often are. Though I'm ashamed to admit to privileging any color over another, darkness is where I have located the beauty that moves me, the beauty that sets my stomach twitching and my mind dreaming. Darkness is graceful, mellifluous, haunting. Darkness is deeper, smarter, more lovable.

This narrative I've attributed to darkness goes on and on, as obsessive fantasy projections often do. It includes words like *community, belonging, stability, justice, righteousness* and *moral superiority*. In weak moments, my mind construes dark skin as a passport that facilitates admittance to cultures that do not disown, that never fail to claim. I imagine that the darkness provides a ready-made identity, a neat sense of knowing as clear and pure and self-evident as skin itself. I think that to be darker is to be on the "right" side of the powerless/powerful, oppressed/oppressor equation. To be black is to be part of the solution. Black Is Beautiful, remember? But what about beige, I wonder. Is beige beautiful, too? Or am I only half of the thing itself, muddied, watered down and eternally ambivalent?

I'm not the only one reading more into the surface of the body than meets the eye. In our North American culture, and indeed in cultures around the world, the body is a sign, a text to be read and interpreted. For each body part there is at least one widely accepted script already written, a bit of subtext that fleshes out, so to speak, the extremity in question. Long fingers foretell musical agility (and sexual prowess). Big hands and big feet promise a great big juicy you-know-what. Big breasts bespeak fertility. A long neck is elegant. Full lips are sexy. Fat is slothful. A big nose is awkward. Nappy is unhappy. Bald women are unfeminine.

While these scripts purport to be objective observations, they are more often propagandistic narratives, self-serving tracts that operate primarily in the construction of community, be it based on ideology, race, vocation or class, on a local, national or international level. As long as there is a standard of beauty, a set of positive attributes assigned arbitrarily to a particular set of body parts, there are two camps locked in a xenophobic embrace: those who have the good parts, and those who do not: those who are on the inside of the community, and those who, tragically, are relegated to its margins.

Enter the civil rights and feminist movements; the gay, lesbian, bisexual, and transgender movement; the Chicano student movement. Enter dyke, hip-hop, cholo, biker, skater, tribal, punk, and neo-Nubian aesthetics. Whether it's multiple piercings, femme girls with no hair, two-foot-high head wraps, or skin so covered with tats that the whole idea of clear and blemish free seems hopelessly naive, finally it is clear that as a result of artistic and political movements, new and different scripts are being written. The body—a blank page waiting for words—and beauty—a subjective idea looking for a location—have been liberated to meet up in a variety of unique and often surprising ways, Barbie, with her pert nose and shoulder-length blond hair, no longer reigns supreme.

Yet as we stand at the millennium, patting ourselves on the back for making it this far, so many of us still struggle to claim our shape and size, color and hue. What compels us to even consider ads exhorting us to reshape, resculpt and remake aspects of ourselves that our parents made just fine in the first place? It would be foolish to minimize the power of societal pressure, the waifish models screaming out from every newsstand and supermarket checkout line, nor can we ignore the self-esteem crisis permeating every cell of our culture. But I think there is something else, too, an overlooked by-product of the hysteria to control and commodify an image of ideal beauty: a crisis of the imagination, a dearth of stories, a shocking lack of alternative narratives.

Where are the stories that challenge the notion that perfect happiness can be found in a perfect body? Where are the anecdotes about learning to love parts of ourselves not because of how they look or how they measure up to Cindy Crawford, but because of how they feel to us, or how they tell a unique part of our personal history? Where, in this ongoing cultural discourse of body image, is the story of the lover who celebrated the hips we found too narrow or too wide, and caused us to see ourselves anew: the story of the Jewish nose that connects us to an ancestral past; the testimony about that "extra" thirty pounds that make us feel solid and abundant rather than slovenly and unattractive?

Recently, an article on body shapes caught my eye. "Death to Diets!" the headline caroled. "Figure out which of these four types you are, then follow this strategy for your best body ever." Apparently the more than two billion females on the planet fall into four neat but definitive categories. Forget genes, socioeconomic status, and individual soul destiny. According to this article, character, diet, and even career are indicated by the size and placement of your hips, breasts, and thighs. Wow! I thought, scanning to find a celebrity body that matched my own. Think of all the money I could have saved on therapy!

The fact is that we say a lot about how the standard of beauty needs to change, and even find some creative ways to revision it, but I know that in my own life and, I presume, in the lives of many others, that abstract and theoretical discussion simply has not done the trick. Rigorous deconstruction may lay the new foundation for personal change, but it does not rebuild the house. That work calls for new materials; we need to do more than articulate what is wrong with the standard; we need to document and tell our very personal stories of confronting that standard. I want to read new scripts based not on what the culture dictates but on what we have come to know and experience in the intimate moments of our day-to-day lives. The body tells its own story, and it is usually not the one you expect. We need to listen for and nurture those stories, the stories that are true.

Until recently I, too, have been decidedly without vision when it comes to accepting, rather than outright hating, my color. For most of my life I have been unable to love my honey thighs, to smile back into my fair-skinned face because I lacked a story I could live with, a story that made sense to me. I have hated my proximity to whiteness, the colonizing tinge that taints and marks me as an outsider and pushes me to the periphery of brown and black worlds I have longed to call my own. Looking down the length of my barely brown body, I have felt revulsion, a horrifying lack that runs deep. Years of comparing myself to brown-skinned sisters with bangles and curves, abundant head wraps and well-shaped thighs has left me dissatisfied in my angularity and running a constant critique of the sharpness of my profile and the unwillingness of my flesh.

But I have finally begun to tell a better story. It is far from a complete or cohesive narrative, but it begins and ends with my maternal grandmother, her beloved place in her southern rural community, my grandfather's abiding love for her, the upright way she walked, her wide and easy smile. By the time I knew her, she was already a woman's woman, not slight but solid, and with an air of experience so profound that when she spoke her mind—which was often—everyone present listened with their full attention, even as their eyes turned toward the television, or their hands moved busily over the stove.

She was a woman of appetite, and could, even paralyzed by stroke, cruise through a plate of chicken legs and collard greens with grace and appreciation. Even though I have always, my whole life since I was a little girl and holding her hand in the Kingdom Hall, loved and admired her, I have of late begun to notice and prize our similarities. We share full pinkish brown lips and what is called yellow skin but is more like a light, light oak; we both turn our heads to the side in photographs, a gesture that highlights our high, well-defined cheekbones. We both love the natural beauty of the earth and turn our dark eyes to it as often as we can, not letting any little creature go unnoticed, unseen, unappreciated. When I look at her photograph, which hangs above my desk, I see fullness, a life lived and enjoyed. I do not see a lack. I see a haunting, regal beauty. I recognize a smoldering intensity that sparks, too, behind my own eyes.

And there are other women. Lena Horne is in the story too, also staring down from a photo above my desk with an awesome fearlessness. In this Carl van Vechten photo, she is in her early twenties, not much older than I was when I found the postcard in a Vermont bookstore. I imagine she is out for a day in the country, her glowing well-scrubbed face facing forward, her small brown eyes smiling honestly and shamelessly into the camera. There is an uprightness, a sad, hard-won pride in her bearing, a moving wistfulness in her startlingly direct stare that I find familiar and reassuring: My path has been walked before. I am not alone. I am kin to these striking, self-made women, and because of this, granted a new and fragile pride before the looking glass, a surety of belonging I have never known.

My lover is in the story, too, tender and attentive, telling me again and again, as many times as it takes, that I am sexy and beautiful and perfectly complete, my beloved who likes my color and the fact that I am neither black nor white but both, some land in the middle that is, miraculously, not too threatening to love. And there are others: the striking light-skinned sisters on the subway who move with an awkward grace, the wiry-haired and olive-skinned brother/friend who wraps his strong arms around me, enveloping me in a musky and powerful but culturally undefined masculinity, the playful and self-possessed biracial children of dear and daring friends.

These affirming bits are punctuated by moments I have more and more often when I look down the length of my body and feel not disgust but a tender gratitude for what I do have: skin that covers and protects, that loves to be lotioned and stroked, that is responsive to touch and fundamentally resilient. Skin that is a record, a kind of testimony to who I am, and what my history is. I am the child of a black mother and a white father; I fell from my bicycle when I was four and got this scar; this mark came from a trip to Cuba and this one from a fight with some girls in the Bronx. My body is its own kind of camera, and what it records reminds me that I am constantly changing, moving from day to day and year to year, toward the final physical change of this life, when my body finally falls away, when my body speaks for itself the final chapter.

I know I have a long way to go before I can unequivocally groove on my paleness, but I consider getting this far to be a major accomplishment. To look at the ways we judge and contort ourselves is a radical and self-affirming act in a culture where altering oneself for admission and approval is the norm. To do the actual work of reprogramming, rewriting the words that we have been taught go with the picture, is a much more strenuous and exacting task. That journey to survival is mapped on the body's surface and begins as we extend to our most hated features the first tremblings of compassion.

ANTHONY WALTON

b. 1960

Anthony Walton burst onto the national stage with his 1989 article "Willie Horton and Me" in *The New York Times Sunday Magazine*. That essay examined the stereotypical black threat invoked in the election campaign of President Bush and its relation to Walton's growing self-awareness as a black man in America. Since then, Walton has moved further into poetry and nonfiction, both editing *Every Shut Eye Ain't Asleep: An Anthology of Poetry by African Americans Since 1945* with Michael S. Harper and helping to write the autobiography of the Reverend Al Sharpton.

Walton's book *Mississippi: An American Journey* (1996) considers the complex legacy of his parents' home state (and its state of mind) through memoir, cultural history, and even poetry. By confronting southern history and his own family heritage, Walton explores his roles as "a black person, a black male, a colored man, a Negro, and sometimes, certainly sometimes in Mississippi, a nigger." In the book's last section, "Walkin' Blues," excerpted here, Walton travels with his father through the state his father left years before, telling a story much like the writer's Richard Wright's.

FROM *MISSISSIPPI*

By the time I went to homecoming at Ole Miss I had traversed Mississippi for several years, had renewed relationships with family and made
new friends, had read volumes of books and documents, and had,
through all of this, endured a steady darkening of my outlook. American
history, and the future possibilities it implied, were becoming in my eyes
a net of irony and sorrow from which I could not free myself. I was a
young man, with a young person's taste for certainty and closure. But
in sifting the complexities of Mississippi I found that each question I
answered branched into three more, into infinitudes I could not grasp.

I couldn't believe how naive I had been about both history and its
processes, and could not reconcile my growing knowledge with what I'd
previously thought about my own life. On one level I felt privileged and
lucky, the winner, as a black American, of a kind of lottery; but on a
much deeper and darker level, I felt undeserving of my privilege. This
feeling of unworthiness had grown from the initial impulse that led me
to Mississippi, an impulse I'd thought my search would stay, and its
increase had much to do, I realized, with my father.

From the things I'd learned I was beginning to see more fully than
ever before just what my father had accomplished. He had created my
privilege when he himself had none. My life was something he had
dreamed and hoped and planned for, an extension of his own; and in
order to see and understand myself I first would have to see him. My
father's life was the Rubicon of my own imagination. Yet for years I had
hardly considered him a part of my story; rural Mississippi had no clear
ties to suburban Chicago. But I realized now that the one would not
exist for me without the other.

What had happened to my father in Mississippi? How had he become
the taciturn, often remote, yet unflaggingly resolute and loyal man he
was? I needed to find out, and was scared to, concerned that I, in whom
he had put so much faith, was not worthy.

*   *   *

When my father boarded a Greyhound bus in Memphis, Tennessee, one warm Saturday evening in the summer of 1952, he had forty dollars and one suitcase, which contained everything he owned: two cotton suits, two pairs of pants and three shirts, underwear, socks, a toothbrush, baking soda, soap and a Bible, the only book he had ever owned. He was seventeen years old.

The suitcase was a step up. When Claude had arrived in Memphis from Mississippi two years earlier, he carried a shopping bag containing his work clothes, a denim shirt and a pair of blue jeans. Everything else he owned he'd worn: his "good jeans," a cotton T-shirt, his sturdy boots and a denim jacket. He had no money, having spent all his savings on the bus ticket from Holly Springs: he was dependent upon his cousin, Edgar, who had promised a couple of weeks' lodging and help in finding a job, and on the kindness of strangers.

In Memphis Claude had worked construction, retrofitting a building from an aircraft plant to a paper factory, then in an automotive repair shop rebuilding engines, carburetors and the like. He has said about leaving Memphis, "I felt that my time was up there. There didn't seem to be any interest in having black people employed on any kind of steady basis. Memphis was a permanent recession for black men." Claude had cousins in the North, and on trips home they flaunted evidence of the promising things he'd heard about Chicago all his life. "Everybody in the North seemed to have a car, they had better clothes. I wanted to get in on that action. I wanted to try for some security. In Memphis they always treated you like a boy. I wanted to be a man. I was tired of the racism, the steady meanness."

So Claude set off on a journey, an odyssey even: in his search for a home he was leaving everything he knew and carrying only his memories. Those details, the specific slights, injuries, and humiliations he'd suffered as a black man in the South, things he would recount to his children about forty and fifty years later, would supply the fire he needed to endure lonely, barely literate years in Illinois, working in foundries and digging ditches, trying to figure out what to do next. He was one of millions of blacks who were willing, or forced, to leave Mississippi, headed for Chicago, Detroit, Milwaukee, Los Angeles. Robert Johnson sings, "I woke up this mornin' feelin' round for my shoes/I know about that, I got them old walkin' blues." Suddenly, strangely, I see my father as a young man, stuck in a dead-end job in Memphis, Tennessee, plot-ting, plotting, plotting his next move.

Claude was born in 1935 in Marshall County, near the town of Holly Springs. In a story much like Richard Wright's, he started his life in poverty and degradation on a cotton plantation, born to uneducated and sometimes violent parents. His grandparents on both sides had been born into slavery and had become sharecroppers during Reconstruction. Some of Claude's uncles and cousins worked in construction, developing their own business years after he left. Claude, with only a grammar-school education, unknowingly traced Wright's path from Mississippi to Memphis, then Chicago, in search of liberty and something that could be called a better life.

On a humid summer afternoon we sat in the shade of a maple tree in a hill pasture southwest of Holly Springs—the site of Claude's gram-mar school, a wooden one-room building now nearly collapsed and faded from white to gray.

"Dad," I said, "tell me about what it was like when you were growing up down here."

"Ain't nothing to tell." Among black males of a certain age, reticence is a way of life, and I've never known whether my father truly dislikes talking about the past, or whether the habit of few words has simply become part of who he is. As he likes to say, "I did not get to be fifty and black by being stupid." By which he means silence is sometimes, especially in Mississippi, the easiest way for a black man to survive.

"What's the first thing you remember?"

"Bigotry." He said this quietly, as if there were nothing else to report and this single word explained it all.

"You were conscious of that as a little boy?"

He laughed. "Even when I was little, my mother would tell me about the things white people did, the things they wouldn't let black people do." This he said with an air of matter-of-factness. "They did not allow black men good jobs where they could make any money; I remember my mother telling me that, and that we couldn't drink out of the drinking fountains on the corners in town that the white people used. I remember her showing me the one in the courthouse that the colored could use. When we were in town we couldn't use the bathroom, we always had to go to some out-of-the-way place."

"White people did all this?"

"*Hell,* yes. They didn't want us to live as they lived, or have the means to."

"How old were you when you figured this out?"

"Three or four." He became, curiously, expressionless. "All I can say it did for me at the time was make me think that white people were awful mean."

"Do you think that now?"

"That was my thinking at the time. They had no right—I don't know that I could have figured it out it in those terms then, but in my heart that's what I felt, that they were unfair and unkind. I didn't think I could treat anyone like that. I knew there were rules black people had to follow, and I knew I was going to have to follow those rules as well, unless I found a way whereby white people wouldn't or couldn't lynch me like I'd heard they'd done to any number of black folks who wouldn't obey, or were considered to be unruly, or a threat. I didn't like it, but I can't say that as a child I knew what I was going to do about it."

Claude paused, then continued in a monotone. "It was a matter of getting old enough, then I was going to find someplace. I didn't know exactly where it would be, but that place was where I was going to move, someplace where I wouldn't be brutalized by men I didn't even know."

"What's the first bad thing you remember happening to you?"

He shrugged, then spoke as if the events he described had happened to someone else. "There were so many things that could happen and did. At school we would get our books and in the cover there would be this person's name; our schoolbooks were always used books. I remember this was like the second or third grade. There would be a person's name in there, and grade, and race, and it would always be 'white.' "

I expressed surprise. He chuckled, without smiling. "Sure. We always got the old books, the white kids got 'em first. And there'd always be pages missing, where if you read two chapters relative to something, you couldn't finish. If the third chapter completed the subject matter, then that chapter would be deliberately cut out, or the pages torn up, and you'd never know how it finished. I didn't understand it, why it was happening, but I talked to my parents and teachers and they said there was this school superintendent, a white woman, and she did this on purpose. She also never gave us enough books, or all the units in a particular subject. I think it was to keep us from doing enough work to get a high school diploma. She succeeded in my case.

"In those days black kids didn't ride the bus, we walked, sometimes miles. The white kids did get to ride, and the reason we knew it was because they'd ride past us on their buses and insult us, or yell something racist and laugh, and you'd be there out in the rain. This was 1941, '42, '43, in there. It was a little country school, one room, one teacher for nine or ten grades. The teacher handled all of them with the help of the older children. She had a lot of kids, as many as two hundred, and she had it organized so that some of them would be outside playing while others were getting their math class, then she'd switch. It was kind of amazing when I think about it. She did this all day, working her way up through the children. She'd use the older girls who could read and write well to fill in and help out."

"When did you decide to leave?"

"I had probably started to hear about Chicago, but I didn't know where it was or what it was like. I heard that black people lived there, that they seemed to live pretty good. They had things we didn't have. Cars, plumbing, electricity, money. So I knew I was going to go away to one of those cities where blacks could make it better. In Mississippi I was watching people work twelve hours a day for two dollars. This was like '46,'47,'48. You had to be on the truck or in the field at six o'clock and you didn't get off until six. And your travel time was on *you*. So sometimes, if the work was far enough away, it was really fourteen hours for two dollars. I figured if I had to work, why not go where I could make some money? I was only ten or eleven at that point, I wasn't old enough to leave, but I was planning on it by the time I was sixteen, eighteen at the oldest. If I worked and got paid, I figured I could get some of the things we didn't have." He stopped to think. "I couldn't see letting white people continually take advantage of me. I had to leave Mississippi because there was nothing I could do about that there, there was no way to confront them.

"Let me tell you a story. I worked for this man, his name was Smith. I think he was a Klansman, he had so much hatred in him. We were digging foundations to houses; he was paying fifty cents an hour. We dug five or six of these foundations, me and another guy, in two or three days. Smith wanted you to *get at it*. Ninety-, hundred-degree temperatures. This was July and August, after we'd laid by the crops. I remember we finished on a Wednesday, then it was time for the white men to come in and take over, pour the foundation, do the carpentry; they wouldn't let us do that. Anyway, Smith said he'd pay us on Friday, so I went over there about ten o'clock in the morning and asked him for my money. He got upset, said he would pay me when he paid everybody else, but I wanted to ride up to Memphis with my cousins and they were leaving. Besides, I wasn't one of his regulars. So he went inside, wrote the check, threw it out on the ground and told me I'd never work for him again, in fact, I was never to set foot on his property again. I figured, 'Why take this?' "

"Did you ever want to hurt white people?"

He flashed an ironic smile. "Most definitely. I hated white people, with a passion." Then the good Baptist in him reasserted itself. "Not all of them, of course. If I happened to know that the man was a good man and was straight and would treat me human, give me water if I was working for him, maybe even food, then I didn't have any problem with him. One man I worked with would even have his wife fix me something to eat. In those days that was important because a lot of the time black people only had food like greens and black-eyed peas and it's hard to carry that for lunch. A man like that, who treated you better, he might want you to stay in your place, but you didn't think about it much, at least he acknowledged that you were a person. I didn't think about him being white. But people that I knew were racists, that did not care for blacks—well, I didn't care for them. I hated them as much as they hated me. I often had visions of wiping out the entire white community."

As I listened I was stunned, because for so long I'd seen my father as a sincere Christian, virtually a pacifist, and now wondered if his dedication to nonviolence had been more a strategy than a belief. I asked why he and the other blacks had never lashed out.

"There was nobody to organize us. The people around me, my peer group, were as young and inexperienced as me. We weren't advanced enough, educated. We didn't know where to get the guns, the ammunition. We didn't know how to plan it so we could win. What was the use of starting something like that, getting caught and getting hung?"

"But you thought of it?"

"Hell, yes. There were times when somebody white did something to you that really hurt, really stung. You'd want to hurt them back. When

I got older I understood that the reason white folks were so sure of themselves in their brutality to us was because the government, the politicians, the merchants and the rich people was all behind it. It came down from the top, from Washington, D.C., right on down: *Keep them niggers in their place.*"

When we were children, my brother and sister and I loved music. We still do, but not with the same fanatical purity that comes from not having much else on your mind. We'd wake up and put on records first thing in the morning: Aretha Franklin, B. B. King, Andrae Crouch and the Disciples or Al Green. We'd spend summer afternoons on the porch happily boogalooing to "Tighten Up," "Cold Sweat," "I Want You Back" and "Jimmy Mack." At night we'd lie awake in the dark and listen to the radio—WCFL, WGRT, WLS and WVON—until our parents yelled at us from the living room to knock it off. My father would sit in the yard with his friends sometimes, shaking his head and saying, "Them children *wake up* with the blues, sing the blues all day and then sleep with 'em." We'd just laugh and say, "Dad, what do you know about it?"

Memories of those days, and the irony of our arrogance, were in my thoughts as I drove down the rough and winding old Mississippi Highway 4 with Claude. My siblings and I actually thought our father knew nothing about "the blues," or the music we called by that name, which was really pop music. Whenever we'd impugn his understanding he'd only grunt or say something like "Everything in its place," or in a good mood he'd laugh and say, "I hope I never know as much about it as y'all." In a bad mood he'd say, "I have forgotten more about the blues than you will ever know." This last was, I now realize, closest to the truth.

What *did* I know about the blues? What could I? The landscape before me, Marshall County, five miles out of Holly Springs, couldn't have looked much different when Claude lived here in a tin-roofed log cabin tucked away in a bottom on Howard Jones's plantation. The land consists of rolling shallow hills covered with kudzu, hay fields, scrub fields, pine trees, oak trees and, in the bottoms, cleared fields bristling with endless cotton. The plants stood as small green shoots this May afternoon but were already in need of chopping. All of this was canopied by a huge blue sky, so bright the sunlight seemed to come from everywhere. In places, the kudzu—a weedy vine, *Pueraria lobata*, that can easily spread a foot a day—had overgrown everything, giving the landscape the feel of a science-fiction movie or a children's book, kudzu everywhere. The hilly vista was gentle and pretty—and full of rage; specifically, now, the dark undercurrent of my father's.

"Last time I was on this road, it was gravel," Claude said matter-of-factly. He had avoided Mississippi—excluding official occasions, mostly weddings and funerals—not enjoying the trip as my mother did and certainly not relishing his memories. *"I call it 'sippi 'cause I don't miss it,"* he'd often say. He had been back to Holly Springs, but never out here to the Jones farm. We stopped the car on a flat stretch of road, got out and walked down a muddy path. "We lived over there." Claude pointed down into the recesses of the bottom, where the ramshackle remains of a tenant cabin stood. Then he moved his left arm from noon to ten o'clock to indicate another run-down structure a short distance from the first. "Uncle Isaac lived down there." He pointed in a forty-five-degree angle away from the cabin at a small and faded, though still inhabited, white frame house on the top of a nearby hill. "And Big Mama"—his grandmother—"up there."

This was the place, the landscape, the image that had been in his mind, his memory, as he struck out from Mississippi for Chicago more than forty years earlier. He had been thinking about these hills and trees and fields spreading on either side of a winding gravel road that, aside from being paved, has not changed much since that time. My father's life had not immediately eased after he left Mississippi; he eventually went north, joined the air force, was honorably discharged and returned to Chicago, where he began working at a taxing factory job, a job he held for the next thirty-eight years, at which he still is working. I often wondered what could drive a man to work that hard that long, and here in Mississippi all around us were the roots of his ferocity and discontent.

Earlier that day we'd been up Highway 4 on the other side of Holly Springs, where the road swings northeast toward the town of Ashland and Benton County. The physical landscape is the same out there, rolling hills, hay fields and ever-thickening clumps of trees, all covered in kudzu. We chose to take that road because Claude had worked on the crew that put in the highway, his first job away from the farm. He was fourteen when he started in 1949, and the crew built the approximately forty-mile stretch that snakes through the Holly Springs National Forest to Ripley.

"Our job," Claude said, "was to plant the sod and grass along the side of the highway. The black men did all the heavy work, the dirty work, planting, tamping the sod into place. We had a machine, a big heavy tool that tamped the sod into place, and you had to be strong to lift it all day. The white guys drove the trucks. They were from the Delta, and they didn't believe in calling you by your name, they'd either call you 'boy' or 'nigger.' It didn't make them no difference." He half laughed, half winced at the memory. "They were a loud and rough bunch. It didn't seem to me like they did anything but booze and chase women and fight, and sit on the top of the truck and tell you what to do. When they got to the site, they felt they were on break and wouldn't do any-thing but wait for the blacks to unload. Some days the temperature would be as hot as one hundred one, one hundred two, one hundred three degrees, even one hundred four; you could bet that every single day it would be at least ninety-five degrees. We worked out here from April to September."

This sort of thing had fascinated and intimidated me about him even before I became fully aware of what he'd been through. When I was fourteen, my chief worry was not embarrassing myself on the freshman football team; Claude had been out in the world doing a man's job with men. "Dad," I said, "this may be a dumb question, but why were you out working?"

"We needed the money." His standard answer.

"Don't you think you were too young to be out on your own like that?"

"Yep."

"Then why'd you do it?"

He was calm. "I'm trying to tell you, I had no choice."

"But why not stay on the farm?"

"There wasn't any money on the farm. I could make thirty dollars a week for six days' work on the road, five dollars a day for ten hours. I'd worked jobs before, two dollars a day for a twelve-hour day. Living on Howard Jones's place was like being under a tyrant. He specialized in keeping black folks down. He took everything we earned. You had to buy everything from his store. He accounted for *everything*, kept the records. Some of the black folks couldn't read and write, some of them didn't think they needed to. Mr. Jones had gained their confidence. I used to think he was a hypnotist, that he could hypnotize black folks and make 'em think he was a good guy. Deep down inside you didn't believe that, but on the surface of your mind, maybe as a way of not facing reality, you'd want to believe whatever he'd told you. He had ways of making it seem like you were working together, you and him, like you were partners in the farm, and you'd accept less, even if you knew he was lying."

"How did *you* know he was lying?"

"I'd had other little jobs, working for white people in town. They were the ones that could pay to have work done in those days. I'd trim hedges, around the sidewalk, maybe somebody'd pay you a dollar and a half. They might cut their own grass but they might not like to trim, so I'd come along with my clippers and my hoe and I'd get that dollar and a half. Some of 'em would let me cut the grass. You'd have to hit as many as you could before noon, because if you waited much past one o'clock, somebody else'd be done cut that yard."

I laughed. "You and the other little black kids were in competition as businessmen?"

Claude didn't find this funny. "That happened all the time. If I could get to these places by the time I needed to be there, I could make six or seven dollars. This was when I was ten years old. I could make more cutting grass in half a day than I could working twelve hours for Howard Jones. I figured it out. I did not like it. I knew I could do better. You could make ten or twelve dollars a week off three, four yards. That was good money for a kid. The highway was the only job I could get that summer. I didn't think the man would hire me because I was skinny and didn't have no weight, but I went and asked him and he said, 'Get on the truck.'

"One day I pointed out to the foreman a place where a mistake had been made and needed fixing." Claude took a sharp breath. "One of his assistants said to him, 'This nigger knows everything.' All I recall from the rest of that is a cold chill going through me. Why was I a 'nigger' when all I was trying to do was work hard, do a good job? That day changed me. I just wanted to make a living and not depend on anybody, not be dependent on anybody else.

"To get to a day's job we had to ride on a flatbed truck with them hillbillies driving sixty, seventy miles an hour down them gravel roads like they were trying to knock us off. We could barely hang on, we'd be thinking we were going to be thrown off the truck. They had no respect for us at all, and any way they could think of to humiliate or embarrass us, they took it.

"When there was one around, he would be nice, but when there were three or four, then all of 'em got filthy-mouthed and disrespectful. Suddenly, anything that happened was 'the nigger's fault.' I think they thought that we might jump on one of 'em, plus, when they were all together, they wanted to impress each other and show off. They liked to say to each other, 'You sure know how to handle them niggers.' They were cowards. They knew they had the upper hand. They were white trash who got treated like upper class and it went to their heads. In them days any white man, whether he could read or write, was above any black man, whether he had a college diploma or a master's or a Ph.D. The black man would have to be beneath the white man and address him as 'sir,' whether he could read or write or anything else. But I learned something out there working on that highway: I learned that I could do whatever they could do; I learned that I could have put that road in if I had the same equipment, the trucks and graders and bulldozers. It gave me confidence. I wasn't as afraid as I had been. The work wasn't that hard and they weren't that smart. And I was able to provide money for my family at a time when we needed it."

Back in the fields and woods where he had grown up, Claude waved his arm in a wide sweep across the horizon. "Black folks owned this land! A black man named Good Nunnally, between 1880, '90, and 1920, managed to get all this land. He had eight or nine families working for him and he was good to them, but his son managed to mess it all up. White folks tricked him, they'd say, 'Virgil,' that was his name, 'Virgil, whatever you need, come and let us know.' Virgil'd go to the bank to borrow a thousand dollars, and the white folks would encourage him to take even more. He run up twenty or thirty thousand at the bank like that. Then they called his loan. A lot of people had been slaves here on this land and somehow his father had bought it from the owners, but white folks got it back."

"What was an average day like on the farm?"

"From the time I was big enough to get the mules, we worked from about four-thirty in the morning until nine at night, taking off about an hour from twelve until one or one-thirty in the middle of the day."

This was taking me back to the talks and riffs of my childhood, him telling me about how hard he'd had it in Mississippi, and how, by contrast, I "had it made." I asked, "What kind of work?"

"Well, I'd get up and get dressed and go out to look for the mules— they'd be out in the pasture—with a stick in my hands to make sure I didn't get bit by a snake." He laughed. "I had this long stick I'd bang through the weeds so anything in there would come out. Once I found the mules, I'd bring 'em back to the house and feed 'em, look 'em over and stuff. Then maybe I'd cut some wood so my mother could finish breakfast, or feed the hogs, whatever needed to be done. Then I'd go in and get something for breakfast, which usually wasn't much. We'd leave for the field by six-thirty, trying to be there by seven, and then we'd work until lunch."

"What was field work like?" This was an aspect of Mississippi black life I could not imagine, even beyond the racism. This inability indicates how privileged, relatively, my generation of blacks has been.

Claude walked a few steps down an incline into a stand of cotton. "Come here." I followed. "This was it. We'd plow, plant, chop cotton. You see this cotton here? Well, weeds start springing up and you have to keep 'em down, so the sunlight can get to the seedlings. That's chopping cotton, out there with a hoe all day."

I shook my head. "How long do you have to do that?"

"Chopping was usually the month of June, in there, until the plant was big enough. Sometimes there was other work, cutting trees and clearing land for more fields, but we'd usually done that in advance. We'd come home at noon to eat what we called dinner, and we'd rest until one o'clock. If it was really hot, over one hundred degrees, we'd wait a little bit longer. We'd have our sun hats on and we'd work until six or seven, sometimes dark, until we got done with whatever it was we had to do."

United States Highway Number 61 is a black asphalt ribbon rolling straight through the quiet, squalid towns of the Mississippi Delta: Tunica, Clarksdale, Alligator and Shelby, Mound Bayou, Cleveland, Leland and Rolling Fork. Towns along the highway tend to consist of a train station across from a gas station and several stores—hardware, grocery, five-and-dime. Nearby towns off the highway usually contain a general store, a garage and several houses ranging in form from splendid to abandoned. Whatever its appearance, a Delta town is likely as not to have a cotton gin.

Highway 61 rides out of Memphis through DeSoto County, Mississippi, and hits the vast cotton, milo and soybean fields of the Delta in the next county, Tunica, fields stretching from there all the way to Vicksburg. The land is flat, the road is straight, the sky huge, a high, pale blue, and the horizon endless. For me and for many others, this is the hard-core Mississippi, home of Robert Johnson, *Cat on a Hot Tin Roof*, the poorest sixteen or seventeen counties in the country; the place where, as my father might say darkly, "you had to know the difference between 'come here,' and 'sic 'em.'" It's the place the writer Richard Ford calls "the South of the South."

But the Delta is also a place where ordinary, daily life goes on, amid millions of acres of farmland, some of the most fertile on the planet. This land was wrested from swamp and river bottom by men like Will Dockery, planters and railroaders and merchants of such ferocity they carved empires out of the wilderness where they reigned over thousands of men and women, black men and women, men and women like my parents and grandparents and their ancestors who drained the land, cleared it, built dikes and levees and then tilled it, raising the cotton that changed the world. Those men and women also invented the blues, which would likewise change the world, though they would never see that change, and wouldn't get paid for it either.

As I rode down Highway 61 with my father, thoughts on the confluence of the words "travel" and "travail," and on how those words were connected to the abstractions of black folks, cotton and the blues, played through my mind like some hallucinogenic, experimental film, images of black people traveling to and from the fields, the fields full of cotton, the white man's white gold, the work day after day, the constant dream of Chicago or Los Angeles, of getting away. In several places Highway 61 is paralleled by the tracks of the Illinois Central Railroad, another dream and road to freedom. Looking down the highway, over the fields and train tracks with Claude next to me in the car, I began to understand that his regular wisecrack, "It wasn't Lincoln who freed the slaves, it was the Illinois Central," was more than a joke. I also heard Robert Johnson's lines again:

I woke up this mornin' feelin' round for my shoes
I know about that, I got them old walkin' blues. . . .

Clarksdale is the seat and largest town of Coahoma County. It's a "Saturday town," the center of commerce and social life for a twenty-mile radius, and has been home, at various times, to men as disparate and as influential in American culture as Tennessee Williams and McKinley "Muddy Waters" Morganfield. The town contains comfortable middle-class neighborhoods of brick-and-wood bungalows under mature oak and dogwoods, horribly decrepit blocks of shotgun houses, worn-looking housing projects, and, just west of downtown, a district of splendid mansions still kept with exacting care. As it passes through Clarksdale, Highway 61 is bordered by strip malls, gas stations and shopping plazas. The intersection of 61 and U.S. 49, rumored to be the legendary "crossroads" where Robert Johnson sold his soul to the devil, is now marked by a Kentucky Fried Chicken, a dilapidated gas station and several boarded-up storefronts.

Claude and I had driven to Clarksdale to visit the Delta Blues Museum, located downtown in a second-floor room in the older of the two buildings that make up the Carnegie Library. The museum holds bookshelves of blues literature and scholarship; glass display cases containing rare records, instruments and documents; and, lining its walls, paintings and photographs of blues greats. The museum collection also contains a bronze bust of Muddy Waters and a mockup of a statue of him that will be a feature of the planned future museum. In light of the fundamental role the blues, along with its stepchild jazz, has played in American culture, the museum appears oddly small and obscure, as if Charley Patton, Skip James, Kokomo Arnold, Robert Johnson, Muddy Waters, Howlin' Wolf et al. were destined to be neglected not only in life but even in monuments to their achievement.

When one listens to Jimi Hendrix, the Rolling Stones, Led Zeppelin, Bonnie Raitt, Prince or their legions of imitators, one is hearing permutations and echoes of the Delta bluesmen. Elvis Presley's first hit, "That's All Right, Mama," is a direct copy of an earlier record by Arthur "Big Boy" Crudup; Bob Dylan's pose of bemused resignation as cultural stance is at least partly traceable to the styles and, more important, the *attitudes* of blues musicians and their songs. Those attitudes gradually became a permanent way of being an American as young whites in the fifties, sixties and seventies became aware (as blacks always had been) of the treachery and duplicity inherent in American society. On a more superficial level, "I got the blues," "I'm a little blue" and scores of other folk sayings have become shorthand fixtures of our culture, and it all started or at least cohered here in the Delta, in the regions around Clarksdale and farther south, where the field hollers and work chants of slaves, sharecroppers, prisoners and heavy laborers evolved into the art form that would become rock and roll, the voice of young America and the world.

Standing there in that room dedicated to the blues, my father and I talked of how far these men and women had gone beyond Mississippi, and of how at the time no one could have predicted their reach. The blues had not been a large part of my father's life; I think he always regarded them like whiskey and voodoo, as a form of darkness, best avoided in a considered existence. He'd listen to a little B. B. King, but even this was tempered by my mother's taste, which came from the other side of the spiritual tracks in the black musical community. Over there were gospel and hymns, the patron saints being Thomas Dorsey and Mahalia Jackson, not Robert Johnson and Bessie Smith. This spiritual divide had been a source of mild conflict during my childhood and adolescence: Dorothy was constantly leading me and my siblings along the straight and narrow, backing this course with stiff doses of "Standing on the Promises," "Trust and Obey," "Just a Closer Walk with Thee" and "Amazing Grace"; we were *much* more interested in "Love and Happiness," "I Can't Quit You, Baby," "When a Man Loves a Woman" and "Ain't No Sunshine."

To be fair, my mother could, in certain moods, enjoy a good blues song, but she still felt that the blues were the Devil's Music, one step from perdition, a grave threat to the salvation of any soul. By contrast, I thought that the blues reflected what life was like *here*, on this plane of existence, and that the hereafter could take care of itself. This conflict, between the sinner begging forgiveness on Sunday morning and the sinner longing for another Saturday night—often one and the same person—is a commonplace of black life in America.

But as I've gotten older, I've seen that the conflict between sinner and would-be saint is highly nuanced, and the two states seem part of the same larger whole. To me, increasingly, the blues shadow everything, my own worldview and those of both my parents. When Dorothy was in church, wasn't she fighting, or running from, Robert Johnson's hellhound? When Claude was a boy on Howard Jones's plantation pining and plotting his escape, did he not have the walking blues *and* the dream of a kind of salvation?

❑

WALKING WITH MY FATHER THROUGH THE FIELDS OF HIS YOUTH

Muddy red fallow this year,
    he stares as though these acres
were bristling green, demanding
    his hoe, plow and back.

The sweat of fifty years
    ago wells from the cloud
of his brow as he says
    a white man name of Howard

Jones owned all this,
    his gesture sweeping across
the sky. We used to do it
    by hand, Howard Jones

wanted you to work, boy,
    I'm talking hands full
of cotton, bags full
    of cotton, cotton as far

as you could see, cotton
    in your sleep. Wiping his face
with his sleeve, he takes
    a long moment and breathes

a smile. By the time I turned
    thirteen I couldn't dream
any more cotton, that plow
    dragged me clear to Chicago.

PHILIPPE WAMBA

b. 1970

Dubbed the "best book dealing with the African half of the compound African-American" by *Kirkus Reviews*, Philippe Wamba's *Kinship* explores the complexities of identity and language, creating a "strange, wonderful hybrid of memoir and history." While telling the story of his African American mother from Ohio and his African father from the Congo, Wamba relates his family's history to the spiritual, musical, and political heritage that connects us all. In doing so, Wamba complicates not just Du Bois's notion of double consciousness—being both African and American—but also parallels Du Bois's journey from historian to political activist (which ended in his eventual relocation to Africa). Wamba moves comfortably between worlds and between essay and memoir in "Of Prophets and Madmen," ultimately reconciling our seemingly conflicting conditions—African and American, "madman" and "prophet."

OF PROPHETS AND MADMEN

"Breda John is having a party," Victor told me as he walked in the door and tossed his wet towel onto the foot of the bed. I looked at him with interest from my prostrate position on the bed; I had just been wondering what I was going to do on yet another no-money day. Victor and I had been hustling cash here and there for a couple of weeks now, and while relief in the form of his meager paycheck and my scholarship award was anticipated any day now, even worse than the lean and beer-less belt-tightening that poverty entailed for us was the boredom of having no money with which to go anywhere or do anything; a party sounded like just the distraction we needed. Victor was returning from a shower at the dorm of our friend Andy and had run into Ian on his way back (the tiny bathroom in the little room we rented behind the campus' most popular restaurant and bar had only a toilet and sink). Ian worked at one of the university cafeterias and had said that Breda John had come by the kitchen early that morning; apparently John had passed his law school examinations and wanted a cake and some food made for the party he was having that night. After ordering the food, Breda John had bustled off again, apparently on his way to make other arrangements for the celebration.

Hearing this I felt a strange and relieved exultation. Breda John's academic success was truly something to celebrate, and not just because the University of the West Indies law course was notoriously difficult; few of us had expected John to make it, even as we hoped for him to. He was obviously bright and passionate about his chosen field. But he had many obstacles to overcome. In the colorful opinion of many, friends and foes alike, Breda John was a "madman."

Victor described a lot of his friends as "mad," but he was only half joking when he said that about Breda John. John had been institution-alized several times in his life, and episodes of "madness" had inter-rupted his law course on more than one occasion. And though his incidents of irrationality seemed cyclical, even his closest friends agreed that Breda John's periods of relative "normalcy" were dotted with eccentricity. Most would even hazard that Breda John did smoke too much ganja, as his family and doctors apparently often complained. Some of us smoked the occasional spliff, especially on Thursday nights when, funds permitting, we went to hear Stone Love, the preferred sound system of the day, mash up the dance in New Kingston. And Mellow, a perpetual graduate student, even seemed to smoke ganja constantly, often appearing with a cone-shaped joint between his lips and a heavy-lidded, bloodshot sleepiness in his eyes. Still, though some of us indulged, it was common knowledge that some temperaments were not well-suited to chronic herb intake, and it was generally felt that Breda John's bouts of madness were not unrelated to his several spliffs a day. Maybe we were just looking for something on which to blame his occasional trips in and out of the mental hospital, a trend that saddened and worried us, and his frequent odd behavior.

I had always been fascinated by mental illness, and the seeming preponderance of madmen on the streets of Kingston was one more thing about Jamaica that reminded me of the urban East African environment in which I had grown up. As a kid in Dar es Salaam, Tanzania, I thought that *vichaa* (Kiswahili for "madmen") were everywhere. Our neighborhood, for example, was patrolled by a seemingly harmless transient who became something of a local celebrity. He would always stride by purposefully, locked strands of his dirty, matted hair jiggling with each step, the dust spurting up in clouds between his bare toes and further layering his filthy clothes, his raggedy burlap sack of collected belongings slung heavily over his shoulder, eyes staring straight ahead as though trained on a distant destination. We would look up from our soccer game whenever he passed, and the bolder kids would call out to him. "Where you going, Miraji?" they'd tease playfully. Sometimes he would grunt and mumble distractedly in response, to the giggles of my friends, but he never really answered the question.

I never knew if "Miraji" was his real name or how my friends had learned it if it was, but stories and rumors abounded to explain how Miraji had fallen on such hard times. Some of my friends told me that Miraji had been a top student at the University of Dar es Salaam until jealous classmates had used witchcraft to drive him mad; others said he had merely blown a mental fuse by studying too hard, and that his sanity had been crushed under the burden of excessive knowledge. Whatever his true past or the reasons for his illness, Miraji quietly wandered our area for most of my childhood years. I used to watch him go by with great curiosity and sympathy, but also with fear. I had never heard of Miraji hurting anyone, but I knew that mad people could become violent without warning because a friend of my father's had once been walking down the road, minding his own business, when an anonymous *kichaa* (the singular of *vichaa*) had struck him in the head with a *panga* (machete). And once, while on one of our regular excursions into the bush near our neighborhood, my friends and I had been trying to knock a ripe mango from a tree when a wild-eyed man in rags had suddenly emerged from the undergrowth to chase us away, laughing maniacally and shouting threateningly as he pursued us.

My childhood world seemed filled with such characters. At Mwenge market my brothers and I had once watched a rag-clad man chastise a large muddy puddle for baring itself in front of the crowds of people who frequented the market. And downtown we sometimes caught sight of an eccentric street dweller who seemed to take pains to dress himself in the most outlandish cast-off clothes and accessories he could find: balding wigs, pink plastic sunglasses with one lens missing, colorful tattered sweaters, and disintegrating American goodwill sneakers. Closer to home was a neighborhood friend named Steveni who only occasionally seemed to live up to the nickname with which the local kids taunted him; despite his protests, they called him "Milembe," after Tanzania's most infamous mental hospital. Though he lived with his uncle and was usually clean and relatively kempt, Steveni rarely obeyed social conventions and often seemed to struggle with episodes of irrationality when he would go fishing at the local sewage treatment ponds and expose himself or make lewd sexual gestures in public. On one occasion he even ingested a potentially lethal dose of anti-malarial medicine to quickly cure his malaria, he said, so he could go to town. After his near "suicide," my friends and I visited Steveni at the local dispensary and joked that he should be careful not to mistake medicine for candy in the future. We had chalked this latest crisis up to Steveni's well-known instances of dementia, and we tried to make light of the situation to ease some of the tension. To us, madness was beyond anyone's control or understanding, and humor helped us to avoid confronting the fear and uncertainty it stirred up.

The madman was a powerful symbol in the East African culture in which I grew up. Since sorcery was so often said to cause madness, mental illness was often associated with evil. The stories about madness that I heard as a youth often depicted madmen as dangerous and sinister characters, and though children often mocked and taunted those who were said to be mad, they also learned to look on them with fear. But in addition to feeling threatened by the mentally ill, my friends and I were also titillated and fascinated by the fact that they said and did things that no one else would dare to. They were free of social restrictions and not obligated to respect any boundaries. Madmen had no control of their actions and neglected to clean and groom themselves. They talked to themselves and to people who weren't there. Mad people walked the streets and ate garbage, and their hair grew in caked, dangling clumps and strands. They were the ultimate transgressors of local custom and respectability. In my teenage years, when I became an ardent reggae fan and was tempted to grow dreadlocks, older family friends dissuaded me, for fear that my hairstyle lead people to mistake me for a *kichaa*.

Figures like Miraji and the other madmen who roamed the city were tragically isolated fixtures on Dar es Salaam's social landscape, where madness was regarded as an essentially incurable condition, a stigma that earned its victims derisive scorn, fear and ostracism. Institutions like Milembe Hospital in Dodoma and the mental ward at Muhimbili Hospital in Dar es Salaam were not usually seen as sources of treatment; instead they were popularly regarded as prisons for the insane, a perception that was perhaps not that far from the truth. The homeless *vichaa* on the streets, and many of those whose experiences with mental illness seemed more sporadic, rarely seemed to get the help they needed, often shunned by family, community and the medical establishment alike. Like lepers, Tanzania's mentally ill tended to be written off and disregarded; local understandings of both madness and leprosy were tied up in superstition and social taboos, and most thought it wise to steer clear of those who were so afflicted. But in disregarding Miraji's mumbles, a madman's vexed ranting at a mud puddle, and Steveni Milembe's exhibitionistic cries for help, I wondered if we might have been missing something they were all trying to tell us.

I had traveled to Jamaica to study for a semester at the University of the West Indies in Kingston and found many echoes of my East African childhood in the gritty Caribbean city I came to love. The tropical panorama, replete with palm and mango trees, the dilapidated Third World infrastructure, the overcrowded buses, and the warmth and wit of people who were often self-consciously celebratory of an African past, all reminded me of home. I made friends on campus and around the city and even ran into a South African refugee, Victor, who had lived for a number of years in Tanzania and was fluent in Kiswahili. Victor had already been studying and working in Jamaica for a few years when I met him and he became my primary guide to Kingston's far-ranging pleasures. Most days after work and class we would sip cold Red Stripes in the shady yard of the campus bar, chatting with friends as they slammed dominoes into the table, making all of the bottles jump and rattle. Other days we made outings to Port Royal for fish dinners, to Hellshire Beach for swimming and festival (tasty ovals of fried dough), to Devon House for free rum drinks from our bartender friend, or to West Kingston for extended discussions on politics over beers with a Rastafarian friend who called himself the Professor of Poverty. And on nights when we could afford it we made our rounds of the Kingston night spots, following sound systems and reggae bands wherever they happened to be playing that night, bouncing to blaring bass lines alongside the raucous dance-hall faithful.

At the university I took classes on Caribbean history and society, and twice a week I interned at a number of the island's largest trade unions, attending union meetings and wage negotiations and touring rural sugar and canning factories, where I helped to catalogue workers' complaints and was often welcomed enthusiastically as a son of the motherland. I immersed myself in Jamaican culture and developed an ear for patois, the local pidgin that to me seemed to echo many African languages in its grammar, rhythm and style. A Jamaican once asked an African friend of mine what it was like in Africa. Look around," my friend replied, gesturing to the Jamaica scenery. I, too, quickly felt at home in this strange, familiar place.

Kingston provided some reminders of my youth in Tanzania that were more unsettling. On my first afternoon in Kingston, on Old Hope Road, one of the city's major thoroughfares, I saw a bearded man in rags who lived in a roadside tree decorated with hundreds of cardboard signs he had scribbled with apocalyptic messages like "The End Is Near." Although no one seemed to pay much mind to his warnings, his tree was a well-known landmark, and he was a source of great amusement and curiosity to passersby. Downtown Kingston, like Dar es Salaam, was home to many ragged eccentrics who endured teasing by schoolchildren and were feared and avoided by more sensible folk. And like in Tanzania, madness in Jamaica seemed to occupy a privileged position in the popular consciousness, where it was also often associated with witchcraft and seemed a source of strong fascination as much as it was also a powerful social stigma. "You mad?!" seemed a common accusation shouted by Jamaicans jokingly expressing disbelief at a socially inappropriate statement or action, and Bellevue, the local mental hospital, seemed to loom large in the local psyche, as both a source of madness and a rightful repository for the mentally ill. In some ways, madness seemed a label for any sort of unconventional, eccentric or antisocial behavior; as in Tanzania, madmen were those who refused to live by societal rules and norms, and in general they were thought to deserve imprisonment if they could not conform to social standards.

In Tanzania I had worried that if I adopted a "dread" appearance I would be mistaken for a madman, and in Jamaica I found that the association of madness with a Rastafarian belief system and lifestyle was a common one. Rastas, especially when the religion first emerged in the 1930s, had often been stigmatized as madmen, whether actually suffering from mental illness or not. Rastafarians took their name from Ras Tafari, the pre-coronation title of Emperor Haile Selassie I, who was revered by Rastas as the earthly incarnation of God ("Jah"). Rastas believed that black people in the west ("Babylon") were living in a state of exile, and that they would ultimately return to freedom in Africa ("Zion"). As a self-consciously Afrocentric movement of black pride, Rastafarianism defined itself in explicit opposition to mainstream colonial culture and society, and as such, became a vehicle for cultural resistance to the white supremacist legacy of slavery. Rastas taught a revised reading of the Bible, which treated blacks as God's chosen people; they promoted a natural "ital" diet of fruit and vegetables, and made liberal use of marijuana for medicinal and religious purposes. Dreadlocks, matted strands of hair identified with a number of African tribal groups, became the most visible signifiers of membership in the movement, and adherents took pride in the length of their locks, at once a symbol of religious devotion, identification with a black African aesthetic, and masculine vigor, thought to resemble a lion's mane. Dreadlocks were the evidence of an individual's spiritual effort to overcome the "dread"-ful experience of bondage in Babylon, and constituted a rejection of European standards of beauty and "proper" grooming. But while dreads became a source of pride for young "lions," the hairstyle became a badge of notoriety to the colonial authorities and to many mainstream Jamaicans, who frowned on the Rasta aesthetic and lifestyle, and attempted to disregard Rastafarians as mad, misguided misfits. Bunny Wailer had lamented as much in the song "Blackheart Man," in which a mother warned her children to beware "the Blackheart Man," the fearsome bearded and dreadlocked crazy man who would steal them away, a homegrown boogeyman who served to reinforce mainstream social values. "Tikya the Blackheart Man, children," the Bunny sang. "I say don't go near him. Tikya the Blackheart Man, children. For even lions fear him." I even heard stories of privileged families having their teenage sons committed to mental institutions when they became Rastas and grew dreadlocks, as though the rebellious desire to adopt a new religion and outlook were itself indicative of mental illness.

Rastas, of course, viewed mainstream society with similar suspicion and scorn. Rastas saw themselves as devotees of the true faith, as followers of the true teachings of God, destined to enjoy divine rewards and repatriation to an African paradise for their loyalty to Jah Rastafari, His Imperial Majesty, Haile Selassie I. If Rastas viewed themselves as the purveyors of spiritual truth, it therefore followed that the unbelievers who scoffed at the notion of Selassie's divinity were the insane, or at least sorely mistaken, ones. The Rastafarian worldview highlighted the rotten foundation of colonial Jamaican society and provided a version of religious truth that rejected and reversed the prevailing social hierarchy; to Rastas, it was the black "sufferahs" who enjoyed God's blessing, while the rich agents of exploitation, the "downpressors," would soon have their fall. Polite Jamaican society said Rastas were mad, but Rastas said it was the nonbelievers who were the crazy ones, clinging to an erroneous white interpretation of religion and turning their backs on their motherland. As every Rasta knew, "Who Jah bless, no man curse," and they had faith that with Jah's backing they would triumph, while non-Rastas, the dreadless "baldheads," would suffer His wrath. "Dem crazy, dem crazy," Bob Marley sang on the classic Wailers song, "Crazy Baldheads." "We gonna chase those crazy baldheads out of town."

With the collision of such disparate views on madness, discussions of mental health in Jamaica unfolded on highly embattled terrain. For the ruling elite, the power to define madness seemed a potent mechanism of social coercion and control. The downtrodden, for their part, were sometimes able to glean a sense of empowerment and self-worth by asserting their own sanity and the corrupt madness of the society in which they lived. In Jamaica it sometimes seemed as if madness was less a question of actual mental health than of who was doing the labeling, adding further complexity to a deeply layered cultural concept.

I quickly learned that the madman had multiple meanings and associations in Jamaican culture. In addition to being thought of as a boogeyman, the madman could also be seen as a prophet, as someone who was tuned into aspects of reality that "normal" people were not. The Prophet of Old Hope Road, with his signs foretelling the end of the world, had his precedent in Jamaican history. I learned that in the 1920s, when a Jamaican trade unionist named Marcus Garvey was leading the world's largest black mass movement, another Jamaican "prophet" named Alexander Bedward was mobilizing another following. Bedward said he wanted to "fly to heaven" and his message seemed to resonate among a significant portion of the population. Bedward's followers said he was the reincarnation of Aaron, the younger sibling to Garvey's Moses, and his utopian message was embraced by poor people who hoped he might deliver them from poverty and exploitation by leading them to a promised land. Bedward led over eight hundred people on a march to Kingston, where he preached against colonial authority and foretold the dawn of a new era before eager audiences in the ghetto of August Town. The authorities were quick to take note, and the rally was disrupted; Bedward was arrested, tried, pronounced a "lunatic" and locked in a mental institution for the rest of his life. But his movement proved greatly influential as a precursor to Rastafarianism, and he was remembered in Jamaican history as the other important prophet of the 1920s.

Madmen were perhaps most threatening to the ruling elite when seen as self-styled prophets, but they also had other, more benign incarnations. And in some ways, Jamaican culture at large preferred to see madmen as childlike jesters, an unthreatening source of comic relief, than to confront the more sinister implications of their condition. While in Kingston I read a book called *The Lunatic,* by a popular Jamaican writer, Anthony Winkler. Winkler's lunatic, a lovable character named

Aloysius who converses with trees, cows and cricket balls but seems harmless and good-natured, highlights the lunacy of a society that looks on his simple ways with scorn, and stresses the humanity of a man who is honest and decent but clearly troubled. Like many, I found Aloysius's quirks hilarious and Winkler's depiction of the village madman endearing. Aloysius is more than a little off, but his life seems romantic; he sleeps out under the stars, he gets by doing odd jobs, bowls for the local cricket team, and seems content with his life. The book ends with his adoption by a village widow who seems willing to overlook his occasional eccentricities in return for his affection, but the challenge of his clearly ailing mental health is not really confronted. Aloysius is painted as an entertaining and sympathetic buffoon, but there is little to suggest that he will, or even should, abandon his mad antics. In the end I felt that the fond and amusing portrait of a genial fool whose best friend is a tree might be oversimplifying a very real problem.

I found the madmen who populated the literary world of Trinidadian writer V. S. Naipaul more complex. "Everybody in Miguel Street said that Man-man was mad, and so they left him alone," begins a story about a local madman in the book *Miguel Street*. "But I am not so sure now that he was mad, and I can think of many people much madder than Man-man ever was." Man-man supports himself by conniving local households into giving him laundry that his dog has soiled and selling it to unsuspecting buyers elsewhere. He exacts revenge on a café owner who was unkind to him by allowing his dog to defecate all over the man's establishment. He expresses his disdain for the colonial educational system and repeatedly runs for local elected office, always garnering three votes. And, at the end of the story, he offers to crucify himself for Trinidad's salvation but quickly changes his mind when the crowd that he urges to kill him begins to hurl stones at him. "Cut this stupidness out," he yells as the first projectiles strike him in the chest. "I finish with this arseness, you hear." Man-man is perhaps not as mad as we might have thought. In fact, his apparent "sanity" calls into question the mental health of the rest of the book's characters, for it is difficult to distinguish Man-man from the gallery of failed carpenters, poets, teachers and hustlers who inhabit Miguel Street.

As the narrator implies, there are many others in the neighborhood who seem to deserve the label of madman more than Man-man ever did. The same sentiment is expressed in another of Naipaul's books, by a character who observes that "[Trinidad] is full of mad people, for truth. And, you know, once you realize you have madmen running about the place, you start seeing them everywhere." It almost seems as though, in the world of the postcolonial West Indies, where it sometimes appears that everyone is mad, the so-called madman is the only one who speaks the truth and makes any sense. After just a few months in Jamaica, I began to think I saw what Naipaul meant.

Victor called many of his friends madmen in a playfully affectionate way, and I suppose most of us probably did have a few issues. Desmond came from an affluent, well-respected, brown (light-skinned) family but seemed to love badness. He was tight with the gangster set and was always having to watch his back at parties. Kwesi, a Rasta who usually tied his long locks into a neat bow, went from obsession to obsession (painting, farming, drumming, bee-keeping, Thoreau-style wilderness living) trying to find spiritual fulfillment and refused to get a real job, often depending on the kindness of friends for food and shelter. Donovan stalked women with an insatiable appetite, and often preyed on giggling teenage schoolgirls and adventurous white women who strayed into his path. We all struggled to support ourselves and constantly complained about being broke, but we always seemed to have money for liquor. And of course, Breda John's quirks and brushes with the Jamaican mental health establishment were well documented, although they had apparently not prevented him from successfully completing a law school degree.

A tall and wiry man, Breda John wandered the campus with a distinctive energetic stride that was recognizable from great distances. He talked rapidly and his mind often seemed to jump from idea to idea, even as his eyes would often seem to scan a room wildly, flitting about like they were trained upon nervous butterflies. A self-declared Rastafarian, Breda John was always trying to grow himself a flowing crown of Marley-style dreadlocks, but his hair always seemed stuck in the wild-haired Afro stage of dreadlock growth. Rumor had it that whenever he reentered the university hospital's mental ward after one of his episodes (apparently it was his family that usually delivered him, insisting that he be confined there), the orderlies would shave his head clean, ending the progress his dreadlocks had begun since his last visit. When he was eventually released he would have to begin growing his dreads afresh. While his aspirations toward the physical image of the politically outspoken, clean-living, herb-smoking, religious Rasta ghetto prophet were thus frustrated, Breda John made up for his hair's shortcomings with the loud and angry Rasta-influenced populist and pan-Africanist rhetoric that constantly poured from his mouth. He ranted about the plight of Jamaica's poor to whoever cared to listen, and encouraged all to make plans, as he was, to return to Africa, as Garvey, one of his heroes, had decreed. He often discussed his romantic desire to move to Africa with Victor and me, the university's local Africans. Once he knocked on Victor's window at three in the morning to consult him on the issue. Victor tumbled out of bed in a panic, assuming some terrible accident had occurred, but instead of the police or a frantic friend, he found a chatty and relaxed Breda John on the doorstep.

"Wha' ya say, Vic," John greeted Victor easily. He paused, and then asked Victor the burning question that apparently couldn't wait until morning. "So, when you a go back to Africa?"

Victor was dumbfounded. "You wake me fi ask dat?" he said crankily through his sleepiness. He yawned and murmured crossly. "Wha'appen, you nah sleep?"

"I man ragamuffin soljah," replied Breda John proudly. "Mi nah sleep."

Victor shooed him away and went back to bed.

Sometimes Breda John's outspokenness landed him in trouble. Once he ran afoul of Country, my and Victor's landlord who ran the bar that was the usual gathering and drinking spot for our group of friends. Country, especially when he had been downing cues of rum all night and drunkenly calling us his sons, usually allowed Victor and me to put the beer, white rum, and curry chicken that we consumed in heroic amounts onto our tab, appending it to our rent each month. But when our no-money days and Red Stripe bills piled up too menacingly, Country would deny us credit and threaten us with eviction. On one such occasion Breda John interrupted Country's standard diatribe with a lecture of his own. "You see you, you nah love black people," he accused venomously, going on to denounce Country as a money-hungry vampire bent on sucking the lifeblood of the students and working people who frequented his establishment.

While it was true, among other perceived slights, that Country begrudged his black tenants (namely Victor and myself) mangoes from the tree in his yard but seemed to make extraordinary efforts to please the white Americans and Europeans who occasionally patronized his restaurant as a quaint alternative to the cafeteria, Breda John's accusations were probably unfair, even ungrateful. Country had proven helpful to many of us on many occasions, and seemed to regard himself as a sort of patriarch to the youthful regulars who spent so much time in his establishment. Country responded to Breda John's speech with indignant and self-righteous outrage, calling him a "likkle blood claat" with no respect. He shouted that John was banned from the bar "for life."

Country, who was well known for his temper, had thrown people out of his place before, but I had always thought John was one of his favorites. Breda John backed out of the bar but was still defiant, keeping the stream of insults and denunciations going long after he was no longer in sight. Flud, a loudmouth in his own right and a close friend of John's, protested the expulsion. He felt that Country wasn't being sensitive to Breda John's special circumstance.

"It no right fi treat im so," Flud objected. When Flud's complaints got louder and angrier, Country kicked him out too. The rest of us stayed away from Country's for a few days (though Victor and I of course had to keep living in the little back room), but since there weren't really many other places to go to in the area, especially places where we had credit, we grudgingly returned to Country's eventually. In time, when tempers had cooled enough to pretend to forget what had happened, Flud returned as well. But Breda John never came to the bar anymore, though he would come to see Victor and me at our place out back. To avoid another explosion we tried to make sure he and Country stayed clear of each other.

In addition to loud public proclamations on the evils of white people and Babylon, and denunciations of accused "downpressors" like Country, Breda John's antics included mysterious disappearances in which he would apparently wander Kingston ghettos for days on end. When such behavior would escalate, Victor and I would worry that John would once again be institutionalized. And we worried that even if he managed to stay out of the hospital, the hours he lost to his mania would leave him unprepared for the exams that would complete his course of law. But apparently, in spite of our fears, Breda John had made it through, and we looked forward to commemorating his moment of triumph with him that night.

Talking to Mellow about Breda John's success that afternoon, I was reminded of how amazing John's accomplishment really was. "It's actually quite impressive. Rasta, dat yout' mus' brilliant, y'know?" Mellow said thoughtfully, switching to Jamaican patois when he wanted to emphasize his point. "Apparently he not only passed his exams, but he did well. An im no really study, im jus go in an tek it."

News of Breda John's good fortune, and of his party, spread quickly. Soon Flud, Donovan, Capo, Dedi, Donny Wonder, Desmond, Jungle, Mellow, Victor, and I were all at Country's, drinking Guinness, beer, and rum and telling affectionate Breda John stories while we basked in good feeling. Flud told of the time Breda John had accompanied him to his workplace and how when Flud's boss had requested a moment of silence in honor of a colleague who had recently died, Breda John had loudly exclaimed, "A waste a time, im already dead." Mellow told how Breda John said he planned to use his position as a lawyer to "plant a 'ole 'eap a callaloo" in August Town "to feed poor people dem."

And everyone talked about the party. Apparently it was shaping up to be quite an affair; Capo said he had seen Jugu, who had told him that Breda John had recruited the sound system services of Stone Love and Silverhawk. Someone else had heard that Breda John was trying to get Shabba Ranks and Ninja Man to perform at his party. And Clarkie, Country's teenage son, bartender, waiter, general slave, and resident practical joker, swore that he had heard Breda John's party announced on Irie FM. I found all of this hard to believe but couldn't help but hope that even a quarter of the rumors about Breda John's party were true. Even a single sound system would have ensured a good time. Victor assured me that the food alone would be worth it; he had visited Ian earlier that afternoon and found him hard at work frying fish and putting the final flourishes on a beautiful cake with white icing, a green map of Africa and the words "One Love Breda John" on it. With the promise of such fancy fare we realized that we couldn't lose, and we eagerly anticipated the night's festivities.

The guys didn't start nibbling at the fried fish until we had waited in the Chancellor Hall common room for over an hour, with Breda John yet to make an appearance at his own party. I don't think anyone had really expected the sound systems and performers to show up, so we hadn't missed them when they didn't, but we did assume that Breda John himself would be present. A substantial flow of Red Stripes and white rum carried over from Country's improved our patience, but after an hour the fish started to look pretty good. Once we had eaten the fish, licking the hot, salty flavor off our greasy fingers and sucking the tiny bones clean, the cake started to look even better. It was Ian who insisted that we at least await Breda John's arrival before digging in, but I thought it was more out of a desire to relish the artistic pride in his handiwork (he kept gazing lovingly at the colorful icing and modestly accepted praise of his efforts) than out of politeness.

After three hours of waiting, Jugu arrived and said he had heard that Breda John had been sighted in August Town, trailed by a retinue of area kids, babbling excitedly about his party and how "all de ghetto youth dem" were invited. The news was greeted with a mixture of amusement and impatience. Breda John was obviously up to his usual escapades, but how long were we supposed to wait before we could expect him to show up? Victor jokingly suggested that we eat the cake now, since we didn't know when he was coming and it sounded like a gang of people were on their way, which would mean less cake to go around anyway. We all laughed appreciatively, but I think we all knew that Ian's beautiful cake would not survive for much longer in Breda John's absence.

After yet another hour, several more beers and cups of white rum, and still no sign of Breda John, the cake's end was swift and delicious. I think it was Victor who started the spontaneous rush for the table, but it could have been anyone. Within seconds the cake was reduced to crumbs, its green and white icing smeared all over the plate and table, our faces and hands sticky with confectioner's sugar. It was truly a delectable cake, we all agreed, offering our thanks to Ian while licking our lips. It was too bad Breda John had never gotten to see it. When the cake disappeared, the party pretty much broke up, people slowly staggering away to their respective beds, grunting good night and cursing Breda John for never having appeared. Victor and I headed off toward Country's, Victor keeping up a stream of abusive complaints at Breda John's expense for keeping us waiting, me silently hoping that John was all right.

We heard the next day that Breda John's brother had eventually been dispatched to find him and had picked him up in August Town, where John was still wandering the streets, by then yelling hysterically about something unintelligible and tearing his clothing from his body. We were told that John had once again been hospitalized at the university mental ward, and once again his head had been shaved. It seemed that his by now familiar cycle had begun afresh. We were all somewhat sobered to hear the news.

"At least," I reasoned, "now he has his law degree."

"And at least," added Victor, "we ate a good cake."

COLSON WHITEHEAD

b. 1969

Colson Whitehead's debut, *The Intuitionist* (1999), merges modern and classic fiction, blending the postmodern prose of Thomas Pynchon with good old-fashioned storytelling. The result is a mystery about elevator operators that comments on racial progress, integration, and "movin' on up." Called by *Time* magazine "the freshest racial allegory since Ralph Ellison's *Invisible Man* and Toni Morrison's *The Bluest Eye*," the novel also revels in a Gotham as surreal and satirical as in the work of Charles Wright, the underappreciated black novelist Whitehead cites as an influence.

Whitehead's second novel takes on the myth and meaning of John Henry, tracing the folk legend through various characters—including a freeloading journalist (J.) sent to report on the unveiling of the John Henry commemorative stamp. As the following excerpt from *John Henry Days* reveals, Whitehead's epic in progress achieves the reveries and social commentary not fully realized in Ralph Ellison's unfinished second novel, using John Henry to explore our complex, ever-changing American character.

THE ALL-NIGHT BODEGA OF SOULS

At the all-night bodega of souls the crackheads promenade, jigger and shimmy, trade palsies in fitful games of one-upmanship, count coins beneath the corrugated tin of the yellow canopy. The bodega never closes. At midnight the night man removes the brick from the front door and transactions proceed through bulletproof plastic. He takes requests. He strains to hear the crackheads. When he withdraws into the recesses of his mercantile domain to retrieve malt liquor and potato chips of anonymous manufacture, protein shakes if that's all the customer can keep down, the crackheads etch nonsense slogans and their names into the plastic with keys or dimes, halfhearted dispatches from under- ground. They look over their shoulders for 5–0; if they pooled their resources they could come up with two dozen warrants and summons between them, surely. They taunt the night man for no reason, reason enough. They deprecate his sensory apparatus. Yo, you deaf? I wanted one St. Ides and two O.E.s, motherfucker, not two St. Ides, shit. I wanted those Lays chips you got right there, not that plantain shit, shit, you blind? They talk through the bulletproof plastic about the state of the economy. What, you want another ten cent? Day before yesterday it was a dollar ninety-five, now you trying to tell me it's another ten cent? My boy was down here two hours ago, nigger, he got the same shit and it wasn't no ten cent more. You Dominican niggers try to rip a nigger off. If the night man is too tired to grant this impromptu haggling session the attention it deserves, he'll let the guy off the hook and hear his name cursed by the man to the other crackheads down the line. If he feels like standing his ground, he'll turn the revolving bulletproof box around so that the man sees his insufficient coin there on the clear plastic, a museum exhibit on ghetto commerce. He can come up with that dime or he can leave. Cigarettes and condoms may be purchased singly. The new demand for Phillies cigars is accounted for. The night man runs back and forth. Even a request for simple orange juice from this crowd, at this time of night, gathers licentious aspect. These people take ordinary items from his uncle's shelves and convert them into crim- inal accessories. The same faces night after night. Crackheads and drug dealers and here's that guy for three Coronas.

J. Sutter on deadline queues up with crackheads in the sinister a.m. His fingers hurt from late employment at the tiny buttons of J.'s microcassette recorder, where they teased shrill idiocy from metallic spools. On the tape the actor and pinup expounded on Tantric sex and the Dalai Lama, from a white table poolside at a hotel in Los Angeles. That day a year ago, J. sipped a margarita and squinted at his notes in the bleaching sunlight. He felt himself getting soft and overripe in the sunlight just like everything else in the state, his brain splitting and spilling juices. Brody Mills had just finished a stint at a court-appointed substance abuse rehabilitation facility. "Four weeks of seriously getting my head together," as he described it that day, and a year later in J.'s apartment through diminutive technology. He tapped ash on the coarse tile of the hotel Sun Deck Lounge, eschewing for reasons of his own the elegant ashtray proximate his hand. "I'm clean for the first time in years and it feels so great," he said, while eyeing and coveting J.'s frothy blue margarita like a bedlam fiend.

Brody Mills dispensed rehearsed penance as the viscount of the studio publicity mechanism nodded and smiled and tapped Brody's tanned forearm when he wandered too close to the demilitarized zone between their agreed-upon orchestrations and the facts themselves. His implosion had announced itself for months, first as nameless ectoplasm in blind items of gossip pages, then as boldfaced and named instigator in a brawl at a Manhattan after-hours club, finally no longer omen but event itself, as Brody Mills was cast against type in a hooded sweatshirt and detectives led him into the precinct at the top of the nightly news. On every channel. He was Wednesday's scandal, he took a wrong turn after an afternoon spent with his surgeon-sculpted proboscis deep in cocaine anthill, slapped his longtime model girlfriend around, and bit the arresting officer on the ass when he came to investigate the noise complaint delivered to 911 by fellow residents of the upscale downtown coop. The judge gave the actor and heartthrob probation and ordered a mandatory stay in rehab. J. was one of ten journalists scheduled for poolside chats that day, one of pop's own parole review board. Brody certainly looked better than in his now-infamous mugshot: the goatee shreds in a Beverly Hills sink; the black haloes around his eyes trod away by step after step (numbering twelve in total) of self-awakening. J. was there to force the man to his mark, the X of tape where the public wanted him to stand, centered beneath the cleansing spotlight of contrition. Brody moved obediently. "Fame came so quickly," he conceded, "I never had a chance to grow up."

When J. got to that part of the tape, a few days later, when he was back in the civilized regions of Brooklyn, that quotation insisted on itself as an obvious and natural segue for a recap of Brody's early career. He grows up before the public's eyes but the child remains inside him. It was obvious, blunt, and ready for copy.

The magazine called him up, asked J. if he wanted to fly to L.A. to interview the actor and idol on his release from rehabilitation. J. flew out, interviewed this nipple-pierced Lazarus, and filed the piece on time. But Fellini died. The great director Federico Fellini was dead in Italy and the managing editor wanted to run a package on the man's demise: capsule reviews of his key movies rated by one to four stars for video-store convenience; brief statements by leading American directors (no one too art-housey) who were influenced by his work; and an essay on his impact on the world of film, the peculiar economy of postwar Italian life and how it produced idiosyncratic and beautiful art, this essay prepared months before when the man first checked into the hospital, just in case. There's a protocol for such things. J.'s piece on the Confessions of Brody Mills, Actor and Superstar, was pushed back a week to make room for the package, and then another week, and then no one cared and a kill fee (full) arrived in the mail. That was a year ago.

Then this morning J. got a call rousing him from a dream, one of the agitated type that he gets only when the noon light gushes full and accusatory on his face through the bedroom window. Brody was in trouble again, falling naturally to mischief just as he did in the show that made him famous, the Fox television program *Quaker's Dozen*, a situation comedy concerning twelve orphans of different ethnic backgrounds and the hip preacher who is their guardian. (When one of the child actors wanted to leave the show, or was eliminated by the producers' caprices, they were "adopted" at the end of the season, a truly successful adaptation in the Darwinian jungle hell of modern entertainment, rarely a dry eye in the house when this stunt was performed and seismic, Nielsen-wise.) Brody arrested yet again, and on the eve of the premiere of his new action film, yet. Will neighbors ever refrain from calling the police over loud noises that disturb the early morning metropolitan calm? When the constables arrived at the Paramount Hotel this morning and knocked down the door, Brody Mills was as naked as a babe (or the famous bare-ass scene in *Ten Miles*, the first film he made after he was adopted from the hip priest's orphanage) and arguing with invisible critics and studio executives (for the unseen goblins he harangued must have surely been critics and studio executives) while the paraphernalia of narcotics abuse lay in plain sight and the hotel reservoir of pay-per-view pornography inundated the well-appointed suite at high volume. "It took half a dozen of New York's Finest to restrain him," the magazine editor related to J. from the AP wire, and would J. mind fixing up his piece from last year, two thousand words if possible, buck a word and by tomorrow noon?

J. put down the phone and went back to sleep. Paid twice for basically the same thing: he slept unperturbed by hectoring afternoon light, tranquilized by the thought of taking money off the troubled celeb. He woke and mulled over, guzzling coffee, the talk-show disaster on his TV screen. At five he strolled to Fort Greene Park for what he reckoned might be a pleasant hour of meditation, but he bored quickly with the pavement and pit bulls and wilted condoms and beat it home after five minutes. His thoughts did not touch on the assignment for more than a few moments through the evening. Pop a few details into the original fifteen-hundred-word piece, no sweat, snatching lollipops from a baby, the tykes have no grip yet, he could get up early and do that easy. He ordered Chinese food and watched television until eleven o'clock, when the faint angel of professionalism perched on his shoulder, implored in a whisper, and he went to check the file. Place the X-rays up to the light and see exactly where the fractures were, what needed mending tomorrow, so to speak. When he called up the file he found gibberish, a glyphic conspiracy of pixilated symbols he didn't even know how to muster from his keys; it was a language from a cranky sect deep within the motherboard. He couldn't explain it. He had fifteen hundred words of shit when he called up the file *B. Mills Repentance Spiel*.

But he still had the interview tape in his income tax receipt drawer, and he had coffee beans. J. knocked back a pot of coffee and transcribed once again the actor and teen scream's confessional peregrinations. J. fast-forwarded past his own voice; he loathed the sound of his voice through the tiny speaker, it was amplified and remastered by the machine so that it contained a quality of earnestness and sincerity that he did not truly possess. Since Brody Mills never answered any of his questions, preferring instead a dada discourse, it did not matter that J. did not hear his questions. But two and a half hours into his reconstructions, J.'s fingers were rebellious from rewinding and fast-forwarding, and his stomach and heart convulsed with the cocoa bean's harassment. He was so jazzed up that he needed to calm down if he was going to get, what, two hours sleep maybe and be fresh for the morning's foray to the happy hunting grounds of hackery. And that meant an expedition to the only establishment open at this time of night. He must make his descent.

There was a time that whenever he suited up for a late-night bodega run, J. would take the necessary bills and leave his wallet behind. Crackheads begging for change, knuckleheads out on the prowl: best to make a strategic withdrawal. But nothing ever happened and he stopped. More dreadful than becoming a participant in the city's most popular street theater (the mugging on darkened corner, a spectacle tourists from all over the globe line up to get see, easier to get than Broadway tickets) are the black windows in all the buildings. Surely, he thinks when he sees them, he cannot be the only one awake at this hour, he is not alone. But in all the buildings and brownstones the neighbors sleep. The decent folk forsake these hours. Blue TV flicker in some windows tell him there are a few like him awake at this time, not many. Always the same windows too, he's noticed, scattered and well dispersed from block to block so as to adumbrate this nocturnal isolation to best effect. He waves at one blue dancer. No response. It's a four-block walk to the trading post with only two sketchy parts: the blind turn from Carlton to Lafayette (who knows what kind of scene he'll stumble into rounding that building's blade); and that block where streetlights stare blindly, handicapped by vandalism and city neglect, where shadows confab to trade samizdat decrying illumination. But nothing has ever happened on the walk. Two blocks down he sees the huddled masses group outside the bodega. He takes a deep breath and sallies forth.

The freaks come out at night.

He gets in line behind the crackhead who sometime dons a subway worker's reflective orange vest, a souvenir he picked up somewhere in the tunnels. This character likes to tell passersby he needs a token to get home, the orange vest intended to provide evidence of solid citizenship; why he'd need a token if he worked for the Metropolitan Transit Authority has apparently never occurred to the man. J. sizes up the group before him. They are travelers who have come a long way, certainly troubadours finally come to this neck of the woods: the most popular entertainment troupe in all of ShabbyLand, the Freebase Players. Yayo the Clown, his face rouged by dried blood and nose swollen after a recent third fracture, stands in his gay gray attire; he prefers to play the dignified gentleman raconteur down on his luck, happy to share a comedic tale of woe for some change. Those dynamic men on the flying trapeze, Gordy and Morty, who zoom on leave from gravity through alkaloid extracted from cocoa leaves, death defying, without a net worth, falling to earth only at dawn, when this team is too exhausted to perform any trick except attempting sleep while wired to the limits of human endurance. And of course the elders, Ma and Pa, married for twenty years, half that on the pipe, God bless 'em, keeping vigil over the dirty garage bags containing the cherished props of their act, deposit bottles and broken toasters. And at the fringes of this group, mingling with the celebrities, are assorted teenagers just ducking around the corner for supplies, some malt liquor and Newports, identifiable by their baggy jeans and beepers and youthful joie de vivre, so refreshing beneath the timer-controlled beam of the streetlight.

The line progresses slowly. Tonight everybody hassles the night man, they denounce the service at this establishment. But there are no questionable characters hanging around who fall outside the usual disrepute of the crowd, so J. starts thinking about the article; he leaves this corner and is conveyed to its double on Grub Street. Then J. sees him.

J. sees him zigzagging down the street, stymieing any snipers of euthanasiac bent who might be roosting on the Brooklyn rooftops, an out-of-control prop plane in for an uneasy landing. Tony darts here to finger the coin slot of a pay phone, diddling around in luckless pursuit of change, scrambles there to see if that glint (bottle top) is a dime or—mirabile dictu—a quarter. J. sees Tony, the ghoul's fingers wiggling in the air like crab's legs over wharf-bottom detritus. Tony lopes down the avenue, scanning and panning, and J. knows that with Yayo the Clown's meticulous and agonized counting of pennies (always that same deficient sum, the limited number of pockets in which to search), there is no way J. will get clear before Tony lands at the bodega.

J. is the only mark in the ragged assembly on the corner; Tony will not approach the malt liquor boys, contusions have taught him better, and the crackheads are his comrade connoisseurs of the pipe and competitors for change, outside the game. During the day the street has enough traffic that J. is not always discovered as the object of Tony's salvage operation. During the day Tony is a puppy; at night he's a damned barnacle, strung out on an odyssey for the next piece of rock, and there's no shaking him. J. and Tony have a relationship at this point, going back to when J. first moved to Brooklyn and had a pocket full of change. Tony looked more craving than hungry, but he needed the change more than J., fuck it, J. was in a good mood. Tony smiled and memorized the sucker's stupid face. The act wed them as mark and conman, til zip code do you part. That first contribution was binding contract (everyone at the bodega now would attest to its legality), although J. hadn't bothered to read all those subclauses; the fine print he couldn't see in the bright and easy light of that aimless afternoon. They have a relationship, with rules. During the day "Sorry, man," will dispatch Tony to the next mark down the street, that bohemian homesteader of these Brooklyn badlands, the goofy white dude with the goatee. Plenty of marks on the afternoon street, such is the bounty of the neighborhood. Another rule: Tony won't beg for change if J.'s escorting a lady; he'll tip an nonexistent hat, but that's it. At night, though, times are tough, and tonight J.'s the only sap around.

Tony's evidently having a bad night. All sorts of tectonic mayhem afoot in Tony's face this eve: his troubled visage bursts with subcutaneous lumps of calcified ooze and porous eruptions trickling a clear fluid. The hair he managed to grow last week and was quite proud of (they talked about it while J. walked briskly for the subway, forbidden turf for the shambling man; the subway cops had beat him up once, or so Tony claimed), has evacuated in patches, exposing old and angry scabby flesh. Tony arrives just after J. asks the man behind the bulletproof glass for three Coronas. He assumes his hovering remora position and says, "Hey, Mickey Mouse man, you having a good night?"

"All right," J. responds, glancing at Tony and then staring dead into the store. J. was wearing a freebie T-shirt from Disney that first day Tony hit him up for cash. Remembering and filing his clients' distinguishing characteristics helps the crackhead keep his various pitches in order.

"That's good, that's good," Tony says, nodding to comrades down the line, who pantomime back things seen. "Say, listen, listen, could you spare a few dollars for some food? I haven't eaten all day, man, and I'm hungry." Holding his stomach urchinwise.

"We'll see," J. says. This is one night he should have left his wallet behind. In a few moments J. will open his wallet and Tony will take a big thirsty peek at the cash. Can't really say he doesn't have any cash when there's a sheaf of twenties in there.

"Sure am hungry," Tony says, nonchalant.

"Maybe," J. says. He withdraws a five, holding his wallet close. He thinks of soldiers in trenches cupping their cigarette tips so that the Kaiser's goons won't see the flame and draw a bead. The night man returns with three Coronas and rings it up, cue now for J. to slide the money into the bulletproof box and spin it around for approval. The night man slips his agile fingers into the register and drops the change and the bottles into the box, slides it around, transaction complete.

Tony bobs happily next to him. J. stuffs the dollar twenty-five into his jeans and withdraws from the crackhead bazaar. "Hey, brotherman, how about that change?" Tony murmurs.

"Sorry, man," J. says. Cradles beer to his chest and strides.

Tony's head rocks back and forth and he pulls up next to J. "But you said so."

Semantics now. "I said maybe. Can't help you out tonight." He just got two checks in yesterday, so giving the man a quarter is no big deal. Tony can have the change and smoke himself to death, no big deal, it's spare change. But J. has that article due, he's been transcribing word for word a Hollywood junkie's incoherent speeches, and he's had enough of junkies tonight. Coffee curdling in him, deadline creeping: he's in servitude to one druggie tonight and that leaves him with empty pockets for this neighborhood nuisance. "See ya later," J. says.

They're the same age, J. found out one day. Tony trotted next to him, like he is now, halfheartedly rapping about needing some Similac for his baby, a ploy Tony used the first few months after their original meeting but eventually dropped when he realized that he didn't come off as a dutiful daddy (no one glows that maniacally with the joys of paternity). Tony said, "How old do you think I am?" and J. guessed forty-five. Tony grinned broken teeth and giggled, "I'm twenty-nine! Twenty-nine years old! Today's my birthday!" And with that he cackled away down the block.

Tony is not giving up so easily tonight. He's hurting for a little something. Tony says, stepping closer than J. would like, "You want some LPs? Cause I know a Guy that got some. You like that old funk? I could hook you up." Switching tactics tonight. He knows a Guy, a Guy who

J. has learned is a truly enterprising individual. Over the years this Guy, with Tony as the middle man, has been able to furnish stereos ("Real cheap!"), VCRs of the finest Japanese craftsmanship ("Videos too! You like porno?"), sticky weed ("I saw you walking with that dread last week. Maybe he wants some smoke"), and women ("The night guy at the old people home pays me five bucks to get a woman for him—I could hook you up!"). The Guy Tony knew was a true entrepreneur. Perhaps one day J. will ask if the Guy has a line on devices that make receipts, but not tonight. Nor is he interested in a bunch of old records that the Guy robbed from someone's house.

"No thanks," J. says.

"I haven't eaten all day, man, please."

"No."

"What do you mean, no? I see you every day, motherfucker, and now you can't even help a nigger out with some money to eat. That's terrible." A boil splits on Tony's face and drips. "Can't even help a nigger out with a sandwich. I saw you got plenty of money on you."

"No." They're on the block of broken streetlights. Tony's mother lives on this block. Tony's pointed it out to J. before, it's a nice old brownstone in the middle of the block. Family discord: Tony lives a few streets away in a vacant lot shack. Or he used to. The habitation burned down a few weeks ago and Tony pointed to a glistening pink burn on his arm for proof. A problem with the wiring, no doubt.

"You got money for alcohol, but I can't eat," Tony says. As if this suppurating shade wanted the money for food, strung out like he was. No one on the street but them, and all the windows dark. Tony takes the advantage on his opponent and leans up and whispers, "I'm so hungry I might have to take it then, I'm so hungry," and the threat sits there in J.'s ear. There was that night when J. was heading for the subway to make it to a book party in Manhattan and he saw Tony prowling around, cussing. His clothes were inside out and blood seeped from a gash above his eye. When he saw J. he asked him if he'd seen these three knuckleheads walking around anywhere. J. replied he hadn't and Tony said that he got into a beef with them and they beat him up and made him take off his clothes and put them on inside out. Or maybe they made him put his clothes on inside out and then beat him up. At any rate, he was looking for them and he had something: he pulled up his shirt and pointed to the long carving knife tucked into his belt. He was going to cut them when he found them. J. told him to calm down and get himself cleaned up. He wasn't going to cut anybody. Tony considered this possibility, nodded, and agreed. He pulled his shirt down over the knife. Then he asked J. for some change.

J. doesn't respond to the threat. They walk in silence for a few feet, and they leave the threat on the pavement behind them. They move into the next streetlight's circle and Tony says, "Hey, you know I wouldn't do that. I ain't like those other crazy niggers they got up in here. But I gotta eat. What do you want me to do?"

"Can't help you, man." If he gave into the crackhead now, it would look as if he was giving into the threat, even with Tony's withdrawal of it. A principle involved: he doesn't want to be punked out. There's one more block before he gets to his house and he doesn't want Tony there when he gets to his front door.

"You want me to sing for my supper?" Tony asks. "You want me to sing for my supper? I'll sing for my supper." He spits a gremlin of phlegm to the pavement and scratches his foot across the sidewalk like a pitcher taming his mound for a pitch. Then he jumps up and down and sings from his singed throat, "This old hammer killed John Henry, but it won't kill me! This old hammer killed John Henry, but it won't kill me!" J. looks back at the crackhead. Tony's eyes bulge out with the strain of producing that gross racket. "This old hammer killed John Henry, but it won't kill me!" And here, J. thinks, this is the essential difference between this neighborhood and those of Brody Mills's orbit. No one here will call the police about the noise. They hear gunshots and arguments in the middle of the night and they might creep to the window to see what's going on, but they won't call the police. They'll pray they don't hear a rape, something that will force them to get involved, or consider getting involved, but the people behind the black windows will not call the police at this. "This old hammer killed John Henry, but it won't kill me!" It's up to J. He has no more resistance. He pulls out the change from the five dollars and gives it to the crackhead. Without touching the man's palm. Who knows what the guy wipes his ass with.

"You like that song?" Tony asks.

"You won," J. responds. Yards between them now, the distance between the mark and the expert con.

J. hears Tony yell, "Hey, brotherman, brotherman, wait a minute!"

J. turns, knowing from the volume of the man's voice that there are distances, old distances, between them. Tony jabs his finger at him and says, "You're a solid brother, Mickey Mouse, you're a solid citizen." He bows and scampers away in the direction of a building without a door, a building with secret steps and codes.

At his desk J. sips his first Corona and looks down at his notes. He calculates what he'll get done before he's dampened enough to fall asleep. He considers how much sleep he'll get and through the calculus of doggerel arrives at how many words per hour he has to produce by noon. He presses a button and listens to the lying junkie. Only variety of junkie awake at this hour.

DANIEL JEROME WIDEMAN

b. 1968

Daniel Jerome Wideman has established a strong foothold in both nonfiction and fiction, while serving as co-editor of *Soul-fires: Young Black Men on Love and Violence*. Son of acclaimed writer John Edgar Wideman, Daniel Wideman recently completed writing about the African slave forts in *Singing Sankofa,* a nonfiction book questioning the relationship between African culture, slavery, and American society. As seen in the following selection, Daniel Jerome Wideman writes with a natural lyricism, his work combining the strength of song and a freedom usually reserved for fiction, resulting in a myth-filled yet investigative prose style reminiscent of Zora Neale Hurston.

SINGING SANKOFA

Where does your story begin?

All of our stories begin in the womb. In darkness, surrounded by water. The world we are about to join just a series of echoes, muffled rumors from beyond the warm walls. The womb our first colony. Attachment to the mother-land a visceral cord of connection. Womb-colony utterly dependent, yet this tunnel between two worlds accommodates two-way traffic flow. A relationship so close that what is exchanged is not just the means of sustenance, the deliquescent waste, but the effluvia of consciousness itself. The mother's sense of self originating in her awareness of the child; the child existing only in relation to the rhythms deep enough to rock its mother's belly.

Birth is always bloody: the violence of it intended to imprint the permanence of severance, yet the trauma insures a memory deeper than blood will remain, a connection beyond memory that will forever exist. A piece of the womb, the nourishing part, the wholesome part, is destroyed at birth. It collapses in despair at the sudden departure, disintegrates into a heap of messy, viscous tears and vainly chases the child down the birth canal.

Nearly every culture in the world recognizes the restless grief of the placenta, has concocted a ritual palliative. Peoples everywhere understand, despite the fireworks and fanfare of physical birth, that nothing is truly *born* through that particular rupture. What emerges is a life already created, dreamed up, made flesh long ago. A story that's been told and retold, a myth reinvented. A life destined to be submerged, cocooned, barricaded, incubated and hatched again and again. Resurrected, revealed, reinterred and reborn in a continuous cycle. We are all eternally wombed and dewombed. Wounded and unwound.

But the first womb, the first birth, the original connecting cord is special. So we *canonize* or *cannibalize* the evidence. Bury the placenta or swallow it whole. Revere the child born with a caul, then strip it from her and stir it into the cauldron. Somehow we build into all our ceremonies surrounding original birth the concept of closure. Passage through a cosmic seam that parts but once for each of us.

It is more than just the notion of gateways, bridges, doors closing firmly behind you. These are all transitional constructs which leave evidence (and the potential for re-entry) behind. Gates swing both ways, doors can be taken off their hinges to reconnect rooms. But the womb, the first womb, is mystic because it is forever inaccessible. Your birth changes its very shape so it is never again the place you once inhabited, which contained and contented you so completely. A dark universe, you its lone star that departs and leaves a black hole behind.

One transcendent truth, unanimously accepted, about that first birth: once you're out, you're out. You can never go back. You can dig a hole and hide, hibernate in a cave, swim deep below the surface, blind yourself to restore the darkness—but nothing, not even death, can take you back whence you came.

You have passed through the door of no return.

The hole cut into the rock where African captives passed from fort to ship, from dungeon to hold, from land to sea, from homeland to exile, was known locally as the door of no return because nobody herded through that doorway was heard from again. Nobody ever made it back. It was the gateway to oblivion.

Vodoun is a New African religion developed on the island of Saint Domingue (Haiti) by African slaves. Many refer to it as a "syncretic" faith since it incorporates elements of Christianity, traditional African religious praxis, and new beliefs which evolved during the middle passage. One of these new beliefs, which became a central part of vodoun, is that *Guinée* (Africa) is no longer part of this world. It exists, rather, as an underwater island, resting on the ocean floor. An inverted heaven to which only the spirits had constant access. Practitioners of vodoun believe death is the sole portal, the only way for human beings to return to true Africa.

Deep blue sea, baby
deep blue sea

> *it was Willy*
> *What got drownded*
> *in the deep blue sea*

Many Africans leapt out of the canoes carrying them to slave ships, some escaped even after being boarded and jumped into the ocean, but only while the mainland was still in sight, still visibly attainable. A slave ship captain noted that:

> *the only danger [of leaping] is while we are in sight of their own country, which they are loath to part with, but once out of sight out of mind . . .*

He goes on to talk of the way captives would swim beneath the surface and exhale, intentionally drowning themselves

> *to avoid being taken up and saved by our boats, which pursued them; they having a more dreadful apprehension of Barbadoes than we can have of hell, tho' in reality they live much better there than in their own country, but home is home, etc.*

Twenty years ago, scuba divers off Key West in Florida searching for pirates' gold and other treasures buried with the ancient wrecks along the treacherous Peninsula reefs began to bring bits of Africa to the surface. Amidst the rotted wood, plankton, and detritus of yet another unremarkable wreck a white gleam caught one of the diver's eyes. Incongruously bright in the dark depths.

Imagine the looks on the faces of those on board the trawler. A worrying of water just beyond the deck. Bubbles and ripples break the spell of stillness cast across the placid bay. A diver returning, completing his measured ascent. Discoloration, angled half-shapes beginning to be visible through the blue-green scrim of surface water. Stories passed from one mouth, one tribe, one generation to the next mutate like the features of faces viewed through a few inches of water. They are hopelessly distorted and distended. Funhouse mirror caricatures of the original. An embryo encased in amniotic swirl, growing blurry and enormous as it jostles against its transparent sac, receding into focus as it floats back to the center of its waterworld.

A sense of humor. Instead of scuba gear, air tank, floppy fin, a solitary sword cuts through the waves off deck and erupts skyward. An ivory dagger thrust aloft, dripping brine and mollusks. The crew of the salvage ship waits to see what will emerge at the end of this ancient tusk. But instead of some prehistoric walrus, the diver appears, pulls the second of the pair up with his other hand.

"Elephants! African ivory down there!"

The ship is the *Henrietta Marie*. A slave ship. The first such ship recovered and traced to its origin. In addition to the tusks, divers (including black scuba divers! Black scuba divers?!) will salvage a crate load of beads intended to be used as barter for human beings. These particular beads, due to color, style, size or the whim of the elite had fallen out of fashion along the Gold Coast and thus made the return voyage to the New World. Dusty and useless, taking up valuable space intended for more profitable cargo. Hunks of twisted metal, corroded chains and collars and coffles and cuffs will be dredged up. Other trinkets and ship instruments which have survived the brutal assaults of time and salt water will be rescued. An exhibit at a Miami museum will be mounted.

The African leg bones formerly attached to the chains will not be found. They have long since dissolved, become fish meal, black bone and flesh passing back into the food chain, absorbed into the continuous life cycle of the sea.

The way I was taught about the door of no return—about the fantastic, phantasmagoric character of darkest Africa, about the Middle Passage, about the unswerving parabola of progress in matters Racial—all starkly reinforced a belief in the irreversible current of history: you cannot wade in the same river twice. Marcus Garvey failed because he tried to "go back" to an Africa that no longer existed independent of his wild imagination—of all the circumstances surrounding emigration to America, black people's story alone is invested with a weighty character of finality. We were forced here in chains, and due to the unfortunate fact that nobody bothered to record where they snatched each of us from, we can never go home. Worse, our fate is to never be permitted or empowered to imagine where home might be, let alone revisit, repatriate, return.

But what if you could name all the dungeons you'd found yourself in throughout your life? If you could make them manifest, conjure cold stone rising, rising and molder and moil and light cuckolded, light ren-

dered not just dark but betrayed and weeping. What if you could construct a forbidding but magnificent fortress to house your most profound
grief, your deepest shame, the moment you were farthest lost to yourself,
to the world. Make it all tangible. Locate suffering in a series of citadels,
crumbling now, collapsing into ruins, but for today anyway still standing.
Extant. Strong enough to withstand your touch; sufficiently solid to resist
toppling at the drum, drumming of angry, despairing fists seeking belated ablution, resolution, restitution. What if you could travel to your
own personal wailing walls, propped up and serene by the sea? What if
someone closed their eyes, waved a wand and created all this, conjured
edifices of pain and sprinkled them across a stretch of distant coastline?
If they built it, would you come? Would you dare to cross the moat,
step inside, bear witness?

What if all the prisons the world has ever seen were still populated?
Every inmate still *in*, every cot occupied, every bar still in place, each
sentry still standing? What if the smell of incarceration, of living flesh
putrefying, dreams drying up in pools of evaporating tears and piss?
What if these odors did not fade over time but rather distilled, worked
themselves into the pores of the rock in these dungeons, colonized the
living, breathing spaces we know exist within all stones and survived,
gradually becoming the sole accessible scent, for those foolish enough
to re-enter the room? Would you come? Would you breathe?

What if you made this trip? Hijacked Charon's ferry and returned to
the land of the living dead. Stepped off the boat into darkness. Could
there be anodyne in this journey? Could you meet your ancestors in a
dungeon, chained, etiolated, moaning out the last measures of their
lives, and survive to tell the tale?

When I first stepped into the women's dungeon at Cape Coast Castle
in Ghana, I was standing in the very room where one of my distant
grandmothers had been imprisoned, inspected, purchased, deracinated,
relieved of her freedom and dignity, sold into slavery. Transformed into
chattel and yoked with a misery so many-tentacled it would greedily
clutch not just her own soul but the souls and bodies of her children,
of unborn generations not yet imagined.

I stood there waiting for my eyes to adjust to a pitch blackness so
deep I'd never encountered it in other dimensions of consciousness like
sleep, let alone in the waking world. The concept of magnification re-

volves around light, around clarifying and enhancing the territory of the visible. Standing in that room I discovered darkness can be magnified as well. The enhancement of invisible space. Darkness expanding and crowding out more than light, displacing the very air it floated in on until I found myself gasping for breath. Is it my imagination or is that closeness, the cloying, almost fleshly taste of the small gulps of air I manage to swallow really there? Can the smell of slavery possibly linger in a place that hasn't seen slaves in a century and a half? Can the fetid tropical humidity, the porous rock, the saline in Oceanside air alchemize, cooperate, function as supernatural preservative?

I swear I can detect unmistakably human overtones in the pervasive stink of mildew in the dungeon. A claustral heaviness in the air that is unnatural, surreal, frightening. I stand very still, try to slough off and tune out all my other senses. The way bloodhounds "point": frozen, noses thrust aloft, an entire complex organism reduced to pulsing olfactory gland. Still the smell remains. It is enough for me. I believe it is real.

Later—years later—I will realize it was neither the darkness nor the pungency that took my breath away. It was the emptiness. I anthropomorphized the darkness and the air because I was not prepared to enter that dungeon and discover . . . nothing. Surely, the atrocities committed in that room, the suffering of hundreds, thousands of souls, the violence and neglect and sickness and despair would leave stains as indissoluble as blood on the Cross. Certainly you cannot pack so much devastation into such a small space and not leave evidence that would last until the end of time. A testament to which we could perpetually return, a record to reread, lives to reanimate and remember. Of all the horrible and triumphant images I had dreamed of discovering passing back through the door of no return into the first prison of my people—fantastic images that alternately filled me with profound excitement and abject terror—the notion that I might walk into that room and find it empty never occurred to me. I had prepared myself for everything, anything but absence. Blank space. Mute walls, stone floor, cavernous silence.

If this place didn't speak to me, didn't cry out and echo in my inner chambers then no place in the world ever could. If I didn't begin to hear the articulation of my story, see the shape of roots and home in the shadows here where else could I possibly look?

It was the emptiness that disturbed me, rocked my organs into rebellion. Heart racing, lungs searing, knees buckling, I slowly stumbled backward, retracing my steps in a desperate effort to escape, and backed right into the wall. I couldn't see anything. The group of friends I had come down with gone now, leaving me alone in the room. Legs gone numb. I just slid down the wall and came to rest on the floor. The stone against my spine somehow not as cold as I had imagined, and I clung to that tiny bit of warmth with all my soul—the only evidence of life in the room.

She spoke for a long while before I noticed her voice. As close, as real as the voice in my own mouth, the voice running through my head. Perhaps she just picked up the frozen words where I'd dropped them in despair, breathed on them till they warmed in her hands, became pliable again, then released them, watched them take wobbly flight like injured birds healed in captivity. Setting loose the same story I'd suddenly found myself paralyzed to tell.

Her voice was soothing, quiet, and strong. It did not echo or crash around the cave recklessly like the screams I wanted to unleash. A steady, almost sweet voice nearly subsumed in the sibilance of the sea slamming the thick stone borders of the fort mere feet beyond the space in which we sat.

"We" now. I am no longer alone. I am sitting next to a pregnant young woman. An expectant mother is speaking to me. Or speaking to herself and her unborn child and allowing, encouraging me to listen in. When I finally realize and accept the reality of her presence, I begin to hear her words. Words which reveal her as an ancestor, a prisoner of this place back when what you purchased at the door was not a visitor's pass but a seat at auction.

I'd been tuning out her voice for the first few minutes, ignoring the calm cadence both because of its subtlety and because of its incongruousness, the sheer implausibility of *company* in a darkened dungeon. A place so empty I'd felt not just alone but dissipated, evaporating. I'd begun to doubt whether I was actually present: did I exist here, and, if so, on whose terms? Where could I possibly be more invisible than buried beneath this ancient rock? So impenetrable was the sense of isolation that a shard of light entering that room would have startled me. A gust of wind would have caught me completely by surprise. To suddenly become aware of a human's warm, welcoming, living presence was totally unnerving.

But there she was, just off my left shoulder, a nebulous heat on the port side. Her words billowing forth in the darkness, taking shape in front of us like bursts of hot breath on a midwinter night. Breath you're sure you could see if only the moon was a bit higher. Smoke wisps of words wrapping round and round each other, a story cloud barely masked by the blackness of the dungeon . . .

Perhaps I can tell you of the color of light in Okponglo, my child. It is different here. Here the light brings blindness and pain. We live in dark-ness, and, when they drag us up into the courtyard each day, there is no color in the light—it is like silver, glittering spears thrust into our eyes or the glare of hot sand when the sun burns fiercely. My eyes are swollen now, and water spills from them even after I've finished crying, but I re-member the color of light in the village. It is soft and green in the morning when the cockcrow stirs the crickets to song. It is red in the yam hills where your father goes each afternoon, and, even after the sun sinks into the sea each evening, there is light. It is grey and thick and blends smoothly with the smoke from the evening cooking fires. The light of the moon paints Okponglo the color of ghosts, and, each time the moon shrivels to a sliver, a new girl joins us in the forest to let her womanly blood flow back into the earth. It is very dark then. But there is no darkness as black as this cave, my-child-who-rumbles-in-me. They have surrounded us with stone, and even in daytime the light is afraid to come in because it hears the chains rattling and knows if it comes it may never get out again. The moon has deserted us. The sun hides and trembles. Do not come here from the other place, little one. Hold on. Keep my stomach company a while longer. I remember the color of light in Okponglo. How did they trap so much night in this room?

Her story, the capture of her voice eventually became a literary project for me. A play I thought I was writing to elucidate her identity. But that is a different chapter. Trying to tell your own version of a great story someone else told you is, in all but the best hands, inept hearsay, bun-gling plagiarism rendered no less awkward and wooden by acknowledg-ing the theft. I wrote and rewrote what I remembered of the tale she told me but never got it quite right. Eventually crafted a serviceable but unremarkable piece of theater out of that afternoon, but never felt I had adequately honored or reciprocated the inestimable gift she bestowed upon me. Watching the production of my play only made the sense of failure more acute.

When I proposed a book about the slave forts, I knew that inevitably I would have to revisit the woman who manufactured light in the Ninth Circle that day at Cape Coast Castle. I dreaded the prospect of wrestling with her story again, failing to get it right again. Dreaded the horrible feeling of volunteering your services as a translator only to discover you've forgotten—or never knew—the language you've been entrusted to decipher. Turning back only to realize you've misplaced your native tongue as well. Language, history, a river running at crosscurrents so whichever direction you try to swim leads you into the vortex of a whirlpool, spinning you in place, leaving you dizzy and wet but no further along in the journey.

Her speech, the contours of her voice, the arc of the epic she spun out as I sat silent and transfixed beside her was beyond any register of language I'd ever encountered; yet I understood, *felt* every syllable as thoroughly as if it had spilled forth undiluted directly from my own soul. When, after what seemed like hours, her voice trailed off and I could hear the soft brushrustle of cotton cloth as she gathered her garments about her and grew silent, I knew I had gone as far into the fort as I ever could. Knew I wouldn't move on and try to catch the group in the men's dungeon, or visit the chapel further on. I stood up, turned slowly in circles until my eyes locked on a vague dimness in the corner of the room. A breach in the black hull which grew larger and brighter as I approached, became the narrow archway I'd passed through to enter the dungeon. I walked into the stairwell and climbed the steps back into the 20th century, back into my own beige skin.

Who was she? In Chicago, after returning from Africa, a friend made me a tape of Roberta Flack performing live at Elmina Castle in Ghana. The track begins with gentle whispers. The rhythmic lull of waves breaking softly against rock. You could be anywhere in the world, asleep on the Riviera in the courtyard of an opulent chateau. You could be anywhere you want until Roberta starts to sing. When she holds the first note forever, unrelenting, the letting go of it like hearing a soul expire, you know you can only be one place in the world. In trouble.

Ohhhh, Freedom.
Ohhhh, Freedom.
Ohhhh, Freedom, over me.
And before I'd be a slave
I'll be buried,
buried in my grave,
And come home,
to my Lord,
and I'll be free . . .

The same voice. The same strength and clarity, the magical melodious weave of pain and simple, stark beauty. The purity born of depthless sorrow courageously defeated. I heard it all again in the song. Realized perhaps there is one ancient voice still singing—or at least a traceable lineage. I began to realize my story, my life is the evidence. I am a survivor of the slave forts and so telling my story, tracing it there, is itself an act of restoring continuity, healing the breach that divorces us from the past, casts us as isolated in time and space. Perhaps continuity can be rescued and restored out of even the most violent of ruptures. Perhaps failing to transcribe the story that ancestor told me in the dungeon would be acceptable if my failure was faithful, if in the act of trying to get it right I could open up just enough space for a sliver of her song to filter through.

JOE WOOD

b. 1964

"When I was a child I wasn't Black enough, but Malcolm X helped me turn things around," Joe Wood writes in his introduction to *Malcolm X: In Our Own Image* (1992), an anthology of essays about the leader and his influence, which Wood edited. For a young Wood, "Malcolm was making blackness Black: *The masses of Black people today think in terms of Black. And this Black thinking enables them to see beyond the confines of America.* Quietly, without fully realizing how much, I began to embrace this thinking, despite its strange incongruity—no one in my Black, working-class neighborhood seemed to be spending much time thinking about America *or* Blackness. Or Malcolm."

Wood's thinking about all three led him to be one of our most brilliant writers and critics, whether in his *Village Voice* columns, such as "The Creole Museum," or in his insightful articles for journals such as *Transition* and *Dissent*. His willingness to see beyond the confines of America brought him to Japan and its hip-hop and "blackface" subcultures, allowing him to question Asian, American, and African American identity in his beautiful essay "The Yellow Negro." Wood was writing a memoir which further investigated identity and family here in the United States when he disappeared while birdwatching on Mount Rainier in the summer of 1999.

THE YELLOW NEGRO

As I unpacked my bags, I assigned the strange feeling in my head—a sense of isolation fastened on my brain like a lump of ice—to the unnatural ease of my passage. It had taken only thirteen hours to cross twelve time zones and thousands of miles of indiscernible land and water; according to the clocks, I arrived in Tokyo three hours after I had left New York.

Even finding a hotel room seemed unnaturally easy. My guidebooks explained that cheap Japanese hotels prefer not to deal with *gaijin* (foreigners), so I'd asked a friendly face at the airport tourism desk for assistance. The room she procured for me turned out to be smaller than a college dorm room, and about as well furnished. There was a bed and a tiny desk unit crowded into one tight corner; the television tinted everything a celestial blue. I took comfort in the vaguely familiar images: game shows and panel discussions, serious-faced newscasters, sumo wrestling tournaments. Out at Shinjuku Station, the nearest train stop, everyone had studiously ignored me and my obvious struggle to figure out where I was going. In the room, I felt safe. Soon as I could, this foreigner slept a few hours.

When I awoke in the evening, the heavenly blue light of the television had turned cold; all traces of home were gone. My headache had subsided, and I realized with a certain smiling fear that I was now a dark American cipher in the Japanese empire of signs.

They say that Shinjuku, the largest precinct on Tokyo's west side, contains the most typical commercial district in the city. Lights and smiling billboards compete to outshine each other; a gallery of earnest advertisements for department stores, films, luxury foods, and sporting goods shouts down at crowds of rushing consumers on the street. Until very recently, some of the most popular icons on display in Shinjuku and across the country were Little Black Sambo and his liver-lipped cousins.

I had been worried about facing those Sambos. Boatloads of typeface have been devoted to Japan in recent years, and one of the more persistent themes has been the peculiar fact of Japanese racism: the Sambo iconography, the coldness toward *gaijin*, the occasional outrageous comment from a prominent politician. In 1990, for instance, then-Justice Minister Seiroku Kajiyama was cited in the *New York Times* as "compar[ing] prostitutes in Japan to black Americans who move into white neighborhoods and 'ruin the atmosphere.'"

Kajiyama made this enlightened analogy after observing a nighttime raid of brothels in Shinjuku, a pebble's throw away from the sign-filled streets where I now stood, feeling like a ripple in some vast unrippled pond. Much has been written about the nation's "island mentality" and insensitivity to foreigners. The Japanese have long perceived themselves, and been perceived by others, as one homogenous group, racially, ethnically, and culturally identical. The purported homogeneity has alternately been cited as the cause of the nation's rapid economic growth, on the one hand, and its insularity, on the other.

Walking around Shinjuku, I thought I could detect an ugly fascination in the eyes of the people around me. How bizarre that there should be such malevolence toward blacks in a country with almost no black people. There are, by some estimates, 50,000 African Americans in this country of 125 million people, and most of them are soldiers temporarily assigned to the area. While the infamous rape of a teenager in Okinawa by black servicemen in 1995 probably exacerbated Japanese attitudes toward blacks, the hostility predates that crime. I couldn't help but wonder whether the racism expressed by Seiroko Kajiyama was identical to that of a white landlord in Queens who refuses to rent to a black family.

I had not come to Japan to examine hostility toward blacks, however. On the contrary, I had been drawn by another much-noted facet of Japanese culture: its profound attraction to black music and style. Even as the Japanese have hung their Sambo signs, they have embraced jazz, rock 'n' roll, funk, and other forms of African American expression. In recent years, this fascination has widened to include Jes Grew's latest incarnation: hip-hop. And, like the children of that white landlord in Queens, many young Japanese closely imitate the styles of the rappers they see on the screens in their living rooms.

"Jiggers" come in several flavors. The most curious are undoubtedly the blackfacers, b-boys and girls who darken their skin with ultraviolet rays. When I first heard about them, years ago, I was bothered by the idea of young Japanese blacking up like the American minstrels of old. But when the opportunity arose to go to Japan to study them, I couldn't resist. I hoped that they might surprise me.

In Tokyo, I was told that blackface Japanese are ordinary high school and college kids. Even their darkened skin doesn't particularly set them apart; surfers, another well-defined Japanese subculture, spend a lot of time in the tanning booth, too. What does separate the small sect of blackfacers from their peers—even their hip-hopping peers—is the ardor with which they pursue African American "blackness."

The blackfacers work it hard. While they bear an obvious resemblance to old-fashioned minstrels, their "performances" do not seem to be aimed at other Japanese. Blackfacers (especially the females) tend to party where natural blacks party, especially black American soldiers. Blackfacers are even proud of their assumed skin color. That, of course, is the strangest thing about them: they wear blackface in order to embrace black people. This is more baffling than anything white America has ever attempted; try to imagine Al Jolson or Sophie Tucker or even Bert Williams wearing their blackface with pride, going out on the town, trying to seduce black people. There's an old Creole proverb: "Show me who you love, and I'll show you who you are." Who were these Japanese who chose to wear my face?

Most people I talked to hadn't heard of the blackfacers. The ones who had thought I shouldn't be taking them so seriously. I interviewed Japanese professors, black American soldiers, entertainers, businessmen, teachers, and former clubgoers. They were sometimes amused, sometimes dismissive, but none of them seemed to think much of the blackfacers. Wherever I went, I encountered the ubiquitous wallpaper of black American music: Billie Holiday, Sly Stone, Cassandra Wilson, Ella Fitzgerald, Eric B. and Rakim, Ray Charles, De La Soul, Aretha Franklin, Al Green, Tammi Terrel, Nina Simone, Funkadelic, Sidney Bechet, James Brown, and KRS-One.

On a local black journalist's tip, I went to Kings, a nightclub frequented by *kokujin* (black foreigners) and their blackfaced admirers. When I asked him to come along, he demurred. "*They* like it there," he said. I suppose I should be embarrassed to confess that my heart was actually racing when I saw my first one of *them*.

The blackface girl and her black boyfriend were one spot ahead of me in a line of about fifteen people, crammed into a small third-floor hallway. The club wasn't open yet; the Africans who ran the place were late. By the hallway's fluorescent lights, I examined the girl: her crimped hair, her darkened skin, her figure swamped by an oversized shirt and a pair of Tommy Hilfiger jeans. She moved well, too, as did the other six or seven blackfacers, a couple of whom she seemed to know. The trio conversed in a body language that would not have seemed out of place on a New York subway: a kind of feinting in which the speakers lead with their shoulders, and then fade back, hands kept low but occasionally flying sharply upward to make a point stick. I recognized the b-girl adolescence, the combination of macho swagger and dancer's grace—just like home, almost, lacking only a little of the homegirl's street-level preparedness. But certainly the girls were more fluid than the men—black American soldiers and African partygoers—who stood like trees among their blackface partners.

I followed the girl and her companion, a well-muscled bush of a man. He sounded African. They stopped at the bar. I suddenly felt self-conscious. I got a drink and wandered over to see what the DJ was spinning. His records looked interesting: solid West Coast hip-hop, and a couple of rappers I'd only heard on New York college radio stations. There was a good crowd, but no one was dancing yet. Off-duty American soldiers stood at the edge of the square dance floor, poised like sprinters; women huddled in groups of two or three.

I waded my way through the thick waves of rhythm to the blackfaced girl at the bar. She was a young nineteen, beautiful and cheesy at the same time: her crinkly hair was pulled up and back, the curls sprouting from the top of her head; her lips were painted with dark, almost black, lipstick. She looked real: a good fake. She could have been a Dominican schoolgirl in the Bronx. Her T-shirt announced that "Black Women Are the Salt of the Earth." I could almost hear the laughter of the black women back home.

I managed to start a conversation with her in elementary English. Her name was Miho. "Do the people in school think you look good?" I asked her.

"No," she said. "But it doesn't matter."

"Why do you choose to look like me?" I asked.

"You?" she asked. "Who?"

"Black," I clarified. I pointed to myself and to her African boyfriend. She turned to her companion. There was a shuffle of discussion in Japanese; the African spoke it effortlessly. "Because it's cool," the girl said, shrugging her shoulders.

"Cool" is everywhere in Japan. There are seemingly endless numbers of subcultures and sub-subcultures. I soon discovered that, for many young Japanese devotees of black culture, the blackfacers are decidedly uncool. In fact, they're considered an embarrassment. These hardcore kids dismiss blackfacers as fools, or as not "real"—the worst thing one hip-hopper can say about another. According to the tan-free aficionados of black culture, the point is not to imitate black people's skin tones but to participate in the graffiti-writing, break-dancing, loose-fitting-clothes culture of hip-hop.

But even as they put down blackfacers, tan-free hip-hoppers are still playing by similar rules. For both groups, black culture is worth being part of because it's cool. This "black cool" is distinctly reminiscent of the subversive hipness Norman Mailer described in "The White Negro" (1957), an essay about white Americans of the Beatnik era. The hipster sets himself apart, Mailer writes, in order to

> encourage the psychopath in oneself, to explore that domain of experience where security is boredom and therefore sickness, and one exists in the present, in that enormous present which is without past or future, memory or planned intention, the life where a man must go until he is beat.

The hipster heralded a new white generation which believed that purchasing a bit of black earth would lend their lives in Cold War America some badly needed vitality. "Hip," Mailer goes on to suggest, "is the affirmation of the barbarian."

Breaking the Eisenhower ice, we can all agree, was a very good thing. But the beatniks' celebrations of a loose-limbed, vital "blackness" only succeeded in confirming their own whiteness. The line is straight and narrow between the beatnik's fetishizations of Dizzy Gillespie and Thelonious Monk, and the rap-loving, phat-styling wigger children of today. Today's white Negroes consume black culture with only a fantastically vague sense of what it might mean to do so, and no appreciation of the ironies involved. Whiteness rules their minds in stealth.

Japan in the eighties seemed a lot like America in the fifties. American white Negroes and Japanese blackfacers had prosperity in common: like Mailer's pals, the *kokujin ni naritai wakamono* (one of the Japanese media's monikers for black-oriented subcultures in general) were middle-class kids rebelling against a conformist society—in their case, Japan, Inc. Beatniks had cheap apartments and low gasoline prices to fuel their road trips; Tokyo blackfacers, until recently, lived off the cushion of wealth that constitutes the Japanese miracle.

Even before I arrived, I had discovered other similarities. The white Negro loved the (black) Negro's music, Mailer wrote, because it "gave voice to the character and quality of his existence, to his rage and the infinite variations of joy, lust, languor, growl, cramp, pinch, scream and despair of his orgasm." The "primitive passion about human nature," which Mailer described as the hallmark of beatnik culture, seemed to be at work in many of the most popular postwar Japanese novels. "Jackson shot heroin into the palm of Reiko's hand; maybe it hurt, her face twitched," wrote Ryu Murakami in *Almost Transparent Blue* (1976):

> The black woman was already drunk on something. She put her hands under my armpits and made me stand up, then stood up herself and began to dance. . . . At the smell of the black woman, clinging to me with her sweat, I almost fell. The smell was fierce, as if she were fermenting inside. . . . Her smell completely enveloped me; I felt nauseated.

Similarly, Nobel laureate Kenzaburo Oe opened his famous *A Personal Matter* (1964) with an almost nauseating vision of Africa:

> The continent itself resembled the skull of a man who had hung his head. . . . The miniature Africa indicating population distribution in a lower corner of the map was like a dead head beginning to decompose; another, veined with transportation routes, was a skinned head with the capillaries painfully exposed. Both these Africas suggested unnatural death, raw and violent.

The uneasy response to blackness and black culture—the combined attraction and repulsion, the "affirmation of the barbarian"—did seem to unite these disparate works, linking contemporary blackfacers to an earlier moment in Japanese culture, and to American white culture as well.

In the nineties, the Japanese miracle has been significantly demystified. Though the times are not austere, there is an increasing sense that Japan, Inc., isn't doing so well—especially since the collapse of the East Asian "miracle." Nevertheless, Japanese kids are still in a better position to purchase, say, the new Dr. Dre record than are middle-class teens in Liberia. This sort of power results in more Dr. Dre records and more photographs of kids in Newark demonstrating how to wear a hat backward with aplomb—so that Japanese kids can do the same at a club like Kings.

I forget who told me to telephone Mikako and Hiroshi. I met them about two weeks after I'd landed. I was ecstatic to find people I could really like. Mikako, a fresh-faced twenty-four-year-old, had an infectiously happy face. Hiroshi, twenty-six, had wiry and studious features; he reminded me of John Lennon. They both had good jobs: Hiroshi was an editor at a big publishing company, and Mikako analyzed fashion trends in one of the company's marketing divisions.

They took me to a soba shop. Mikako described some of the research her office had conducted on *burapan* fashion, which is the name given to the fashion sensibilities of all black wannabes, including blackfacers. Fashion communities among teenagers in Tokyo are numberless and strict, she said. *Bodykasi* wear the casual clothes a European supermodel might put on in her free time, while the *bodykons* dress more slinkily. *Co-gals* are would-be *bodykons*, with bodies too young and linear to achieve slinkiness. *Femi-o* guys wear flare pants, platform shoes, and feminine shirts. *Burapan*, she said, is on a downswing, so the "cool" my friend at the nightclub aspired to wouldn't be "cool" for very long. By the time you publish your essay, she told me, blackface costumes will be dead, relegated to the backs of closets and the bottoms of drawers.

Toward the end of a delicious soba meal I asked Mikako and Hiroshi what Japanese people thought of black people.

Mikako wrinkled her face; what a huge, unanswerable question I had asked. I was trying to understand whether Japanese attitudes toward blacks were really analogous to American attitudes. Although I often felt slighted here, I couldn't say for certain that people were treating me badly because I was black. My feeling of isolation could have been the loneliness any Western tourist might feel in Tokyo. Or I could simply have been taking personally the studied indifference I saw on the streets, a blankness that seemed to shut out everyone, including other Japanese.

One of my interviewees had emphasized that the Japanese are a mask-wearing culture. "Think of *noh*, or *kabuki*," he had said. Everyone wears his mask in the office, on the subway, at the restaurant, and even at home.

Still, I couldn't shake the feeling that there was something more to it. I told Mikako how people ignored me when I first arrived, how I'd never felt this foreign in any other country. I was surprised by how angry I was getting as I talked, but I didn't think it showed. I heard myself say that most foreigners probably have the same complaints.

The blacks in the Roppongi section make people afraid, Mikako said. But usually Japanese people do not think anything about black people. They like Michael Jordan and black American music, yes. She smiled broadly.

"I know," I agreed. "It's wild to hear. I love how much of it is played here. It's almost like home. But why do you think blacks make people afraid? Is it because you've *heard* African Americans are violent? Or is it because soldiers keep getting into fights?"

"Yes," Mikako said, nodding vigorously.

I hoped she meant the latter. "All soldiers get into fights," I assured her.

I told her a story about how, late one evening, when I was walking back to my hotel, I noticed two elderly women riding bicycles. They did not flinch at the sight of my black face. I compared this with the starchy fear on the white faces I routinely encountered in Park Slope, in Brooklyn, late at night, on the way home from the subway. I didn't tell Mikako that I was unsure what those elderly women were thinking. She didn't say what she thought they were thinking, either.

Hiroshi liked to chew his thoughts before speaking. Like many arts workers in his age group, he planned to come to America to study. He would study fashion, he said. He told me that the infamous "darky" trademarks had been discontinued because of local protests and the negative press they generated internationally. Today there is little evidence that Sambo ever gazed out from Japanese billboards or magazine covers, except for the occasional racist comic book—and, of course, the blackface Japanese.

I asked Hiroshi if he'd ever heard the term *minstrel*. He hadn't. I told him about the cartoons I'd seen on the television in my hotel room, examples of *anime*, Japan's world-famous animation. Almost all of the characters appeared to be white. Though they spoke Japanese, the characters had upturned noses and large, round eyes, sometimes colored blue. Minstrelsy is imitation like that, I explained, except usually it's imitation of people you think are lower than you.

Hiroshi nodded. The animation used to be worse, he said. The scenarios used to take place in Paris or London, never Japan. The characters had names like Mary or Jane. "I would say it's changing," he said. "Young people don't feel inferior any more."

My next question was nearly as huge as the one about what Japanese thought about blacks. It turned out to be unanswerable. "Do you think Japanese people see a colored person when they look in the mirror?"

I knew it was absurd to ask them to take sides in a racial system born and bred in the United States, the most race-conscious country in the world. But perhaps not completely absurd. America has been exporting its race problem around the globe for at least a century, and the Japanese *have* taken sides—both sides, as it happens.

The Japanese encounter with modernity began in 1853, when Commodore Matthew Perry "re-opened" Japan. The Japanese encounter with blackface dates back to the same year: Perry brought a troop of minstrels along with him. After Perry's visit, trade with Europe and the United States was established, and the country undertook a massive modernization drive. As with many modernizing countries, Japan's drive to "catch up" with the world's financial powers was accompanied by a powerful movement to preserve the country's cultural traditions. To Westerners, however, Japan was just another Asiatic country—more mysterious, perhaps, for its centuries of isolation from colonial depredations, but still little more than what we would today call an "emerging market."

In 1905, Japan defeated Russia in the Russo-Japanese War: the West now had to take the island nation seriously. The rise of Japan was also celebrated in Asia as a sign that the time had come for other countries in the region, as well. Sun Yat-sen, the father of Chinese nationalism, wrote:

> Since the rise of the Japanese, the Caucasians dare not look down upon other Asiatic peoples. Thus the power of Japan not only enables the Japanese to enjoy the privileges of a first-class nation, but enhances the international position of other Asiatic peoples. It used to be the general belief that the Asiatics could not

do what the Europeans could do. Because the Japanese have learned so well from Europe, and because we know we Chinese can do as well as the Japanese, we see the possibility of doing as well as the Europeans.

For a time, the Japanese were considered "colored" (both inside and outside Japan), and the nation enjoyed a brilliant stardom among the "darker peoples" of the world.

In the United States, Negro race-men made the idea of an Afro-Asiatic people an abiding theme of early-twentieth-century racialist thought. Figures like Booker T. Washington, W. E. B. Du Bois, and Marcus Garvey all considered Japan a model of "colored" progress. Black Muslim leader Elijah Muhammad spent four years in prison for urging black Americans to evade the draft rather than fight the Japanese. More surprisingly, perhaps, Japanese nationals of various ideological stripes made contact with American blacks. Langston Hughes spent time with Japanese leftists before being deported from Japan in 1933. On the right, and much more visible, were ultranationalist figures like Satokata "Little Major" Takahashi, who founded several organizations in 1930s Detroit to stir up pro-Japanese sentiment among U.S. blacks. (Some of the most receptive were early members of the Nation of Islam.) Even as late as 1942, Japanese fascists tried to rally fellow "colored people" around the world to support their national cause.

At home, however, the fascists were more interested in promoting their version of the Shinto religion and the contention that the emperor was divine: *He descends from the sun goddess Ameraterasu Omikami, He is a living testament to the divine origins of the Japanese people.* A key component of ultranationalist ideology was a belief in the ethnic purity of the nation. The superiority of the "Yamato race" (as the Japanese called themselves) was used to justify Japan's brutal annexation of Korea in 1910, its massacres in China in 1937, and its terrorism of other Asian nations during World War II. After the Japanese surrender, the American occupation forces demanded an end to emperor worship. The Japanese complied and established a political democracy modeled on the American system.

What happened next is less clear. The horrific defeat of the nationalist cause in World War II, and the American occupation, scholars agree, was the source of Japan's renewed "inferiority complex" vis-à-vis the West. This is where John Russell comes in. Russell, an African American scholar at Japan's Gifu University, has done the most thorough work documenting the meaning of race in postwar Japan. His writings fed my suspicion that the postwar explosion of negative depictions of blackness represented an attempt to soothe a Japanese inferiority complex. Russell contends that the appropriation of antiblack racism was a sign of iden-tification with white Americans, a bid for equality. Or even superiority: by the eighties, as Japanese companies came to dominate the American automotive and electronics industries, America's decline could be as-cribed to American racial heterogeneity. As then–Prime Minister Ya-suhiro Nakasone argued in 1986, America's declining competitiveness was a consequence of the low intelligence of its black and Hispanic populations.

What has complicated this, of course, is the small but significant population of black people in Japan—most notably the black American soldiers who frequent the entertainment precinct of Roppongi. While the presence of these black soldiers undoubtedly plays some role in fanning Japanese stereotypes, it is also the context for the *vogue negre* among Japanese youth, especially among women. Russell sees the fash-ion for blackness typified by *kokujin ni naritai wakamono* as akin to white appropriations of black culture:

> *Just as the white minstrel/White Negro acted out his racial and sexual fantasies in a bid to transcend Whiteness, so the current Japanese obsession with blackness allows Japanese youth a freedom of expression they are unable to experience in their circumscribed social role as "Japanese." Additionally, it has allowed both to celebrate "non-whiteness" while remaining embedded in the political economy of "Westerness/Whiteness."*

In a word, then, Hiroshi and Mikako's parents went white over black. In their Japan, there was no room for being "colored" anymore.

Many of the black people in Tokyo are soldiers. The soldiers are the blacks on the ground, so to speak, and treat the city with equal measures of fear and condescension. You never see soldiers on the subway until the weekend, when they train in from their suburban bases in search of fun. Usually, they end up in places like Roppongi.

There are several types of black Americans in Roppongi. There are "refugees," out-of-work entertainers who spend what little money they have trying to pick up Japanese women, who lend them money to eat and go out. Sooner or later these guys get tired of the life, or they get deported. Then there are the "professionals," businesspeople, teachers, and students, only a small number of whom hit Roppongi on the weekends. And there are the servicemen, the largest black contingent in Roppongi. The black military men behave—well, like military men. They wear buzz cuts, they eat and party where other Americans do, they get into drunken fights. They spend a lot of time in the nightclubs.

I spent a lot of time in those clubs, too, trying to figure out their intricate sociology. Although most of the clubs are open to all races, and Japanese predominate everywhere, the kind of music played depends on the race of the next largest racial group. That is, all-Japanese clubs play Asian pop, with a little black pop music (à la Janet Jackson) for style; clubs patronized by whites feature dance pop and rock, with a little hip-hop for style; clubs frequented by blacks offer reggae and hip-hop, and nothing else. In the Japanese clubs, there is an even mix of Japanese men and women; in the white clubs, an even proportion of men to women, across racial lines. But in the black clubs, almost all the men are black, and almost all the women are Japanese.

The black scene in Tokyo is highly diverse. Besides the Americans, there is a sizable population of Africans, mostly from Ghana, Kenya, and Nigeria. You see them milling about outside the Roppongi subway station, passing out flyers for the most popular black clubs. The clubs are owned by Africans, although the businesses are recorded in their Japanese wives' names, in compliance with Japanese law. The Africans actually cause American blacks considerable discomfort, in part because they can "pass" for American. They walk around "head-to-toe in Karl Kani," one American complained to me. "Nobody who knows anything about hip-hop culture would go out looking like that. They don't know any better. And the Japanese girls can't tell the difference." This last point hints at the real issue: the soldiers don't mind the blackface Japanese, whose tans they see as flattery or beauty or silliness, but they do mind the competition from the Africans. A couple years ago, a black crew from the battleship *Independence* nearly beat to death the son of a Ghanaian diplomat, allegedly over the attention of a Japanese woman. The group called themselves the G's, gangsta style, but no one believes they were real gangsters, or that they were only fighting for the woman's affections. The issue is authenticity. In Roppongi, where everybody consumes everybody, the real question is who gets to be an African American.

One morning I boarded one of Japan's famous supertrains. I was going to speak with John Russell about his life and work, and to do that I had to get to his house in Gifu, way out in the country. Even after the supertrain ride to Nagoya, I had to take two or three local trains, and then a bus, to get to Gifu.

The entire neighborhood was roofed with those beautiful traditional tiles rarely seen in Tokyo. The small two-story building where the professor lived was full of Japanese books. He spoke Japanese with his Japanese wife, and even carried himself with a rather Japanese restraint. He was as Japanese as an outsider could get. Still, he told me, the nation had "been a disappointment."

Living in Japan, Russell explained, meant contending with "the Ellisonian invisible man syndrome." The cultural deluge from the West made it hard for Japanese to actually see black people. For example, even though he wrote essays and books in Japanese, Russell's mastery of the language was sometimes greeted with disbelief. *Gaijin* familiarity with Japanese culture always seems to surprise the Japanese; apparently *kokujin* familiarity is even more astonishing. Russell's blackness marked him as somehow less weighty, and, for all his learnedness, his skin color put him in much the same category as the black boys who go to play in Roppongi.

I felt sorry for Russell. My own appreciation of his work undoubtedly had something to do with our shared experience of race, American style. Russell had hoped to leave behind America's strict racial categories on the voyage over. Alas, they trailed him well, those stupid categories.

I guess I wanted to know what race Hiroshi and Mikako considered themselves because I didn't really know how to place my new friends. As Asians, perhaps, but "Asian" has taken a battering from this century's many inter-Asian conflicts, and "Asian American" is a category under construction, at best, despite nearly two hundred years of yellow and brown faces on our shores. The act of designating oneself black or white is so basic to American culture that I found it hard to believe that Hiroshi and Mikako had not chosen sides, too.

I couldn't shake the suspicion that the Japanese still secretly want to be white. When I asked Hiroshi about how Japanese see themselves, I already knew what I wanted him to say: "We hate black people. We love white people." I wanted to hear him say, "We see ourselves as white." Like Russell, I believed that the Japanese see themselves as white, even when they black up.

Reginald Kearney disagreed. Kearney was a long-time African American resident of Japan and a professor at the Kanda University of International Studies. Black people in Japan shouldn't obsess about race, he insisted. "When we are referred to as *gaijin*," he told me, "they don't care what color you are." Japanese prejudice against foreigners is undiscriminating, he assured me: "There are signs in Shinjuku that say 'Japanese Only' in other Asian languages: Korean, Chinese, Tagalog." Still, it was possible to be accepted, he said, as long as one respected the Japanese. There was even a black sumo wrestler.

"I came from Virginia," Kearney said. "I can remember the last time I was called a nigger. It was not in Japan."

"I see," I told the professor, remembering those unafraid elderly women on bicycles. But black sumo wrestlers notwithstanding, it wasn't particularly reassuring. Still, I did have occasion to revisit his argument days later, after I got to know a couple of white people.

Let me tell you about my dinner at Anne and John's house. Anne is a homemaker in a swank neighborhood; her husband John directs the Tokyo branch of a mammoth American bank. She invited me over for dinner because she thought I should meet her friend Lance Lee, a black American entrepreneur who has already been the subject of several "blacks in Japan" articles. "Lance Lee knows everybody," she said. "He's probably the type who would do well anywhere."

While waiting for Lance, Anne and I sipped beer from tall glasses and discussed the local schools. John arrived. He had the boyish, blond confidence of a well-to-do surfer. He went to college in the United States but grew up in Japan. His family had been doing business here for generations. "You speak more Japanese than my father did," he said, laughing, upon discovering my minimal proficiency. It seemed like a family joke.

When Lance Lee appeared, he shook everyone's hands gracefully. He apologized for his lateness, explaining that he had wanted to make sure the hosts were home before he arrived. The caution fit his appearance. Lance had a tightly buttoned face with straight regimented teeth, and his hair was cut neat and close to his head. His Japan story began when he came from California with the Air Force, after which he'd planted roots, and made a lot of money. "Money makes you more yourself," he said.

John nodded in agreement. "I'm an extreme optimist," he exclaimed. "Whatever happens, happens for the best!" I folded my arms. There was a certain confrontational quality to Lance's voice when he said, "I'm optimistic, too!"

Anne had mostly been listening, but now she had something important to get off her chest. Warning Lance and me not to take it the wrong way, Anne explained that she never understood why black people on the street in, say, Queens, where she grew up, would pass her enraged. Occasionally she would encounter a man grumbling something to the effect of, "I hate white people," and it would always bother her.

But Tokyo was making her sympathetic, Anne said. She was endlessly frustrated by her interactions with the Japanese. Her social circle consisted largely of Japanese women—other bankers' wives—from whom she felt estranged. Some of this was positioning: as the boss's wife, she had to be boss to all the wives: as a higher-up in a very hierarchical system, she could never be considered an equal. But the women also excluded her, she thought, because she was white. They were awed by her and they disliked her because of her race. They never talked to her and it was driving her crazy; she was terribly lonely. For the first time in her life, she concluded with angry penitence, she knew how black people must feel.

A week later Lance told me that he wanted to tell Anne she could never understand how a black person felt. "The reason a black person is cursing at white people is that he's a victim of his American system. White people come over here, and for the first time in [their] lives [they] aren't running things." I agreed that Anne's analogy was faulty, and I was also glad, in a way, that one white person had felt some racial pain. But the more time I spent in Japan, talking to dozens of people, the more I realized that Anne did have a point, and that it was simpatico with the one Kearney had been making. Anne could never be accepted in Japan because she is a *gaijin*, and therefore not Japanese—which means that the color of a Japanese face could not possibly be white.

Because my dinner with Hiroshi and Mikako had broken down when I attempted to broach the race question, I decided to try another tack.

Hiroshi became quite engaging when the subject turned to Japanese culture. The fact that I had read Japanese writers appeared to surprise him.

"You like Oe?" Hiroshi asked.

"Very much. I want to interview him," I said. Kenzaburo Oe writes autobiographical fiction. *A Personal Matter*, his most famous book, is based on the unwelcome birth of his autistic son. "Oe's self-absorption strikes me as similar to Southern American modernism," I said, trying to be generous. "Black American writers tend to be extremely self-absorbed, too. To extremes."

"Some people think he writes about himself and his son because he wants to have something to write about. I think it is hard for the Japanese writer. He has to find some problem to write about," Hiroshi said.

"You mean because there aren't too many problems in Japan?"

"I think so." He considered his words carefully. "In my opinion, the Japanese people are not interested in ethnicity, for example, because they feel the same."

"But the sameness is not at all real, is it?" I asked.

"No."

"Look at all the different faces on the subway," I said. I had spent countless hours marveling at the range of features I had seen riding around Tokyo: the sizes of nose, the shapes of eyes, the coarseness of hair and darkness of skin. "People from the north as light as Russians. People from the southern isles as dark as me. Almost."

He smiled. "I think," he said patiently, "that this might be true."

I had done my homework and wanted my dinner companions to know. We talked about the different dialects spoken in Japan, and how difficult it is for some Japanese to understand each other, literally. We talked about the Ainu of the North, and about the Okinawans and others from the South: all Japanese with distinct cultural traditions. I mentioned the plight of the Koreans in Japan, and brought up the *burakumin*, a class of Japanese historically excluded from Japanese society because of their association with occupations considered unclean (for example, leatherwork and the disposal of dead oxen and cattle). Until the beginning of this century, *burakumin* lived in specially designated areas.

"Yes," said Hiroshi. "There are some problems with *burakumin* people." Where Hiroshi grew up, in Osaka, he explained, *burakumin* were a vocal political force. A *buraku* friend of his used to complain about discrimination endlessly. After a while the complaining started to get on Hiroshi's nerves, because he himself hadn't discriminated against anybody.

I've heard that before, I thought to myself.

"The Japanese people don't want to upset each other," he told me, "by thinking about other people deeply. Japanese people are good at assimilating other cultures."

I broke the quail egg over my last few soba noodles. "Do you worry that thinking about others less superficially will force Japanese to think about themselves too much?" I asked.

Hiroshi thought a long time before he answered. "I think so."

A few days later I interviewed Yoshimoto Sakamoto, the head of the Buraku Liberation League. I asked him whether there were any *buraku* in Tokyo. He told me I'd probably seen many *burakumin*. No one knows how many there are in Japan. There may be three million; by some estimates, everyone in Japan is in fact descended from a *buraku*. "What we're doing is waking up the sleeping babes," said Sakamoto. "It requires courage to openly state you are a *buraku*, not to conceal your identity."

I laughed, and told him that some members of my family in South Carolina had left home and disappeared into the white world. Genes travel farthest in the secrecy of night, but most people don't like to think about it. Few white Southerners want to talk about the black genes in their bodies, or the black words in their mouths. And many blacks prefer to let sleeping dogs lie.

The situation is not very good for *buraku*, Sakamoto continued. The income gap between *buraku* and non-*buraku* is about one million yen (almost 8,000 dollars). While there has been some public assistance for *burakumin* over the last few decades—for housing and education, primarily—Sakemoto suspects that the government is planning to discontinue it, using the current economic recession as an excuse.

Buraku are still stigmatized, he told me. Japan has yet to overcome the feudal association of *burakumin* and uncleanliness. Families still investigate the histories of potential marriage partners to screen out *buraku*, even though almost everybody has some, somewhere. The point is you wouldn't know, because *buraku* never acknowledge their identities in public. Some of Japan's most famous politicians, businessmen, and artists are *buraku*, Sakamoto said. But *buraku* faces look Japanese enough, and it is easiest to pretend away the difference.

My next trip was to Kawasaki, just south of Tokyo, to visit the Reverend Lee Inha. We met in his small church off one of the main avenues in Kawasaki, where Lee is a leader of the large Korean community.

There are approximately a million Koreans in Japan. Though a large percentage of them have lived in Japan for generations, they are still required to carry alien registration cards, and they haven't yet won the right to vote in national elections. The Japanese government only recently acknowledged that many Korean women were forced to serve as prostitutes for Japanese soldiers during World War II. Although few Koreans are middle class, they had been barred from receiving welfare, health care, and other social benefits until 1982.

"Socially speaking," Lee told me, "black fate in the States and ours are almost the same." Koreans are denied access to the tightly knit world of Japanese business, and after the Kobe earthquake, Korean refugees were segregated from Japanese in refugee camps. Most Koreans look nearly the same as Japanese, so many try to pass. After the war, Japan offered to naturalize its Korean population, a process that involved adopting a Japanese name. Although most Koreans didn't accept the deal, a sizable number did try to protect their children from discrimination by sending them to school with Japanese names. As a result, some young Koreans don't even know their true background.

The reverend said nothing about the bombs—but certainly he knew that most of the non-Japanese victims in Hiroshima and Nagasaki were Koreans. Tens of thousands of Koreans died in those unnecessary attacks, which means that Korean nationals in Japan, some of whom were enslaved by the Japanese for the war effort, were victims of both Japanese masters and American liberators, a terrible irony. In much the same way, black American soldiers are walking ironies. African American soldiers enforce the policies of a nation that does not like black people very much. In Japan, a nation that could conceivably offer them a blank slate, they are instead handed back an imperfect version of American racism.

When the reverend and I met, we recognized what we had in common: we had both suffered at the hands of an oppressive majority. We were both outsiders. Each saw himself in the other: Reverend Lee saw the Korean in my face, and I saw the black in his. We realized we shared a job description.

"Japan needs us," Lee said, because otherwise it will remain an island nation with no regard for others. The Japanese believe that they are one big family, but the Koreans make the Japanese respectful of differences. "That can make a good contribution to the Japanese society. One day they will be surprised to wake up and find out the name of the prime minister is Mr. Kim." The reverend laughed. "That is a joke, of course!"

My forty-five minutes were up. "I wish I had known you were African American," he told me in parting. "We could have had more time."

The next time I saw Hiroshi and Mikako, we had a French meal and repaired to a tiny jazz bar, underground. We sat on high chairs and talked about Hiroshi's plans to get out of Japan for graduate school.

The couple inquired about my previous travels. I described a trip I took to New Orleans and the Creoles I had met there. I explained what light-skin privilege means to black Americans, and how it is a legacy of slavery. Both my new friends seemed baffled, even though light skin and feminine beauty are to some extent equated in Japan.

"Koreans," Hiroshi said, "are rumored to be more beautiful than the Japanese." Many people say that they are the most beautiful actresses. Groups of businessmen are known to take sex tours of Seoul, he told me.

"But I thought you can't tell the difference," I said. "At least that's what I've been told."

"There is a rumor," Hiroshi confided, "that Japanese eyes turn down, while the eyes of Koreans and other Asians turn upward."

"That's a joke, right?"

"It's the rumor," said Hiroshi.

"Like my eyes," said Mikako, pointing. I couldn't really tell; if anything. I thought they pointed down a little. "They are up, maybe?" she said.

"I see," I said, not seeing at all.

Mikako nodded her head.

"Do people think you're Korean?" I asked.

"Oh, but I am Japanese," Mikako said, her happy face bleached with a startling sincerity—almost strong enough to wash away the variety of Japanese features in this restaurant, on the train, everywhere in Tokyo.

No wonder the young blackfacer in that "Black Women" T-shirt felt shunned in school; no wonder none of my other correspondents wanted to talk about the phenomenon. The source of Mikako's sincerity, her perfect belief in the mask of Japanese homogeneity, had to be the very thing blackfacers were poking fun at with their silly getups.

A couple of nights before I was scheduled to leave Japan, I paid my way into one more Tokyo club. The brooding music of Dr. Dre and several other Los Angeles rappers filled the tight basement room; the music hugged everyone with its familiar warmth. I was waiting by the DJ booth, all alone, when the owner brought me and the other black man in the place a can of beer each, gratis.

We hadn't met before, but I was happy to find another black American in an all-Japanese club, especially in Shinjuku. I stood for a minute before I said emptily, "Feels like we're the entertainment."

The other guy grunted inconclusively. I thought maybe he hadn't heard me. But perhaps he didn't find it funny because he had in fact come to Japan to entertain. He called himself J. J., and he was trying to be a rap star. He said he'd been flown here by a Japanese business-man to play, in effect, himself.

We spent half an hour looking at the dancers on the floor. Boys and girls were hunched in separate bundles, hurling small sharp eyes at each other. Those few who did dance were pretty much alone, dressed in brand new hip-hop gear, working out the spacious clothing heartily, and being teenagers.

I drank my free drink and noted with a little unease that an undis-criminating eye might see more blackness in J. J. than in me. My new pal told me about being raised in Arkansas, slinging guns and whatnot, then traveling out to L.A., and slinging guns and whatnot. J. J. was an authentic member of the Crips, and he had spent time in an authentic California prison: he was as real a ghetto gangsta as any hip-hopper could wish to be. But the way J. J. told his story made poverty sound boring, not like in the movies. The narrative produced a squall of bour-geois nervousness and shame; I could remember being younger and wishing I could act more like J. J. Back then, I didn't see that I could be him much more easily than he could be me.

We went outside to get some air. A Japanese teenager followed us out, tanned with processed curls, nattily dressed in *burapan* apparel. At first, I thought he had come outside to cool off, too, but soon realized he was watching us. I raised my eyebrows and bobbed my head. He did the same.

"See that?" I said to my companion.

"Yeah," said J. J.

"What do you think about the blackface?" I said. "I guess he wants to look like me and you. Yellow Negroes."

"Yeah," said J. J., uninterested.

When we went back downstairs, I was rethinking my resentment toward the blackfaces. Give them some space, I told myself. Which attitude is preferable: theirs or Mikako's? Japan incorporated Chinese characters into its alphabet; sushi supposedly comes from Korea; the word *arigato* comes from *obrigado*, the Portuguese word for *thank you*—but the average Japanese still doesn't think of his or her culture as creolized. Hiroshi had said that the Japanese were good at assimilating other cultures superficially; maybe that was fine. Everyone at this club shared a desire to shift, change, morph, copycat, *and* stay the same. Hell, one of the CDs being played was by a black American group that calls itself the Wu-Tang Clan, in homage to a posse of film gangsters from Hong Kong. Maybe this kind of shifty identity is the nature of things in a global economy: pop culture moving in strange ways, its wonders to perform.

I was wondering, then, whether the existence of *kokujin ni naritai wakamono* might even be a good thing: whether we *kokujin* might consider their celebration of black culture a progressive stance, especially in a country where Sambo was the norm just a few years ago. Maybe Japanese who act black are ten years ahead of their time, proof that Japan is changing, that the mask of Japanese sameness is being shown up for what it is: an illusion. Maybe the sooty faces of the blackfacers are the first signs of a tidal wave in the unrippled pond. Maybe, I thought, we "blacks" *are* ruining the atmosphere. For good.

"I'd guess those misguided Yellow Negroes are foolish childish consumers just like any other foolish childish consumers," one drunken Marxist had suggested back in the States, by phone, before I left for Japan. "Buy shit. Buy more shit. Buy better shit. More efficient multinational corporations, more continental coalescings of nations, more transnational bodies ignoring borders and helping corporations use cheap labor to make more shit to sell. Somebody gets those jazz records to the Japanese. The triumph has a black American face, but the triumph isn't black or American. It's capital." His argument was that race was obsolescent: "Black is one more solid that melts into air; so will every other minority in the world. In time everybody must exist to be a consumer. Even Japan, Inc., and the American empire are eroding at the edges. The question is what big, mean capitalist beast will rise from the ashes and eat us all up. Because everybody is being encouraged to chew, chew, chew." I heard the tinkling of ice in a glass. "Which circle of Hell is the one where people feed on each other?" my friend had asked.

As I sat with J. J., I thought of my friend's diatribe. Maybe he was right. Maybe we're all minstrels now, the opening act on an emerging global stage.

But my Marxist friend didn't quite have it right. See, I know that when that wild "transnational" world finally arrives, race is still going to matter. There will still be plenty of sufferers, probably many of the same people who are suffering now. I wanted to ask J. J. what he thought we would take from the Japanese if we wanted to imitate them. But then I realized that I was asking the wrong questions. I should have been asking whether we *could* ever emulate them. Consider where J. J. had come from. How many items of Japanese pop culture can a black ghetto kid buy? How expensive would Japface be, assuming that kid could figure out how to wear it?

Tanning oneself in emulation of black people or wearing black hipster's clothing needn't mean anything; Mikako and Hiroshi, two young, thoughtful, open-minded people, showed no sign of feeling strained by the existence of blackfacers. And the sexualized "cool" that Japanese attribute to blackness doesn't leave much space for the black humanity. They know very little about us. The clubowner gave me and J. J. our drinks, I knew, for our cool. The implications were disturbing: if American blacks could be appropriated by the Japanese, could Japan's own minorities be far behind? Look ahead to a fashion sense that imitates Japan's own *internal* outsiders—Korean chic, or *burakumin* cool. The sad, exhausted feeling I'd had when I first heard about Japanese kids wearing blackface came back to me in a rush.

Then, on my last day in Japan, I found solace in Hell.

I walked through a small entryway, put my boots in a locker, and entered a large hallway. I paid the attendant. I removed my clothes, careful to step on the cold wood of the floor with the outsides of my feet. I pulled a towel and soap from my bag. I closed the door of a second locker, pulled the elastic band of its key around my wrist, and passed through the sliding doors of the bathing area.

Sentos, public baths, are segregated by gender. The practice of going to them is losing ground to showers at home and the comforts of private health clubs, but sentos are publicly subsidized out of respect for tradition. The washing process is simple: you scrub under faucets before entering a hot pool of water. The water softens the dead skin, which you then scrub off, repeating the process until you are clean.

One of my interviewees, a man named Curtis, went to a sento in Osaka once. He said when he got into the water everyone got out: *Gaijin! Kokujin!* He said he never went back. I wasn't deterred, though, because I had paid thousands of dollars to experience the real Japan.

There was no black music in this Shinjuku sento, no music at all. There was a row of green stools by the sliding doors, and a set of yellow plastic basins. I picked up one of each and placed them in front of the wall of faucets. The faucets were set in pairs, two feet above the tile floor. On my left, there was a naked man scrubbing. Behind him was a pool of hot water; above it was a clock and some dials for telling the water's temperature. The pool looked hot.

I turned to my faucets and scrubbed. I washed my face first, and then my neck, my shoulders, my back, chest, and stomach. I filled the basin and made a lather; suds slipped toward the wall, inching down the sloping tile to the drain by the door. I washed my arms and hands, my thighs and my backside, my genitals and my knees. I washed my legs and the tops of my feet, then between the toes, and then the white undersides. Everything except my hair.

The man entered the pool and stayed in for a minute or so. He emerged enervated: he was a beet red yellow man. I made my way into the pool. It was hot. After a few minutes, I started to feel dizzy. I thought of the way Africans are said to be more resistant to heat, how science says our skins were made for heat, how they said we were made for working in the sun.

The other man was chatting to himself in silence: *He is a kokujin. His skin is dark dark dark.* I could tell—I saw my skin in his eyes and I knew that look and what it meant. I knew! I hated him until the heat in the hot bath settled things. For a second I forgot what my dark skin meant. *It is black. It is dirty like the jungle. It is American.* I forgot that I am not Japanese like he is, and that he is not black like me.

I nearly passed out. With effort I rose, went to the faucets, scrubbed my body once more. I washed hard, cleaned everything again, including my hair this time. The other man left. I went back to the tub. My skin felt raw and good. I let my muscles go and submitted to the hold of weightlessness. My head began to pulse once more, a good warm pulsing. *So warm are the ashes of burning empires.* I got out and repeated the process several times. With a new car owner's pride I celebrated my small triumphs: how I'd brought myself to Japan, how I'd found this truly Japanese sento, how I felt right at home. *This is the cleanest I've been since my mother let me out of her belly,* I thought, as I eyed the blackfaced Japanese in the mirror.

KEVIN YOUNG

b. 1970

Kevin Young's first book, *Most Way Home*, won the National Poetry Series and the Zacharis First Book Prize from *Ploughshares;* the volume considers the possibilities and limits of home, particularly for his parents and grandparents in rural Louisiana. *Booklist* said of his debut, "Young engages the material of African American history the way Yeats did Irish history and García Márquez the history of Latin American economic colonization. That is, he engages and transforms it with his language and compassion."

Young's new work, *To Repel Ghosts*, takes up the history of black and popular culture through the figure of the late artist Jean-Michel Basquiat; these "riffs" may start with Basquiat as inspiration but more often than not end up taking on race ("Negative") and popular culture ("Charlie Chan on Horn"). Like the jazz musicians and black artists who influence him, Young constructs his own tradition, whether through family, a blues for "Langston Hughes," or an "Homage to Phillis Wheatley," the first African American published poet.

NINETEEN SEVENTY-FIVE

Since there was no better color
or name, we called the dog
Blackie, insurance no one would forget
the obvious. One of the few dark ones
in the bunch, the only male,
he died twelve human years later
standing on a vet's table;
when the news came Mama
Lucille, visiting, gathered us
in a circle of hands, called up
Jesus to the touch, to protect.

But that year when beautiful
still meant Black, when I carried
home my first dog full of whimpers
& sudden dukey, we warmed him
in our basement with a bottle disguised
as his mother, we let his hair grow long
around his feet, just as ours did

around ears, unbent necks. Back
in the day, my mother cut my afro
every few months, bathroom layered
with headlines proclaiming the world's end,
our revolution. I cannot recall
when I first stepped into the reclining
thrones of the barbershop
when I first demanded to go there alone,
motherless, past the spinning white
& red sign left over from days of giving
blood, to ask for my head turned
clean, shorn, for the cold to hold.

I only remember how back then the room
seemed to fill with darkness as she trimmed

my globe of hair, curls falling like an earth
I never thought would be anywhere
but at my feet, how the scissors twanged
by these ears like the raised voice
of a Southern gentleman the moment after
some beautiful boy segregates coffee, no cream,
black, onto his creased & bleached lap.

NO OFFENSE

If you wonder why
I'm not laughing, go ask
Brian, the sixth grade cut-up
the one with the most dirty jokes
who requested the tribal African song
Tina Singu, each music class, black
vinyl spinning while Brian made
faces, knocked his knees together
like eggs. If you are curious about
me, just ask the boy who riddled
the whole playground or me
& my friends walking
home: *What do you get*
when you cross a black person

with a smurf? I am sure today
he would answer you, would explain
now that he meant No offense just
like he did then above the crowd
of girls leaning close or the boys
trying to get his timing down,
just as after the punchline
he always said *You know I don't*
mean you. It's OK. And when
you see that boy whose last name
I don't seem to remember, be sure
to tell him that this here Smigger

could care less yet could never care
more, that my blue
& brown body is more
than willing to inform
him offense is one hostage
I have never taken.

NEGATIVE

Wake to find everything black
what was white, all the vice
versa—white maids on TV, black

sitcoms that star white dwarfs
cute as pearl buttons. Black Presidents,
Black Houses. White horse

candidates. All bleach burns
clothes black. Drive roads
white as you are, white songs

on the radio stolen by black bands
like secret pancake recipes, white back-up
singers, ball-players & boxers all

white as tar. Feathers on chickens
dark as everything, boiling in the pot
that called the kettle honky. Even

whites of the eye turn dark, pupils
clear & changing as a cat's.
Is this what we've wanted

& waited for? to see snow
covering everything black
as Christmas, dark pages written

white upon? All our eclipses bright,
dark stars shooting across pale
sky, glowing like ash in fire, shower

every skin. Only money keeps
green, still grows & burns like grass
under dark daylight.

CHARLIE CHAN ON HORN

For Prestige

Bird records
a few sides
(for contract

reasons) as Mr Charlie
Chan—no matter
the name his blues

sound the same,
same alto blaring
ALCHEMY,

licks exotic
as *Charlie Chan*
in Black Magic—

Chan's dark sidekick
Birmingham Brown
(aka Man-

tan Moreland)
seeing ghosts,
fleeing. *Feets*

do yo stuff—
THRIVING ON A RIFF,
Bird on a run

(in one place)
eyes bugged out
blowing

like Gabriel.
Solos snorted—
in one nose

& out the other.
Gone. Number one
son—don't they know

Charlie Chan
is a white man?
Fu Manchu too.

(Bless you.)
Parker play
your horn, not

no coon
no coolie in a white
suit. Bird's shot

his way to the top—
made a fist, tied off
& caught

the first vein
out of town.
Laying tracks—

NOWS THE TIME
NOWS THE TIME
BIRD GETS THE WORM—

Now dig
this—Basquiat
lit, lidded, does

a gravestone—
CPRKR
in the Stan-

hope Hotel,
the one Bird bit
the dust in (ON AIR)

high. TEETH.
HALOES
FIFTY NINE CENT.

Who knew how well
Basquiat would follow—
feet (six deep) first.

LANGSTON HUGHES

LANGSTON HUGHES
LANGSTON HUGHES
          O come now
          & sang
them weary blues—

Been tired here
feelin' low down
          Real
          tired here
since you quit town

GIANT STEPS

Our ears no longer trumpets
Our mouths no more bells
    FAMOUS POET©—
    Busboy—Do tell
us of hell—

Mr. Shakespeare in Harlem
Mr. Theme for English B
    Preach on
    kind sir
of death, if it please—

We got no more promise
We only got ain't
    Let us in
    on how
you 'came a saint

LANGSTON
LANGSTON
    LANGSTON HUGHES
    Won't you send
all heaven's news

HOMAGE TO PHILLIS WHEATLEY

Poet & Servant to Mr. Wheatley of Boston,
on her Maiden Voyage to Britain

There are days I can understand
why you would want to board
broad back of some ship
and sail: venture, not homeward
but toward Civilization's

Cold seat,—having from wild
been stolen, and sent into more wild
of Columbia, our exiles

and Christians clamoring upon
the cobblestones of Bostontown—

Sail across an Atlantic (this time) mild,
the ship's polite and consumptive
passengers proud. Your sickness
quit soon as you disembarked in mist
of England—free, finally, of our Republic's

Rough clime, its late converts who thought
they would not die, or die simply
in struggle, martyr to some God,—
you know of gods there
are many, who is really only

One—and that sleep, restless fever
would take most you loved. Why
fate fight? Death, dark mistress,
would come a-heralding silent
the streets,—no door to her closed,

No stair (servant or front) too steep.
Gen. Washington, whom you praise,
victorious, knows this—will even admit
you to his parlor. Who could resist a Negress
who can recite Latin and speak the Queen's?

Docked among the fog and slight sun
of London, you know who you are not
but that is little new. Native
of nowhere,—you'll stay a spell, return,
write, grow still. I wake with you

In my mind, leaning, learning
to write—your slight profile
that long pull of lower lip, its pout
proving you rescued by
some sadness too large to name.

My Most Excellence, my quill
and ink lady, you spill such script
no translation it needs—
your need is what's missing, unwritten
wish to cross back but not back

Into that land (for you) of the dead—
you want to see from above
deck the sea, to pluck from wind
a sense no Land can
give: drifting, looking not

For Leviathan's breath, nor waves
made of tea, nor for mermen half-
out of water (as you)—down
in the deep is not the narwhal enough real?
Beneath our wind-whipt banner you smile

At Sea which owns no country.

SELECT BIBLIOGRAPHY

Anthologies
Listed alphabetically by last name of editor.

Anderson, S. E., and Tony Medina. *In Defense of Mumia*. Writers & Readers, 1996.

Anglesey, Zoe. *Listen Up! Spoken Word Poetry*. One World, 1999.

Asim, Jabari, and Kevin Powell. *Young Tongues: A Poetic Exchange*. First Civilizations, 1992.

Austin, DorisJean, and Martin Simmons. *Streetlights: Illuminating Tales of the Urban Black Experience*. Penguin, 1996.

Baraka, Imamu Amiri, and Larry Neal. *Black Fire: An Anthology of Afro-American Writing*. Morrow, 1968.

Boyd, Herb, and Robert L. Allen. *Brotherman: The Odyssey of Black Men in America*. Ballantine, 1995.

Callaloo: A Journal of African American and African Arts and Letters. University of Virginia. Edited by Charles H. Rowell.

Chapman, Abraham. *New Black Voices: An Anthology of Contemporary Afro-American Literature*. New American Library, 1972.

Datcher, Michael. *My Brother's Keeper: Blackmen's Poetry Anthology*. S.I., 1992. (Introduction by Yusef Komunyakaa)

Davis, Arthur P., et al. *The New CALVACADE: African American Writing from 1760 to the Present*. 2 vols. Howard University Press, 1992.

Ellis, Thomas Sayers, and Joseph Lease. *Standing on the Verge: Emerging Poets*. Boston, 1993. (Plus Emerging Massachusetts Artists)

Gates, Henry Louis, Jr., and Nellie Y. McKay, gen. eds. *The Norton Anthology of African American Literature*. Norton, 1997.

Gilbert, Derrick I. M. (with Tony Medina). *Catch the Fire!!!: A Cross-Generational Anthology of Contemporary African-American Poetry*. Berkley, 1998.

Gilyard, Keith. *Spirit & Flame: An Anthology of Contemporary African American Poetry*. Syracuse University Press, 1997.

Golden, Thelma. *Black Male: Representations of Masculinity in Contemporary American Art*. Whitney Museum of Art, 1994.

Hamer, Judith, and Martin J. Hamer. *Centers of the Self: Stories by Black American Women, from the Nineteenth Century to the Present*. Hill and Wang, 1994.

Harper, Michael, and Anthony Walton. *Every Shut Eye Ain't Asleep: An Anthology of Poetry by African Americans Since 1945*. Little, Brown, 1994. (From Robert Hayden to Elizabeth Alexander)

Hayden, Robert. *Kaleidoscope: Poems by American Negro Poets*. Harcourt Brace & World, 1967.

Hemphill, Essex. *Brother to Brother: New Writings by Black Gay Men*. Alyson, 1991.

Hill, Patricia Liggins, et al. *Call and Response: The Riverside Anthology of the African American Literary Tradition*. Houghton Mifflin, 1998.

Kallenbach, Jessamine S. *Index to Black American Literary Anthologies*. G. K. Hall, 1979.

Kanwar, Asha. *The Unforgetting Heart: An Anthology of Short Stories by African-American Women, 1859–1993*. Aunt Lute Books, 1993.

King, Woodie, Jr. *The Forerunners: Black Poets in America*. Howard University Press, 1975.

———. *The National Black Drama Anthology: Eleven Plays from America's Leading African American Theaters*. Applause, 1995.

Locke, Alain. *The New Negro*. With an Introduction by Arnold Rampersad. Atheneum, 1992. (originally 1925)

Major, Clarence. *The Garden Thrives: Twentieth-Century African-American Poetry*. Harper, 1996.

———. *Calling the Wind: Twentieth Century African-American Short Stories*. Harper, 1993.

———. *The New Black Poetry*. International Publishers, 1969.

McMillan, Terry. *Breaking Ice: An Anthology of Contemporary African American Fiction*. Penguin, 1990.

Miller, Adam David. *DICES or Black Bones: Black Voices of the Seventies*. Houghton Mifflin, 1970.

Miller, Ethelbert. *In Search of Color Everywhere: A Collection of African-American Poetry*. Stewart, Tabori & Chang, 1994.

Morrow, Bruce, and Charles H. Rowell. *Shade: An Anthology of Fiction by Gay Men of African Descent*. Avon, 1996. (Introduction by Samuel Delany)

Naylor, Gloria. *Children of the Night: The Best Short Stories by Black Writers, 1967 to the Present*. Little, Brown, 1995.

O'Hearn, Claudine Chiawei. *Half and Half: Writers on Growing Up Biracial and Bicultural*. Pantheon, 1998.

Okwu, Julian C. R. *Face Forward: Young African American Men in a Critical Age*. Chronicle Books, 1997. (Photos and interviews)

———. *As I Am: Young African American Women in a Critical Age*. Chronicle Books, 1999. (Photos and interviews)

Oxford Companion to African American Literature. William L. Andrews, Frances Smith Foster, Trudier Harris, eds. Oxford University Press, 1997.

Powell, Kevin, and Ras Baraka. *In the Tradition: An Anthology of Young Black Writers*. Harlem River Press, 1992.

Reed, Ishmael. *19 Necromancers from Now*. Anchor, 1970.

Rowell, Charles H. *Ancestral House: The Black Short Story in the Americas and Europe*. Westview Press, 1995.

Salaam, Kalamu ya, and Kwame Alexander. *360°: A Revolution of Black Poets*. Black Words, 1998.

Sherman, Joan R. *African-American Poetry of the Nineteenth Century: An Anthology*. University of Illinois Press, 1992.

Tarpley, Natasha, ed., *Testimony: Young African-Americans on Self-Discovery & Black Identity*. Beacon, 1994.

Turner, Darwin T. *Black American Literature: Essays, Poetry, Fiction, Drama*. Charles E. Merrill, 1970.

Walker, Rebecca. *To Be Real: Telling the Truth and Changing the Face of Feminism*. Anchor, 1995. (Foreword by Gloria Steinem; Afterword by Angela Y. Davis)

Wideman, Daniel J., and Rohan Preston. *Soulfires: Young Black Men on Love & Violence*. Viking Penguin, 1996.

Wilentz, Ted, and Tom Weatherly. *Natural Process: An Anthology of New Black Poetry*. Hill and Wang, 1970.

Woods, Paula L., and Felix H. Liddell. *I Hear a Symphony: African Americans Celebrate Love*. Doubleday, 1994.

Worley, Demetrice A., and Jesse Perry, Jr. *African American Literature: An Anthology of Nonfiction, Fiction, Poetry, and Drama*. Lincolnwood, Ill.: National Textbook Company, 1993.

Young, Al. *African American Literature: A Brief Introduction and Anthology*. HarperCollins, 1996. (Series editor Ishmael Reed)

Contributors

Year of birth in parentheses.
Cities are given below names to indicate the range of places where these writers live and work; if associated with a university, only the institution and city are listed.
Abbreviated citations refer to anthologies listed above. Individual volumes listed in reverse chronological order (most recent first).

ALEXANDER, Elizabeth (1962)
New Haven, Connecticut
Body of Life. Tia Chucha Press, 1996.
The Venus Hottentot. University Press of Virginia, 1990.
"Introduction," Melvin Dixon, *Love's Instruments*. Tia Chucha Press, 1995.
Anthologized in *Callaloo* 19:2 Ellis and Lease; Golden; Harper and Walton; Major, *Garden*; E. Miller; Powell and Baraka; Wood and Liddell.

ALS, Hilton (1960)
New York City
The Women. Farrar, Straus & Giroux, 1996.
"The Garden Party," in *Our Town: Images & Stories from the Museum of the City of New York*. Abrams, 1997.

BUTTS, Anthony (1969)
University of Dayton
Dayton, Ohio
Fifth Season. New Issues Press, 1997.
Evolution. Sutton Hoo Press, 1997. (Chapbook with woodcuts.)

DANTICAT, Edwidge (1969)
Brooklyn, New York
The Farming of Bones. Soho Press, 1998.

Krik? Krak!: Stories. Soho Press, 1995.

Breath, Eyes, Memory. Soho Press, 1994.

Estepa, Andrea, and Philip Kay, eds. *Starting with "I": Personal Essays by Teenagers.* With an Afterword by Edwidge Danticat. Persea Books, 1997.

Anthologized in Naylor.

ELLIS, Thomas Sayers (1963)
Case Western Reserve University
Cleveland, Ohio

The Good Junk in *Take Three: AGNI New Poets Series.* Vol. 1. Graywolf, 1996. (Three-in-one volume of emerging poets)

Ellis, Thomas Sayers, and Joseph Lease, eds. *Standing on the Verge: Emerging Poets.* Boston, 1993.

Anthologized in *Callaloo* 21:2; Major, *Garden;* Powell and Baraka; Salaam and Alexander.

FERRELL, Carolyn (1962)
New York City

Don't Erase Me: Stories. Houghton Mifflin, 1997.

Anthologized in *Streetlights; Best American Short Stories 1994;* Austin Naylor.

FORMAN, Ruth (1968)
Los Angeles, California

Renaissance. Beacon Press, 1998.

We Are the Young Magicians. Beacon Press, 1993.

Anthologized in Gilyard; Salaam and Alexander; Woods and Liddell.

HAYES, Terrance (1971)
Xavier University
New Orleans, Louisiana

Muscular Music. Tia Chucha Press, 1999.

JOSEPH, Allison (1967)
Southern Illinois University
Carbondale, Illinois

In Every Seam. University of Pittsburgh, 1997.

Soul Train. Carnegie-Mellon University Press, 1997.

What Keeps Us Here. Ampersand Press, 1992.

Anthologized in Ellis and Lease.

KEENE, John (1965)
New York University

Annotations. New Directions, 1995.

Anthologized in *Callaloo* 19:2 Hemphill; Morrow and Rowell; Powell and Baraka; Rowell.

KENAN, Randall (1963)
University of Memphis
Memphis, Tennessee

Walking on Water: Black America on the Eve of the Twenty-first Century. Knopf, 1999. (Nonfiction)

James Baldwin. Chelsea House, 1994. (Biography for young adults)

Let the Dead Bury Their Dead. Harcourt Brace, 1993. (Short stories)

A Visitation of Spirits. Grove/Atlantic, 1989. (Novel)

Afterword, in W.E.B. Du Bois, *The Souls of Black Folk.* NAL/Dutton, 1995.

Anthologized in Boyd; *Callaloo* 21.1; McMillan; Naylor; Morrow and Rowell; Rowell; Harris, Trudier. *The Power of the Porch: The Storyteller's Craft in Zora Neale Hurston, Gloria Naylor, and Randall Kenan.* University of Georgia, 1996. (Mercer University Lamar Memorial Lectures, No. 39)

MULLEN, Harryette (1960)

University of California, Los Angeles

Los Angeles, California

Freeing the Soul: Race, Subjectivity, and Difference in Slave Narratives. Cambridge University Press, forthcoming fall 1999. (Critical study)

Muse & Drudge. Singing Horse Press, 1995.

S*Perm*K*T. Singing Horse Press, 1992.

Trimmings. Tender Buttons, 1991.

Anthologized in Miller; Young.

POWELL, Kevin (1968)

New York City

Keepin' It Real: Post-MTV Reflections on Race, Sex, and Politics. Ballantine Books, 1997.

Recognize. Writers & Readers Publishing, 1995. (Poems)

Anthologized in Anderson; Asim and Powell; Boyd; Gilbert; Powell and Baraka; Wideman and Preston.

Powell, Kevin, and Ras Baraka, eds. *In the Tradition: An Anthology of Young Black Writers.* Writers & Readers Publishing, 1993.

RANKINE, Claudia (1963)

Barnard College

New York City

The End of the Alphabet: Poems. Grove/Atlantic, 1998.

Nothing in Nature Is Private. Cleveland State University Poetry Center, 1995.

Anthologized in Ellis and Lease; Major, *Garden.*

SCOTT, Darieck (1964)

University of Texas

Austin, Texas

Traitor to the Race. Dutton, 1995.

Anthologized in *Callaloo* 21.1; Morrow and Rowell; Okwu, *Face Forward*; Rowell.

SENNA, Danzy (1970)

Los Angeles, California

Caucasia. Berkley Publishing, 1998.

Anthologized in O'Hearn; Okwu, *As I Am*; Walker.

SHEPHERD, Reginald (1963)
Cornell University
Ithaca, New York
Wrong. University of Pittsburgh Press, 1999.
Angel, Interrupted. University of Pittsburgh Press, 1996.
Some Are Drowning. University of Pittsburgh Press, 1994.
Anthologized in *Callaloo* 21.2; Ellis and Lease; Major, *Garden*; Morrow and Rowell.

TARPLEY, Natasha (1971)
New York City
Girl in the Mirror: Three Generations of Black Women in Motion. Beacon, 1998.
I Love My Hair! Little, Brown, 1998. (Children's book)
Editor, *Testimony: Young African-Americans on Self-Discovery and Black Identity.* Beacon, 1994.
Anthologized in Miller, *Color*; Tarpley; *City River of Voices.* Denise Bergman, ed. West End Press, 1992. Spears, Alan. *Fast Talk, Full Volume.* Gut Punch Press, 1993.

TRETHEWEY, Natasha (1966)
Auburn University
Auburn, Alabama
Domestic Work. Graywolf Press, 2000.
Anthologized in *Callaloo* 19:2 Ellis and Lease; Gilyard; *Two Worlds Walking: Short Stories, Essays, and Poetry by Writers with Mixed Heritages.* Diane Glancy and C. W. Truesdale, eds. New Rivers Press, 1994.

WALKER, Rebecca (1969)
Los Angeles and New York City
Editor, *To Be Real: Telling the Truth and Changing the Face of Feminism.* Anchor, 1995. (Foreword by Gloria Steinem; Afterword by Angela Y. Davis)
"The Initiate's Journey." *House and Home: Spirits of the South.* Addison Gallery of American Art (Philips Andover Academy), 1994. (Introduction to traveling show of Max Belcher, Beverly Buchanan, and William Christenberry)

WALTON, Anthony (1960)
Bowdoin College
Bowdoin, Maine
Mississippi: An American Journey. Knopf, 1996.
Cricket Weather. Blackberry, 1995. (Poems)
Harper, Michael, and Anthony Walton, eds. *Every Shut Eye Ain't Asleep: An Anthology of Poetry by African Americans since 1945.* Little, Brown & Co., 1994.
Sharpton, Al, and Anthony Walton. *Go and Tell Pharaoh: The Autobiography of Reverend Al Sharpton.* Doubleday, 1996.

WAMBA, Philippe (1970)
Boston, Massachusetts
Kinship: A Family's Journey in Africa and America. Dutton, 1999.
Anthologized in O'Hearn.

WHITEHEAD, Colson (1969)
Brooklyn, New York
The Intuitionist: A Novel. Doubleday, 1998.
John Henry Days. Doubleday, forthcoming 2001.

WIDEMAN, Daniel Jerome (1968)
Durham, North Carolina
Singing Sankofa. (Forthcoming 2000, Nonfiction)
Wideman, Daniel J., and Rohan Preston, eds. *Soulfires: Young Black Men on Love and Violence*. Viking/Penguin, 1996.
Anthologized in *Callaloo* 21.1.

WOOD, Joe (1964–1999)
Editor, *Malcolm X: In Our Own Image*. St. Martin's, 1992.
"It's a Trick." *World Tour: Renée Green*. Los Angeles Museum of Contemporary Art, 1993. (Catalog essay)

YOUNG, Kevin (1970)
University of Georgia
Athens, Georgia
Most Way Home. William Morrow, 1995. Reprint edition, Zoland Books, 2000.
Two Cents: Works on Paper by Jean-Michel Basquiat and Poetry by Kevin Young. Miami Dade, 1995. (Exhibit catalog)
Anthologized in *Callaloo* 21.1; Ellis and Lease; Gilyard; Major, *Garden*; Tarpley.

DISCOGRAPHY

We submit these lists to reminisce over, to start an argument, or to start listening to the music of this generation—to go beyond a "best of" or compilation. The following recordings are in order of significance, judged by influence, importance, and general groove.

Useful sources and suggested further reading: LeRoi Jones, *Blues People*; Nelson George, *The Death of Rhythm and Blues*; Tricia Rose, *Black Noise*; Craig Werner, *A Change Is Gonna Come*; Phil Hardy and Dave Laing, *The Faber Companion to 20th-Century Popular Music*; *Music Hound. R and B: The Essential* Album Guide..

Top 50 Records (1960–1990)

These albums are the very best from an era that began when albums were records and had themes—best experienced as one long groove, flipped over in the middle. While the list of artists and albums to own before 1960 is fairly set—we suggest Langston Hughes's *First Book of Jazz* for pointers—after that time, things may be open for discussion. Please note that this list excludes hip-hop and greatest-hits compilations, and in cases where no one album by an artist dominates but a list without the artist seems ludicrous, only the name of the artist is listed.

1. John Coltrane, *A Love Supreme* (1964)
2. James Brown, "Say It Loud (I'm Black & I'm Proud)" (1968)
3. Stevie Wonder, *Innervisions* (1973)
4. Aretha Franklin
5. Curtis Mayfield, *Curtis Live!* (1971)
6. Bob Marley & the Wailers, *Burnin'* (1973)
7. Marvin Gaye, *What's Going On* (1971)
8. Al Green, *I'm Still in Love with You* (1972)
9. Curtis Mayfield, *Superfly* (1972)
10. The Shirelles, "Will You Still Love Me Tomorrow?" (1960)
11. Richard Pryor, *That Nigger's Crazy*
12. Jimi Hendrix, *Are You Experienced?* (1967)
13. Supremes, "Love Child" (1968)
14. Parliament-Funkadelic
15. Prince, *Sign o' the Times* (1987)
16. James Brown, *In the Jungle Groove*
17. Staple Singers, "I'll Take You There" (1972)

18. Sly & the Family Stone
19. Jimmy Cliff, *The Harder They Come* (1972)
20. Fishbone, *Fishbone* (1985)
21. Ray Charles, *Modern Sounds in Country & Western Music* (1963)
22. John Coltrane & Johnny Hartman, "Lush Life"
23. Marvin Gaye, *Trouble Man* (1972)
24. Desmond Dekker & the Aces, "The Israelites" (1968)
25. The Temptations
26. Charles Mingus, *Mingus Plays Piano* (1963)
27. Jackson 5, *ABC* (1970)
28. Miles Davis, *Jack Johnson* (1969)
29. Donna Summer, "Love to Love You Baby" (1975)
30. Archie Schepp, *Fire Music* (1968)
31. Stevie Wonder, *Hotter Than July* (1980)
32. Kool & the Gang, *Wild and Peaceful* (1973)
33. Isaac Hayes, "By the Time I Get to Phoenix" (17-minute version, 1969)
34. Prince, *Dirty Mind* (1980)
35. Gloria Gaynor, "I Will Survive" (1978)
36. Nina Simone, *Nina Simone Sings the Blues* (1968)
37. Chic, "Good Times" (1979)
38. O'Jays, *Back Stabbers* (1972)
39. Michael Jackson, *Thriller* (1982)
40. Tina Turner, *Private Dancer* (1984)
41. Terence Trent D'Arby, *Introducing the Hardline According to Terence Trent D'Arby* (1987)
42. Janet Jackson, *Control* (1986)
43. Soul II Soul, *Keep on Movin'* (1989)
44. Earth, Wind and Fire, "Reasons" (Live) (1975)
45. Chubby Checker, "The Twist" (1960)
46. Charley Pride, *The Best of Charley Pride* (1969)
47. Grace Jones, *Nightclubbing* (1981)
48. Smokey Robinson
49. Tracy Chapman, *Crossroads* (1989)
50. Living Colour, "Elvis Is Dead" (1990)

40 Top Hip-Hop Albums of All Time

Listed in order of importance and influence, these albums are those that changed the music, refining and redefining hip-hop through concept (*Three Feet High*), style (*Paid in Full*), subject (*Straight Outta Compton*), and vision (*The Miseducation of Lauryn Hill*). We honor records here that expand what hip-hop can and must be.

1. Run-D.M.C., *Run-D.M.C.* (1984)
2. Eric B. & Rakim, *Paid in Full* (1986)
3. Public Enemy, *It Takes a Nation of Millions to Hold Us Back* (1988)
4. De La Soul, *Three Feet High and Rising* (1989)
5. N.W.A., *Straight Outta Compton* (1989)

6. A Tribe Called Quest, *The Low End Theory* (1991)
7. Ice Cube, *Amerikkka's Most Wanted* (1990)
8. Public Enemy, *Fear of a Black Planet* (1990)
9. Queen Latifah, *All Hail the Queen* (1989)
10. Dr. Dre, *The Chronic* (1992)
11. Boogie Down Productions, *Criminal Minded* (1987)
12. EPMD, *Strictly Business* (1988)
13. L. L. Cool J, *Bigger & Deffer* (1987)
14. Salt-n-Pepa, *Hot, Cool & Vicious* (1986)
15. Beastie Boys, *Licensed to Ill* (1986)
16. Schooly D, *Saturday Night* (1987)
17. Wu-Tang Clan, *Enter the Wu-Tang (36 Chambers)* (1993)
18. Lauryn Hill, *The Miseducation of Lauryn Hill* (1998)
19. Notorious B.I.G., *Ready to Die* (1994)
20. Pharcyde, *Bizarre Ride II the Pharcyde* (1992)
21. Poor Righteous Teachers, *Holy Intellect* (1990)
22. Tricky, *Maxinquaye* (1995)
23. Ice Cube, *The Predator* (1992)
24. Cypress Hill, *Cypress Hill* (1991)
25. Brand Nubian, *One for All* (1990)
26. Basehead, *Play with Toys* (1992)
27. De La Soul, *Buhloone Mind State* (1993)
28. Son of Bazerk, *Son of Bazerk Featuring No Self Control and The Band* (1991)
29. Digable Planets, *Reachin' (A New Definition of Time and Space)* (1993)
30. MC Solaar, *Prose Combat* (1993)
31. Nas, *Illmatic* (1994)
32. Various Artists, *Juice: Original Motion Picture Soundtrack* (1992)
33. Black Sheep, *A Wolf in Sheep's Clothing* (1991)
34. Ultramagnetic MC's, *Critical Beatdown* (1988)
35. DJ Shadow, *Endtroducing . . .* (1996)
36. Del the Funky Homosapien, *I Wish My Brother George Was Here*
37. Fugees, *The Score* (1996)
38. Erykah Badu, *Baduizm* (1997)
39. Outkast, *Aquemini* (1998)
40. The Roots, *Things Fall Apart* (1999)

75 Top Hip-Hop Singles

The following singles represent those songs that changed music, making us move and think. These are not only "favorite jams"—there are many more that we could produce if that were the case—but those that affected the genre. Often when no one song could be pulled from a classic album (Public Enemy's *It Takes a Nation of Millions*, for instance), we have chosen to point to cuts that are equally important, but not on the record (as with "Fight the Power").

1. Sugar Hill Gang, "Rapper's Delight" (1979)
2. Grandmaster Flash & the Furious Five, "The Message" (1982)

3. Run-D.M.C., "It's Like That" b/w "Sucker MC's" (1983)
4. UTFO, "Roxanne, Roxanne" (1985)
5. Roxanne Shanté, "Roxanne's Revenge" (1985)
6. Afrika Bambaata & the Furious Five, "Planet Rock"
7. Doug E. Fresh & Slick Rick, "La Di Da Di" (1985)
8. Eric B. & Rakim, "Eric B. Is President" (1986)
9. L.L. Cool J, "I Need Love" (1987)
10. Slick Rick, "Children's Story" (1988)
11. Public Enemy, "Fight the Power" (1989)
12. M.C. Shan, "The Bridge" (1987)
13. Boogie Down Productions, "The Bridge Is Over" (1987)
14. NWA, "Fuck tha Police" (1989)
15. "The Adventures of Grandmaster Flash on the Wheels of Steel" (1981)
16. Jungle Brothers, "Girl, I'll House You" (1988)
17. Herbie Hancock, "Rockit" (1983)
18. Ice Cube, "The Nigga You Love to Hate" (1990)
19. Salt-n-Pepa, "Push It" (1986)
20. Audio Two, "Top Billin'" (1988)
21. A Tribe Called Quest, "The Scenario" (Remix) (1992)
22. MC Lyte, "I Cram to Understand You (Sam)" (1987)
23. Rob Base & DJ E-Z Rock, "It Takes Two" (1998)
24. Tom Tom Club, "Genius of Love" (1981)
25. Arrested Development, "Tennessee" (1992)
27. Queen Latifah (with Monie Love), "Ladies First" (1989)
28. Geto Boys, "My Mind's Playin Tricks on Me" (1991)
29. Run-D.M.C., "Walk This Way" (1986)
30. Dr. Dre & Snoop Doggy Dogg, "Nothin' but a G Thang" (1992)
31. Wu-Tang Clan, "C.R.E.A.M." (1993)
32. Notorious B.I.G., "Big Poppa" (1994)
33. Pete Rock & C.L. Smooth, "They Reminisce Over You (T.R.O.Y.)" (1992)
34. Fugees, "Vocab" (1994)
35. De La Soul (with Native Tongues), "Buddy" (Remix) (1990)
36. 2Pac, "Dear Mama" (1995)
37. Paris, "Break the Grip of Shame" (1992)
38. Method Man (with Mary J. Blige), "You're All I Need to Get By" (1995)
39. Ice-T, "Colors" (1988)
40. Stetsasonic, "Talkin' All That Jazz" (1988)
41. Big Daddy Kane, "Ain't No Half-Steppin'" (1986)
42. Digital Underground, "Humpty Dance" (1990)
43. Lauryn Hill (with Refugee All Stars), "The Sweetest Thing" (1997)
44. Brand Nubian, "Slow Down" (1990)
45. Boogie Down Productions, "Love's Gonna Get You (Material Love)" (1990)
46. Master P (with No Limit Soldiers), "Make Em Say Uhhh" (1998)
47. The Last Poets, "Niggers Are Scared of Revolution"
48. L.L. Cool J, "Mama Said Knock You Out" (1990)
49. M/A/R/R/S, "Pump Up the Volume" (1988)
50. The D.O.C., "It's Funky Enough" (1989)
51. De La Soul, "Millie Pulled a Pistol on Santa" (1991)

52. Craig Mack, "Flava in Ya Ear (Remix)" (1994)
53. EPMD, "You Gots to Chill" (1988)
54. Main Source, "Friendly Game of Baseball" (1991)
55. Dr. Dre & Snoop Doggy Dogg, "Deep Cover" (1992)
56. Ice Cube, "Dead Homiez" (1990)
57. Gang Starr, "Just to Get a Rep" (1991)
58. Jay-Z, "Hard Knock Life" (1998)
59. Mobb Deep, "Shook Ones (Part II)" (1996)
60. Goldie, "Inner City Life" (1997)
61. Missy "Misdemeanor" Elliott, "The Rain" (1997)
62. Outkast, "Rosa Parks" (1998)
63. Das EFX, "They Want EFX" (1992)
64. Urban Dance Squad, "Deeper Shade of Soul" (1990)
65. Tricky, "Black Steel in the Hour of Chaos" (1995)
66. 3rd Base, "Gas Face" (1989)
67. Digable Planets, "Rebirth of Slick (Cool Like Dat)" (1993)
68. Busta Rhymes, "Woo Hah!!! Got You All in Check" (1996)
69. Ol' Dirty Bastard, "Shimmy Shimmy Ya" (1995)
70. Gil Scott-Heron, "The Revolution" (1972)
71. Kool Moe Dee, "How Ya Like Me Now?" (1987)
72. Noreaga, "Superthug" (1998)
73. Blondie, "Rapture" (1981)
74. Souls of Mischief, " '93 Til Infinity" (1993)
75. Mike Ladd (with Company Flow), "Blade Runners" (1998)

ACKNOWLEDGMENTS

First I would like to thank my agent, Eileen Cope, who supported this anthology and helped find it a home. She is, as my mother would say, "a classy lady." At that home, William Morrow and Company, I would like to thank my editor, Zach Schisgal, for making this second book as easy and pleasant as he helped make the first; thanks also to his fearless assistant, Taije Silverman, for her insights into poetry and the editing process.

On the home front, I would like to thank the University of Georgia's Departments of English and of African American Studies for their support, particularly my understanding heads Dr. Anne Williams and Dr. R. Baxter Miller. Thanks too to Julie Checkoway and Lee Thomsen; Sean Hill and Philippe Wamba for help with the Discography; and Michelle Ballif for last-minute help with the Intro. Thanks also to Barbara MacCaskill, Steve Lickteig, Laura Wexler, and all others, too many to mention by name, who encouraged me along the way.

Thanks to my early research assistants, Eric Rochester and Michael Hill, who helped lay the groundwork for what would eventually become this book.

Special thanks goes to my research assistant, Stefan Potzner, who set the highest standard possible for any who might dare follow, offering me invaluable information, timely reminders about returning books, vital help with the Bibliography, and a wonderful spirit that I looked forward to weekly. Without him I would still be working on narrowing the field, instead of publishing what I found.

For his moral support, his editorial suggestions, and his unerring friendship I would like to thank Colson Whitehead—without his steady encouragement this book would simply not have been possible. Last but not least I would like to especially thank Kim Cretors, not just for her invaluable proofreading and computer help, but for her loving support, which saw me through to the end. She made me a better man and *Giant Steps* a better book.

ACKNOWLEDGMENTS

Thanks also for the following authors and publishers who granted permission to reprint the following work:

"Nineteen," "Stella by Starlight," and "Deadwood Dick" from *The Venus Hottentot*, University Press of Virginia, 1990; "What I Am Telling You," "Frank Willis," and "Blues" from *Body of Life*, Tia Chucha Press, 1996; "Race," "Overture: Watermelon City," and "Feminist Poem Number One" by Elizabeth Alexander. All poems printed by permission of the author.

Excerpt from *The Women* by Hilton Als. Copyright © 1996 by Hilton Als. Reprinted by permission of Farrar, Straus and Giroux.

"A Poe Story" first published as "Coasters" in *Crab Orchard Review*. "Becoming the Ghost," "Self-Portrait with Clark Street Cadillac," "Detroit, One A.M." published in *Fifth Season*, New Issues Press. "The Loudest Sound" first appeared in *Pleiades*. "Machines" by Anthony Butts. All poems reprinted by permission of the author.

"The Book of the Dead" first published in *The New Yorker*. Reprinted by permission of Edwidge Danticat and the Watkins/Loomis Agency.

"View of the Library of Congress from Paul Laurence Dunbar High School," "Fatal April," and "Being There" first published in *The Good Junk* in *Take Three*, Graywolf Press, 1996. "Hush Yo Mouf," "Photograph of Dr. Funkenstein," and "Atomic Bride" by Thomas Sayers Ellis. All poems reprinted by permission of the author.

"Can You Say My Name?" from *Don't Erase Me* by Carolyn Ferrell. Copyright © 1997 by Carolyn Ferrell. Reprinted by permission of Houghton Mifflin Company. All rights reserved.

"Haiku I" and "Blues Poem III" from *We Are the Young Magicians* by Ruth Forman. Copyright © 1993 by Ruth Forman. Reprinted by permission of Beacon Press, Boston. "The Williams Side of the Family," "Cancer," "Momma Died When My Wisdom Teeth Come In," and "Even if I Was Cleopatra Jones" from *Renaissance* by Ruth Forman. Copyright © 1997 by Ruth Forman. "Show Me the Ankles of Justice" by Ruth Forman reprinted by permission from the February 1, 1993, issue of *The Nation*.

"Neckbones" and "Candied Yams" were published in *Obsidian II: Black Literature in Review*; all other poems by Terrance Hayes were published in *Muscular Music* by Tia Chucha Press. Reprinted by permission of the author.

"Salt" appeared in *New Delta Review*, Volume 13, Number 1, 1995. "On Being Told I Don't Speak Like a Black Person" appeared in *Many Mountains Moving*, Volume II, Number 1, 1995. "Family Life" and "Learning the Blues" appeared in *What Keeps Us Here*, Ampersand Press, 1992. Copyright © 1992 by Allison Joseph. Reprinted by permission of the author. "Home Girl Talks Girlhood" reprinted from Allison Joseph, *Soul Train* by permission of Carnegie Mellon University Press, Copyright © 1997 by Allison Joseph.

"Jackie Robinson in Sportsmen's Park, 1949," "Winter Elegy," "Cecil's Consolation (1942)," "One Revolution," and "Why I Love My Father" copyright © 1999, 2000 by John Keene. Reprinted by permission of the author.

"Now Why Come That Is?" by Randall Kenan from *Callaloo*, Volume 21, Issue 1. Reprinted by permission of the author.

"She Landed on the Moon" published in *Quilt* 5, 1986, ed. Ishmael Reed and Al Young. Reprinted in *African American Literature: A Brief Introduction and Anthology*, HarperCollins, 1996, ed. Al Young. "Roadmap" published in *Tree Tall Woman: Poems by Harryette Mullen*, 1981. Reprinted in *In Search of Color Everywhere: A Collection of African-American Poetry*, 1994, ed. E. Ethelbert Miller. Selections from *Muse & Drudge* by Harryette Mullen, published by Singing Horse Press, 1995. "Suzuki Method" published in *Parnassus*, edited by Herbert Leibowitz, 1998. "Black Nikes" published in *Santa Monica Review*, edited by Lee Montgomery, 1997. All works copyright © by Harryette Mullen. Reprinted by permission of the author.

"Letter to My Father" from *Keepin' It Real* by Kevin Powell. Copyright © 1997 by Kevin Powell. Reprinted by permission of Ballantine Books, a Division of Random House, Inc.

"American Light" and "Him" published in *Nothing in Nature Is Private*, Cleveland State Poetry Press. "Overview Is a Place" and "The Quotidian" published in *The End of the Alphabet*, Grove Press. "This Life" appeared in *Southern Review*. All poems reprinted by permission of the author.

"1979" by Darieck Scott reprinted by permission of the author.

"The Land of Beulah" reprinted by permission of International Creative Management, Inc. Copyright © 1999 by Danzy Senna.

"The Difficult Music" published in *Some Are Drowning* by the University of Pittsburgh Press, 1994. Reprinted by permission of the University of Pittsburgh Press and the author. "Desire and the Slave Trade" and "Skin Trade" published in *Angel, Interrupted* by the University of Pittsburgh Press, 1996. Reprinted by permission of the University of Pittsburgh Press and the author. "Antibody," "S'il Meurt," "Icarus on Fire Island," and "At the Grave of Hart Crane" published in *Wrong* by the University of Pittsburgh Press, 1999. Reprinted by permission of the University of Pittsburgh Press and the author.

Selections from *Girl in the Mirror* by Natasha Tarpley. Copyright © 1998 by Natasha Tarpley. Reprinted by permission of Beacon Press, Boston.

"At the Station" published in *Southern Review*, "Speculation, 1939" published in *Greensboro Review*, "Drapery Factory, Gulfport, Mississippi, 1956" published in *Agni*, "Flounder" published in *Callaloo*, "Saturday Matinee" published in *Painted Bride Quarterly*, and "Bellocq's Ophelia" published in *Southern Review*. All poems by Natasha Trethewey, reprinted by permission of the author.

An earlier version of "Higher Yellow," Rebecca Walker, appeared as "Foreword" in *Adios! Barbie*, Seal Press, 1998. Copyright © 1998, 1999 by Rebecca Walker. Reprinted by permission of the author.

Selections from *Mississippi* by Anthony Walton. Copyright © 1996 by Anthony Walton. Reprinted by permission of Alfred A. Knopf, Inc.

"Of Prophets and Madmen" by Philippe Wamba reprinted by permission of the author.

ACKNOWLEDGMENTS

"The All-Night Bodega of Souls" reprinted by permission of Colson Whitehead and the Watkins/Loomis Agency.

Selection from *Singing Sankofa* by Daniel Jerome Wideman, to be published
by Scribner in 2000. Reprinted by permission of the author.

"The Yellow Negro" by Joe Wood from *Transition* 73 (Volume 7, Number 1,
1998). Copyright © 1998 by W.E.B. Du Bois Institute and Duke University
Press. All rights reserved. Reprinted with permission.

"Nineteen Seventy-five" first published in *Callaloo*, "No Offense" published
in *Kenyon Review*, "Negative" published in *Double Take*, "Charlie Chan on
Horn" published in *Gulf Coast*, "Langston Hughes" published in *The New
Yorker*, and "Homage to Phillis Wheatley" published in *The Paris Review*. All
poems copyright © 1995, 1999 by Kevin Young. Reprinted by permission of the
author.

INDEX BY GENRE